Praise
ELEMENTA.

"Fantasy author Sharon Shinn is known for her brilliant world-building and the layered richness of her characterizations, and she's in top form with her new Elemental Blessings novel, *Whispering Wood*. This is the long-awaited book of the hunti, the people of wood and bone, who are known for unbreakable strength, but are too often inflexible. *Whispering Wood*'s heroine, Valentina Serlast, is the younger sister of Darien Serlast and is hunti to the bone. Though Val doesn't want to leave her quiet life in a forest, she reluctantly visits the capital for her brother's coronation as king. Forced out of her comfort zone, Val finds new friends, new challenges, and an impossible old love—and learns that even a hunti soul can change."
 — Mary Jo Putney
 New York Times bestselling author of The Rogues Redeemed series

Troubled Waters
"Shinn carries readers away into a vivid new fantasy world where the five elements control everyone's lives."
 — *Publishers Weekly*

Royal Airs
"When it comes to vividly layered characters and detailed world building, Shinn is a master at her craft."
 — *RT Book Reviews*

Jeweled Fire
"The amazing Shinn returns to the world of her Elemental Blessing series by following the exploits of a young princess determined to chart her own course."
 — *The Romantic Times*

Unquiet Land
"A world that is completely believable and magical at the same time."
 — *Fantasy Literature*

Whispering Wood

Also by Sharon Shinn

Uncommon Echoes
Echo in Onyx
Echo in Emerald
Echo in Amethyst

The Samaria series
Archangel
Jovah's Angel
The Alleluia Files
Angelica
Angel-Seeker

The Twelve Houses series
Mystic and Rider
The Thirteenth House
Dark Moon Defender
Reader and Raelynx
Fortune and Fate

The Elemental Blessings series
Troubled Waters
Royal Airs
Jeweled Fire
Unquiet Land

The Shifting Circle series
The Shape of Desire
Still-Life with Shape-Shifter
The Turning Season

Young adult novels
The Safe-Keeper's Secret
The Truth-Teller's Tale
The Dream-Maker's Magic
General Winston's Daughter
Gateway

Standalones and Graphic Novels
The Shuddering City
The Shape-Changer's Wife
Wrapt in Crystal
Heart of Gold
Summers at Castle Auburn
Jenna Starborn
Shattered Warrior

Collections
Quatrain
Shadows of the Past
Angels and Other Extraordinary Beings

Whispering Wood

AN ELEMENTAL BLESSINGS NOVEL

Sharon Shinn

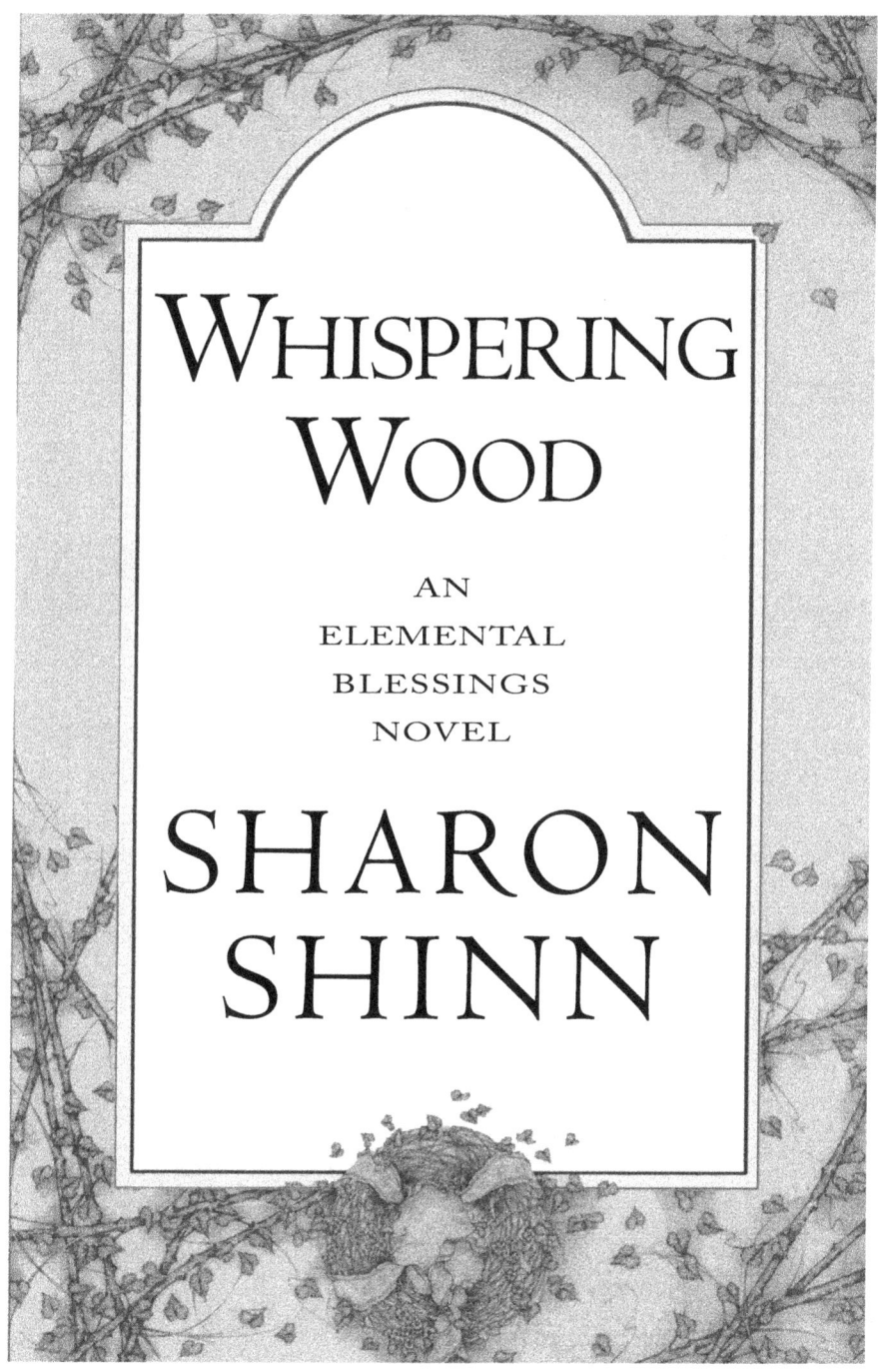

FAIRWOOD PRESS
Bonney Lake, WA

WHISPERING WOOD
A Fairwood PressBook
November 2023
Copyright © 2023 by Sharon Shinn

All Rights Reserved

No part of this book may be reproduced or transmitted in any form or by any means, electronic or mechanical, including photocopying, recording, or by any information storage and retrieval system, without permission in writing from the publisher.

First Edition

Fairwood Press
21528 104th Street Court East
Bonney Lake, WA 98391
www.fairwoodpress.com

Cover image © 2023 by Tom Canty
Cover and book design by Patrick Swenson
Initials design by Artemis Swenson

ISBN: 978-1-958880-13-5
Fairwood Press Trade Edition: November 2023

A note to readers:

You might find yourself thinking, "I didn't know Darien Serlast had a sister!" Indeed, he only mentions her once, early in *Troubled Waters* when he is taking Zoe to Chialto. Of course, he says he has two sisters and that his mother is hunti, when (it turns out) he only has one sister and his mother is torz. The only way to explain the discrepancy is to assume that Zoe's presence left him almost too flustered to think clearly. He didn't show it, but it was obviously true.

WHO'S WHO IN WELCE

The Serlast Family & Their Connections

Darien Serlast, the king
Valentina Serlast, his sister
Zoe Lalindar, the coru prime and Darien's wife
Celia, Darien's daughter with Zoe
Corene, Darien's daughter with Alys
Foley, Corene's personal guard
Damon Serlast, Darien & Val's father, the former
   hunti prime (now deceased)
Merra Serlast, Darien and Val's mother (now deceased)
Jenty and Lissa, Merra's sisters
Saska, Jenty's daughter
Morgan, Lissa's son

The Primes & Their Relations

Mirti Serlast, the hunti prime; aunt to Val and Darien
Nelson Ardelay, the elay prime
Beccan Ardelay, Nelson's wife
Sebastian Ardelay, the bastard son of one of Nelson's
   remote cousins
Taro Frothen, the torz prime
Virrie Frothen, his wife
Leah Frothen, Taro's niece
Mally, Leah's daughter and Taro's heir
Kayle Dochenza, the elay prime

Other Prominent Royals

King Vernon (now deceased)
Queen Elidon, Vernon's first wife
Queen Seterre, Vernon's second wife
Queen Alys, Vernon's third wife
Queen Romelle, Vernon's fourth wife
Josetta, Seterre's daughter
Rafe Adova, Josetta's husband
Natalie, Romelle's oldest daughter
Odelia, Romelle's youngest daughter

Friends, Enemies, & Foreigners

Geoffrey, a restaurant owner
Jodar, an enterprising criminal
Yori, a soldier in the royal guard
Melissande, a princess from Cozique
Alette, a princess from Dhonsho who is a friend
   to Melissande and Corene

THE BLESSINGS

ELAY (air/soul)	HUNTI (wood/bone)	SWEELA (fire/mind)
joy	courage	innovation
hope	strength	love
kindness	steadfastness	imagination
beauty	loyalty	clarity
vision	certainty	intelligence
grace	resolve	charm
honor	determination	talent
spirituality	power	creativity

CORU (water/blood)	TORZ (earth/flesh)	EXTRAORDINARY BLESSINGS
change	serenity	synthesis
travel	honesty	triumph
flexibility	health	time
swiftness	fertility	
resilience	contentment	
luck	patience	
persistence	endurance	
surprise	wealth	

MONEY

5 quint-coppers make one copper (5 cents --> 25 cents)
8 coppers make one quint silver ($2)
5 quint silvers make one silver ($10)
8 silvers make one quint gold ($80)
5 quint golds make one gold ($400)

QUINTILES & CHANGEDAYS

The calendar of Welce is divided into five quintiles. A quintile consists of eight "weeks," each nine days long. Most shops and other businesses are closed on the firstdays of each nineday.

The first quintile of the year, Quinnelay, stretches from early to deep winter. It is followed by Quinncoru, which encompasses late winter to mid-spring; Quinnahunti, late spring to mid-summer; Quinnatorz, late summer to fall; and Quinnasweela, fall to early winter.

The quintiles are separated by changedays, generally celebrated as holidays. Quinnelay changeday is the first day of every new year. Since there are five changedays, and five seventy-two-day quintiles, the Welce year is 365 days long.

Whispering Wood

Chapter One

Valentina Serlast spent the entire two hours of the coronation ceremony trying to convince herself that she didn't hate every other person in attendance. She didn't succeed particularly well.

She certainly hated the crowds of enthusiastic and overdressed people who filled the palace's vast foyer and pressed so close to the dais that she could feel it trembling under their weight. Theoretically, any urchin off the street was welcome to attend the event and watch the installation of the new king. But in actuality, almost everyone who'd clustered inside the palace was wealthy or politically important, and at least half of them came from one of the prominent families of the country of Welce. Val was never comfortable around large gatherings of the rich and ambitious, and today far too many of them were crammed into one room, flaunting their fine clothes, their sparkling jewels, and their close connections to the king. They all wanted to make sure their friends and rivals saw them in the crowd on this most momentous day, and they spent more time scanning the faces of their fellow revelers than watching the activities on the stage.

She had never had much use for the new king's wife, the woman who had arrived in the city of Chialto almost eight years ago and upended everything. Careless, chaotic, and completely unpredictable, Zoe Lalindar had disrupted the power balance at court, set the four queens at each other's throats, brought to light shocking secrets about the old king, and—in a moment of uncontrolled fury—flooded half the city. And then she had married Val's brother and he had completely abandoned Val and her mother so he could lavish all his attention on his new family.

And now he was being crowned King Darien. And she hated him most of all.

Except she didn't. Except sometimes she did.

For a moment, she turned her eyes away from the jostling crowd to survey the apparently interminable action on the stage. Val was one of the thirty people who had been deemed important enough to have a place on the raised dais while the ceremony was underway. It was supposed to be an honor but, practically speaking, it meant she couldn't slip away while the coronation went on and on. There had been speeches by each of the five primes—the heads of the Five Families, the ones who had the strongest affiliations with the five elements—and then various politicians had stood up to make their own declarations. Now someone was rattling off some sort of incantation about the blessings and the elements. Val thought the speaker might be an acolyte from one of the temples, but she barely listened. She let her eyes rest on Darien's face, wondering what he was thinking.

It was impossible ever to know, of course. Darien had never been open or easy to read, and he certainly had never felt any impulse to confide in the sister who was twelve years his junior, despite the fact that she had absolutely adored him and would have kept any small nugget of personal information entirely to herself. His wary aloofness had not been softened at all by nearly a decade as the most powerful figure in Welce—first as advisor to the ailing King Vernon, then as regent to Vernon's infant daughter, then as designated heir to the throne himself. What was he feeling as the speaker gabbled on about power and responsibility? Was he excited? Pleased? Anxious? Triumphant? Unmoved? Nothing could be discerned on his lean face, which remained unsmiling, watchful, alert, and composed. As if this was any other day. As if his life was not changing forever.

Val's gaze wandered over to Zoe, who sat in a high gilded chair next to the thronelike seat where Darien endured his coronation. Zoe was suitably dressed, in a blue tunic so heavily embroidered with glittering beads that her body flashed every time she made the smallest movement, but she hadn't managed to make her expression properly reverent or solemn. In fact, she lounged back in her chair as if it was actually comfortable (Val knew it wasn't) and seemed to be struggling to keep a look of boredom off her face. When she caught Val's eyes on her, she offered up a grin and a wink.

Val glanced away.

Maybe no one would notice if she left the stage. She could rise to a half-crouch, wind stealthily through the row of chairs to the back edge of the raised platform, then jump lightly to the floor. Within a few moments, she could blend in with the crowd, work her way to the outer perimeter, and slip away. Darien obviously wouldn't notice. Zoe might, but she was such a care-for-nobody that she would only laugh.

Val straightened in her seat, gathering her legs under her. *I'm doing it*, she thought. She glanced around one more time to make sure no one was paying attention, and found Mirti Serlast scowling at her. Val slumped back into her chair, unable to keep the surly expression from her face.

Mirti was the reason Val was at the coronation in the first place, because Val had *not* intended to come. She hadn't even responded to Darien's formal invitation, and when he followed up with a handwritten note, she had simply answered, "I don't think I can make it." She didn't know if he had asked Mirti to intervene or if Mirti had come up with that idea all on her own, but a little over a nineday ago, the hunti prime had showed up at Val's house and said, "Start packing."

Val had acted like she had no idea what Mirti meant. "Packing for where?"

"Chialto. You're going to see your brother named king of Welce."

"Well, I'm not."

Mirti had snorted and headed to Val's bedroom as if she planned to root through Val's closet and choose the most appropriate outfits. Indignant, Val had followed. It was a small house, only ten rooms, nothing like the place she and her mother had owned in the city, nothing like the sprawling estate where Val had grown up and where Mirti now resided. It was only a few steps to Val's bedroom.

"You'll have to stay at the palace, of course, so you'll need your fancy clothes. There will be dinners and whatnot. All very tedious, but it can't be helped." Mirti had indeed gone to the closet and began working her way through all the tunics and trousers hung carefully in place. They were arranged by color, the pale shades giving way to the darker ones, matching shoes and accessories lined up on the shelf above and the floor below. Mirti pulled out a black silk outfit lightened by spangles at the collar and cuffs. "That's pretty. You could wear that to the coronation."

"I'm not going to the coronation."

"Darien wants you there."

"Darien doesn't always get everything he wants."

Mirti's dry, wrinkled face looked amused. "Doesn't he? Seems like he does."

Val stiffened. "Not this time."

Mirti turned back to the closet, pulling out pants and long jackets in sage green, in cobalt blue, in variegated gold. "Your mother would want you to go."

"I haven't been to Chialto in three years. I don't like the city. I feel awkward and clumsy at state dinners and political events. Darien will be so busy he won't even know I'm not there."

Mirti had stepped back from the closet, her hands filled with the soft folds of a prim black shawl. "You're the daughter of the previous hunti prime. You're the niece of the current hunti prime. Your brother is going to be crowned king. Your place is there, for the honor of the family. You have to go."

Val had stared at her aunt with bitterness and resignation. It was an incontestable argument, and Mirti knew it. There were rules in life, and everyone knew what they were, and they were incontrovertible. Val had to attend the stupid coronation.

So here she was, loathing every second of it, pinned in her seat by Mirti's relentless glare. She added Mirti to the roster of people she hated. Pretty soon there would be nobody who wasn't on the list.

The speaker came to the end of his homily and Val returned her attention to the figures at the head of the stage. The acolyte was smiling, and even Darien looked less remote.

"To mark your first day as king of Welce, would you like to invite three people to pull blessings that will inform your reign for all of your days?"

"I would," said Darien in a clear, carrying voice.

Someone handed the acolyte a heavily carved canister of richly polished wood. Above the murmuring of the crowd, Val could hear the slight clink of the metal coins inside. She estimated that the container was big enough to hold several sets of blessings, a couple hundred in all. That meant Darien easily could be gifted with duplicates. She wouldn't be surprised to see him walk away with power, power, and power—or certainty, certainty, and certainty. Of all the hunti people who had ever been born, Darien was the one who most completely embodied the unyielding elemental traits of wood and bone.

"Who would you ask to draw your first blessing?" the acolyte asked.

"My wife, Zoe Lalindar, the coru prime."

The crowd cooed in response, though it would have been astonishing if he had made any other choice. Zoe grinned again as she stood up and plunged her fingers into the container. She spent a moment stirring through the coins as if waiting for a specific one to burn against her fingers. Her grin grew wider as she retrieved her hand, glanced at the disk, and handed it to the acolyte.

"Steadfastness," he intoned. "A most excellent attribute for a king. Who would you like to pull your second blessing?"

"My daughter Corene."

A second figure jumped up and hurried to Darien's side, her delicate face alive with excitement. It still seemed strange to think of Corene as Darien's daughter. She had been born to Vernon's third wife, Alys, and it wasn't until Corene was eleven years old that everyone realized Vernon was almost impotent and three of his four daughters had been sired by other men. Val found the whole tale both sordid and horrifying. First, adultery was *wrong,* and Val could see no excuse for it, even if the goal was to make sure the kingdom had a set of heirs. Second, how could Darien have been so misguided as to fall in love with *Alys,* the most manipulative and despicable of women? He detested Alys now, of course, but it seemed at one point he had been besotted with her. It was the worst thing Val knew about him.

Corene spent even longer than Zoe had fishing through the coins, looking for exactly the right one. She was small-boned and red-haired and wild straight through. She had been the most unlikable child imaginable, back in the days when Val lived at court. Mirti swore that Corene had greatly improved, though she was still sharp-tongued and outspoken and frankly brazen. Val didn't have any desire to find out for herself if any better qualities had surfaced.

Finally, Corene pulled out a blessing—then dropped it back into the pot and stirred again. She did that twice more, while the acolyte frowned and Zoe looked like she was trying not to laugh, before she finally handed over her prize.

"Vision," said the acolyte. "Another propitious sign."

Val was surprised. Vision was an elay trait, and Darien had never shown any affinity for the element of air and spirit. And Corene was sweela down to her soul. She could have been sculpted out of fire; she had a mind that was constantly racing to the next idea. Who would have expected such a girl to pull such a coin for such a man? And yet Val couldn't disagree. Vision would be essential for the new king.

"I'm glad to receive such a blessing," Darien said gravely.

"Who would you like to pull your third one?"

Val's eyes went instantly to Celia, the cherubic-looking almost-three-year-old sitting next to Zoe. How the crowd would murmur and sigh when he called out his youngest daughter's name! How darling everyone would think it was to watch her thrust her chubby little hands into the container and offer her innocent's benediction on her father's reign!

"My sister, Valentina."

For a moment, Val sat frozen in place, not certain she had heard correctly. Then she was washed with a wave of horror. She had to stand up in front of all these people and participate in one of the most solemn rituals the country offered? What if she tripped, what if she knocked the container out of the acolyte's hands, what if she fell off the edge of the stage? She couldn't do it. She couldn't even stand up. She sat on the edge of her seat as motionless as if she had been carved from a block of wood.

Rescue came from an unexpected source. "Here, I'll help you up. Those shoes don't look easy to walk in," said a man sitting next to her, kindly pulling her to her feet. She thanked him blindly, not registering his face or his identity, and tried to gather the shreds of her composure as she advanced across the stage. She stiffened her spine, lifting her chin and letting her bones take her weight. She was the daughter of one hunti prime, the niece of another. Nothing could break her.

Darien gave her the slightest nod as she reached his side. The acolyte proffered the small barrel and Val dipped her hand into the cool metal. Instantly, her anxiety evaporated; it was as if mere contact with all the blessings of the world restored her sense of balance. She allowed her fingers to clench and relax, feeling the disks slide across her skin, but hesitated a moment before plucking one from the pile.

If she could pick what blessing to bestow on the new king of Welce, what would she choose? If she could select one for her brother, would it be the same one? What if she pulled something disquieting like surprise or a ghost coin that offered no guidance at all? She clenched her fingers again, told herself sternly to stop agonizing, and grabbed the first coin that she could. She didn't even look at it before handing it to the acolyte.

Whose face reflected deep pleasure as he showed the glyph to Darien. "Time," he said. "A great gift both to you and our country."

At that, Darien's face relaxed into the slightest smile, and Val found herself smiling at him in response. Maybe she didn't hate Darien after all.

She picked her way back to her seat, remembering to whisper a thank you to the man who had helped her to her feet. He was older, with a friendly expression that made her think he must be torz, but she didn't recognize him. She wondered how many people sitting on the dais recognized *her*. Well, of course, now that she had been so publicly identified, everyone would know who she was, but five minutes ago? Would any of them have been able to recall her name? She wished she was back home, where such questions wouldn't even have occurred to her.

To distract herself from uncomfortable thoughts, she turned her attention back to the crowd below. She could tell that people were starting to get restless, and she guessed it was time for the long ceremony to be over. She even saw a few people edging toward the open doors, their shapes backlit against the brilliant sunlight as they eased themselves outside. At the same time, one or two stragglers stepped in through the wide archways—probably people who hadn't been able to push themselves inside while the crowd was at its densest, hoping they still might have a chance to gawk at royalty. There was a cluster of teenaged girls, smiling and pointing at the stage, maybe sighing over Darien's stern good looks. There was a father who'd hoisted his young son to his shoulders; he was holding onto the boy's ankles and standing on his tiptoes, trying to get a better view.

There was a tall man lurking in the shadows at the very back of the hall, as far as he could be from the stage and still be inside the palace. He had a slim build and a crown of curly dark red hair and a smile that could be seen from across the city. He was looking straight at Val.

She stopped breathing.

Sebastian?

She wanted to rub her eyes and stare in his direction but instead she averted her gaze so that no one—not her brother, not her aunt, not any of the dozens of palace guards patrolling the foyer with the explicit intention of keeping the new king safe—*no one* noticed where her attention was focused.

I'd be risking my life if one of Darien's soldiers apprehended me, he had said in his last letter.

She hadn't told him she was coming to Chialto. She hadn't had time to write him and receive his reply, so she hadn't bothered to try to set up a meeting. And she couldn't stop fretting over Sebastian's last communication. Darien was entirely capable of assigning a guard to follow her around the city; if Sebastian was engaged in criminal activities, Val did not want to lead a soldier straight to his door.

So Sebastian couldn't have known for certain that Val would be in Chialto, though he obviously could have guessed that she might put in an appearance at her brother's coronation. But surely he was too clever to make his way to the ceremony just to get a glimpse of her. It couldn't possibly be Sebastian. There was no need to worry.

She spent five minutes staring straight ahead of her, listening to but not comprehending the acolyte's final summation and benediction, holding her body so still she didn't even flinch when the woman next to her accidentally elbowed her in the arm. Then she slowly, casually, turned her head to sweep the whole foyer with a single comprehensive glance.

The shadows were empty. The red-haired man was gone.

Chapter Two

Val had recovered her equanimity by the time the coronation finally ended, but the interminable day was far from over. Once the ceremony was done, there was a great deal of milling about in the great hall and the courtyard just outside the palace, and then there was a reception, and then there was a dinner, and then there was another reception.

Her only consolation was that progressively fewer people attended each of these events, so that by the time everyone had gathered for the final round of drinks and conversation, fewer than fifty remained. And they had moved from the cavernous formal dining hall to the space her mother used to refer to as "the lesser ballroom." It was spacious enough to accommodate a hundred guests, but its pale colors and comfortable furniture made it feel cozier than many of the grand rooms at the palace. Little alcoves behind big plants offered places for someone to sit if she was trying to avoid attention, and tall windows with narrow balconies provided an escape if she needed to feel cool air on her cheeks.

It was close to midnight when Val took refuge on one of these balconies. There were no chairs, but she leaned her elbows on the iron railing and let some of the tension seep from her shoulders.

The view was enough to make anyone go slack with awe. The lesser ballroom was on the second floor of the palace, and its windows looked out over the southeastern walls. From here, she could see the broad, still surface of the small lake that lay just past the courtyard, a pool of blackness just barely illuminated by the lights thrown from the palace windows. It was formed by the Marisi River, which paused here just long enough to fill the shallow basin before rushing down a short drop and a narrow canyon to form the ragged eastern edge of the city. Val thought she could make out flickers of light on its restless currents, and she could certainly hear the low rumble of its incessant fall.

If she turned her head to the right, she could see most of Chialto laid out before her. The palace was situated halfway up a low mountain, visible from every point in the city that spread out over the flat plain below. Even this late at night, there were enough gaslit streetlamps and candlelit windows to suggest the outlines of houses. She could see the great imperfect circle of the Cinque cutting its pattern through the neighborhoods, tying the whole city together. Fast-moving lights indicated the passage of elaymotives; slower ones were probably carts and carriages. In the years since Val had been in the city, the elaymotives had become vastly more popular, outnumbering the horse-drawn conveyances by two to one. Until she'd ridden in one, Val had thought she would hate the new machines, powered by some mysterious gas manufactured by the elay prime. But she'd instantly loved the luxurious interior, the smooth ride, the swift transit.

It wasn't true that a hunti woman could never change her mind. It was just rare.

Behind her, there was a brief swell of sound as the door to the balcony opened and closed, and someone stepped outside. Val half-turned to frown at the newcomer, hoping the person would slip back inside once it was clear the space was already occupied. In the dark, she didn't immediately recognize who had joined her, but she could tell it was a woman.

"I thought I saw you sneak out here," the new arrival said in a tone of satisfaction.

Val was surprised to recognize Corene's voice. The sweela princess might be the last person she would have expected to seek her out. "It's been a long day," she answered. "I'm not sure I have one more conversation left in me."

She intended it as a hint, but Corene chose to ignore it. "No, this has been even worse than some of the state dinners for foreign royalty who came to visit, and I thought nothing could be more dreadful," she said. "I don't know how Darien is still on his feet, but he doesn't even look tired. That's a hunti man for you."

"Darien is inhuman," Val said. "Nothing ever wearies him."

"It's one of the most annoying things about him," Corene agreed. "Though to be fair, there are many annoying things about Darien."

Val couldn't help a small snort of laughter at that. "Did he become more annoying or less so once you discovered he was your father?"

Corene crossed the small space to lean her elbows on the railing, so Val resumed her former position, and they both looked out over the city. "Well, so many other things were going on right then that it was hard to separate out the Darien part of it from all the rest," she said. "I was eleven, and I didn't understand how much was about to change." She glanced at Val, then back at the view. "But when Darien got involved in my life—some of it was a lot better. He protected me. He gave me a refuge from my mother. But he also made it harder for me to figure out who I really wanted to be."

"They say you ran away to Malinqua with a palace guard."

Corene laughed. "I did run away to Malinqua! I thought it would be an adventure. And it was, though *nothing* like what I expected. Foley came with me, but it was only later that we became lovers."

Val almost flinched at the word *lovers*. Who talked so openly of such things, especially to someone who was practically a stranger? She spoke stiffly. "I suppose many people frown at the notion of a princess taking up with a common soldier." Val was one of them; she had always believed there were certain rules about who made a suitable partner for whom, and she was always a little shocked when other people didn't respect those conventions.

"Oh, I've heard plenty of whispers since I've been back," Corene said, sounding amused. "Nothing the Five Families love more than a scandal! It doesn't bother me."

"What has Darien said?"

"He's been careful not to say anything. I think he's hoping it's an infatuation that I'll outgrow, so he figures he'll just let it burn itself out."

And is it? Val thought about asking. She was curious, but not curious enough to invite more confidences. She was somewhat uncomfortable with the easy intimacy Corene seemed to offer. It took Val much longer to warm up to people, to want to share dreams and secrets. "Maybe he's hoping one day you'll make a strategic marriage with a political ally," she said instead.

"Maybe, but the two times anyone considered me as a bride to a foreign prince, everything was pretty disastrous, so I'm not sure Darien would want to try it again," Corene said cheerfully. "Anyway, I think he's figured out he can't make me do anything I don't want to do, so I don't expect him to be making plans for me any time soon."

"Well, that's an achievement," Val said. "Getting your own way with Darien."

For a moment, silence fell between them as they watched the lights below them wink and fade. Val wondered if the whole city ever went dark at any point. Or was someone always awake, no matter the time of day? She always felt a slight disapproval for people who kept irregular hours. She could think of no good reason anyone would want to be roaming the streets or even sitting up at home in the middle of the night.

Val was hoping Corene would find the silence awkward enough to make her excuses and leave, but apparently that was not the case. "So I suppose you're my aunt," the princess said next.

Val didn't put any warmth into her voice. "I suppose I am."

"It seems very strange. I mean, you're hardly any older than me."

"Eight years," Val said promptly, since this was the sort of thing she always kept track of. "If you're nineteen, as I believe you are."

"I am," said Corene. "But it still feels odd. I mean, even before I knew Darien was my father, I *knew* him. The last few years Vernon was alive,

Darien practically lived at the palace. But I hardly remember ever seeing *you*."

Val was surprised by her complex reaction to that, a mix of anger and sadness and irritation. Why should she have to explain anything to this insensitive girl? And was Corene only saying out loud what everyone else at court was thinking? *Valentina Serlast? You mean, she's still alive? I haven't thought of her for the past ten years.*

"I spent about a third of my life in Chialto until I was sixteen," she said, keeping her voice even. "My father kept a set of apartments in the palace, so I was here whenever we weren't on the hunti estates in the country. But my father and Darien were in the city almost all the time. Darien is twelve years older than I am, and our father would bring him to all his important meetings. Once my father died, I thought Darien would step back from the court life, but if anything, he just got more involved. Vernon started to count on him for everything. My mother and I almost never saw him anymore."

"Did you stay in the city after your father died?"

"Part of the time. Mirti asked us to keep living at the estates, because she didn't have much interest in managing the property, so we did that for a while. And we spent some time in Chialto at a house Darien had found for us. But I hated it. My mother hated it. Five or six years ago, we moved back to the countryside to be near one of my mother's sisters. I've only been to the city a couple of times since then."

Corene appeared to be listening closely to the timeline. "So were you already gone by the time—" She made a sweeping gesture. "Everything happened?"

That fetched another slight laugh from Val. "You mean, when Zoe arrived and she turned everything upside down and Vernon died and everyone found out all his secrets? No, I was still here."

Something in her tone of voice seemed to catch Corene's attention, because she turned to appraise Val in the dark. "You don't like Zoe," she observed.

"I didn't say that."

Corene ignored this. "Is it because she brings so much chaos with her?"

It's because I thought I would get my brother back after Vernon died, but Zoe took him even farther away from me. "She does do that."

Corene nodded. "But all the primes do—or could—if they wanted to," she said. "I mean, Nelson could burn the city down! Taro can cause mountains to collapse. Kayle could whip up such a storm that it would blow houses over. And let's face it, Kayle is so odd that he causes a disruption just by walking into the room," she finished with a laugh.

"Mirti doesn't cause chaos," Val said defensively. "She's the *opposite* of chaos. She brings order and—and—solidity."

"It's hard to imagine what the hunti prime would do," Corene admitted. "Knock over a bunch of trees on someone's head? But I still think she could cause a lot of damage if she wanted to."

"She wouldn't want to," Val said.

Corene shrugged. "I suppose it depends on the provocation. And I've never seen Zoe do anything spectacular without a really good reason."

"So you like her. Your stepmother."

"I adore her. She saved my life. She saved Josetta's life."

Josetta was the daughter of Vernon's second queen; it turned out *she* had been sired by Zoe's father. It was almost impossible to keep track of all the tangled bloodlines, and some days Val didn't even feel like trying.

Corene wasn't done yet. "But it's more than that. Zoe loves me in ways no one else in my family does. She would flood Chialto to keep me safe, but she'd never hold on to me so tightly I couldn't breathe. She *believes* in me. And she's just likable. Friendly. Funny. And kind. And she's the best thing that ever happened to Darien. He's almost relaxed when he's around her."

She's so much more important to him than any sister could ever be. "I'm sure I'll have a chance to get to know her better while I'm here."

"How long do you plan to stay?"

"I don't know. Maybe a day or two, and then I'll go home."

"Where's that?"

"The house I lived in with my mother before she died. It's out in the country, and we rent land to several families, so I have a lot of details to take care of."

"Like what?"

Well, this was a tiresome interrogation. "Like, what crops should we plant this year, because last year's harvest wasn't so good but maybe that was because of the weather, and is it time to invest in new equipment, and if one farmer is about to retire should I split his land among the other renters or look for a new tenant? Maybe it doesn't sound like much, but it can take a lot of time."

She thought Corene might roll her eyes and exclaim, *How unutterably boring!* but the princess just nodded. "It sounds more like a torz life than a hunti one."

"My mother was torz," Val admitted. "She loved everything that had to do with land management. It doesn't come as naturally to me, but it keeps me busy."

"Who's watching the place while you're gone?"

"I have an estate manager who's very reliable."

"So you could stay longer if you wanted. A whole quintile, maybe."

"I don't think I'll want to be in Chialto that long." *I didn't want to come here to begin with.*

"Why? Is there someone waiting for you back home? Someone you're in love with?"

Val stared at her resentfully in dark. Who would ask such personal questions? "I don't think that's any of your business."

"Oooh, there is, isn't there? Someone unsuitable? Someone Darien wouldn't approve of?"

"You mean, like a palace guard?" Val said sharply.

Corene laughed. "Or worse! A gardener! An illiterate laborer with a good heart and soulful eyes. Oh, now I'm hoping that's who it is."

"I didn't say there was anyone."

Corene shrugged. "Sweela people always suspect a hidden romance. And we're right more times than not."

Unbidden, Val's mind called up that face she thought she'd seen in the crowd. Surely that hadn't been Sebastian. *We all know I'm not a careful man,* he'd written in his last note, his tone as jaunty as ever. *But these are particularly hazardous enterprises and I don't want to catch your brother's attention. It's a little too dramatic to say I'd be risking my life if one of Darien's soldiers apprehended me, but it certainly would be unpleasant, so I'm being as cautious as I can be. But I've never had this much fun before.*

If he was being cautious, he wouldn't have showed his face in the most public venue in the city, on a day when palace guards were on the highest possible alert. Right? Even Sebastian wouldn't have been that careless.

Of course Sebastian would be that careless.

"Indulging in doomed romances has always seemed like a waste of time to me," Val said coolly. "If there's no future, what's the point?"

"Feelings don't care if there's a future," Corene said. It was clear from her voice that she was smiling. "Feelings don't care if there's a point."

"I don't think I'll ever understand the sweela mind," Val said.

That wasn't entirely true. Sebastian was sweela, and Val understood him as well as she understood anybody. But that was only because she'd known him since she was eight years old.

Corene was laughing. "I've had a lot of practice learning the hunti mind, and I'm starting to figure it out," she said. "I think we'll manage to be friends."

Val couldn't keep herself from staring at Corene in shock. "We *will*?"

"Oh, yes. You'll see. It will be fun."

Chapter Three

Fortunately, there was no real opportunity for Corene to pursue this newfound friendship right away. The evening finally ended and Val was able to retreat to her bedroom, collapse on her bed, and sleep until late morning. At which point the maid who arrived to help her dress informed her that Darien was hosting an informal luncheon for the family members and primes who had remained at the palace, and she should put in an appearance within the hour. Val groaned but climbed out of bed and proceeded to make herself presentable.

Contrary to her expectations, the luncheon was indeed a casual affair with only about a dozen people in attendance, and she actually liked one of them. She filled her plate from the sideboard then made her way directly toward Taro Frothen, the torz prime, and one of her favorite people in the world. He was a big, rumpled, comfortable man who looked like he'd come straight off the farm even on the days he was dressed in formal attire and about to meet foreign royalty. Today he hadn't bothered with the pretense. He wore wrinkled trousers and a loose, overlarge tunic marked with several visible repairs. It was possible he hadn't combed his hair, or even washed it. But as Val set her plate down next to his and pulled up a chair, he gave her a warm smile that bathed her whole body in sunshine.

"There you are," he said. "I haven't had a chance to talk to you since you've been in Chialto. How are you doing?"

"I hate it here," she replied promptly. "I want to go home."

He nodded. "So do I. Let's leave right after we eat."

She laughed. Taro was famous for refusing to travel to the city except when it was absolutely imperative, which usually was less often than either Vernon or Darien would have liked. "Maybe I'll come visit you for a while," she said.

He nodded at his wife, who was sitting at the other end of the table. She was holding Celia on her lap and having an animated conversation with Mirti and Zoe. "We'd be happy to have you. Stay as long as you like."

"And you could tell me what I should do with the smaller farm," she said, and launched into a recitation of her latest crop troubles. He listened intently and made a few suggestions, and she felt herself growing more cheerful than she had since her arrival in Chialto. Taro always had that effect on her. Well, he had that effect on most people. The torz prime was affiliated with the land and the body, and he personified the joy of earthly pleasures, simple touch, fellowship, solidity, and nurturing plenty. Everyone drew strength from the torz prime.

She was related to him somehow through her mother, though her mother hadn't been a Frothen by birth. "You can just consider me your uncle," he had told Val when she was a little girl, and so she had. She suspected he extended the same offer to everyone, but not everyone needed it as much as she had. Sometimes it was hard to be hunti, all precise angles and strict rules. Sometimes she had to rest all those edges against something a little more forgiving.

They had been talking for twenty minutes when someone tapped a fork against a glass goblet to gather the attention of everyone in the room. "Who would be so rude?" Val huffed under her breath.

"Nelson," Taro replied. "Of course."

Nelson Ardelay was the sweela prime, a loud, cheerful man with the red hair and ruddy coloring that characterized most of his clan. He perfectly modeled the sweela traits of fire and mind, as he was both restless and brilliant. He was close to Zoe, whose father had been Nelson's brother; and given that Corene was sitting right next to him, Val suspected that he was close to the princess as well. Val had always found him a bit overbearing and not entirely comfortable to be around, but it was impossible not to like him.

"Let us all drink a toast to our new king!" Nelson exclaimed, holding aloft a glass of fruited water. "Maybe he rule long and peacefully, and may Welce prosper under his hand."

Everyone else greeted this proposal with murmurs of agreement, raising their own glasses and tilting them in Darien's direction. Darien responded with a nod and a cool smile, his expression as composed as ever.

Nelson dropped back to his seat and leaned across the table in Darien's direction. "So tell us! What great plans do you have in store for the first year of your glorious reign?"

"No great plans," Darien said, though everyone in the room knew he wouldn't share them if he had them. "I hope to continue expanding our international trade, particularly developing more agreements with Malinqua and Cozique. I hope to maintain peace with Soeche-Tas—though, as you know, that's always a fraught and fragile endeavor. But at the moment, their leaders aren't agitating for any impossible arrangements, so our current treaties hold."

Nelson sipped at his water with such enthusiasm that Val suspected he might have added a measure of alcohol to spice it up. "But there's a little trouble brewing with Soeche-Tas, isn't there? Wasn't there a skirmish along the border just a couple of days ago?"

Welce shared a small continent with Soeche-Tas, though the two nations were divided by an inhospitable mountain range that discouraged large-scale conflicts. Val's father had once said that if any of the mountain passes had been wide enough to allow three men to walk through side-by-side, the countries would have been permanently at war. But they both maintained excellent navies and patrolled their ocean approaches so diligently that there had never been any reason to open hostilities.

Darien nodded again. Val couldn't tell from his impassive expression if he was annoyed that Nelson had introduced the topic. "There was. There have been a number of these small skirmishes, as you call them, over the past five or six months. I am working to contain them. I am not sure yet how ruthless I will have to be."

Mirti looked over with a frown. "What's the problem?"

Darien toyed with the stem of his own water glass. "International commerce, in fact, is the root cause. Soeche-Tas has been ramping up its exportation of sirix, which, for those of you who don't know, is a specialty wine with a rapidly growing popularity. The government has been subsidizing small vineyards in an effort to increase production, while buying up larger operations to run under its own auspices. Their goal, as I understand it, is to make sirix a luxury product famous the world over—or at least, famous among the southern nations."

"Everybody in Cozique was mad for it when I was there," Corene said. "But you could hardly ever find it and it was *so* expensive. If you were at a party and the hostess served sirix, you knew the event would be a success."

Val shared a glance with Taro and they both rolled their eyes. As if anyone could care that much about a drink. As if anyone could care that much about a party.

"On the face of it," Mirti said in her usual dry way, "this doesn't seem to concern Welce at all."

"It wouldn't, except that there is a thriving black market in smuggled sirix."

"Which, again, Welce shouldn't care about," Nelson said.

"Except that much of the contraband is going through Welchin hands and Welchin ports."

"Ahhhh." Nelson leaned back in his chair, still fiddling with his glass. "So the Soechin government is losing profits because of the illegal activities of its own countrymen—but it's blaming Welce for making those illegal activities possible."

"Precisely," said Darien. "And it's not just that the government is losing revenue. It wants to position itself as the source of a luxury product, but sometimes the smugglers are exporting inferior products and marketing them under pirated labels."

"Diluting the quality of the brand and making buyers more skittish, thus depressing the market further," Nelson said.

Corene unexpectedly entered the conversation. "I don't see that as a problem at all," she said. "The authentic vintners simply have to find ways to guarantee their products. They can raise their prices and gain even *more* cachet because what they're selling is genuine."

"Except some buyers don't care if what they have is genuine or not," Nelson said. "They just like to *appear* as if they're up on the latest fashions."

"It doesn't really matter to me what motivates the people who buy the pirated sirix," said Darien. "If Soeche-Tas is distressed by the smugglers and blames Welce for providing safe passage, my concern is figuring how to shut down the illegal operations on this side of the border."

Taro lifted his voice. "What have you done so far?"

Darien looked frustrated. "Very little. As far as I can tell, there is no real centralized operation—just a network of loosely connected confederates who follow dozens if not hundreds of different routes to bring the contraband into the country."

"Are they coming across the mountains?" Taro asked.

"Sometimes. Sometimes they're coming in at the smaller ports."

"You mean like the one up by the northwest border?" Zoe said.

"Unfortunately, no," Darien said. "I could set up a blockade there. But the wine fetches such a high price that they don't need much to make a profit. So they're bringing it in barrel by barrel, using small private docks and fishermen's piers and narrow coves that barely accommodate a rowboat."

Nelson looked both appalled and amused. Val had the sense that he might be on the side of the smugglers. He loved an enterprising scoundrel. "There must be thousands of docks like that on the western seaboard."

"Exactly. I cannot possibly patrol every one."

"And I suppose the problem is the same with the mountain passes," said Taro. "There are countless places where a single man can squeeze through with a small cargo. You'd have to spread an army across the continent to guard them all."

"Exactly," Darien repeated. "All I can really do is heighten security in the main harbor south of Chialto, but that's a delicate balance. I don't want to make the port unfriendly to the foreign merchants I have been working so hard to entice to Welce. And I certainly don't want to give them reasons to head for Soeche-Tas ports instead."

"Well, it's a conundrum," Nelson said. His voice was edged with boredom; clearly, he was less excited about the challenges of law enforcement than the logistics of smuggling. "I'm sure you'll figure something out."

Darien rested his gray eyes on Nelson's face. "I certainly hope so," he said. "Let me know if any clever ideas occur to you."

After that, conversation became general again. Taro's attention was claimed by Mirti, but his wife took his place at Val's side. Since she was also a warm torz presence, Val barely minded the substitution. But she was just as glad when people started leaving and it looked like the last celebration of the coronation might finally, finally be over.

Maybe she could go home tomorrow or the day after. She could leave Chialto behind so quickly she would barely remember she'd been here at all.

It turned out Darien had other plans.

Late in the afternoon, he asked her to meet him in his office, a comfortable room with high ceilings and plush furniture. He'd placed a couple of chairs before the tall windows and set up a tray of refreshments between them, as if he thought they would have a cozy chat. Val warily sank into a seat and accepted a glass of fruited water from his hand.

"Are you enjoying your visit?" he asked.

She didn't particularly want to antagonize him, so she shaded the truth. "It's been interesting to be back in Chialto after so long," she said. "But I miss the quiet of my house."

He held a glass of his own but didn't sip from it; instead, he studied her for a moment. "I find myself wondering if the house might be *too* quiet for you."

"What? Why would you think that?"

"There's nothing but farms and small towns for a hundred miles. I can't think you have much in the way of entertainment or companionship."

"Fortunately, I don't require entertainment and I don't need much companionship," she snapped.

He tilted his head to one side. "I am not certain it is good for you to be buried in the countryside as you are," he said.

"I am not certain you're an expert on what's good for me."

"You have to realize I have your best interests at heart."

She remained silent and just watched him. Darien was the most determined and unyielding person she had ever met. If he had a plan in mind, he was all but certain to execute it. He almost always got his way.

Of course, Val herself was hunti to the bone. She prided herself on being one of the few people who had occasionally refused to yield to Darien's wishes.

"I've been thinking you might come stay in Chialto for some time," he said. "A few ninedays. Maybe a quintile or two."

"No."

"You haven't even heard my reasons."

She remembered her conversation with Corene the night before. "You don't want to try to marry me off to some foreign dignitary, do you?"

His face lightened with one of his rare smiles. "I can imagine few schemes more destined for failure! Unless you had someone in mind?"

She felt an unexpected smile tug at her own mouth. "I've met very few of them, but the stories I've heard make most of them sound dreadful."

"I would lock you in your room if you wanted to run away with a viceroy from Soeche-Tas," he agreed. "Or a prince from Berringuey. *Or* the Karkades. *Or* Dhonsho. Each nation barbaric and terrifying in its own way, at least when it comes to the customs at court. I believe the heirs to the throne in Malinqua are more sophisticated and less blood-thirsty, so I wouldn't stop you if you wanted to take up residence there. Though Cozique would be your best choice, from everything I hear. A beautiful country, an enlightened queen, and a very civilized society. Corene lived there for a couple of quintiles, and she makes it sound most attractive."

"I've learned to speak Coziquela," Val said, "but I have no desire to visit the country. I'm not much for travel, as you know."

"I'm happy to have you stay in Welce, but I wish you would extend your visit to Chialto."

That quickly he had managed to turn the conversation back to his original topic. "I don't want to remain in Chialto," she said. "I like my life at home. I miss my house."

"It's been an empty house since our mother died," he said deliberately.

It had been obvious that would be his attack, so she was braced for it; she didn't even flinch. "I employ half-a-dozen workers who share the property, and I have daily interactions with tenants, neighbors, merchants, and friends. I can't remember the last time I was truly alone. I don't think you need to picture me sobbing in solitude."

"I still believe a change would do you good," he said. "I would like you to come to Chialto."

She permitted herself a small, cold smile, not really a smile at all. "Why now? Our mother has been dead for nearly two years."

"And I have invited you here many times," he reminded her. "This is the first chance I have had to make the offer in person."

"Why would that be?" she asked. "Oh, because you've rarely bothered to come to the house in the past six years?"

"More often than you've come to the city."

"I don't like the city."

"You don't like change."

"An interesting accusation from a hunti man."

"But your life has changed around you against your will," he went on. "And unless I miss my guess, you're still grieving."

In an instant, she lost her calm control. "And unless I miss mine, you never grieved at all."

He didn't look hurt or surprised, though his expression turned a shade more sober. "Our mother's death hit me harder than anything since our father died. Some days the world still seems off-balance."

"And yet you left me wholly alone to care for her while she was sick."

"That's not true," he said. "I was there five times that last year."

"Five times! Five ninedays at most! I was there every *hour*. Every *minute*. Every chore fell to me, every decision. Should I try this treatment, should I move her to this room, should I bring in her closest friends or should I keep her quiet to conserve her strength? The burden was so heavy and I had no one to share it with. *You* were the one who should have shared it. But you weren't there. Even before she was sick—all those years, as she began failing—I had to take care of everything because *you weren't there*."

A shade of anger crossed his face, a rare display of emotion from Darien. "No. I was trying to shore up a dying king and prevent the country from falling apart. I was chasing down criminals who had tried to kill a princess and serving as regent for a child too fragile to ever take the throne. I had responsibilities so numerous and so immense that some days I did not think I could perform them. And you would have asked me to walk away from them?"

"Someone else could have performed them! You're not the only man who can govern a kingdom."

He struck back hard. "You're not the only woman who can manage a sickroom. Would you have trusted someone else to take care of our mother?"

She stared at him and did not have an answer.

"I did not believe anyone else could do the job I had to do," he said more quietly. "And so I stayed."

She found her voice. "And if I hadn't been there? Would you have let our mother die alone?"

"I would have brought her to Chialto and had her cared for here. Or I would have installed someone at the house who answered to me night and day. It is *because* you were with her that I could take up my tasks here. It is not that I abandoned you. It is that I had faith in you."

"I *needed* you," she whispered. "And you weren't there."

He watched her for a long moment, nothing to be read behind his set expression. Darien never believed he was in the wrong, so she waited bitterly for him to refuse to apologize now. But his voice, when he spoke, was softer than she expected. "Faced with the same situation today, I would make the same choice," he said. "But I am sorry your burden was so crushing. And I am sorry that you are still so angry at me. I had hoped we could find a way to close some of the distance that has grown up between us."

She would not let herself even think about crying. "Your life has taken you far from me. I think some of that distance is inevitable."

He nodded. "It's true. I cannot easily leave the city, because so many threads tie me in place. Which is why I wish *you* would come *here*. I cannot come to you and I miss you."

Her lips parted. *That* she had not expected—that Darien would resort to vulnerability. She had no defense against it. She could resist pressure all day long, leaning stubbornly against it with her own intransigence, but take away the opposing force and she stumbled forward, absolutely powerless.

"I'm no different than I ever was," she managed.

He smiled and held his hand out to her. "Really?" he said. "I am as hunti as you are, and even I have changed. Surely you have as well."

"I don't want to stay in Chialto," she said, but she laid her hand in his anyway. His fingers closed over hers, warm and reassuring.

"I can't make you," he said.

She choked on a laugh. "You make people do things all the *time!*"

He smiled back. "Not when I don't want them to hate me."

"I don't *hate* you."

"Then will you stay?"

She looked at him helplessly. "How long?"

"A quintile? Maybe to the end of Quinnatorz? Of course, if you can't bear it, you can always leave sooner."

It was a hollow reassurance; he knew that she would honor any promise she made. If she said she would stay for a quintile, she would not leave a day sooner. "What will I *do* while I'm here?"

"Meet foreign princes?"

"I mean *really*."

He stood up, tugging her to her feet before he dropped her hand. "Just see where the days take you," he said. "It might be more interesting than you think."

Chapter Four

The next day was anything but interesting, as heavy rains kept everyone indoors unless they had inflexible commitments. Val had only one thing she had to do, and that was quickly accomplished: write a letter to her estate agent, telling him she would be away for a few ninedays and authorizing him to make day-to-day decisions.

She signed the note with her usual precise flourish. *Valentina Serlast*, the V cut in half by a sweeping horizontal line that crossed the t in *tina*. It was a signature she had perfected when she was ten, having spent hours getting the decorative line perfectly placed. As an adult, she knew it was an overdramatic affectation, and yet she couldn't force herself to abandon it. She even retained the ornamentation when she was simply using her initials—the V bisected by the curving line, the S tucked against the severe slant. *This is me. This is who I was as a child and this is who I am today.*

But once the letter was finished, there wasn't much else on her agenda to absorb her time. Darien was closeted all day with advisors and visitors, so Val only saw him at breakfast and dinner, and even then he was preoccupied. She spent a couple of hours trying to get to know her youngest niece, but Val had never been particularly good with children and Celia's inexhaustible energy quickly wore her out. She thought hopefully that the little girl might get more interesting when she was older. Most people did.

The following day was still overcast and gloomy, but at least the rain had stopped. Val took refuge in the conservatory, a large, humid room of high glass walls and overbearing greenery, and hid behind a tall, thick-stemmed plant. She'd brought a book and a handful of snacks, and the gardeners left her alone, so all in all she passed a pleasant few hours between late morning and early afternoon.

Which was when Corene found her.

"Look, the sun's coming out" was Corene's greeting. "Put on some comfortable shoes. We're going to have an adventure."

Val couldn't restrain a frown. "I don't think I want an adventure."

"Of course you do. You can't just sit here all day." As Val opened her mouth to say that, in fact, that was exactly what she wanted to do, Corene went on. "And if you don't come with me, I'll just stay here and keep talking to you anyway, so you might as well agree now. Come on. Let's go."

It was all too easy to imagine Corene carrying out this threat. Unexpectedly, Val felt a surge of restlessness. She'd been cooped up in the palace too long. And the sun *was* shining.

"All right," she said, closing her book. "What do you want to do?"

Corene's eyes gleamed with mischief. "We're going to find some sirix."

※

When Val and Corene stepped out of the grand front doors, they found a compact elaymotive idling at one end of the broad stone courtyard. Years ago, when Val had been a child living at the palace, the easiest way to get from the royal court to the city below was on one of the public omnibuses that continually traveled the route back and forth. Then, all the conveyances had been horse-drawn, smelly, and slow. She had noticed that many of the current omnibuses were elaymotives, which was probably a decided improvement.

"Darien lets me borrow one of his smoker cars whenever I want to," Corene explained as they headed to the vehicle.

"Are you planning to drive it?"

"I *can* drive, but I'm not very good at it. Foley will take us."

Foley turned out to be a strongly built young man with light brown hair, an open face, and a watchful attitude. He just nodded when Corene made careless introductions as she and Val climbed into the back seat. Val studied his profile and wondered what had drawn the vivacious princess to the taciturn soldier. He looked most ordinary.

"So how do you think we're going to find sirix?" Val said as Foley eased the car forward and headed down the steep road.

"Mmm, well, it's not illegal to sell it—if a bar owner has purchased it from a Soechin trader," Corene said. "So I would think it would be available at any of the upscale places around the plazas."

"So we're staying in the nicer parts of town," Val said with some relief.

The mischief was back on Corene's face. "No! We want to try smuggled sirix. So we're going southside."

Val groaned, but Foley turned his head to glance back at them. "No, we're not," he said. "I'm not taking one of your father's cars across the canal."

"So we'll park it somewhere safe and cross on foot."

"No, we won't," he answered. He didn't say it, but the corollary hung in the air. *I'm not taking* you *across the canal, either.*

Corene hunched a shoulder but didn't argue. It was the first thing that made Val actually like her. She was a headlong sweela girl, but she wasn't foolhardy. She would listen to reason. Or at least she would listen to Foley.

"Then let's go to the bachelor district," she said. "There must be all kinds of questionable venues there."

Foley's silence seemed to indicate assent. They continued down the mountain until he turned onto the Cinque, the five-sided boulevard that made a loop around the outer perimeter of the city. Val gazed out the windows, intrigued. Foley immediately headed east and south so their route was bordered by the tumbling Marisi River. This was not a direction that was familiar to Val—she had spent most of her time in the northwest quadrant of the city where the rich families had their homes and the most exclusive merchants set up their shops. But in this part of town, there was a jumble of different styles and neighborhoods, changing almost block by block. On one street were what appeared to be small individual homes for prosperous tradesmen; on another, rows of somewhat dreary apartments where laborers and working-class families might live. Farther down were clusters of well-kept buildings of varying sizes and styles, not opulent but not cheap, either. Some appeared to be residences, while others were storefronts for shops or clubs. Foley slowed and turned off the Cinque into one of the side roads lined with commercial establishments.

"This is the bachelor's district?" Val asked. "I've never been here before."

"I haven't been here *often*," Corene said. "Rafe says—"

"Who's Rafe?"

"Josetta's husband. He used to be a gambler across the canal. He says this part of town is like a more respectable version of the southside. You can get in trouble here, but only if you're looking for it. You're not likely to get assaulted in the streets, but you can indulge your vices if you want."

Val looked out a little fearfully. In the afternoon sunshine, the brick and wood and plaster buildings looked perfectly ordinary, even welcoming. Not dangerous at all. "I don't have any vices I want to indulge."

"Well, you can pretend, can't you?"

Foley found a place to park the elaymotive, a lot watched over by a bored young man who charged them a quint-silver. Corene stood on the street corner, hands on her hips, critically eying the options. "Those two look like restaurants—those two look like bars—which one would be most likely to have contraband sirix?"

"The seedy one," Val said, pointing.

"Maybe," Corene said. "But I think the fancy restaurant is a better bet. Because sirix is expensive and if you can't afford a pricey meal, you probably can't afford imported wine."

"I guess that makes sense," Val said.

"Then let's go."

Foley followed them to the building, a well-maintained two-story structure of white stone softened by climbing ivy. The front door and the window shutters were all made of wide slabs of dark wood, and they were all tightly shut, but appealing odors of onions and spices scented the air just outside.

"I won't come in," Foley said. "But I'll be right here. Shout if you need me."

Corene stepped inside, Val on her heels. Despite the shuttered windows, the place projected a warm and cozy air. The floor and lower half of the walls were covered with the same dark polished wood, brightened by a cheerful fire in a large pit in the center of the room, candles on every table, and discreet gaslight that illuminated the whitewashed ceiling. At this time of day, the place had a somewhat somnolent feel. Only a few of the high-backed booths were occupied and no one sat at the freestanding tables surrounding the fire pit.

"Should we sit at a booth?" asked Val, who liked her privacy.

But Corene shook her head and made straight for the table closest to the door. "Too easy for someone to trap you in booth," she said. "And Foley could hear us better from here if we started screaming for help."

They took their seats across from each other. Val moved the candles from the center of the table so she could study Corene's face without anything getting in her way. "Those aren't things I've ever considered before."

Corene grimaced. "I've had reason to run away from someone more than once. I start looking for escape routes the minute I walk into someplace new. It's become a habit."

Val felt her eyebrows rise. "You've had to run away from people? While you were in Malinqua?"

"Yes, and even when I was in Welce." She grinned. "I've had a rather adventurous life."

"Now I want to hear some of those stories."

A smiling man approached the table. He wore neat black clothing designed to draw no attention, and kept his long hair tied back in a ponytail. He wasn't particularly young, and the wrinkles around his eyes and the scar on his right cheek hinted at a life even more adventurous than Corene's. Val thought he might be the owner instead of a mere employee; he had a clever aspect and an air of authority. He had recognized rich young women when they came through his door, and he wanted to make sure they received the proper attention.

"Good afternoon," he greeted them. "I'm Geoffrey. Welcome to my establishment. Is there something I can get you? Are you hungry or thirsty?"

"Both, I think," Corene said. "But could we start with food? What would you recommend?"

"What does the princess like?" he countered.

So he had, indeed, recognized them, or at least one of them. Corene laughed, and Val was relieved. It seemed even less likely that they would come to harm if the proprietor knew he was dealing with Darien's daughter. "It is very hard for me to be incognito in this city," she said, faking a pout. "I'm so disappointed! I never get a chance to behave badly and have no one be the wiser."

"I can pretend you are just another rich girl testing the limits of her father's patience," Geoffrey replied with a grin. Val thought with indignation that they were actually flirting with each other. "In what small way can I contribute to your afternoon of mild debauchery?"

Now Corene glanced at Val, a smile spreading across her face. "I do like a sweela rogue, don't you?" she said.

Val couldn't emulate Corene's reckless insouciance, but she tried to make her own contribution to the charade. She puckered her forehead and infused worry into her voice. "Oh, I hope we won't get into trouble," she said.

Geoffrey gave her a quick, polite glance, but clearly the king's sister was a stranger to him. Val was both piqued and relieved. "No trouble," he said. "Just—a taste of life that might not normally come your way."

Corene leaned toward him in a conspiratorial fashion, clearly ready to share secrets, and he returned all his attention to her. "I wondered—do you have—I have been hearing about this marvelous new drink from Soeche-Tas. But nobody has it, or nobody is *supposed* to have it, and I don't know what all the fuss is about. And I want to know."

The bar owner was smiling. "Perhaps you mean sirix?"

"Corene," Val hissed. "Your father said people could be *arrested* for drinking that."

"He's not going to arrest *me*."

"I don't think we should stay here."

"Nobody is going to arrest anybody," Geoffrey said smoothly. "It is true sirix is not widely available, but it's delightful, and I think you should try it if you like. But it is quite strong, and if you're not used to it, you should make sure you have a little food in your stomach before you take the first sip."

Corene was practically bouncing in her seat. "But you have some? You aren't just *saying* you have some so we'll order an expensive meal?"

He laughed at that. "The devious sweela mind," he said. "You're as much a rogue as I am."

"I doubt that," she said, but she was grinning. Val was starting to lose track of whether Corene was playing a part or showing her true self.

"I swear I will bring you the sirix once you've had a bite to eat," he said.

"And you won't send someone off to the palace to tell my father where I am?"

He laughed again. "Princess, your father is the last man I want to notice me."

"Then yes. Bring us a meal. Something tasty."

He glanced at Val to see if she had anything more specific to add, but she just shrugged and nodded. He smiled again and headed back toward the kitchen.

"That was well done!" Corene whispered as soon as he was too far away to hear. "That made him *want* to give us the sirix."

"He still might send a courier to Darien."

"He might," Corene said. "But I don't think so. I think he wants to impress us with his smuggled goods. Show off to a couple of Five Family girls."

"I'm beginning to see why you've had to run away from so much trouble in the past. Because you ran *toward* so much trouble to begin with."

"Well, some of it was my fault," Corene admitted. "But not all of it."

"So tell me some stories."

Val spent the next hour listening to heart-stopping tales and eating one of the best meals of her life. Corene would interrupt her own dramatic recitations to exclaim over an unexpected flavor or a particularly delicious garnish. "That's a spice from Berringuey but I've never had that other seasoning before," she would say, or "Oh! I had that in Cozique, but I didn't know they imported it to Welce."

As they finished the meal, she said, "I think Geoffrey is smuggling more than sirix. But he certainly has an exquisite sense of taste."

"Too bad we can't recommend this place to any of our friends," Val said, taking the last bite. "Because we can't ever admit we were here."

Corene was grinning. "Speak for yourself. *I* have friends who would come here, no questions asked."

Val couldn't help smiling in response. "Maybe Darien is the only one we can't tell."

Geoffrey was approaching the table again, carrying a tray with three cut-glass tumblers, each one about a quarter full of amber liquid. He set the glasses on the table with the air of someone producing magic and then pulled up a chair. "Sirix," he said grandly. "Let the first sip sit on your tongue for a bit, just until it starts to burn. Drink the rest of it slowly. It will go to your head fast."

Val was shocked that Geoffrey considered himself welcome to join them, but Corene appeared delighted. Corene lifted her glass to clink against his, and Val felt compelled to do the same. Then she took a cautious sip and, as instructed, let the wine linger in her mouth. It had a sweet, heady flavor that made her think of tangled patches of wildflowers too thorny to harvest. When she swallowed, she could feel the fire trail down her throat. She took another sip, and then another.

"I can actually taste the color," she said.

Geoffrey turned his smile on her, and it was as warm as the sirix. "Now, that's interesting," he said. "What color do you think it is?"

"Red and amber and really dark green. Like it's made from blooms that grow near a hidden waterfall under a pile of boulders that are always in shadow."

Geoffrey and Corene both burst out laughing. "Oh, that's perfect," Corene exclaimed. "Don't tell us if she's wrong. That's how I want to picture it from now on."

"I won't correct her, then—but she's not far off. Well done."

Corene turned wide eyes in Val's direction. "But I wouldn't have expected *you* to start spouting poetry over a glass of booze."

Val was a little embarrassed, but that didn't keep her from drinking a little more sirix. "I just had the thought."

"I told you it would go quickly to your head," Geoffrey warned.

Now Val eyed her glass with doubt. Maybe half of the liquid remained. She felt like she had hardly had any and she wanted to finish the rest. But maybe that was a bad idea. "Am I drunk?"

"Have you ever been drunk before?" Corene asked.

"Not really."

Corene shared a glance with Geoffrey and he reached over to take Val's glass away. "That might be enough for you. It's very potent."

Val couldn't help a frown of disappointment. "Maybe I could take the rest of it home with me."

"Not if you're going to the palace, you can't."

Corene smiled at him. "Maybe we'll just have to come back some other day."

"That would be most acceptable to me."

"Just one more sip," Val said.

Geoffrey returned the glass. Val considered downing the rest of the liquid in one quick gulp, but she had always heard such repulsive things about people who became inebriated. She didn't want to lose her stern self-control and begin doing irrational things. So she took one more small taste and held it on her tongue until her whole mouth was tingling.

"I really do like that," she said.

"You are not alone," Geoffrey replied.

Sunlight made a harsh bright arc at the front of the room as the door opened and Foley stuck his head inside. He didn't say anything or even cross the threshold, but it was plain he thought it was time for them to leave. Corene nodded at him and finished off her own sirix.

"This has been *most* enjoyable, but it's time for us to be getting back," she said. "We'll settle up the bill and be on our way."

Geoffrey named a sum and Corene handed over a couple of quint-gold coins. More expensive than Val would have thought, but the princess hadn't even blinked. "I owe you a little change," Geoffrey said, and headed back to the kitchen.

"Do you feel dizzy? Or just a little giddy?" Corene asked. "I can't believe I got you drunk the very first time I took you outside of the palace."

"I think I'm fine," Val said uncertainly. "But I wouldn't want to have to think too hard about anything."

"I can certainly see why people want to be smuggling sirix all over the world," Corene said. "I'll have to tell Zoe to buy some for the next state dinner. Buy it from a respectable merchant, of course."

"Zoe doesn't seem like she would care that much about what's legal and what isn't," Val remarked.

Corene laughed. "Generally that's true! But if it's something that matters to Darien, she's very strict about observing the rules."

It was an opportunity to ask something that had been on Val's mind for the past few days. "I was surprised Zoe wasn't crowned queen when Darien became king," she said.

"Oh, that's because of some old rule of law." Corene waved a vague hand. "Whoever marries the monarch has to forfeit other lands and titles. But Zoe can hardly stop being prime. So it was decided that she could keep her property and status as long as she was never named queen."

Geoffrey returned, jingling a pile of coins in his hand. "Your change," he said, setting a stack of coppers in front of Corene. "And a little bit of whimsy. My cook keeps a cauldron of blessings in the back, and he likes to pull some for every customer."

"That's charming!" Corene exclaimed. "What did he draw for me?"

Geoffrey dribbled three coins onto the table. They looked thin and cheap, not temple-quality, and they made a cheerful tinny sound as they landed.

"Courage," Corene said, picking up the first one. "Oh, he cheated! Everyone knows that's one of my random blessings!"

Geoffrey maintained a serious expression, but his eyes were merry. "He would never do such a thing."

She checked the other two. "And, let's see—grace and charm. Oh, I think *you* must have picked these out for me!"

Geoffrey placed a hand to his heart. "The blessings seem most apt for the sweela princess."

If Geoffrey was sorting through the glyphs to find the ones he thought would please his customers, Val was a little nervous to discover what he thought *she* deserved. It was probably her imagination that he watched her with a barely suppressed look of amusement as he dropped three more disks in front of her.

She turned over the first one. "Loyalty."

"A fine hunti trait," Corene pronounced.

It also happened to be one of the random blessings that had been bestowed upon Val at birth, but there seemed to be no way Geoffrey could have known that. She picked up the second one and made a face. "Surprise."

"Oh, I *love* surprise," Corene said.

"Of course you do," Val said. "I hate it."

"Of course you do."

Someone from the kitchen called Geoffrey's name. "I've got a crisis to attend to in the back," he said. "I have thoroughly enjoyed your patronage this afternoon, and I hope you return often." He bowed and hurried off.

"What's the third blessing?" Corene asked.

Val lifted it up to study the glyph in the poor light—and felt everything else fall away. Noise disappeared, the edges of her vision blurred. Even her breathing stopped.

Etched into the smooth tin surface was a set of initials nestled together. *V* and *S*, with a swooping arc cutting through the *V*.

Slowly, carefully, barely feeling the edges of the metal against her fingers, she rotated the coin so the glyph was upside down. And now she was looking at an *S* and an *A*.

Sebastian Ardelay.

"Well? Don't you recognize it? I have to admit, there are some of the symbols that I simply can't remember."

"It's a ghost coin," Val managed to say. "Nothing on it."

"Ooooh, I like that even better than surprise!" Corene said. "You're a woman of mystery!"

Val summoned a wan smile. "Do you think we're supposed to keep these or give them back?" she asked.

"Keep them, of course. They're so inexpensive Geoffrey must commission them by the hundreds. I'm surprised he doesn't have the name of the restaurant embossed on the back. Think what a great marketing tool that would be!"

"I suppose if you sell contraband sirix, you don't need to do any other marketing." Despite her shaking hands, Val managed to slip the coins in her pocket without dropping any on the floor.

She glanced around casually, trying to get a better look at the other diners. Sebastian must be here somewhere. But he wasn't one of the three men arguing in a corner booth and he wasn't at the table on the other side of the fire pit. Maybe he was working in the kitchen. Maybe he was the cook who liked to draw blessings for special customers. He had peered out when Geoffrey relayed the order for sirix, and he had recognized Val, and he had quickly snatched up some sharp, pointed kitchen tool and gouged their mirrored initials into the metal . . .

The coincidence was too fantastical. Hundreds of restaurants scattered across Chialto, and Val happened to wander into the place where Sebastian worked? Not possible.

More likely—she didn't want to think it—but more likely he had been aware of her presence in the city ever since she arrived. Maybe he'd been loitering around the palace, waiting for the day she left on an excursion, hoping to approach her casually in some public spot. He'd followed their elaymotive to the bachelor's district, and slipped around back, and wheedled his way into Geoffrey's good graces. One sweela rogue would recognize another, after all.

Val's thoughts stuttered to a halt. Or maybe Sebastian had been on the premises, delivering a contraband cargo, when he happened to spot Val sharing a meal with the sweela princess.

I'd be risking my life if one of Darien's soldiers apprehended me, Sebastian had written.

I am not sure yet how ruthless I will have to be, Darien had said.

Was it possible Sebastian was smuggling sirix into and out of Chialto?

What would happen when Darien found out?

Chapter Five

In the morning, Val was awake and out of bed shortly after sunrise. No one was in the small family dining room having breakfast, but servants hastily brought her a plate of food, which she scarcely tasted. It wasn't long before she was sitting on a wooden bench in the courtyard, staring moodily at the placid water feature and waiting for the first omnibus of the day to show up.

It lumbered up the long drive fifteen minutes later, the gas-powered motor almost noiseless. Probably twenty people disembarked—more palace staff, as well as petitioners determined to get an early audience with Darien—and a handful climbed on. The interior was empty enough that it seemed much more spacious than its horse-drawn counterparts, though Val guessed it would feel a lot less roomy when the regular crowds started boarding.

In a few minutes, they were headed back down the mountain road, swaying on the wider turns and encountering an increasing level of traffic going the other way. Val gazed sightlessly out the window as the driver turned west onto the Cinque, heading toward the wealthy districts she remembered from her childhood. She knew she should be paying attention to the changes in the familiar skyline, noting new buildings and parks, nodding approvingly at some municipal improvement. But she couldn't concentrate on anything over the low buzz of alarm in her head.

Other passengers hopped on and off, and the seats started filling up. But almost everyone exited when Val did, at the Plaza of Women. It was a large, paved open-air market where every curve and corner was crammed with booths and wagons selling an amazing array of offerings. When she'd been a little girl, it had been her favorite spot in the city, filled with the promise of such rich delights. Who knew what merchant would be selling a beautiful silver bracelet just right for a child's wrist? Who could guess what vendor might be offering sweet cakes or honeyed bread, treats that an indulgent parent would buy after only a few pleas?

Her mother could almost always be counted on to get Val a trinket or at least a piece of candy. But the ideal companion was her father, though he rarely had the time to take her on frivolous excursions. If he had decided to spend the day with her, he would give her every scrap of his attention. He would stop to look over any piece of merchandise, he would encourage her to try any item that caught her fancy. He wasn't a profligate spender, but he would buy her *something* on every outing. He would gravely tell her the budget for the day, and they would pause at every booth that interested them, and Val would make a list of the things she wanted the most. Then they would stop at one of the outdoor cafés and have flavored ices or spiced tea and debate the attractions of every item on her list. She always came away feeling deeply satisfied, certain she had chosen wisely, happy with her purchases. She had always come away secure in the knowledge that her father loved her.

Well. It had been a long time since anyone had showered her with useless presents and made her feel like she was the center of the world. She shook her head and walked on.

She didn't know if Darien had set a guard to trail after her. It seemed like the sort of thing he might do just as a general precaution. She didn't have the skills to elude a truly skilled watcher, but she also didn't have to make it easy for anyone to keep track of her. She stopped at a few booths, ducked into a couple of the more permanent storefronts, wound around the backs of a couple of buildings, and attached herself to a small vivacious crowd of brightly dressed young women who tumbled through the narrow streets like escaping toddlers. When they moved as one body toward an oncoming omnibus, she followed them, and managed to be in the very middle of the group as they scrambled aboard. No one who looked like a soldier boarded in their wake.

The large elaymotive rocked gently as it headed south, stopping so often that Val sometimes wondered if it would be faster to walk. The girls were still chattering together in high, excited voices when the bus made its gradual turn left to travel along the southernmost leg of the Cinque. Val slipped off as five people boarded, hoping she looked inconspicuous, and began hiking down a narrow side street that pointed in a northeasterly direction.

The first few blocks were a little dicey, since the southside slums lay only a mile or so away, but soon enough she was in a respectable part of town. There were many small family dwellings, some storefronts and corner markets, and buildings that looked like schools and offices. Not a bad place to live, her father had said, if you didn't mind being surrounded by stone and bare dirt. If you didn't care if you never saw a rosebush or could rest your hand against a tree.

But then there it was, just ahead of her, a small green haven in the middle of a seemingly endless stretch of urban dreariness. Her father and Taro had decided one day that they would commission a park and build it in a neighborhood that offered no similar amenities. They would fill it with greenery—torz flowers and hunti trees—and make it a restful haven.

The trees that ringed the spot had grown significantly since she had last visited, creating a curtain of low branches she had to push aside to step into the velvety green heart of the park. On this early summer day in Quinnahunti, the whole space was carpeted in thick grass, with an inner perimeter of flowering bushes that offered a pleasing mix of scents and colors. Just inside the circle of bushes was a ring of five wooden benches, a bit battered from years of exposure to the weather, but still inviting to the footsore wanderer. Each one was a different color to correspond with the elemental affiliations—white for elay, blue for coru, red for sweela, green for torz, and black for hunti.

In the center of the enclosure was a pot-bellied metal cauldron that came up to Val's knees. It was sheltered by a peaked wooden roof, but otherwise wholly open to the elements. Inside the cauldron, she knew, were hundreds of blessing coins, ready for anyone to pull if they came to the park and needed reassurance or guidance. Because this place was a temple as well as a sanctuary.

Although for Val, it had always, first and foremost, been a sanctuary—the place she went when there was no other solace, no other rest. When she was a child, she had run away one day after an argument with her mother, and this was where she had gone. Her father had found her within the hour. After he died, when Val and her mother were living in the town house and Darien was so busy attending King Vernon, Val had visited the park almost daily. One summer evening she had even spent the night there, sleeping on the hunti bench as the anxious stars peered down. She had been surprised, when she returned home in the morning, to find her mother so worried. *I thought you would realize I was at the park.* Even Darien, who seemed to have abandoned her, knew that this was the place Val would go when she was troubled and on edge.

Sebastian certainly knew.

She took a seat on the hunti bench and waited.

Barely an hour had passed before she heard footsteps approaching at a steady pace. She stood up and faced the small break in the treeline that led to the street. She had had time to compose herself, but it hardly mattered. Sebastian could always read the emotions on her face.

Another moment, and he was inside the park. He was dressed in his usual careless style, a nondescript brown jacket over wrinkled trousers; his dark red hair was long enough to brush his shoulders and looked as if he might have forgotten to comb it this morning. But he was smiling as he threw his hands in the air.

"Finally! I've been here every afternoon for the past nineday. What took you so long?"

"I wasn't even sure you knew I was in the city."

"And that's another thing! Why didn't you tell me you'd be in Chialto?"

"I didn't want to come. But Mirti made me, and I didn't have time to let you know I would be here."

He cocked his head to one side. "You could have sent a note once you arrived."

"I've barely had time to think, let alone get in touch with anyone."

"How long are you staying? Let me guess, you're planning to leave tomorrow."

She couldn't help a wry smile. "If I had my way," she agreed. "But Darien is trying to convince me to spend a quintile in the city. He seems worried that I'm isolated and lonely, that I need to be out in society more."

"Finally, something Darien and I agree on."

"I'm *not* isolated and lonely! There are people everywhere and there's a great deal to do."

Sebastian bestowed a warm smile on her. "But Valentina Serlast should be at court, dining with rich merchants and clever politicians and taking up the accustomed life of a daughter of the Five Families."

"You know I've never cared about that."

"You haven't," he said. "But you deserve a better life than the one you've been living."

"I don't think," she said, "that you should be giving other people advice about how to live their lives."

His smile turned devilish. "Now what would bring you to that conclusion?"

"You're smuggling sirix, aren't you?"

He burst out laughing. "That's my Tina. Always straight to the point."

"Do you have any idea how dangerous it is?"

"Oh, there are a few hazards on the road, but so far the Soechins selling the merchandise have been trustworthy enough. No one's knifed anyone in the back, anyway, as far as I know."

"That's not what I meant," she said. "Darien has started to pay attention. He thinks the Soechins blame the Welchins for providing open harbors to the smugglers, and he wants to shut down the illegal operations so there isn't some kind of diplomatic crisis."

Sebastian put a hand to his chest. "My heart pounds in fear!"

"Don't be stupid," she said sharply. "You know Darien can be relentless. And he's the *king* now. He's got all the resources of the country behind him. If he realizes you're involved—"

Sebastian shrugged. "Darien has never liked me. He'll hardly think less of me for being a free trader."

"I don't care what he *thinks* of you! I care what he might *do* to you!"

"Well, I wouldn't worry about it, if I were you. I'm careful. I don't think Darien's spies will catch me."

She stared at him. "You're *never* careful."

He laughed. "It only seems that way to you because you're so cautious about *everything*. In fact, I have a very well-developed sense of self-preservation. I am smart about my choices, and I minimize my risks. I'll be fine."

"But Sebastian," she said helplessly. "Why sirix? Why *smuggling?*"

He glanced over his shoulder and nodded at the sweela bench, so they sat down side by side. The sun was beaming enthusiastically, but the trees provided just enough shade to keep the temperature tolerable.

"Oh, you know that I'm too restless for an ordinary job and a steady life," he said. "This kind of work suits me. I like the buying and selling. I like finding the merchandise and matching it to the outlet. I like putting puzzle pieces together. Who would want *this?* How much would they pay?"

"Very well, but there are plenty of traders who handle *legal* goods, and they're traveling all across Welce, and they seem to lead fine lives."

He shrugged and spread his hands. "There's no edge to it. It's too easy. The contraband goods—I *like* that I have to be one step ahead, that I always have to be watching, that there could be a trap behind any door. It keeps me on my mettle. It makes every day exciting."

She shook her head. She couldn't understand it. Oh, she understood that *Sebastian* felt that way. He had said variants of the same thing dozens of times in the past nineteen years. But it made no sense to her. She had never been attracted to risk. Never seduced by danger. She was happiest when she felt most secure. "But why sirix? If it has to be something illegal, why not pick something that won't start a war at the border?"

His lively, laughing face became unexpectedly somber. "I've tried other contraband," he admitted. "Veneben. Renaissance. Drugs are a whole lot easier than liquor to transport and sell. The packages are smaller and the buyers are numerous."

She was shocked. She'd known he dabbled in illicit activities, but she hadn't realized which ones. "But veneben is—and renaissance—"

"I know. I'd tried them myself, but only a few times. They're not my style, though I can see why people get addicted." He sobered still more. "That's what stopped me. Meeting a couple of addicts. I'd always thought—" He shrugged. "I'm nobody's moral compass. If a man has a craving and I have the goods, why shouldn't I sell him what he wants? But then I saw—" He shook his head. "So I decided I didn't want to be part of that chain any more. I didn't want to be the link that enabled that kind of devastation."

Val remembered how quickly the sirix had gone to her head when she and Corene were at Geoffrey's restaurant yesterday. "I'm not sure your current product is much better."

Sebastian was grinning again. "Maybe, but it's more elegant, you have to agree! And sirix is a banquet for the senses. The taste, the smell, the color, the effect—it's all exquisite. As you should know, since you tried a sample of it for yourself."

"Did you follow me yesterday? Is that how you found me?"

He burst out laughing. "I did not! It was absolute random chance that brought us to Geoffrey's place at the same time. I was making a delivery and Geoffrey was distracted by his clients, so I peered into the taproom to see who had made such an impression on him—"

"It was Corene, not me. He scarcely noticed me."

"His error, then."

"Well, Corene is pretty hard to overlook."

He smiled at her. "You might not be as striking as the princess, but I'd pick you over her any day."

She scoffed. "Only because you don't want to be competing with another sweela person who might get all the attention."

He was still watching her. "That's it, of course. That's the only reason."

Speaking of outsize sweela personalities . . . "I saw Nelson at the coronation the other day."

Sebastian nodded. "We have dinner from time to time."

Nelson was head of the Ardelays, the hot-headed and often feckless sweela clan famous for their indiscretions. As far as Val knew, Nelson had never sired any illegitimate children, but Ardelay bastards could be found across Welce. Nelson had always treated them like any other member of the family. He had been particularly kind to Sebastian when he was young and practically an orphan—his mother dead, his father largely absent.

"And Nelson doesn't lecture you about your illegal activities?"

"It's possible he doesn't know about them."

"I would guess Nelson knows a lot more than you might think."

Sebastian grinned. "Maybe. But he himself is not above the shady deal now and then, so he's unlikely to tell anyone else how to behave."

"I don't think Nelson is *smuggling*."

"Maybe not, but I'd be surprised if he hadn't bought a cask or two of illegal sirix. I think he delights in annoying Darien, at least in small ways."

She snorted. "Everyone delights in annoying Darien. Or trying to. It's very hard to throw him off balance."

Sebastian studied her for a moment. "So how are you doing? Are you getting along with your brother? Do you think you'll be able to enjoy your time in the city?"

"I don't know. I'm not very happy. I'll *try*."

"I can't really stroll up to the palace when I want to see you."

"You were there for the coronation, weren't you?"

"Ha, you did see me! You looked away so fast I couldn't be sure."

"I didn't want anyone else to notice you! And this is *before* I knew about the sirix. I just knew you were involved in something criminal."

"My point stands. I can't come calling on you like a scion of the Five Families. How will I see you again?'

She glanced around the park. "We can meet here every firstday."

"That would work. Say, noon?"

She stood up, smoothing down the front of her tunic. "All right. I'll see you next firstday. But now I need to get back to the palace."

Sebastian jumped to his feet and gestured at the cauldron. "Since we're here, shouldn't we draw blessings for each other?"

She was already headed that way. It was a ritual they often observed when they were together. It was ridiculous, she knew, but she always preferred the blessings that came to her by way of Sebastian. "Of course."

The big kettle was so squat, and the protective overhang so low, that they had to crouch on either side of it. Val reached in and mixed the coins, letting them slide between her fingers and over her palms. "Just one, or three?" she asked.

"Just one for today."

She made her choice and laughed when she glanced at the glyph in her hand. "Honesty."

"Hey, I always tell *you* the truth."

"I don't suppose you can say that about anyone else."

"Not if I'm actually being honest." He plunged his hand into the cauldron, giving the coins a vigorous stir before drawing one out. "And for you—" He presented the disk with a flourish.

"Loyalty," she said. It was the blessing they shared, the single trait in all of human existence that they had in common. "Did you cheat?"

"How could I cheat? You were here before I was! I haven't had a chance to approach the barrel in secret."

"You could have stopped at another temple on the way, and picked through the coins, and then put this one in your pocket."

"Would an honest man do that?"

He hadn't denied it. She was pretty sure she was right, and she should have been scolding him, but she was just a little pleased that he'd gone to the effort. She offered him the coin she'd drawn. "Keep it or throw it back?"

"Keep it," he replied, taking it from her. "I don't think you've ever pulled honesty for me before. Do you want this one?"

"Thank you, but I already have the blessing of loyalty."

"Always and forever."

He tossed the disk into the pot. They began strolling back toward the street, not moving too quickly.

"Did you take the omnibus?" he asked. "I'll walk you to the stop."

"I can't get over how many elaymotives there are on the Cinque these days," she said. "Do you drive?"

"I do. Very fast. I can take you out in one someday if you like."

"That sounds like fun."

"Next firstday, then, when I see you."

She smiled. "Maybe I *will* enjoy a whole quintile in Chialto."

Chapter Six

Val is eight. She is sitting primly in the formal parlor of her father's house, awaiting the arrival of her cousins. The parlor—a big space with heavy, dark furniture, and huge portraits of stern-looking ancestors—is possibly her least favorite room in the entire mansion. But it's the one with the best view of the long, sweeping drive that makes its approach to the house through a double row of majestic oaks. And Val does not want to be surprised by the arrival of visitors. She hates surprises.

Her cousins come every summer to spend three or four ninedays at the house, and Val anticipates the event with mixed feelings. On the one hand, the visitors are noisy and they disrupt her normal routine and they don't always know the rules about how things should be done and they often don't care about the rules even when she's explained them. On the other hand, she mostly likes them and she gets used to them in a few days and, while they're visiting, someone is always available to play a game. For most of the year, she's the only child in the house, and it's sometimes lonely. Now that Darien is twenty, he is indisputably an adult; he almost never wants to spend time with her anymore, and he's gone to the city with their father more than half the time anyway. Sometimes it's nice to be around other children.

There are usually five of them, three boys and two girls. They belong to her mother's two sisters, who also descend on the house for the duration. Her mother and both of her sisters are torz through and through, so nothing makes them happier than gathering in large boisterous groups of people. Her father, like Val, is a little less eager to be surrounded by rambunctious relatives. He usually stays for the first four or five days, then finds a reason to retreat to Chialto.

This year, there will be a sixth child in the mix, another boy, not really a cousin. Aunt Jenty had written to Val's mother to let her know the circumstances, and Val had been in the room when her mother read the letter out loud at the breakfast table.

It's rather a sad story. My sister-in-law died earlier this year, leaving the boy essentially on his own. She was never married to his father—a second cousin of Nelson's, I believe, though I may have that wrong—and the father has never been around much, though apparently he is quite the charmer. Of course I said we could take the boy in. So far he's been quiet and well-behaved, but I glimpse that Ardelay wildness in his eyes from time to time. I think once he recovers from his grief, he will be quite a handful. Anyway, I plan to bring Sebastian this summer, so make sure there's a bed for him! We're all looking forward to coming.

Val isn't sure how she feels about a stranger coming to live in her house for such a long time, but she knows that she has to be polite. It is one of the rules of life that the lady of the house must extend courtesy to every guest.

It is just past noon when two carriages come lumbering up the long drive. Her girl cousins are already leaning out the windows, pointing and calling. The boy cousins have managed to find seats outside with the coachmen, and they appear to be throwing walnuts at each other over the heads of the tired horses. Of the stranger, there is no sign.

Servants have alerted her mother and father, so they are already waiting in the kierten just inside front door when the carriages shudder to a halt and all the passengers start climbing out. Val comes to stand behind her parents, peering between their bodies to see five of the children racing up the walkway while the women follow more sedately. Behind Aunt Jenty and Aunt Lissa is a small solitary figure trudging slowly up the stone path as if not entirely certain he wants to reach the house.

As the newcomers pour into the kierten, there is so much hugging and exclaiming and laughing that it's hard to keep track of everyone, but pretty quickly the whole ball of commotion has moved down the hallway and deeper in the house. Except for Val, who is still patiently waiting at the door, and the last laggard arrival, who is still standing on the front walk. He is fine-boned and red-haired, and his expression is both curious and cautious, as if he wants to know what's on the other side of the door but is afraid he won't like it. He holds himself with a certain coiled readiness, as if he's prepared to take off running at the least provocation. He's properly dressed, in clothes that are as well-made as anything her cousins might wear, but he somehow manages to look a little raffish. Maybe because the jacket is wrinkled from travel. Maybe because the red hair is unkempt. Maybe because there's something untamed behind his wary eyes.

He sees Val waiting and steps inside. She nods gravely and says, "Welcome to our house."

He looks around, glancing down the hallway and noting the wide, restful proportions of the kierten. Every house has a kierten, of course—an area entirely empty of furnishings, proof that a home's owner can afford to waste the space—but Val wonders if he has ever seen one as grand as this. It is almost as large as the parlor, and its two longest walls are lined with huge pots planted with slim, tough, decorative trees. Their narrow trunks grow straight up alongside the walls and their whippy branches spring out from tall crowns, creating an interwoven canopy under the skylight of the high ceiling. Val has always thought that standing in the kierten is as close as anyone can come *inside* to standing outside in a forest.

"It's your house?" he asks. "Your family owns it?"

"It's the house of the hunti prime," she says. "The next prime will live here after my father is gone."

"What's his name?"

"My father and mother are Damon and Merra Serlast. I'm Valentina Serlast, but people call me Val."

"I'm Sebastian Ardelay."

"How old are you?" she asks.

"Seven."

"I'm eight. What are your blessings?"

It is tradition in Welce for every child to receive three random blessings before he or she is five hours old. In the cities, there are stories of dazed and exhausted parents racing out into the night to find the closest temple and hope there are three strangers on hand to pull coins from the barrel. In big houses like the prime's estate, plenty of visitors and staff members are always on hand to perform the ritual—and of course, every large household has a cask of blessings somewhere on the premises. Often more than one.

Val is old enough to know that sometimes people have the most unexpected blessings that do not seem to match them at all. And other times their blessings illuminate who they are down to their very core. She is always intrigued to discover which one it is.

"Luck, innovation, and loyalty," he says.

She tilts her head. "Do you think they suit you?"

He grins and nods. "What are yours?"

"Determination. Certainty." She glances at him. "And loyalty."

"Like me!" When she nods, he adds, "And very hunti."

"Hunti is my elemental affiliation. Like my father. What about you?"

The ghost of a smile crosses his watchful face. "You can't tell from the red hair? Sweela, just like *my* father."

"My mother is torz," she says.

"My mother was torz, too."

"I understand your mother died," Val says gravely. "I'm sorry. That's terrible."

That catches his complete attention, and he fixes his brown eyes on her face. "No one seems to want to talk about it," he says. "No one says her name to me."

"You can talk to *me* about her," Val replies. "*I'll* say her name. What is it?"

"Helia Danzen."

"That's a pretty name."

"*She* was pretty," he says. "She was always laughing."

"You must miss her very much."

"I do. She was never mad at me. She told me stories. She hugged me when I was sad." He shrugs.

"I'll hug you if you want," Val says.

He looks at her a moment, as if judging the sincerity of the offer. "All right."

They each step forward until they are nose to nose, then Val puts her arms around him. He feels thinner than he looks, his bones prominent under the fine clothes. She presses her cool cheek against his warm one and feels his hair tickle her forehead; he is maybe an inch shorter than she is and probably about the same weight. He smells like moss and cedar chips and boy. She thinks it has probably been a while since anyone has held him, so she lets him cling to her as long as he wants. It is a minute or two before he steps away.

"It's not like my mother's hugs," he says. "But it's nice."

"I'm glad. Are you hungry? Everyone else is probably in the dining room."

"I'm starving."

"Then let's go eat."

The first nineday passes in a blur. As expected, Val's father and Darien decamp for the city as soon as they can do so without appearing rude. Her mother and her aunts spend most days lounging outdoors on one of the shaded patios, sipping fruited water and telling each other stories that make them double over in laughter. The seven children go running through the gardens and farther afield. The cousins love playing in the lively stream that borders the southern edge of the property, and in the heat of the day they might spend hours splashing through the cool water, dousing themselves and each other.

Val is the one who organizes expeditions to the forest that spreads out for miles from the northern edge of the estate. Everyone is willing to go in deep enough to get a sense of the profound silence and watchful stillness of the trees, and they welcome the chill created by the dense shade. But not one of them is hunti, and they're all reluctant to wander too far away from the sunlit edges of the woods. They don't believe Val when she says she couldn't possibly get lost in the forest. It's too vast for them, too full of whispers and hazards. Even Sebastian, who doesn't seem to be afraid of much, won't go past a certain safe distance.

Val is disappointed, but not surprised. Her father and Darien are the only ones who have ever been willing to explore the forest with her. There are paths she thinks that no one has ever seen except the three of them. And the other primes, perhaps, the ones who lived here before. The ones who recognized each tree for its own unique beauty and wandered among the great looming trunks as among a crowd of friends.

Because she considers herself the hostess for the youngest visitors, Val pays attention to everyone's well-being. The youngest cousin, a girl who is only five, is coru and absolutely fearless. Someone always has to be chasing after her before she wades out too far in the stream and gets carried away by the water. Val likes little Saska, though, because she says what she thinks and never seems to have any mean thoughts in her head.

Val is less fond of the two oldest boys, who are twelve and thirteen and think it's fun to harass their younger cousins. They'll tip someone over into the water or snatch a pastry right out of someone else's hand, and the games they devise are usually rougher than the others like. One time, the oldest one snatched Saska up in the air and tossed her to his brother, and they passed her back and forth three times before Val could rescue her, screaming at the top of her lungs. Since then, Val keeps Saska close by her side and glares at the boys any time they come near. She hasn't bothered reporting their bad behavior to her mother or theirs, since experience has taught her the adults expect the children to work out their own problems. But she is beginning to think she might dislike them.

Sebastian doesn't seem to mind their boisterous ways, and he has even introduced them to a couple of games that seem to involve a lot of running and shouting. He moves easily between the rowdy activities of the older children and the quieter pastimes of the younger ones, and Val notices that everyone seems to like him. She also notices that, although he appears relaxed and nonchalant, he is always constrained by a certain wariness. He waits to be invited into the circle, waits to be spoken to. He has an uncanny sense of where everyone is at every moment, and the older boys—who love to sneak up on the girls and terrify them with a pounce—have never caught him unaware.

One day, all seven of them are gathered at the edge of the stream, trying to get comfortable on the mingled grass and gravel. Saska is sitting with her feet in the water. Morgan, the oldest, is standing on a level boulder at the water's edge, taking turns balancing on one foot and then the other for as long as he can hold the pose. Sebastian is teaching Val how to toss stones so they skip across the water. The others are lying flat on their backs, drowsy with sun and exercise.

So far, Val has not succeeded in getting a stone to bounce more than once. "I think you have to be torz to have any luck with rocks," she says.

"I'm torz," Morgan says. "Once I skipped a stone seven times before it fell in the water."

Sebastian gives him a considering look. "I'd like to see that."

Morgan shrugs. "I don't feel like doing it *now*."

Sebastian nods, but his expression makes it clear that he doesn't believe this claim. Morgan is instantly irritated.

"So what are you, sweela? What can you do with fire?" he demands.

"I try to be careful with fire," Sebastian replies. "My father says you can't ever forget how dangerous it is."

"Your father," Morgan says, and his voice is taunting. "I bet you don't see much of him."

"I see him enough," Sebastian replies in an even tone.

"*My* father says you're a bastard."

Saska looks up at that. "What's a bastard?"

Val answers before Morgan can give a more hateful definition. "Someone whose parents aren't married to each other."

"Is that bad?"

"No," Val says.

Morgan snorts and switches to his other leg, swaying a little before he regains his balance. "*Some* people think it's bad," he says.

"Why?" Saska wants to know.

"Well, you can't inherit property unless there's a special will or something. And people won't want to marry you."

Saska is concerned. "You mean, no one will marry Sebastian?"

"That's right."

"*I'll* marry him," Saska says.

"You're too young to get married," Morgan scoffs.

"But someday."

Sebastian makes an underhanded throw of a small, flat rock, and it touches the water five times before it disappears. "Thanks, Saska," he says. "But I don't think I want to marry anybody."

She looks worried. "Then what are you going to do?"

"I'll have adventures. I'll travel around the world, maybe."

"You'll get a job, maybe," Morgan says. "Since you don't have any money and you won't get any from your family because you're a bastard."

Val moves closer to where Morgan is standing and bends over to sort through the debris on the bank. She picks up a handful of loose stones. "You're being mean," she says. "I don't like it."

"I'm just being honest," he says.

"What kind of job would you get?" Saska asks Sebastian.

"I don't know. Maybe I'll move to Chialto someday and just look around."

"You can work in the stables somewhere," Morgan says. "You can work down on the docks. I think that's where bastards go to find jobs."

Val throws a small stone and hits him right on the nose.

"Hey!" he shouts, hopping in surprise.

She throws another one, and another one, fast and hard and accurate, striking him on his cheek, his shoulder, and his forehead. He draws his hands up before his face, and her next shots hit his palms and wrists and then his shoulder again. Behind her, she hears Saska shriek and Sebastian say "Stop it" in a quiet voice, but she keeps on flinging the rocks. Morgan jerks back from the assault, slips on the wet surface of the boulder, and tumbles headfirst into the stream.

He's upright in seconds, shaking water out of his hair and spitting with rage. The other cousins are all on their feet, laughing and pointing, as Morgan charges out of the stream as if he wants to barrel right into Val and knock her over. She stands her ground as he splashes onto the bank, soaking her with great gusts of water.

"I ought to throw you in," he snarls.

"You *ought* to be nicer to people," she replies, staring him down.

Sebastian has moved to stand next to her, clearly ready to fight, and Saska has scrambled over to cling to her tunic. "Don't you hurt Val!" Saska wails.

"Don't be a jerk, Morgan," his brother calls. "You deserved it."

For a moment, Val thinks Morgan might hit her anyway, or pick her up and drag her into the water. But instead, he makes a deep growling sound and stomps away, heading back toward the house.

Saska throws her arms around Val and buries her head in Val's stomach. Sebastian gives her a long, steady look.

"You don't have to protect me," he says. "I can take care of myself."

She's annoyed. "You're my *guest*," she says. "You're my responsibility. No one should mistreat you in my house."

"You're just a kid," he says.

"The rules still apply," she answers in a huffy voice.

The other cousins have drawn near to form a circle around them. "You're going to get in so much trouble," says the eleven-year-old girl.

"Only if Morgan tells," says Sebastian.

"He'll tell," his brother replies.

"He's not even hurt," Val said. "He's the one who should get in trouble."

※

As it turns out, both of them receive punishment, but the sentences are light. Morgan's mother draws him aside to deliver a stern lecture about treating other people with respect, and Val's mother sends her to her room before supper. Of course, she also sends up a dinner tray, so Val doesn't really suffer. And Saska and Sebastian join her, so she actually enjoys herself.

An odd thought crosses her mind as they pass around the food. In Welce, the numbers three, five, and eight are considered propitious, and people always try to make sure some combination of these numbers is present at the launch of any new enterprise. At this moment, Val is eight and Saska is five; three people are sitting in the room together. All the coveted numbers have united to preside over this little impromptu meal.

"Lissa thinks your mother needs to come up with a harsher punishment," Sebastian informs her as he helps himself to her potatoes. "But your mother said it wouldn't do any good."

"Why not?" Saska demands.

Sebastian grins at her. "Because she says Valentina never does the wrong thing on purpose. Whatever it is, she thinks it's the right thing to do. Merra said, 'How can you discipline something like that out of a child? And really, how can you want to?' Lissa thought that you should apologize to Morgan, anyway."

"Well, I'm not going to."

"Are you going to have to stay in your room forever?" Saska asks, wide-eyed.

Val gives her an absent pat on the head. "No. Just for tonight. My mother never stays mad for long."

"You didn't have to do it," Sebastian says. "But thank you."

"You're my guest," she says again. "You're my friend. I'll always take care of you."

Chapter Seven

Darien, Zoe, and Corene were all in the breakfast room the next morning when Val made her way down there, still yawning. Zoe, who was usually the most relaxed person in any gathering, looked unusually vexed, but her expression lightened when Val took a seat across the table from her.

"I don't suppose you have the whole day free to help me with something, do you?" she asked.

"Ha," Corene said, speaking with her mouth full. "Tell her you're busy."

Val raised her eyebrows. "I'm at your disposal," she said, not that she really wanted to spend more time with Zoe than she had to. "What do you need?"

Zoe looked with distaste at a sheaf of papers on the table and then nodded at Darien. "Our newly crowned king informs me that a Soechin delegation has arrived in the city and would like to have an informal meeting with someone at the palace."

Val looked at her brother. "And Darien is busy?"

"I feel certain the Soechins realize that I cannot be available to them at a moment's notice, whenever they take it into their heads to visit," he said in his usual maddeningly calm way.

"So you just want to annoy them," Corene said.

"Not at all. Help them gain a certain respect for my station, perhaps."

"Because if you really want to annoy them, you could stop making it illegal for smugglers to sell contraband sirix."

It took all of Val's willpower not to choke on a sip of juice, and she gave Corene a look of burning reproach. They had agreed they would not tell Darien about their clandestine excursion the other day, and Val's meeting with Sebastian had made that secrecy even more urgent. She had hoped the word *sirix* wouldn't even come up in conversation.

Darien patted his mouth with a napkin. "Those are two different things," he said. "I would certainly like to avoid going to war with our nearest neighbors, and thus I will try to keep my countrymen from activities that might incite violence. But that doesn't mean I have to be at the beck and call of every minor politician who decides to grace me with his presence."

Corene glanced at Val. "Was he always this self-important?"

The question was meant as a joke, but Val considered it seriously. "He never liked it when people wasted his time," she said. "You could always count on him when something really mattered, but he usually didn't have time to fix a broken doll or take a walk through the woods."

Darien came to his feet. "Maybe not, but what about finding a missing puppy? Or hearing about a bad dream in the middle of the night?"

She found herself smiling up at him. "You had time for those," she agreed.

"Really? A puppy? You don't even like animals," Corene said.

His eyes rested briefly on Val's face. "It wasn't the dog I was worried about."

"A puppy! Now I know what I need to get your attention!" Zoe exclaimed.

"Indeed, yes, a most excellent idea," Darien said. "But I'm still leaving the Soechins to you."

Zoe sighed, then turned to Val with a beseeching look. "I cannot bear to meet them alone," she said. "Will you join me this afternoon?"

Val was completely taken aback. "Me? I don't have any diplomatic skills."

"Neither does Zoe," Darien murmured.

She favored him with a mock frown, but said, "It's true they bring out the worst in me. Darien thinks I should have someone in the room to encourage me to mind my manners."

"I'd think Corene has more experience dealing with foreign dignitaries than I do."

"Oh, I do," Corene said cheerfully. "And I like doing it! But I'm not going anywhere near a Soechin. I'm always afraid they're going to snatch me up and carry me away across the border."

That was when Val remembered that nearly eight years ago, Vernon had arranged for a marriage between eleven-year-old Corene and the middle-aged viceroy of Soeche-Tas. Zoe had put a stop to it in the most spectacular fashion, calling on her coru powers to raise the Marisi river and flood the palace. Val had been in the courtyard when the water started rising, and for a moment she had thought she might drown. But she'd managed to drag both herself and her mother to safety.

"No one is going to kidnap you," Darien said. His voice was mild, but there was an iron finality in its undertones. He would be even more relentless in the search for a lost daughter than a missing puppy. He considered Corene for a moment, and a faint smile lit his gray eyes. "No, if you disappear, it's because you've slipped off of your own accord."

She smirked back at him. "Probably. But I'm still not meeting with this delegation."

Val looked over at Zoe, whose expression was despondent. "I have to think they aren't particularly fond of you."

"No," Zoe said. "And I have a deep dislike of every Soechin I've ever met. That's why I was hoping someone would bolster me up during the meeting."

When someone asked you for help and had a good reason for it, you couldn't refuse. That was just one of the obligations of life. Besides, Val was starting to feel a bit curious about these unwelcome guests. "I'll do it," she said. "When will they be here?"

The delegation arrived in time for lunch. Zoe had ordered a fancy meal, multiple courses that showcased both traditional Welchin dishes and Soechin delicacies. Val glanced dubiously at a plate full of what looked like fried eyes and decided she wasn't even going to try one.

A servant ushered the three guests into the small sunlit dining room and Zoe made quick introductions. The Soechins were all tall and thin, elaborately dressed, and dripping with jewelry. Two were men who might have been in their late fifties, with lean faces and deep-set eyes; their main differentiator was that one was balding and one had a full head of dark hair. The third was a woman who might have been a decade older. All three of them came to stand right next to Val and Zoe, suffocatingly close, smiling in a fashion that felt oddly appraising. The woman reached out to brush her knuckles against Val's cheek.

"So soft," she murmured.

Val didn't jerk away, but she did take a step backward. "I hope your journey here was pleasant," she said.

One of the men took Zoe's hand in his, turning it palm-up and palm-down as if examining it for flaws. "Uneventful," he said. "We sailed into your harbor and commissioned one of your elaymotives to bring us into the city. Your hands are more muscular than I expect from a woman."

Zoe didn't quite yank herself away, but she wasn't particularly subtle about freeing herself from his grip. "My hands are powerful," she said. "They need to be strong."

The woman looked between Zoe and Val, allowing her eyes to linger on Val. "You are the younger one, I can see that. Your skin is so fresh."

Val was beginning to see why Corene had flatly refused this meeting and why Zoe had dreaded it. She remembered that someone had once told her the Soechins were obsessed with youth. It was the first time in her life she'd wished she was older.

"I have my mother's complexion," she said. "Her skin was beautiful until the day she died."

A slight frown puckered the woman's face. Val wondered if it was the implication of age or death that displeased her. But all she said was, "How fortunate."

Under the guise of shepherding them all to the table, Zoe had taken another step away from her guests. "Are you hungry? Please, sit and eat. Here, Val, you take the seat next to me."

Ah, that was clever. Instead of putting herself at the head of the rectangular table, Zoe had made sure the board was set with two places on one side, three on the other. This meant Val would not have to sit next to one of these disturbing visitors, who would probably crowd close to her and try to touch her throughout the meal.

Of course, now she had to look at all three of them, but that still seemed preferable.

The two men seated themselves on either side of the woman, and all of them murmured their appreciation for the food laid out before them. "You have gone to some trouble to prepare a meal we would enjoy," the woman said. "That was most gracious."

Zoe laughed and picked up a carafe of fruited water, pouring for all of them. "My cook did the work," she said. "But I shall gladly take the credit for requesting the menu."

There was little real conversation as they handed the dishes around and filled their plates. Val skipped the fried eyes but took a spoonful of something that looked like shredded twigs. A very small spoonful. Zoe helped herself to everything. Val guessed that there was very little Zoe wouldn't try at least once. She had that coru love of novelty.

"Welchin provisions do not often make it into Soeche-Tas," one of the men commented. "You will have to tell us which of these items are most popular in your country and why."

So Zoe and Val introduced each dish before their guests took their first bites, and they all shared their opinions. Then Zoe and Val had to try each of the Soechin items, so Val was forced to eat a fried eye after all. It turned out to be the seed pod of some woody plant, chewy and heavily spiced, and she rather liked it. Once Val had eaten the last bite of everything on her plate, she took seconds of a few items, including another seed pod. The Soechins smiled with approval.

"Our menus are not similar in general, but we do share some tastes in common," the Soechin woman pronounced. "I would think we could send more foodstuffs across the border on a regular basis."

Zoe toyed with her silverware. "There is a coalition of Welchin farmers who would be happy to find foreign markets for their crops," she said. "I could set up a meeting for you with some of them as early as tomorrow."

"Your king would have to favor such commerce," one of the men said. "And he would have to take the necessary steps to promote it."

"I don't understand," Zoe said, though Val had the feeling she did.

"The taxes," the Soechin woman said. "In the past, the crown has taken a high percentage of foreign sales, making Welchin business owners less eager to trade outside of their borders."

"Yes, Vernon had lived through years of drought, so he took steps to make sure Welchin products went first to domestic outlets," Zoe said. "But in recent years we have opened up the country to more international markets, and we trade with nations throughout the southern seas."

"But there are still tariffs that discourage Soechin merchants from selling in Welce," the woman said. "For instance, the tariff on sirix is so high that it encourages illegal trafficking. Many Chialto merchants are eager to sell sirix, but they turn to smugglers because the price of legitimate goods is unreasonably high."

"I appreciate your point," Zoe said. "I can certainly bring the matter to the king and see if he's willing to make some adjustments."

The Soechin woman nodded at the bald man, who produced a green bottle holding enough liquid to fill four wineglasses to the brim. "We have brought you a bottle of sirix for your personal use," she said. "I feel certain that once you have tasted it, you will agree that your countrymen will be delighted to have it readily available."

"Thank you," Zoe said. "I will share it with my husband tonight. I look forward to tasting it."

"It has become quite popular in Cozique," the woman boasted. "And you know the people of that country have both sophisticated palates and a high level of wealth. Thus they can both afford and appreciate such an exquisite product."

"Yes, we have been increasing our trade with Cozique as well. And Malinqua and even Dhonsho."

The Soechin woman looked suddenly put out. "We have withdrawn entirely from the Dhonshon market."

Zoe looked genuinely surprised. "Really? We have found them eager to buy many of our crops. But I admit we hesitate to maintain relations with a country that historically treats its subjects so poorly."

The woman brushed that aside. "It is no concern of ours how the king chooses to govern. He might put a thousand people a day to death and be justified for his actions."

That made Val widen her eyes. She wondered what atrocities the Dhonshon crown would have to commit to make Darien abandon any attempts at diplomacy.

"If it is not his governmental policies, what is it you dislike about the king?" Zoe asked.

"He has interfered in our relationship with the Karkades," the dark-haired man burst out. "He has offered the Karkadians a military alliance against Cozique, which they are eager to accept, but only if the Karkadians stop trading with us for certain grains and do all their commerce with Dhonsho instead."

"It has been quite an economic hit to our farmers," the Soechin woman said. "And deliberately done. We have no love for the Dhonshons."

"But of course we cannot strike back in a military fashion," the other man said, his voice glum. "The ships of the Dhonshon navy are far superior to ours."

The woman gave him a quelling look. "More numerous, not superior," she corrected.

"And an armed response is inevitably risky," Zoe said. "War is always a last resort."

"I am not opposed to bloodshed," the Soechin woman said, "but only if something can be gained from it."

Zoe smiled and lifted her hand, turning it from side to side as if to show off the smooth palm, the bony back. "The coru prime deals in water and blood," she said, her tone conversational. "So *bloodshed* of any kind is anathema for me. I honor you for choosing not to engage with Dhonsho on such a petty matter."

The Soechin woman looked so nonplussed that Val had to smother a laugh. Clearly she did not think the matter was petty, and clearly she would like to retaliate against Dhonsho if she could think of a way, but she couldn't reject Zoe's compliment in the middle of a negotiation. "Just so," she murmured.

"But I am glad to hear you are not sending sirix to the Dhonshon ports," Zoe added. "That means we shall see more of it in Chialto."

"That is our hope," the woman said.

That seemed to nicely wrap up the topic of sirix, Val thought in some relief. So far, the whole conversation been very polite and rather boring. Val couldn't see why Zoe had wanted her here.

"Obviously I have much to discuss with Darien," Zoe said. "How long will you be in the city?"

"Less than a nineday, we hope."

"I will engage to discuss these matters with him soon."

"But it is not only *food* that can cross our borders," the dark-haired man said.

"I don't know much about the machines that our enterprising inventors have been building," Zoe said with a smile. "Kayle Dochenza is the one who manufacturers elaymotives and aeromotives! I can introduce you to his business manager if you want to discuss possibilities."

"We've had some dealings with him," the bald man answered. "It is not inanimate objects we would bring into Soeche-Tas."

Val was still trying to puzzle out what that might mean when she felt Zoe tense beside her. But Zoe spoke still in a civil, neutral voice. "Oh? What else?"

The woman frowned, though her irritation did not seem directed at anyone sitting at the table. "Soechin society is changing," she said. "Young men are restless and young women are selfish. Many observers worry that our society is growing too old—that there are not enough young people marrying and having children. There could be drastic economic consequences ten or twenty years from now."

Val had no idea where the conversation was going. But by the hostility she could feel radiating from Zoe's body, the coru prime had a pretty good guess about what the Soechins wanted to discuss, and she didn't like it. But all Zoe said was, "I suppose that's true."

The woman leaned across the table. "Perhaps there are excess members of your own population," she said. "Unwanted children. Perhaps your own social systems are overtaxed by trying to care for them. We could take them off your hands."

Now Val was staring in stupefaction. She couldn't even pretend to keep the astonishment off her face. *What?*

Zoe was practically vibrating with fury, but her voice still sounded serene, even sympathetic. "No, in fact, I do not believe we have overflowing orphanages and small towns overrun with urchins."

"But there is a district in Chialto," the woman said eagerly. "You call it the southside, I believe. Many unfortunate people reside there, and sadly many of them seem to live desperate lives. They are addicted to terrible drugs. They sleep on the streets. What kind of life is that?"

"We walked those streets and witnessed those lost souls," the dark-haired man explained. "We saw dozens. Perhaps hundreds."

"We could offer them much better lives," the woman continued. "Clean homes. Substantial food. Safety. Status."

"Wealthy husbands," the bald man added.

"Husbands?" Zoe repeated.

The woman nodded. "Of course, we would only want the girls. The younger ones. Our well-to-do bachelors are looking for wives and our government is looking for women who will bear the children we need to sustain our population."

"We would expect to pay handsomely, of course," the bald man said. "We have come to very advantageous deals with Berringuey and the Karkades. But Welce is so much closer."

Zoe's voice was cold enough to chill the room. "You want. To take children from the slums. And pay the Welchin government. To enslave them."

The Soechin woman looked shocked. "They would not be slaves! They would be valued members of our society!"

Zoe's fingers curled around the edge of the table. Val suddenly remembered stories she'd heard about how Zoe could call up a bruise on someone else's skin, how she could cause the blood to rise in a stranger's body and stream outward. The coru prime could manipulate both blood and water. *My hands are powerful,* she had said. *They need to be strong.* The Soechins didn't seem to realize how much danger they were in.

"You want—" Zoe began.

Val put an impulsive hand on Zoe's wrist. "Wait, I think we didn't entirely understand," she said. She turned to the Soechins and managed an expression of hopeful confusion. "You surely would not imagine taking anyone against her will, would you?" she said. "You would simply meet with young women and offer them an opportunity in your country?"

"Sometimes young women don't recognize an opportunity when it's presented to them," the dark-haired man said.

The muscles in Zoe's arm tightened under Val's hand, so Val rushed to speak again. "That might be true in Berringuey and the Karkades, but here in Welce, we don't believe in forcing anyone to do anything," she said in a helpful tone. "You understand, of course."

"Well—"

The Soechin woman was frowning. "What would you envision?" she asked.

"Many desperate souls on the southside might value a chance to escape to a new life," Val said. "But they would have to willingly make the choice."

The woman made an impatient gesture. "But some of the Welchin girls we saw were dazed and dizzy with alcohol and drugs! They were barely able to *walk,* let alone think deeply about their futures."

"And yet they have the right to decide their own fate," Val said. Her voice was still agreeable, but it had taken on a tone of finality. "We would never agree to let you take them—but we might let you *recruit* them."

Val had her attention fixed on the Soechins, but out of the corner of her eye she saw Zoe turn and give her a long, appraising look. Some of the tension had left Zoe's arm, but Val wasn't ready to let go just yet.

The Soechin woman spoke reluctantly. "What did you have in mind?"

Val had nothing in mind. She was just trying to ward off Zoe's catastrophic response. "An office in the heart of the slums," she said, improvising madly. "You could have representatives there who would explain what the women would be signing up for. Maybe there would be a few beds, a place where the girls could spend the night and think over the proposition."

The bald man was frowning. "But—that might net us only one or two women every nineday."

"Better than none at all," Val said pleasantly. "And whatever fee you planned to give to the Welchin government, you'd give to the girls instead. So they didn't enter their new lives completely destitute and dependent on their husbands' favor."

"Women like that don't understand the value of money," the dark-haired man said.

Zoe finally spoke again. "Women like that understand more than you think."

She sounded calm enough now that Val thought it safe to drop her hand. She was struck with a sudden inspiration. "So there would be an office in the southside—and there would be another office in Soeche-Tas, one that would be staffed by Welchin representatives. The women could go there for help if they were having difficulties with their new lives."

The Soechin woman threw her hands in the air. "What, and renege on their vows? I don't think so!"

"An unhappy bride will find a way to leave her marriage," Zoe said softly. "She might run. She might dose herself with more drugs. She might put a knife in her heart—or her husband's heart. I think you will find that such an office would do you more good than harm."

"We will discuss it," the Soechin woman said.

Now Zoe looked at Val again. "Josetta runs a shelter in the slums. She could help us with the details. She might even want to oversee the recruiting effort herself."

"Who's Josetta?" one of the men asked.

The Soechin woman scowled at him. "Princess Josetta. The oldest daughter of King Vernon."

Val didn't know much about Josetta, except that she was elay, with all the oddness that implied. "Will she approve of the idea?" she asked.

Zoe nodded slowly. "If certain conditions are in place, I think she will. Actually, we should get her advice before we proceed too far."

"I am not convinced this is the most efficient plan," the Soechin woman said.

"Let me put it this way," Zoe said. "It is the only plan. And if we were to discover that you were acquiring Welchin women in some other fashion—scooping them up off the streets when you thought we weren't paying attention—well, let me assure you that we *are* paying attention. And you would not be happy with our response."

The Soechin woman narrowed her eyes and stared at Zoe across the table. It occurred to Val to wonder how much power this woman wielded in her own country. She seemed unaccustomed to being balked. "Naturally, we would not do such a thing without your consent," she said at last. "We are here to make friends with the Welchins, not anger them."

"Excellent," Zoe said. "Then I will talk with Princess Josetta and see what she recommends. Now, Val, would you like to take one of those powdered cakes and pass the plate around the table? I understand this is a Soechin specialty, and I have been waiting all morning to try it."

The mood at the dinner table was much lighter than the atmosphere at breakfast. They had been joined by Mirti as well as Vernon's first queen, Elidon, both of whom kept apartments at the palace. Over the meal, Zoe recounted the conversation with the Soechins in vivid detail.

"Honestly, at that point, I wasn't sure anyone would have been able to keep me from making the blood boil in that woman's body," Zoe said. She had opened the gift bottle of sirix and was pouring out small measures for everyone at the table. "When Val put her hand on my arm, I was so angry I almost bruised her."

Val felt her eyes grow big. "Really? Then I'm never touching you again."

Darien nodded at her. "Good job. A hunti hand is always the steadiest."

"I'm glad you were there," Zoe said.

Corene sipped her sirix with a contemplative air, as if she'd never tasted it before. "This is delicious," she said. "No wonder everyone wants to smuggle it." She glanced at Val. "It's a good thing *I* wasn't in the room, because I would have been encouraging Zoe to do her worst. I hate those people." She took another sip. "But they make really good wine."

"But what do you think about their proposal to collect wayward girls and send them off to Soeche-Tas? The very idea makes my skin crawl," Zoe said.

Corene shuddered. "Hard to imagine anyone could be that desperate."

"I think your instinct to get Josetta's opinion was a good one," Darien answered. "And I very much like the notion of installing an outpost in Soeche-Tas. A place where Welchins can be seen without causing any suspicion."

"You and your spies," Corene said.

"My spies have proved very useful over the years."

"But aren't our relations with Soeche-Tas stable?" Elidon asked.

"For the moment," Darien said. "But just a year ago, Soeche-Tas was plotting against us with the Karkadians. I watch them more closely than any of our other neighbors. Not just because they are nearest—but because they cannot be trusted."

Val remembered something. "The Soechin woman—she said something about the Dhonshon king killing thousands of his people every day. Is that true?"

"Perhaps not that many. Or perhaps not every day," Darien said. "But he has a vast army of loyal troops, and he tolerates no dissent among his people. He keeps order in a ruthless fashion."

"His daughter was terrified of him," Corene said. When Val looked over in surprise, Corene explained. "I met his daughter Alette when I was in Malinqua. She tried to kill herself rather than return to her father's court. Several of us helped her escape and she's safe in Yorramol now. Her father has many wives and dozens of children and apparently someone in the royal family was always being put to death. Alette's mother and sister were executed while she was in Malinqua." She shook her head. "It was awful."

Val looked back at Darien. "And we're trading partners with Dhonsho?"

"For some items, yes."

"Well, we shouldn't be!"

Darien nodded. "It's always a delicate balance," he said. "Do we treat with them, and in that way seem to validate their policies? Or do we shun them, and thus know nothing about what goes on inside their borders? Including what threat they might pose to us?"

"They're a small nation, and some distance away," Elidon said. "How much could they harm us?"

"Small—but they have a fearsome fighting force, both on land and on sea," Darien said. "They're currently feuding with Soeche-Tas, but in the past, the two nations have been allies. And now the Dhonshons have made friends with the Karkadians. And their relations with Malinqua are always shifting—sometimes friendly, sometimes not. If Soeche-Tas and Malinqua and the Karkades were to band together with Dhonsho, that might put Welce at risk. And don't forget Berringuey, which is another unreliable ally. The only nation in the southern seas I wholly trust is Cozique—but it has the same enemies we do. No, I prefer to keep a pipeline open to Dhonsho if I can. I want to know if the king is arming for conquest. If that requires me to sell him a few bushels of grain, so be it."

Val rubbed her forehead. "I don't know how you keep track of it all."

"Oh, but it's fascinating," Corene said. "Like counters on a game board. If this piece moves here, then this one can move there, but what about this one over in the corner that I forgot all about?"

"Corene is proving to be an admirable ambassador," Darien said. "I think the sweela mind is best suited for diplomacy."

Corene grinned. "We have a devious way of thinking."

"And you aren't restrained by elay scruples," Zoe murmured.

Corene turned a marveling look her way. "*You* should talk about having no restraint!"

"Well, it all gives me a headache," Mirti said. "I am much more focused on what's right in front of me. The here and now."

Darien nodded. "Which also requires constant attention. Is something concerning you?"

"Not at the moment," Mirti said. "But I'm planning to leave the city for a few days and head to the estate. Romelle's going to join me there."

It seemed like an innocuous thing to say, but Val realized that Darien was regarding their aunt with narrowed eyes. "Romelle is coming to the estate again?" he said. "Is she bringing Natalie with her—again?"

Now Zoe looked interested. "Really? Natalie?"

"Well, I'm not sure yet," Mirti answered.

Romelle had been Vernon's fourth and youngest queen. Once the king died, she and her two daughters had gone to live with Taro and his wife, since Romelle was related to the torz prime. No one knew—or at least no one was telling—who had fathered her older daughter Natalie. Her younger daughter had turned out to be Vernon's, but Odelia had a strange condition that made her withdraw from society and live mostly inside her own head. Otherwise, she would have been the heir to Vernon's throne, and Darien would have just been another advisor to the crown.

But Natalie's father could have been anyone. Even someone with a strong hunti affiliation running through his bones—

"You think Natalie is your heir?" Val asked.

"I think she could be."

"This is exciting!" Zoe exclaimed. "I still have no idea who might come after me, and it makes me nervous."

"So what is the strange and secret ritual that reveals the hunti prime?" Corene wanted to know. "We all know that Zoe just fell into the Marisi and didn't drown when she should have, so that's how she found out she was the coru prime. And apparently it was quite spectacular when Taro's heir brought the whole mountain down, though I wasn't there to see it."

"You should be glad you weren't there," Darien said. "The entire day was terrifying."

"The hunti heir is revealed when the trees whisper a name," Mirti said. "You know there's a whole forest attached to the property. People could get lost there for days."

"I never get lost there," Val said.

"But in the middle of the woods, there's a cluster of challinbar trees. When the time is right, they shake their branches in a breeze that does not exist, and their leaves murmur the name of the next prime."

"I've never been in a place that seemed so rife with power," Darien said. "I have stood there sometimes on the calmest day and felt my hair lift from my scalp—felt my arms tingle as if from a charge of lightning."

"I have experienced the same thing," Mirti agreed. "Especially when I'm standing under the challinbar tree at the very center of the grove. Its trunk is so wide it takes five men to encircle it. Its branches reach so high into the sky you cannot see the tops of them. Its roots go down to the center of the world."

"It's the heart tree," Val said. "That's what my father always told me. It ties all the elements together. Its roots soak up nutrients from the soil and water from the underground springs. Its leaves absorb heat from the fire of the sun and scrub color into the wind. The heart tree is the hunti cord that binds together torz and coru, sweela and elay."

"Our father told you that?" Darien asked. "He never said anything like that to me."

"I believe that for a long time your father thought Val would be the next prime," Mirti said. "He took special care with her for that reason."

"*Me?*" Val said. "I always thought it would be Darien."

"Did you want to be prime?" Corene asked Darien.

He shook his head. "No, but I was secretly afraid the power would come to me. I wanted to be in Chialto, which seemed like the center of the world. I wanted to be at court. I already loved politics. I didn't want to be distracted by other responsibilities."

Corene transferred her attention to Val. "Did you?"

Val felt almost blank. "It never even occurred to me." She fought down a spike of sorrow. "It never occurred to me my father might die."

"So how did you find out it was you?" Corene asked Mirti.

"I was living in a cottage not far from the estate. Running a small business that turned lumber scraps into boxes and carvings. Perfectly content with my rather solitary life. And my brother Damon came to my home one day and said, 'It turns out I have an illness that no one can cure. I probably have less than a year to live. You have to come to the estate now.' And I said, 'Of course. Does Merra need help caring for you?' And he said, 'The challinbar trees have whispered your name.'"

Val had never heard this story before. Although she remembered very clearly the day that Mirti had moved into the house. Val had been sixteen and convinced she was fully a grown-up with a grown-up's responsibilities. So she had welcomed Mirti at the door, and showed her to her room, and told her which of the maids would be assigned to her—as if Mirti had never been to the estate before in her life, when she had spent whole quintiles there in the past. And Mirti had just as gravely thanked her, and never mentioned that it was soon to be her house, and that Val's life had just changed beyond recognition. It was the kindest thing anyone had ever done for her.

"Were you shocked when he told you that you would be the prime?" Elidon asked.

"I should have been," Mirti answered. "But instead, I just said, 'Oh.' As if someone had finally explained a math problem to me. Like I understood something that had confused me for a very long time."

"So now you think the trees are all talking about Natalie," Corene said.

Zoe picked up a basket of bread and began passing it around the table. "I have to say, Natalie is an interesting choice," she remarked. "She's very self-assured for someone who's only—nine? ten?—years old."

"She's bossy," Corene muttered.

"But she's hardy," Mirti said. "Think of the storms she's already weathered in her young life. Think of how she protects her little sister. Once she plants herself, she is not easily uprooted."

Admirable and essential hunti traits, to be sure. Val took a roll when the basket came to her, but her mind was on the earlier part of the conversation. Her father had always expected the hunti power to come to her? Was that why he had spent so much time with her, taking her on hikes through the primal forest, patiently naming every tree on the property? Was that why he had always loved her so much? And what had been the flaw in her that turned the power aside, that made her too weak to contain it, accept it into her body? She had been young, yes, but older than Natalie was now. She had endured repeated blows and remained standing. She had been buffeted by powerful storms but never cracked and never yielded. She had placed her palm against the rough surface of the heart tree and *felt* the other four elements cycle through its trunk, transmogrify into a single great symbol of life.

Apparently, that wasn't enough.

She tore the bread into smaller chunks and placed a piece in her mouth, not even tasting it. But to be hunti prime—! Guardian of the challinbar, advisor to the king, feeling in her own bones the shape and weight of every skeleton of every single person who lived in Welce? Just the thought made her feel too heavy to move. She could shoulder a burden, but she wasn't sure she could carry the world.

She lifted her eyes from her plate and found the coru prime watching her from across the table. Zoe's expression was filled with understanding and compassion, as if she could read all the conflicting thoughts in Val's head. She didn't ask any questions, didn't offer any sympathy. Instead, she just gave Val a small smile, and then turned to ask Elidon a question. Val reached for another piece of bread, still shaken, but just a little comforted.

Chapter Eight

Firstday came arrayed in pliant gold and intransigent blue, warm enough by early morning to hint at a hot day ahead. Val wore a lightweight tunic and took the early omnibus south to her father's park, bringing a book and a satchel of snacks. They had agreed to meet at noon, but Sebastian wasn't known for being punctual.

But he surprised her by arriving only ten minutes after she did. "I *knew* you'd be here early," he greeted her. "Come on, let's go."

"Go where?"

"I brought an elaymotive. We can go anywhere we want."

She followed him out through the break in the trees to find a small, sporty vehicle waiting on the street. It looked to be little more than two seats slung between four wheels, with a few metal casings on the front and back. It had no doors, no roof, no spaces for storage.

"You think I'm going to ride in that?" she asked in disbelief.

"It's perfectly safe."

"Until we hit something and it flips over and we land on our heads and die!"

"No, no, it's too low to the ground. We won't flip. We won't smash into a tree. Nothing bad will happen."

They had drawn close enough for Val to touch the sleek metal contours of the almost nonexistent body and peer inside at a bewildering array of levers and dials. "Maybe if you drive really carefully. Where do you want to go?"

"The harbor, maybe? It's a beautiful afternoon for a drive to the coast."

"Won't that take all day?"

"The elaymotive is so much faster than a horse and carriage. We can get there in a couple of hours, have a late lunch, and get home before sunset."

On the one hand, she wasn't sure she believed him. Sebastian was famous for shading the truth when there was something he really wanted.

On the other hand, she had had a difficult nineday, and the idea of leaving Chialto behind even for an afternoon was marvelously appealing. She'd told Corene she would be gone for a few hours because she was meeting with a friend, so she didn't think anyone at the palace would worry about her until nightfall. Even if some mishap stranded them overnight down at the harbor, it wouldn't be a true disaster. The city offered plenty of accommodations, and she had a fair amount of money on her. Assuming they avoided a crash, what was the worst that could happen?

"All right," she said. "Let's go."

※

It turned out that few things were more delightful than tooling along a scenic road in an open vehicle on a sublimely sunny day with your best friend by your side. Val didn't even have to ask Sebastian to keep to a decorous pace, so she didn't have to worry about being thrown over the side of the elaymotive every time they hit a bump.

She was impressed by how much the route had changed since the last time she had traveled this way. Before, it had been a long, relatively lonely two-lane road with the rare isolated business popping up every twenty or so miles to offer travelers a place to rest. Now it was wide enough to allow large transports to pass each other in opposite directions—or impatient elaymotive drivers to whip by slower horse-drawn wagons. And an almost unbroken line of roadside vendors provided food, beds, and opportunities to refuel. Here and there she spotted sprawling complexes that looked as if they might be warehouses or even manufacturing facilities, conveniently situated partway between the harbor and the city proper. A few small neighborhoods had grown up around some of these major outposts. Val wondered if someday the entire route would be one solid settlement, from sea to palace.

They stopped once so she could buy something to use to tie back her hair, which was horribly tangled from the whipping of the wind. They picked a fancy-looking shop in a collection of buildings that appeared to also contain a hotel, a restaurant, and a stable. Most of the merchandise was high-priced and high-quality, and Val was pleased with her eventual selection, a long filmy scarf in a swirling pattern of cinnamon, persimmon, and cherry.

"Sweela colors," Sebastian commented.

"A compliment to my driver."

Back in the car, she found her hair was so knotted she could barely drag a comb through it. "Here, let me," Sebastian said, taking the comb from her hand.

"Don't pull too hard. It'll hurt."

He began gently working his way through the snarls. "I used to help Saska with her hair all the time. I got pretty good at braids and ribbons. But I don't remember your hair being this long before. And so wavy."

He was behind her, so he couldn't see her grimace. "When my mother was sick, I didn't have time to bother with my appearance. I let my hair grow out and stopped styling it. Now I've gotten out of the habit. Maybe while I'm in Chialto, I should find someone who can give me a fashionable cut."

"I like it the way it is. It seems even darker when there's so much of it. Almost black."

"It looks like my hair's too heavy for my head. Like it might tip me over."

He laughed. "Not *quite* that bad. Here, how's that?"

She ran a hand experimentally through the smoothed locks. "Very good, thank you! Let me tie it back and then we can be on our way."

They were quickly back on the road. Even during that short detour, the sun had strengthened considerably, so Val was glad to see the skyline of the harbor taking shape on the horizon. Even from a distance, she could tell it had significantly expanded, spreading out in all directions. Warehouses and storage facilities hunched up along the entire coastline, while shops and residential buildings crept north back up the road toward Chialto. Even the water at the edge of the land had grown more crowded, with hundreds of tall-masted ships and smaller vessels clustering along expanded piers.

"They're going to have to start considering the harbor a city all on its own," Val said.

Sebastian laughed as he steered into an endless stream of elaymotives, wagons, carriages, hand carts, omnibuses, and transports. The streets were narrow and inconvenient, designed for a simpler town with fewer destinations and much less usage. The noise level had jumped so high Val thought they would have to shout the rest of their conversation. The air was dense with a wild variety of scents, the oily odors of machinery mingling with the spicy aroma of cooking meat, the rotting smell of day-old garbage, and the salty freshness of the sea.

"Informally, people have started calling it Vernon Harbor," he answered in a raised voice, "although the elay prime thought they might consider naming it after him."

"Really? Why?"

Sebastian pointed. "He's got a huge complex where he manufactures aeromotives and trains pilots. He and Nelson own half the land around here. They've both gotten very rich as the harbor has expanded, because they invested in property years ago. Kayle Dochenza seems to think it's all because of him that the place has grown so dramatically."

"Sounds like Kayle."

Traffic opened up in fits and starts, allowing Sebastian to drive two or three narrow blocks before he had to slam to a halt again. "It's busy for first-day," Sebastian observed. "As soon as I find a place where I can leave the car, we're getting out and walking. I hope you wore comfortable shoes."

"I did."

It was another fifteen minutes before he turned into a flat, rocky acre that already held a dozen elaymotives jammed together in a way that made Val wonder how the owners would ever get them out again. A small boy demanded three silvers to allow them to park, but at this point Val thought Sebastian would have handed over a gold coin and considered it a bargain. He helped her over the side of the car, then pulled her arm through his.

"In case we get jostled on the street," he said. "Stick close."

But it was more enjoyable to stroll through the harbor town than to drive through it. It was such a haphazard collection of buildings, thrown together with absolutely no forethought or design, that it was impossible to guess what might be around the next corner. A printing office, a cobbler's shop, a small manufacturing site, a cluster of food carts in a narrow open area between what looked like a tavern and a temple. Under their feet, the ground shifted from brick, to stone, to dirt, to some kind of paving.

The people they passed were just as varied. Men who looked like merchants, women who looked like artists, children who darted between carts and pedestrians to carry messages or pilfer packages. Val identified sailors, clerks, footmen, nannies, dock workers, and students. Most interesting, on every third or fourth corner she spotted a quintet of soldiers, wearing dark uniforms ornamented with the Welchin rosette. She wondered if they had always patrolled the harbor in such numbers or if Darien had increased their presence in response to the activity of sirix smugglers.

She found herself fascinated by the fact that so many people they passed seemed to be international visitors. The solidly built men with the dark skin and brightly colored clothing must be from Dhonsho. Those women with olive coloring and silky black hair might be Berringuese. Other groups had lighter skin tones that matched that of the average Welchin, but they wore hairstyles or clothing that marked them as foreigners—Malinquese, perhaps, or Coziquela. Once she noticed a visitor from Soeche-Tas standing completely still in the middle of a crowded sidewalk and staring at the passers-by with a unnervingly intense expression. Almost unconsciously, she drew closer to Sebastian.

"Feeling overwhelmed?" he asked.

"The place has changed so much since the last time I was here. It's exciting but—" She missed an uneven border that changed from gravel to cobblestone, and momentarily lost her footing. "But it's a mess! The streets are so badly laid out and in such disrepair I'd think they'd be better off tearing everything down and rebuilding from scratch."

"Yes, I would expect it to offend your tidy hunti soul, but I love it. You never know what delightful place you'll stumble across on any given day. And then when you come back a week later, you can't find it again because you have no idea how you got there."

"How often are you here?"

"A few times every quintile. I'm in the city more often. Or on the road."

She glanced up at him. "Darien says that most of the contraband sirix comes into the country by way of the smaller ports. Or tiny little docks owned by families along the coastline."

"He's right, as one would expect Darien to be. This—" He gestured at the muddled skyline and the bobbing array of ships on the blue water. "Is much too public for your average cautious smuggler."

"But you still do business here."

He smiled. "I do business everywhere."

The evasive answer perturbed her, but she didn't have time to think about it, since Sebastian immediately steered her toward a doorway. It sat unevenly inside the crooked frame of a low-slung clapboard building, once painted blue but now worn nearly to gray by the incessant assault of the elements. The interior looked equally weatherbeaten, with scuffed wooden tables and mismatched chairs scattered haphazardly across a floor that was one part tile, one part carpet, and one part hardwood. Still, the view from the side windows was spectacular, looking out over the crowded harbor and the limitless sea beyond.

"And my favorite spot is open," Sebastian said, guiding Val toward a small table set in front of the largest window. She would have expected it to be the first place any customer would claim, but the few other patrons in the room seemed to have their minds on matters other than gawking at the ocean vista. At three tables, mixed groups of men and women were deeply engaged in playing penta or some other card game. At two other tables, disreputable-looking characters seemed to be plotting nefarious activities, leaning close to each other to whisper about their plans. A lone man sat on a stool by the bar, nursing a drink and moodily eying the clientele. Val made a point of averting her face.

"Not very fancy," she said, taking her seat. Sebastian dropped down into the chair across from her.

"No, but the food is delicious," he said. "And you don't really like fancy."

"I don't," she acknowledged. "But I would just as soon not be murdered by one of my fellow diners."

He grinned. "I'm sure they're all harmless."

She studied him for a moment. "And you're not."

He tried to look modest. "I could defend myself, if it came to that. And you." His expression became more sardonic. "Growing up as a fatherless boy, you learn a bit about fighting."

She nodded. "How you're raised influences the skills you acquire," she said. "I can't imagine Darien could punch a man in the face or bring him down with a kick."

"Ha. Darien wouldn't have to. He'd walk into a place like this with five soldiers at his back, any one of them ready to kill on his behalf." He raised his hand to signal to someone across the room. "Not that I doubt Darien could kill a man if he wanted to. He'd just be more subtle about it. Untraceable poison in an innocuous glass of wine. Everyone would know he'd done it, but no one would be able to prove it."

"I like to think he's never done that."

Sebastian watched her for a moment. "I'm sure he hasn't."

They were approached by an older, cheerful-looking woman who was drying her hands on her apron as if she'd just washed up after chopping a tubful of fish. "What'll you be having this afternoon?" she asked. "Food or drink?"

Val wondered if Sebastian would order sirix—wondered if this was one of the outlets he did business with—but he instantly put that worry to rest. "Just food today," he said. "What do you have that's fresh-caught?"

She laughed. "All of it!" She pointed to the window. "See that out there? Everything we serve was swimming around in the ocean this morning."

"Then we'll split a platter of whatever you've got on offer, and a plate of bread," Sebastian said. He glanced at Val. "If that's acceptable?"

"That sounds wonderful."

In fifteen minutes, they were sipping fruited water and sampling a spectacular selection of seafood. Even the bread was delicious. As she munched on a crab leg, Val thought that the majority of her time in Chialto had been spent eating extravagant meals, and she had stuffed herself every time. Maybe Darien was right. She had stayed away from the city too long. She had forgotten what profound pleasure could be afforded by a rich, complex meal artfully assembled from uncommon ingredients.

Sebastian seemed to have read her mind. "Nothing like this back home, is there? Maybe a few trout in the local stream, but—" He waved a hand over the platter.

"There are other advantages to country living."

"So you'd never consider moving to the city? Give up the estate, take up a life here?"

"It's not easy for me to uproot and plant myself somewhere else," she said. "There would have to be some powerful incentives."

"I think there must be some coru in me somewhere," he said. "It's hard for me to stay in the same place for long."

"I know," she said, rearranging the items on her plate. "And not a drop of coru in my blood."

She glanced up to find him smiling down at her food. "I'd forgotten you do that," he said.

"Do what?"

"You eat your meal in a precise order. One bite of seafood, one bite of bread, one bite of compote. One sip of water."

"No," she said, somewhat defensively. "I'll take two bites in a row sometimes. But I try to plan it out. I want it to all be even at the end—one bite of everything left. Then I eat them one at a time."

He shook his head, but his expression was fond. "Nobody else does that."

"Well, maybe *you* don't. You just shovel everything into your mouth at once."

"I can savor my food! I just don't make it a *process*."

"You're just careless."

He opened his mouth to answer, then turned his head sharply as a shadow fell across the table. Val looked up to find that someone else had entered the establishment when she wasn't paying attention. He appeared to be forty or fifty years old and wore well-made clothes that looked expensive but nondescript. He had a loose and easy way of moving that suggested a comfort with physical exertion, and a pleasant expression that gave away nothing at all.

His tan face showed a slight smile as he pulled up a chair and sat at their table. "Hello, Sebastian," he said. "I see you've brought a companion to enjoy the fine sights of the harbor."

"Jodar!" Sebastian exclaimed with every evidence of delight. The tone rang false to Val's ears. "I had no idea you were in the city."

"Off and on, my friend. Off and on." He nodded at Val. "Who's the lovely lady?"

"Tina Corro," Sebastian said promptly. He was the only person in Welce who ever called her Tina, and Corro had been her mother's last name. Clearly, whoever this Jodar was, Sebastian did not want him to recognize Val. "She's been mired in the country too long and said she was longing for seafood."

"This is the place to come for it," Jodar said. "Could I buy you a drink to round off your meal?"

"That's kind," Sebastian said. "But we'll be leaving soon. I need to get Tina back to Chialto before nightfall."

"Ah, so you're heading back along the harbor road," Jodar said genially. "In an elaymotive, I take it?"

"Oh yes. I haven't bothered with a wagon since I scraped up enough money to buy a smoker car," Sebastian said. "Never could stand horses. Best day of my life was when I unhitched the last one."

"Smoker cars are fast," Jodar agreed. "I've got one that—" He whistled. "If there wasn't any other traffic on the road, I think I could get from here to the Chialto canal in an hour."

"I drive a little more sedately when I've got a passenger," Sebastian said.

Jodar grinned. "Depends on the passenger."

Every word they exchanged was friendly, but Val could feel herself growing more and more tense. She couldn't see how and didn't know why, but she was certain that Jodar was threatening Sebastian and that Sebastian was furiously trying to come up with ways to neutralize the danger.

Sebastian nodded at her across the table. "Well, *this* passenger has pretty strict ideas about how she likes to be treated," he said. "She's already unhappy with me because I wanted to stop by—ah—a business office while I'm here."

That was her cue to say something, turn the conversation into a different channel, and Val only hoped she had judged correctly. "You *said* you'd spend the whole day with *me*," she complained, trying to strike the right note between petulance and disappointment. "I don't mind five minutes here and there, but why did you even bring me if you were going to be busy half the time?"

Sebastian shrugged and looked at Jodar. "You see?"

"Only a few ways to deal with a woman who's got unrealistic expectations," Jodar said easily.

For a second, Sebastian froze. Val got the impression of great fury and great fear, and then he laughed. "Well, I've never needed advice dealing with women," he said.

Val's stomach was clenched so tightly she thought she might throw up all the excellent seafood she had devoured so greedily. "How long do we have to stay?" she whined. "You know I have to get home soon."

Jodar slapped his hands on his thighs and rose to his feet. "Don't let me be the one to keep you," he said. "Good to run into you, Sebastian."

"Likewise. I'll look you up next time I'm in town."

Jodar's grin widened as he turned away. "You do that." He nodded at Val and sauntered off.

Val watched him until he had stepped through the front door and disappeared into the endless stream of pedestrians. "*What* was that all about?" she demanded, turning back to Sebastian. "That man is absolutely terrifying."

Sebastian had produced a crumpled piece of paper from somewhere and was busily sketching out a simple drawing. He didn't look up. "Even more than you might guess," he said.

"So?" she insisted. "What did he want from you? I had the feeling he was threatening you."

"He was." He shoved the paper over toward her and she could see it was a crude map of streets and buildings. "Here's what we're going to do. We're going to pretend to have a fight and you're going to stalk out of the restaurant. Walk as fast as you can to this corner here—it's got the blue house with the seagull painted on the front—and then turn left and *run*. Keep running till you get here, the new three-story building made of brick. Then duck inside and announce that you're Darien Serlast's sister and someone is trying to kill you."

Val just stared at him.

"It's Kayle Dochenza's business office," Sebastian went on. "Kayle probably won't be there, but *someone* will be, and they'll recognize your name. You'll be safe—Kayle may seem like a dreamy lunatic, but in some ways he's sharp as a razor. He knows what his inventions are worth, and he has guards on hand around the clock."

"What will be happening to *you* while I'm running away?" she asked slowly.

He smiled tightly. "I'll be having a very uncomfortable conversation with Jodar."

"About what?"

"About some business that we did not conclude satisfactorily about a quintile ago."

"Did you cheat him?"

He looked offended. "Why would you assume that I'm the one who's done something wrong?"

"*Are* you?"

"I would say there's fault on both sides."

"What's he going to do to you?"

Sebastian was silent for a moment. He watched her, his brown eyes guarded. She mentally reviewed the conversation, the discussion of elaymotives and their impressive speed.

"He's not—what, you think he might *kill* you? Chase you down the road and—and *murder* you?"

Sebastian shrugged. "It's happened before. People who got on the wrong side of Jodar have died in some spectacular elaymotive wrecks. Or fallen in the canal and drowned. Or had other unfortunate accidents."

Val folded her arms and sat back in her chair. "Then I'm not leaving."

"What? You have to!"

"Not if he's going to kill you the minute I walk out."

"He won't. He'll talk to me first. We might be able to come to terms."

"Then I'll wait to find out what those terms might be."

"You can't," he said urgently. "He was giving me a warning. He was giving me time to get you safely out of here. That was a—a professional courtesy. But if he comes back and you're still with me, he won't care. He'll take you down right alongside me."

She remembered the air of iron menace that Jodar had radiated, even while making jovial conversation, and she knew it was true. She felt her spine tingle with ice. Her hands were already freezing.

"I'm not leaving you behind to die," she said.

He stretched his hands out across the table, an obvious invitation, and she helplessly laid hers in his. His hard grip was warm and reassuring. "I don't think it will come to that," he said. "But you have to understand. I would rather die than see harm come to you. Do you hear me? If Jodar hurt you because of my carelessness, I would kill myself anyway. If you don't leave me here, right now, and Jodar comes back and *touches* you, I am a dead man, anyway. Because I would not be able to live with the knowledge that I had caused you grief."

For a moment, they stared at each other, their hands locked together, their expressions grim. Val knew her own face showed protest and fear, but Sebastian's revealed only bleak, uncompromising determination. Sebastian was a gifted liar, but he wasn't lying now.

She ripped her hands away. "I will never forgive you," she said in a low, furious voice.

"Tina—"

Her voice was loud enough for the other patrons to hear, if they were so inclined. "You buy me presents—you bring me here—you shower me with attention, and I think maybe you've changed—"

She could tell he wasn't certain how much of her rage was real and how much was manufactured for the charade. She wasn't sure she knew, either.

"I *have* changed," he said, trying to recapture her hands, but she jerked them away and scooted back in her chair. "Just give me a chance—"

"There have been too many chances," she said. When he reached for her again, she snatched up her water glass and flung its contents in his face. "Too many disappointments." She jumped to her feet. "Don't come looking for me back in Chialto. I don't want to see you again."

The dismay on his face was swift and genuine. He still couldn't tell whether or not she meant the things she was saying. He stood up more slowly, extending his hand. "Tina—"

"Don't you follow me," she said sharply, putting up her own hand as if to shove him back in place. "You stay here. I'm leaving." She whirled for the door, not bothering to look back. Out of the corner of her eye, she saw the friendly restaurant owner watching her with consternation and the assorted patrons eying her with a mix of amusement and sympathy. She strode past them all and slammed through the door, reaching up to rip off the bright sweela scarf she had worn in her hair all this time.

Outside, she paused on the street just long enough to double over, catching her breath and scrubbing her hands hard across her cheeks. She dug the nails of her right hand into the skin under her jaw and raked down hard, catching her fingers in her collar and tearing off a button as she jerked upright.

Then she began screaming as loud as she could.

A young woman hurrying by glanced at her fearfully without stopping, and two men across the street turned to look at her in astonishment. A couple of Dhonshon merchants peered at her over their shoulders but continued on their brisk walk. Val kept wailing.

The door behind her burst open, and the cheerful bar owner hurried out.

"My dear girl—what happened? Are you all right?"

Val turned away from her and screamed again. As if her heart had broken. Her world had ended. Her life had been rendered forfeit.

She heard the sound of running footsteps, and two five-person squads of soldiers converged from different directions. "What's up? What happened to her?" demanded the lead guard, a small compact woman with an authoritative air.

The restaurant owner shook her head, bewildered. "I don't know! She had a fight with her young man, and she came rushing out here, and then all the sudden she just started shrieking—"

Val stopped screaming and turned away, putting her palms to her face and weeping through her fingers. She felt the guard place a hand on her shoulder.

"Can you tell me what's wrong?" the woman asked, her voice compassionate but brisk. This was someone who liked to know what the problem was so she could put all her energy into solving it.

"I came out—here to—*think* for a minute," Val gasped out between gusty sobs. "And this *man*—came up and attacked me—"

"What did he look like? Can you tell me?"

"No! He grabbed me from the back—and he tore my scarf—and he scratched my face—"

"Did you see anything?" the guard asked the restaurant owner.

"I was inside," the woman answered. "Maybe someone saw something through the window, but it all happened so fast."

Val still had her hands over her eyes, but she could feel the guard turn away to address a couple of the other soldiers. "Look around. Ask a few questions. Find out if anyone noticed anything."

There was the sound of booted footsteps moving off. The hand on Val's shoulder tightened as the guard turned back to her. "Would you like to go in and sit down? Maybe have a glass of water? Maybe you'll feel a little better and you might remember something you can tell me. My name is Yori, by the way."

Val took in a deep exaggerated breath and dropped her hands. "Maybe," she said in a wispy voice. She glanced around in a hopeless fashion, as if despairing of seeing anything useful. It was enough to show her that Sebastian was one of the people inside the restaurant, crowding up at the window to watch the scene outside. Trying to figure out what her game was, though he might have guessed it already. Reflections from the afternoon sun obscured some of his features, but she thought he looked furious.

Good. So was Val.

Her gaze dropped to the pavement. "My scarf!" she exclaimed, bending down to scoop it up, muddied and a little ripped. She cradled it against her cheek. "It was a gift," she explained to the guard.

It was the first good look Val had gotten at the soldier who'd come to her rescue. Yori had short dark hair and an expression of limitless curiosity—and right now her eyes were locked on Val's face with a look of sharp intelligence. It was all Val could do to keep her expression frightened and innocent instead of triumphant.

Val didn't remember ever seeing Yori before, but obviously the guard recognized her.

Obviously, nothing and nobody would be allowed to harm the king's sister. Or her companion.

"Shall we go inside?" Yori said, urging her forward. "Can you tell me your name?"

"Val."

Yori didn't bother saying, "Valentina Serlast?" It was clear she had guessed there was more to this little drama than might be instantly apparent, but also clear that she didn't care. She knew what she had to know and what she had to do, and that was all that mattered to her.

As soon as they stepped inside, Sebastian came rushing up. "What happened? Someone said there was screaming—and suddenly there were guards—are you all right?"

She allowed him to take her in a brief, comforting embrace, aware that every eye in the place was fixed on them with interest. "A man tried to grab me, but I got away—I was so frightened!"

"I think you'd better take a moment to compose yourself and then let us take you home," Yori said. "Do you live nearby?"

Val pulled herself from Sebastian's arms and shook her head. "Back in Chialto. We drove down here for the day." She looked at Sebastian and bit her lip. "And then we had an argument—"

"I'm so sorry," Sebastian said, his voice remorseful. "It's all my fault."

Yori seemed unconvinced by this bit of acting, but all she said was, "Well, why don't you have a glass of water? Then we'll get going."

Val made her eyes big. "You can't take me all the way to Chialto!"

Yori grinned. "We were headed back there tonight anyway. Happy to provide an escort."

"Oh, that would make me feel so much safer!"

Yori nodded over at Sebastian. "If he's not ready to leave yet, we could take you home." Her voice flattened. "Or if you don't feel like riding with him after your argument."

Val didn't even look at Sebastian. Instead, she tried to appear shy and uncertain, though she couldn't manufacture a blush. "Oh—we have so much to talk over," she said breathlessly. "But thank you. That's so kind."

"When you're ready, then."

So Val had to endure a few moments of the owner fussing over her, and the other patrons whispering about her, and Sebastian fuming in silence as she sipped a very tall glass of water and nibbled on a piece of bread that the proprietor seemed to think would restore her spirits. But soon enough she was able to pronounce herself fortified for the journey home. Yori, who appeared to be inordinately capable, had used this interlude to send one of her men off to find a transport, because there was a large official-looking elaymotive idling outside the restaurant when they stepped out.

"Let's get your vehicle and then we can go," Yori said.

In another fifteen minutes, they had retrieved Sebastian's jaunty smoker car, fought through the late-afternoon traffic, and hit the open road to head north to Chialto. Sebastian kept to a sedate pace, and Yori and the elaymotive full of soldiers followed right behind them.

Neither Val nor Sebastian said a word for the entire two hours of the drive. He kept his eyes fixed on the view straight ahead of him, while she rested her elbow on the side of the car and propped her chin in her palm. She hadn't wanted to put the dirty scarf back on her head, so she held her hair back with her free hand and simply watched the scenery flow past. She couldn't tell if Sebastian was so angry he didn't want to speak to her, or if he realized she was so furious she didn't want to speak to him. She wasn't sure it mattered.

They crossed the canal just as the sun was sinking low enough to start tinting the western sky with hazy gold. They were almost to the Cinque when Sebastian steered the car to the side of the road. The transport pulled in smoothly behind them.

"Probably just as well if I'm not the one to drop you off at the palace," Sebastian said in a neutral voice.

"I was thinking the same thing," she said. He didn't get out of the car, so she was going to have to clamber over the side unaided, but he stopped her with a hand on her arm before she could climb out. She looked at him over her shoulder.

"I don't know why I always forget what you're capable of," he said. "It's not that I underestimate you. Never that. I just don't expect you—" He shook his head.

Her voice was absolutely uninflected. "I don't know why I always forget what *you're* capable of."

"I'll take care of the situation," he said.

She freed herself from his grip and turned away, to find Yori standing at the side of the car. "Need a little help getting out? These sporty models are a challenge."

"Yes, thank you." She had barely climbed from the elaymotive before Sebastian took off.

"You can sit in front with me," Yori said as they headed over to the transport. "I'm going to drop this lot off at the barracks."

The four soldiers in back laughed and joked together until they arrived at a blocky institutional-looking building flying the Welchin rosette flag. The barracks, Val supposed, though she'd never had cause to visit the spot before. The guards all waved cheery goodbyes to Yori as they climbed out, confirming Val's impression of Yori's general likability.

Yori pulled back onto the Cinque and—without ever asking Val where she wanted to go—headed up the winding road to the palace.

Almost a dozen smaller elaymotives were clogging up the courtyard and at least that many soldiers were lined up on either side of the great double doors. Which were wide open, showing the enormous kierten brightly lit and filled with a cluster of finely dressed guests.

"I forgot Darien was having some kind of state dinner tonight," Val said as Yori brought the transport to a halt.

"You probably still have time to change clothes and make it to the table."

"No, I told him last night that I didn't want to attend. He knows I hate these sorts of things."

"I think they're fun," Yori said. "Well—usually dull, but always with the possibility of excitement. Someone drawing a knife or rushing in off the street shouting about killing the king."

Val turned to give her a closer examination in the gathering dark. "You have an odd notion of fun."

Yori grinned. "I don't like to be bored."

Val put her hand on the door handle. "I'm never bored. The quieter life is, the better I like it."

Yori jerked her head to indicate the city laid out behind them at the bottom of the mountain road. "Not quiet with a man like that. He's trouble."

"I know," Val said. She opened the door, then turned back. "Thank you."

Yori grinned again. "Not sure exactly what was going on, but I was happy to help."

Val just nodded and stepped out of the car. Yori had driven away before Val had figured out how she was going to sneak in without anyone seeing her. She didn't want to risk someone recognizing her and demanding she join them for whatever the night's festivities held. She thought about circling the palace and going in through one of the servant's doors, but in the end she made her way down to the small lake that rested just outside the palace walls. She would sit here until the crowd moved to the dining hall and no one would see her slip inside.

A handful of picturesque benches were scattered around the shoreline, so she took a seat on one that was out of sight of the first-story windows. The air was still warm enough to feel pleasant against her skin, and she took her shoes off to cool her feet against the smooth paving stones. As the sun sank lower, the surface of the water seemed to change color, moving from clear blue to clouded indigo to spangled black. The lights from the palace danced erratically across the gently lapping waves, and the Marisi made a muted grumble as it streamed down the southern perimeter of the lake to create the eastern border of the city.

She had no idea what she was going to do about Sebastian.

Chapter Nine

Val woke the next morning, her thoughts heavy and her mind in an uproar, and wondered how she could possibly distract herself from worrying about Sebastian all day. And how she could possibly avoid hearing Darien's scathing response to yesterday's misadventure. Salvation came shortly before lunch in the form of an invitation from Saska.

Come see my new play! she wrote in her execrable handwriting, as if she could barely stand to waste the time it took to get her words on paper. *We'll be performing for three nights at a little theater near the Plaza of Women. All experimental and completely incomprehensible. So much fun. Have dinner with me first. Tonight? Don't bring Darien (as if you would).*

Val spent a few minutes trying to decipher the address scrawled at the bottom of the page and then just gave up and hoped she would make it somewhere close to the correct vicinity. She had no idea how a person should dress for such an occasion, so she wore a black tunic and a bright scarf which she figured she could take off if the mood seemed more funereal.

"I'm meeting Saska for dinner," she told Darien on her way out, hurrying a little so he wouldn't try to stop her for a real conversation.

"I didn't even know she was in town."

"I get the sense that it will just be for a few days. You know Saska."

"Indeed. Let me order an elaymotive for you."

The driver had no trouble finding Saska's designated dinner spot, a small seedy-looking place in a row of rundown cafés and shops. The street was overflowing with fashionable young men and women wearing bright clothes, unnatural hairstyles, and expressions of lawless gaiety. The exact sort of place that Val tended to avoid and Saska found almost without trying.

The instant Val stepped out of the elaymotive, she heard Saska calling her name and saw her waving from the restaurant's open window. She felt her frown smooth into the smile that it was impossible to suppress in Saska's sunny presence. She waved back and hurried into the café.

"I got here hours ago so I could get the best table," Saska said, once she had smothered Val in an enthusiastic hug and then dropped back into her seat. This claim was entirely believable, as the table was littered with used plates, crumpled napkins, and four glasses with varying levels of liquid. "How *are* you? You look so serious."

"Don't I always look serious?"

Saska laughed. "Yes, but you should at least seem happy to see me."

"I am *delighted* to see you. You're the best thing about Chialto so far. How long have you been here?"

"We got in on eighthday and leave on fourthday, so it's a short visit. We've been touring all over the provinces but—" She waved her hand in extreme unconcern. "One of the actors wanted to visit his mother, or maybe it was his girlfriend, and the producer found an open theater for a few nights and—you know how it always goes. So here we are."

Val had no idea "how it always goes" with a theater troupe except for what she had gleaned from Saska's letters and visits over the past two years. After adopting and discarding half a dozen other passions, from horseback riding to exotic flower gardening, Saska had decided she wanted to pursue a life in the theater. It seemed like a perfect match for the restless coru girl who got bored with every obsession, since it allowed her to change her circumstances, her appearance, and even her persona every quintile.

"So tell me about the play."

"No, no, you'll see it tonight. Tell me about *you*. I can't believe you actually came to Chialto. How are you getting along with Darien?"

"How does anyone ever get along with Darien?"

Saska grinned. Unlike their other cousins—who had idolized Darien, following him around devotedly on the rare times he was home while they were visiting—Saska had always found him irksome. One of Val's most indelible memories was the time Saska had called him a pompous bore right in the middle of a grand dinner party. Darien, of course, had been unmoved, gravely replying, "As always, Saska, I value your insights." Most of their other interactions had been similar, if less spectacular.

"Well, *some* people must find him tolerable," Saska said. "What about his wife? I've only met her a couple of times. Has she softened any of his hard edges? I still can't believe a coru woman would actually marry him."

Val poured herself a glass of fruited water from a carafe on the table. She wasn't sure how it had happened, but over the past few days, she had come to like Zoe more than she ever had. "I don't think Zoe has softened him, no. He's just as righteous and sure of himself as ever. But she—" Val took a sip. "She makes him seem warmer, somehow. Less rigid in his thinking."

"So you're enjoying your visit."

"No. I can't wait to go home."

Saska laughed. "That's my Val. Never change."

"I probably won't."

"Have you seen Sebastian since you've been here? I haven't had time to track him down."

Saska was the one person who cared about Sebastian as much as Val did, so she would be the one person Val could confide in. Even so, she found herself shying away from sharing details. "A couple of times," she said. "He seems to be involved in some unsavory activities."

"Well, that's hardly a surprise. Give him my love next time you see him."

Whenever that might be. "I will."

They were approached by one of the café workers, a solid Dhonshon woman whose flowing crimson tunic enhanced the rich tone of her dark skin. "Don't bother looking at the menu, by the way," Saska said. "I'm going to order for you."

"I see your friend has joined you," the woman observed in Coziquela.

Saska replied in what sounded like gibberish, though Val quickly realized it must be Dhonshon. The woman snorted with amusement and gave Val one swift, appraising glance before asking what seemed to be a question. Saska's reply was laughing and emphatic, and the woman nodded and left.

"I don't even want to know what terrible thing you told her about me," Val said.

"Just that you're not very adventurous with your food choices but you're too polite to throw your plate against the wall if you don't like something."

Val doubted that was what Saska had really said, but she let it go. "How do you know Dhonshon? I thought it was difficult to learn."

"It *is*. Much harder than Coziquela, or even Soechin, which I'm also pretty good at. But I was seeing a Dhonshon girl for a couple of quintiles, and she taught me a lot."

"But then you got bored and found someone new."

"*No*," Saska said, though that was usually the way of it. "She was even more serious than you, and eventually she found me too frivolous. But I learned some very good words."

"Teach me some. Maybe I'll meet a Dhonshon someday."

So they practiced the pronunciations for *water* and *danger* and *help me* and *friend*, which Saska said were useful words to know in any language. "There are actually two words for 'friend,' and the other one is way more common. But *this* is the word that means you're speaking from the heart. It's the one you use when you're giving a deathbed promise or something. So of course that was the one I wanted to know."

"Of course it was."

"And then I learned a few curse words. Also very useful."

When their food arrived, a platter of five unidentifiable items, Val gamely tried each one. Two were barely edible, in her opinion, and she was forced to leave the last few bites on her plate instead of finishing her meal in a symmetrical fashion. But the other three were surprisingly tasty despite the unfamiliar spices and intense flavors. She was actually disappointed that they didn't have time to sample dessert options because Saska suddenly realized how late it was.

"We have to go!" she said, jumping to her feet and tossing a handful of silvers on the table. "Come on—the theater is just up the street."

Unlike the rest of the establishments in this part of town, the playhouse was relatively new, well-maintained, and perfectly respectable. "It's owned by the hunti queen—Seterre," Saska explained as she pulled Val through the front doors. They were instantly inside a cool, dark space that featured an empty stage facing a couple dozen rows of chairs arranged in a semi circle. "She has another venue that's much finer than this one, and I'd *love* to play there someday, but this is where you want your new production to open. This is where everybody wants to be seen."

Maybe ten audience members were already scattered in seats throughout the auditorium, but Saska drew Val up to the front row. "Sit here," she said. "And wait for me after the play is over so you can tell me what you thought."

"I'm sure I'll find it very interesting."

Saska laughed, blew her a kiss, and hustled off to disappear through a side door. Val resigned herself to a tedious period of waiting, but in fact the space filled up quickly. Apparently, the trendy young theater-goers of Chialto liked to wait until the last possible moment to take their seats. It was only twenty minutes after Val's arrival that the gaslights dimmed and the first actors moved onto the stage.

As Saska had warned, the play was almost impossible to follow, although Val thought it might be about someone named Milton learning that his father was not the man he had always believed. Some of the actors spent the entire performance with their backs to the audience, shouting their lines; some wore light cotton bags over their heads so their faces were invisible; two were naked. Val thought they might be trying to express various ideas about identity—how much a person might choose to hide or reveal and to whom—but she wasn't entirely sure. Nonetheless, she clapped politely when the play was over and the actors took their bows. She was just as glad that the production had been short.

Val came to her feet as the audience started dispersing, but she remained in place, waiting for Saska to come bounding out. Behind her, she heard a surprised laugh, and someone touched her on the sleeve. She turned to find herself facing Corene and a couple of her friends.

"If I had to pick any spot in the city where I would *not* expect to see you, this would be at the top of my list," Corene said. "What are you *doing* here?"

Val felt her face relax into a smile. "My cousin Saska is one of the actors."

"Which one? Not the woman who didn't have any clothes on, I hope."

"No, but that astonishes me, now that I think of it. It's the sort of part Saska would love. But she was the woman who always walked behind Milton, repeating all of his lines."

"Oh! My favorite character! I could understand everything she said, which was very useful, as Milton mumbled his words."

"But what are *you* doing here?" Val asked.

Corene gestured at her companions, a serene-looking woman with long blonde hair, and a slightly older man who had a friendly face and an air of infinite curiosity. "My sister wanted to see it."

The blonde woman smiled. "'Wanted' might be the wrong word," she said. "More like 'agreed to come because my mother asked me to.'"

That was when Val realized who the other woman was. Queen Seterre's daughter, who had been sired by Zoe's father. Corene's sister by tradition and affection, not by blood. "Princess Josetta! My apologies! I didn't recognize you."

"No apologies needed, because I didn't recognize you, either. Corene had to tell me who you were."

"I've been having this conversation with a lot of people," Val said. "Apparently, I've been away from Chialto too long."

"And this is my husband, Rafe."

Val nodded at him, and he smiled back. "I won't even ask how you enjoyed the show," he said. "I will assume you found it as delightful as we did."

Josetta laughed and Corene rolled her eyes. Val said, "Well, Saska did warn me."

Corene squinched up her face as if trying to figure something out. "So if Saska is your cousin—"

"My mother's sister's daughter."

"Then she's Darien's cousin, too. So she's related to me?"

Just then, the door to the stage banged open and Saska came flying out, still wearing dramatic stage makeup and her character's shapeless green sack of a dress. "Well," Val said, "if you want to claim her."

"Val! You're still here!" Saska exclaimed, throwing her arms around Val as if they hadn't seen each other in two years. "Wasn't that fun? I bet you didn't understand a word!"

"I mostly understood the *words* but not what the words were supposed to *mean*," Val replied.

Saska grinned. "We've been performing it for a quintile and I still have no idea what it's about. But who are your friends?"

"I'm your cousin Corene," the princess said promptly.

If she expected to discompose Saska, she was disappointed. "Darien's secret daughter! Of course! Oh, you look much more likable than he is. Are you?"

Corene, Josetta, and Rafe all burst out laughing. "Some days I'm even more disagreeable," Corene said. "This is my sister Josetta and her husband, Rafe."

"Princess," Saska said, addressing Josetta with unexpected earnestness. "I admire all the work you do with charities in the city."

"Thank you. I'm always looking for volunteers, if you ever decide you want to—" She glanced around. "Give up the glamour of the theater."

Val watched a rapt expression pass over Saska's face and wondered if the wayward girl had just stumbled into her new obsession. "Thank you. I'll think about that," she said.

"Have you started your new project for Darien?" Val wanted to know. "Rounding up women for the Soechins?"

"We're trying to work out the logistics," Josetta said. "But I have very mixed feelings about the enterprise. I find the Soechins generally reprehensible, and yet if they do actually represent a viable alternative lifestyle—" She shrugged. "It could be a solution with benefits to all parties."

"I have to say I'm curious to see how it unfolds," Val replied.

There was a bustle behind them, and a small whirlwind of a woman descended on their group. She was fair-haired, extravagantly overdressed, and covered with jewels; she gave the impression of bouncing even when she was standing still. This was the infamous Seterre, old King Vernon's second wife. Val remembered the queen from her childhood visits to the city, but back then, Seterre had been a more typically stoic hunti woman. Trying to stand straight and tall and unbroken against the incessant buffeting of court intrigue. Once she had been freed of her royal responsibilities, she had turned herself into another person entirely, abandoning the political stage to become a patron of the arts. It was the least hunti thing Val had seen any hunti person do.

The queen fluttered her hands around her daughter's face. "Josetta, darling, I'm so pleased to see you! And Rafe, of course. Oh, and you brought Corene! How delightful! Wasn't it the most amazing play?"

"I can truthfully say I have never seen anything like it," Rafe replied.

"Aren't you the dearest man! Saska, how do you know my daughter and her friends?"

"I don't. But Val is my cousin, and she's Darien's sister, so—"

"Valentina!" Seterre cried, enveloping Val in a scented hug. "I cannot even remember the last time I saw you! It must have been when your father was still alive. What a shy and serious young girl you were then."

Val managed a smile. "Still serious. It's good to see you again."

"You must have come to Chialto for the coronation. Are you staying?"

"For a while. Maybe a quintile."

Seterre stepped back so she could rest her eyes on first one of them, and then the next. "So Saska is Val's cousin. Which means Saska is also in some sense Corene's cousin. And Corene is Josetta's sister. And Josetta is my daughter." The queen was beaming. "Isn't that marvelous! All of us related in such unexpected ways!"

"It does seem strange and remarkable," Val admitted.

Seterre put one hand on Val's arm, one on Rafe's, and made as if to draw them all into one untidy embrace. "But that's the hunti gift!" she exclaimed. "To bind the world together! If we would only be bothered to look for the ways, we would find we are all connected in some mysterious fashion." She leaned over to kiss Val on the cheek. "Once you understand that, you understand everything."

Chapter Ten

Val was reminded of this conversation the following day when she had lunch with Elidon in her suite at the palace. Val was still hunting for ways to avoid a confrontation with Darien, or otherwise she might not have accepted the invitation. She had never been particularly comfortable around Elidon, Vernon's first and most powerful queen. She was a majestic, complicated, and not always likable woman who was widely assumed to be Mirti's lover. Val had never asked.

At any rate, the two women had suites that were fairly close together on the same floor of the palace. The bulk of the building was split into two wings branching off of the cavernous foyer, each accessed by its own grand stairwell. In Vernon's day, the queens and their children had all had their quarters in the left-hand wing, while Vernon lived and worked primarily in the rooms on the right.

Zoe had made it clear she was not living apart from her husband or her daughter, so there had been massive upheavals as spaces had been reapportioned and repurposed. Now the right-hand wing served all the needs of the royal family. It was where Darien, Zoe, Celia, and Corene had their bedrooms and took their meals, and where Zoe and Darien kept their formal offices. Val also had been given a room near the rest of the family.

The left half of the building was reserved for what Darien called "affiliates of the crown." The lower floors were made up of offices, meeting rooms, and dining halls, and they were often the busiest sections of the palace. The upper floors were all living spaces. Not only did Elidon and Mirti have suites there, but rooms also were set aside for Kayle, Taro, and the dowager Queen Romelle to use whenever they were in town. Most other guests also were quartered in the left wing.

Mirti was still at the hunti estate, so Val and Elidon were the only ones sharing the meal. The conversation turned out to be a bit more interesting than Val had expected, as the queen spent half an hour outlining, in great and precise detail, plans for revamping the Cinque over a five-year construction period.

"You're so decisive and full of plans," Val said when she was finished. "I would never think you were elay. All the elay people I've known were dreamy and sort of unfocused. They're artists and acolytes, not people who work on metropolitan transit."

"I have the elay trait of vision," Elidon said somewhat grandly. "I imagine a different world. But I work with large canvases, like cities and countries, instead of the small personal projects other artists pursue."

"When I was a little girl, I used to think you should be hunti and Seterre should be elay," Val said. "Because you've got such strength of will and Seterre is so flighty."

Elidon arched her brows. "Ah, that is because you think there is only a single manifestation of the hunti characteristics," she said. "You yourself are like some tenacious challinbar tree, with your roots sunk deep in the ground. You plant yourself someplace and you take hold, and you make sure nothing will displace you. You do not yield and you do not break."

Val thought of her aunt, her father, and her brother. "I'm not the only one."

"But Seterre is like a stand of grasswoods," Elidon said. "Thin and flexible, able to bend with any wind. And under the ground, the grasswood sends out roots and runners, and then it sends up another shoot, and another one, until it creates an entire grove. And if you chop down one or two or a dozen shoots, it will pop up again somewhere else nearby, unless you rip out every single root and burn every trunk to the ground. *That* is the kind of hunti woman Seterre is."

Val shook her head. "I'm not like that at all."

"And yet it is an admirable trait," Elidon said. "There are times we must all stand firm, of course. But there are times it would not hurt us to be more open to change."

"I think if I tried to change as much as Seterre has, I would just come crashing down," said Val. "You'd find me lying helplessly on the ground somewhere."

"You could look at it another way," said Elidon. "A tree in a forest is a beautiful thing. But a tree that has been turned into something else—perhaps timber for a home, or a beautiful piece of furniture—becomes a useful thing. It retains its essence, but it becomes something more. A woman, too, can remake herself while remaining true to herself. It is not impossible to do."

"I think it would be impossible for *me*," Val muttered.

Elidon shrugged and picked up the pitcher of fruited water to refresh their glasses. "Then perhaps you will never be faced with such a necessity. It is hard to predict what our lives might present us with next."

On the morning of fourthday, Val's luck ran out. She was by herself in the breakfast room when Darien came in. "Look at you, sitting here all sad and lonely," he said as he filled a plate and sat across from her.

"I'm never lonely," she said. "But I did start wondering where everybody was."

"Celia has been coughing all night, so Zoe is staying with her."

"Oh, I'm so sorry."

"She'll be fine. Anyway, Zoe is not above commanding the elay prime to drop everything and rush to the palace to clear any infection out of Celia's lungs. All the primes have breathtaking healing powers."

"Our father mended Saska's wrist one summer when she broke it. Do you remember? It was amazing to watch."

He nodded. "They can save people with their elemental powers—and they can hurt people, too." He worked through a bite of sausage before adding, "I'm not sure everyone in Welce really understands the relationship between the primes and the king or queen. When a ruler is chosen, the primes forswear their power against that person. They render their own abilities null for that singular individual."

"So that they can't do any harm," Val guessed.

"Exactly. Because if a rogue prime wanted to take down the monarch—" He snapped his fingers. "It could happen very fast. And no one could stop it."

"I suppose that primes who wanted to bring down a king could *pretend* to nullify their power," Val said. "I mean, if the primes were already evil and planning destruction."

Darien burst out laughing. "I confess I never thought of that, but you're absolutely right. So far, however, that situation hasn't arisen."

"So how does it happen? Is there a secret ritual where all the primes do something to make you immune to them?"

"Apparently, but I haven't undergone it."

"Why not?"

"Because I weighed the risks and benefits and decided I would rather be able to draw on the primes' gifts in a dire situation than feel myself safe from their influence during the normal run of existence."

She leaned back in her chair and regarded him. "That's not the decision I would have expected you to make," she said slowly. "You never gamble. You always take the certain course. It's *possible* you might someday need their healing power. But it's *certain* you'll never want to be vulnerable to their attack."

"I take the certain course when I can," he agreed. "But so many decisions in life are not clear-cut. Maybe it's highly unlikely that a specific risk will occur—but if it does, it's catastrophic. I have to choose the course that promises the best outcome, even if offers a risk of its own."

"Nuanced thinking for a hunti man."

"Yes, I am capable of much more subtlety than people give me credit for."

She grinned at that. "I admit I'm shocked."

"I was in the house when Mirti and Zoe and Nelson saved Taro's life last year. I do not want to give up that option." He laughed. "And, anyway, the coru prime is my wife. I'm not going to make myself invisible to *her* power. And if I can't trust Mirti—and Taro—" He shook his head.

"What about Kayle and Nelson?"

He gave the question a moment's consideration. "Nelson has strong principles and a passionate devotion to the realm," he said. "But he's always thinking about how things could be different. How things could be improved. If a current prime was going to overthrow the king, it would be Nelson—but only if he was absolutely convinced that Welce would be better served in the end."

"And Kayle?"

"Well, who ever knows what Kayle is thinking? He's not a revolutionary. He's certainly not a plotter. If there was an uprising, would he support a rebel cause? I honestly couldn't guess."

"And of course there's a new generation of primes who will someday take over from the ones you have now," Val said. "Who knows if you'll be able to trust them?"

"An excellent point," he said. "I have put some effort into maintaining good relations with the heirs who have already been identified, and I will do the same as the others are named. A way to mitigate risk, if I can."

She remembered that Mirti had made plans to bring Natalie to the hunti estate, and she wondered if the young princess would indeed be revealed as Mirti's heir. It seemed strange to think of her childhood home passing on to someone even farther removed from Val than Mirti. She would have less and less claim to the property, no reason to ever again pace between those massive challinbar trees, practically feeling an exhalation of air as they worked their chemical magic. Almost believing the lowest trailing branches reached out to her, rested their smallest twigs on her shoulder, welcomed her with an intelligence much different from but at least equal to her own.

She shook her head to banish the thought. She couldn't think of an easy way to change the topic, so she refilled her plate at the sideboard. When she took her seat again, she learned Darien already had the next subject in mind.

"So," he said. "You're still keeping company with Sebastian Ardelay?"

All the talk about primes and their powers had lulled her into thinking he wasn't going to ask her about Sebastian after all, so she was taken completely off guard. She tried to cover her sudden unease by making a small scoffing noise. "What a way to put it. As if we're courting."

Darien raised his eyebrows. "And you're not?"

"He's my best friend."

"I hadn't realized you were still in touch."

"Why wouldn't we be?"

"Friendships end. People drift apart. They change."

"I don't."

"He does not seem," Darien said deliberately, "like the kind of person who would merit your attachment."

She decided to attack. "He said you'd never liked him."

"He's likable enough. But I admit I've never had a high opinion of him."

"I can't imagine you hold it against him that he's a bastard."

He laughed. "Of course not. I have an illegitimate daughter of my own."

"I know he tried to torment you when he was a young boy—"

"Oh yes," Darien said in a sardonic voice. "The endless practical jokes. The dead fish in the pocket of my best tunic. The black frogs in my bed."

"Actually, he put frogs in *everyone's* bed that day. Saska thought it was hilarious."

"Saska's approval is hardly a recommendation in *any* situation. And then of course he graduated to crackpot schemes when he was a little older. For instance, there was the summer he encouraged all the young men in the neighborhood to pilfer expensive items from their parents' houses so he could sell them on his own little black market network. He made a fair bit of profit off that, if I recall."

"Aunt Jenty grounded him for the rest of the year."

"I can't imagine the punishment curbed his inventiveness."

"But you can't still be mad at him for things he did ten or twelve years ago!"

"No, but I can see that the adult is much like the child—someone who embodies all the worst of the sweela traits. He's unsteady. Reckless. Attracted to danger. Charming enough, personable when he wants to be, but—a walking bundle of mayhem."

She couldn't exactly deny any of those charges, so she just shrugged. Darien sipped his water and continued laying out his case. "He's been in Chialto for years now, living on the fringes. Never quite breaking the law, but associating with people who do. In my experience, nobody successfully walks that line for long."

"I don't know how you could possibly have any experience in that area," she flashed, "since you've never broken a law in your life."

He smiled. "I've made the acquaintance of a large number of questionable characters since I took my place at court," he said. "You would be surprised at the people I have employed to carry out certain tasks or discover particular pieces of information."

"Your spies."

"And I have found that it takes a very strong personality to withstand the temptations of an underground life. I would be astonished to learn Sebastian

Ardelay has that strength of will."

He hadn't mentioned a suspicion that Sebastian was smuggling sirix, so either he didn't know about that or he thought Val didn't. She said, "*I* am astonished to learn that a collection of petty transgressions has made him instantly recognizable to members of the royal guard."

"Oh, Yori didn't know his name. But she described him to me in enough detail that I felt reasonably certain of who he must be."

And now Yori *would* recognize Sebastian if she ever saw him again. Might even be looking for him. It was possible that Val had saved his life with her theatrics down at the harbor, but she'd also made him highly visible to Darien's soldiers. No wonder Sebastian had been so angry with her. She had thrust him into the bright light of the king's attention.

Val put her chin up. "You never know," she said. "I might have become friends with any number of disreputable people in the years since you've moved away from home. Sebastian might be only one of many."

"Well, if that's the case, I hope you start exercising more caution when you join them on afternoon excursions," he said.

She came to her feet. There didn't seem to be much else to say on this subject. "I'll keep that in mind."

Darien stayed in his chair, keeping his eyes fixed on her. "You could do so much better," he said softly. "You seemed to be afraid I wanted to arrange a political marriage for you, which is the farthest thing from my mind. But I could hardly do worse for you than Sebastian Ardelay."

She made a huffing sound and headed for the door. "You worry about the strangest things," she said over her shoulder as she left the room. "I'm not going to *marry* Sebastian."

She was out in the hallway in two more steps. Behind her, she thought she heard Darien sigh, but she was too far away to be sure.

Chapter Eleven

Val is fourteen.

It is summer and her aunts have descended on the property as they always do, although fewer of the cousins accompany them every year. The two oldest boys are off on their own pursuits, and the oldest girl is spending a year in Chialto with her father's mother. The rest of them still play together, choosing different games as they get older, spending less time splashing in the streams and more time putting on elaborate amateur productions that their mothers pretend to enjoy. Saska is always cast as the beautiful but imperiled princess; Sebastian is always a pirate or a thief. Val is variously a magistrate or a queen or some other person of authority. Neighbor children from nearby estates are usually recruited to play other key roles, and it always ends up being more fun than Val would have expected. She doesn't really approve of pretend, but she does like stories about justice. And she likes telling people what to do, and the plays always provide plenty of opportunity for that.

Still, she is never happy being cooped up indoors for long, particularly during the emerald opulence of summer. At some point every day, she escapes outside to amble through the garden or disappear into the forest. Sebastian usually accompanies her on longer excursions, and they load up on provisions—a blanket or two for picnicking on the grass, baskets of food, jugs of water. They evenly distribute the weight and then skip lightly down the lawns and across the ragged border of the woods.

The trees on the fringes are sparse and solitary, like outcasts who have been shunned from society, but soon enough they grow thicker, fuller, shoulder to shoulder and crown to crown. What light filters down through the dense canopy of leaves is a heavy gold, crafted from the few rays of sunlight that have the weight and mass to penetrate the tightly woven branches. The ground is covered with layers of ancient detritus—fallen leaves, brittle seed pods, broken branches, dead mushrooms, the buried bones of woodland animals—and they make a crunching, swishing sound as Val and Sebastian wade through. To Val, everything smells like rain. Wet and muddy, clean and dirty at the same time.

There are no paths through the woods, at least that most people can discern, but Val knows her way to every separate grove. Sometimes, as she passes specific trees, she reaches out to touch them, as if greeting old friends, as if checking that they're still healthy, still growing, that they still remember her. Sometimes she thinks she feels the sap moving down the thick trunks, the water climbing up the thin ones. Sometimes she feels the lower branches brush against her cheeks and she hears the leaves whisper a greeting.

Sebastian has lost his fear of the forest, but he sticks close to her so he doesn't lose track of her in the gloom. They don't talk much as they tramp through the woods, because it takes most of their energy to climb over dead logs and push their way through undergrowth. It is appreciably cooler in the woods than on the open land, but even so, both of them are starting to perspire by the time they arrive at the stand of challinbar trees.

"Here we are," Sebastian says, dropping his pack. He knows what comes next.

Val moves slowly around the cluster of trees, pausing in front of each one, resting her hand on the corrugated bark for three minutes, five minutes, eight. Maybe no one else can see it, but to her, each tree has its own individual spirit. Shy, or curious, or joyful, or meditative. She feels each one greeting her in its own way, all of them happy to see her.

She stops last at the massive tree that forms the heart of the grove, the heart of the forest—as far as Val is concerned, the heart of the world. She places both her hands against its broad trunk and leans in until her forehead touches the rough bark. She is flooded with a sensation so powerful it makes her dizzy, an indescribable combination of warmth and scent and welcome. She never hears any words, but, as always, she is seized by a conviction that the giant challinbar has offered her a simple, comprehensive benediction. *I approve.*

She stands there a moment, feeling comforted even though she was unaware of needing comfort, and then she straightens and looks around for Sebastian. While she's been greeting the trees, he's been tossing through the fallen branches, looking for one or two that are large enough to have a little heft to them but not so big they're too heavy to carry. He's decided he wants to try his hand at whittling, so he's been gathering up scraps of challinbar every time they've visited the forest this summer.

"Are you hungry?" she asks. "I am. Let's eat."

He shoulders his pack again and follows her as she climbs up into the tree. The lowest part is the hardest, because there are no branches for the first twenty feet, but they can find footholds from gnarls and nubs where branches used to be. The ascent gets easier as they make it to the first broad limbs, thick as the trunks of some lesser trees and extending almost horizontally from the central core. There are days Val keeps climbing and climbing, going as high as she possibly can before the fresh springiness of the boughs warns her that she's arrived at the point where the branches can no longer support her weight.

But today she's feeling lazy, and she only ascends a few levels before choosing her spot for the day. Then she glides out onto a tree limb almost as broad and flat as a kitchen table, entwined so closely with a sister branch that they form a natural bench. She drops down as if settling onto a sofa in her mother's parlor. Sebastian doesn't go quite as far; he sits so that he's able to lean his back against the central trunk and stretch his legs out before him.

"I think the hike through the forest gets longer every year," he says.

"Really? To me it seems shorter every time."

"That's because you're practically a tree yourself."

"That doesn't make any sense," she says severely. "People aren't *trees*."

He grins. "Well, you would be if you could be."

"And trees can't walk."

"You would walk if you were a tree."

She just shakes her head and begins pulling items from her pack. They have to be careful about balancing jugs and loaves on the tilting surface of the boughs, but it's still relatively easy to lay out a meal, and they dig in. As they eat, they share their thoughts about the activities of the past couple of days, the arguments the actors have had about the current script, the news that Aunt Lissa shared over breakfast. She wants to rent a house in Chialto during Quinnasweela, as the weather gets cooler, and bring the whole family with her. Her husband is a banker who spends a good portion of his time in the royal city, and she thinks her children should gain a little town polish. She hopes Jenty and Merra might join her in Chialto, at least for a few ninedays.

"I know Merra would stay in their suite at the palace, but if Jenty wanted to come, we could rent a bigger place," Lissa has said.

Val is not thrilled at the prospect, because she already spends more time in Chialto than she wants to, but she can tell Sebastian is desperate to go. He's only been in the city a handful of times, when his erratic father has shown up to spirit him off for a few days, and he absolutely loves it.

"Jenty will agree if your mother will," he tells Val. "But if she doesn't—"

"Maybe Lissa would let you come with them even if Jenty doesn't go."

He makes a face. "It wouldn't be as much fun without you and Saska."

She nods. It's simply a statement of fact. It wouldn't be. "Well, I'll see what she says. I know my father would be happy to have us there."

There are ripe challin fruits hanging within easy reach, and Sebastian snaps one off the nearest branch. It's about the size of a dried plum but much juicier, and its dusty red skin is almost bursting from the liquid inside. He tosses it in the air and catches it in his mouth. "Your father probably thinks *you* need more 'town polish,' too."

Val makes a face. "No, it's my mother who's been making comments like that. How I need to stop spending so much time running wild and start behaving more like a young woman. Like someone who is comfortable at court, talking to politicians and foreign visitors."

Chewing noisily, Sebastian says, "Do you think she's starting to look for a husband for you?"

Val frowns. "I hope not."

"Isn't that what girls from the Five Families are supposed to do? Find the right man and get married?"

"I suppose so. But I don't think I'll find him in Chialto."

"Why not? Where will you look?"

"I don't want to live in the city. I want to be in the country. Near a forest, if I can. So I'll need to find a landowner. Maybe a farmer. I don't want a banker or a merchant. How boring would that be?"

"I don't want to get married at all," Sebastian said. "Who wants to be tied down to the same place all the time? You have a house and a wife, and you never get a chance to leave."

"My father has a house and a wife, and he leaves all the *time*," Val says.

"It's different for a prime."

"Maybe. Or maybe you'd find a girl who likes to travel as much as you do."

He tosses another challin fruit into his mouth and grins at her. "Guess that knocks you off the list."

She looks at him in surprise. "I could never marry *you*."

He's chomping on the challin fruit, so she can't tell if his face shows a fleeting look of hurt. "Why not? Because I'm a bastard?"

She brushes that aside impatiently. "Who cares about that? No, there's two very good reasons."

"Well, let's hear them."

She shifts on her makeshift chair and leans forward, very intent. "You're younger than I am."

"By one year! Anyway, what does that have to do with anything?"

"Everybody knows that a woman marries a man who's at least a couple of years older than she is."

"That is *not* something everybody knows. Maybe it happens a lot, but it's not a *rule*."

"It's an *unwritten* rule."

"You sure have a lot of those," he said. "Anyway, what if it's a woman marrying a woman or a man marrying a man? Do they have to be exactly the same age?"

She feels a moment's uncertainty. "Well, I don't know. It probably doesn't matter so much then."

"It doesn't matter *ever*."

"I think it does."

He shakes his head. "What's the second reason?"

"You're sweela."

He grins. "Some people say sweela and hunti are a good combination. Fire makes hunti burn. Hunti fuels sweela for a lifetime."

She gives him a quelling look. "Sweela burns through hunti and leaves only ashes behind."

He picks another piece of challin fruit and tosses it to her. "I suppose that depends on the people. You shouldn't rule out every sweela man you ever meet."

She catches the fruit, but holds it in her hand instead of eating it. She shakes her head. "I'm going to marry someone who's torz."

That makes him laugh. "Oh, you are? What if you never meet a torz man you fall in love with?"

"I'm sure there will be one I like enough to marry."

"Why torz?"

"Everyone knows torz people make the best husbands and wives. They're patient and nurturing and loving and kind. They're dependable. They're like Taro."

"They're not *all* like Taro."

She ignores this. Dropping the challin fruit in her lap, she begins ticking items off on her fingers. "A coru man is too restless. An elay man has his head in the clouds. A hunti man is too stubborn. But a torz man is just the right combination of standing firm and giving in." She points a finger at him. "*You* should marry a torz woman. She'll be willing to travel with you, but she'll keep you grounded at the same time."

"I told you, I'm never marrying anyone."

"Well, if you change your mind, remember what I said."

"I won't change my mind."

"You change your mind all the *time!*" she exclaims. "That's because you're sweela."

He grins. "Sometimes even sweela people stick to a notion."

"That's true," she says fair-mindedly. "Loyalty *is* one of your blessings."

"Loyal as you," he says.

She picks up the challin fruit and, instead of eating it whole as he has been doing, takes a delicate bite. The rich, slightly sour juice fills her mouth with a taste she always associates with summer.

"So let's figure out what we can tell my mother," she says, "so she decides to join everybody in Chialto."

Chapter Twelve

Firstday typically began with an air of purpose. Darien was usually preoccupied at the breakfast table, looking over a list of plans for the rest of the nineday. Zoe and Corene were often comparing notes on the various social events they'd committed to, although Zoe frequently was trying to come up with reasons she wouldn't have to attend. Sometimes Elidon joined them and reviewed her own schedule; the dowager queen was almost as busy as Zoe, but much more likely to enjoy the chance to exercise her power and influence. While Celia almost invariably joined them for breakfast, this was the day she was most likely to be turned over to one of the nursemaids when she grew restless.

It was the day everyone was least likely to be paying attention to Val, the day it would be easiest to slip away for an assignation with Sebastian. But she had already made up her mind she wasn't going to the park today; she wasn't ready to see him again. She had no idea what she would say to him, if she would flash with anger or crumple with worry. She had no idea what he would say to her. She wasn't sure she wanted to find out.

So instead she headed to the conservatory and tried to find solace in the humid quiet and restful green. It was harder than she had expected it would be to sit there placidly, resisting the urge to run for the courtyard and catch the next omnibus. She was happy to see Corene when the princess popped her head in and invited her to go the Plaza of Women for the day.

"A lot of the shops will be closed because it's firstday, but all the booths in the plaza will be open, so there should be plenty to look at," Corene said.

Val hardly cared. At least she would be distracted from her constant circling thoughts. She gratefully accepted.

Foley again acted as both their chauffeur and their guard, following them at a discreet distance as they shopped and paused for refreshments at an outdoor café and shopped some more. Val was hardly surprised to see that the princess had expensive tastes, being drawn almost irresistibly to the most costly item in any display, but neither of them had bought much by day's end. It was almost the dinner hour by the time they headed back to the palace. Corene chattered for the whole return trip, while Val mostly just smiled and nodded.

Well, that's over, she was thinking. *Eight more days before I have to do this again.*

Those eight days passed more quickly than she would have expected, and suddenly firstday arrived again, spiky with its unresolvable dilemma. Val spent the whole of the breakfast hour scowling at her plate, convincing herself that she was *not* going to the park today to meet with Sebastian.

"Do you have a headache?" Corene asked.

Zoe looked over from the foot of the table, where she was trying to convince Celia to eat another square of toast. "I have something you can take for that," she offered.

Val was embarrassed to have caught anyone's attention, something she tried not to do even when she wasn't wrestling with a problem. "No—sorry—just thinking about things," she replied.

Before anyone could inquire more closely into what those things might be, someone stepped into the room. Not one of the efficient, noiseless palace servants—this was someone Val had never seen before. He was tall and thin, bald and bland, yet there was something about him that made her think he was anything but boring. Darien looked up sharply at his entrance and did not seem at all annoyed to be interrupted. This must be one of his most trusted associates, someone in whom he had absolute faith and confidence.

"Yes?" Darien said.

"Sire, a ship has been seen sailing into the main harbor flying the Coziquela flag. A courier spotted it this morning and came here directly."

Darien raised his eyebrows. "Ships arrive here daily from Cozique," he said, but he still didn't sound annoyed.

"It also bears the standard of the royal house."

"A messenger from the queen?"

"Perhaps," said the tall man. "But the ship is large and luxuriously appointed. The courier said it looked like a vessel that might carry a member of the royal family."

Darien nodded. "Ah. How soon might its passengers come ashore? Has the harbormaster been alerted? Was anyone on hand to greet the arrivals?"

"The harbormaster indeed has been informed and was mustering staff to prepare a welcome. The courier thought it might be an hour before the ship was safely docked."

Val could see Darien quickly calculating the probable timetable. "Send an honor guard to accompany visitors to the palace. Provide an empty elaymotive—a large one—in case a suitable vehicle is not available at the harbor. Have someone tell the elay prime that his attendance might be required in Chialto very soon. I'll send urgent messenges to Taro and Mirti. Once you know for certain who has arrived, send a courier back to me with all speed."

The tall man bowed and stepped out. Everyone else turned to look expectantly at Darien.

"I take it this is a surprise to you?" Zoe said. "Not one of those things you knew about all along and just didn't bother to mention?"

"No, indeed. I like to marshal all my resources when I'm anticipating a visit from foreign royalty."

"Who do you think it is?" Elidon asked.

Darien looked at Corene and raised his eyebrows. "As the one with some knowledge of the Coziquela court, perhaps you could hazard a guess."

Corene was frowning slightly as she tried to work it out. "It's unlikely to be the be the queen, who doesn't travel much," she said. "It could be one of her brothers or uncles, because they're all involved in trade. But my guess is Melissande."

"Who's Melissande?" Val asked, because everyone else seemed to know.

"The queen's daughter," Darien said. "And Corene's friend."

"Why would she be coming here unannounced?"

"That is exactly the question."

Corene was grinning. "She delights in being unpredictable."

"A coru woman at heart, maybe," Zoe said.

"Yes, but—" Corene spread her arms wide, nearly knocking Elidon in the face. "Broader than that. She contains *all* the elements and probably even more we haven't thought up yet."

"All of us contain all the elements," Elidon said sternly. "We just tend to be ruled by one more than another."

"You'll see what I mean when you meet her."

"It still doesn't answer the question of why she would suddenly put into port," Darien said.

Corene shrugged. "I guess you'll have to ask her."

"I suppose I will," he said. "Now, tell me what we can do to ensure that the princess of Cozique is completely comfortable while she is our guest."

※

A little more than three hours later, Princess Melissande arrived in a bewildering swirl of laughter, color, and pageantry. Half of the royal household had lined up in the courtyard to greet her convoy when it pulled up. Val counted seven capacious elaymotives, though the one in the lead and the one in the rear held soldiers from Darien's hastily assembled honor guard. Everyone else who climbed out of a smoker car, however, was part of the Cozique contingent.

And what a diverse group it was. Most of the twenty or so travelers appeared to be Coziquela, with wide, generous faces in light to medium skin tones. They wore simple clothing of flowing lines but somehow managed to project an air of distinctive elegance. Val thought it might be due to the not-quite-arrogant way they held themselves or their slightly condescending smiles, signaling their conviction that they were the wealthiest, most sophisticated citizens in the southern seas.

But among the entourage were three women that Val would have guessed were Malinquese and two men who had to be Dhonshon. One or two others might have been Berringuese. Cozique was famously cosmopolitan and boasted thriving communities of every nationality, but Val was surprised that foreigners had attained such high rank as to be attendants to the princess. *And doesn't that reveal you for the provincial girl you are?* she chastised herself.

Fifteen of the twenty appeared to be soldiers, neatly dressed in dark, close-fitting uniforms and sporting a few visible weapons. Val remembered stories about the queen of Malinqua's visit to Chialto, when she had brought a hundred soldiers with her and demanded they be housed within call. On the other hand, Corene had fled to Malinqua with only Foley at her side. The Coziquela princess seemed to be aiming for a point somewhere between the two extremes.

Even among all the unfamiliar faces, it was easy to tell which one was Melissande. She didn't so much climb from the elaymotive as float down with an easy grace. She was smaller than most of her escorts, fine-boned, with a pretty, plaintive face. Her eyes were a dangerously deep blue, her mouth a mischievously tilted red, and her hair a tangle of curly black. While she wore an ankle-length sheath dress far finer than the traditional Welchin garb, more than anything she seemed to be clothed in laughter.

"Corene!" she exclaimed, throwing her arms wide. "Oh, I *so* much hoped that you would be here, and not off on one of your unsanctioned adventures!"

Corene laughed and tumbled into her embrace. "I have only had one unsanctioned adventure, and that might have been enough to last me for a lifetime," she said. "But it's wonderful to see you!"

Melissande gave Corene a quick kiss on the mouth, then pulled back to examine her with a critical eye. "You look quite well! I do like that color on you. I cannot *wait* to go shopping at the Plazas that you told me so much about."

"Since you can never find any of the merchandise you want in Cozique's legendary bazaars."

Melissande put a hand to the back of her head. "I need something new. Something different. I have had the same look for too long, and I have become dull. Everyone says so."

It was an extraordinary way for an unannounced foreign dignitary to present herself to her waiting hosts, as if she was a familiar neighbor who had just paused to exchange a breezy greeting on her way to market. Was Melissande really so impetuous and informal? Or was the whole performance coolly calculated to be innocuous and disarming? Val had no idea.

By the slight twist of Darien's lips, she guessed her brother had come to the second conclusion. But as he stepped forward, he showed no trace of impatience or reprimand.

"Perhaps my graceless daughter would deign to introduce us," he said.

Melissande laughed again and threw her hands in the air. She seemed to be someone much given to expressive gestures. "Forgive me for my discourtesy! My mother despairs of me ever learning proper manners. I am Melissande, of course."

"Of course," Darien said, offering her a slight bow. "I am Darien. Corene's father."

"*King* Darien now, I understand," Melissande said swiftly.

"Yes, though very recently crowned."

"My mother sends her felicitations and her hope that there will continue to be excellent relations between our countries."

"I return thanks for the first and reassurances for the second." He motioned behind him, and Zoe stepped forward. "This is my wife, Zoe. She is also the coru prime, which is a role I presume Corene has explained to you in the past."

"Zoe! Yes. Corene speaks of you with such affection," Melissande said. "Is it permitted that I hug you? Or would that be unwelcome? I know that Welchins tend not to indulge in the same familiarities as the Coziquela."

Zoe was smiling, as if she found this whole performance vastly entertaining. "I am not as reserved as some of my fellow countrymen," she said. "But I assume Corene has warned you that I have the ability to decode secrets in the blood of anyone I touch."

Melissande looked intrigued. "Even a stranger's?"

"Yes."

"I am not afraid," Melissande said, opening her arms again to envelop Zoe. "Everybody knows all my secrets."

Zoe hugged the princess and stepped back, still smiling. "Everybody has secrets that nobody knows."

Not giving Melissande time to respond, Darien gestured to Val. "My sister, Valentina."

Val didn't want to be drawn into this strange woman's whirlwind, so she didn't come close enough to be pulled into an embrace. Instead, she inclined her head in a fair imitation of Darien's bow. "It is a pleasure to meet you."

"Valentina," Melissande repeated. "And you are Corene's aunt?"

It was clear she was thinking how odd it was that Corene had never mentioned Val. "I am, but we have not had much time together since we knew of that relationship," she explained. "And I generally live far from the city."

"And you are much too young to be Corene's aunt!" Melissande exclaimed. "You should be playmates instead."

"They are both too old to be thinking of playmates," Darien murmured.

"Conspirators, then. Companions in adventure."

Val couldn't help looking at Corene as she remembered the afternoon excursion in search of sirix. Corene burst out laughing. "What an excellent notion," Corene said.

Darien introduced the others who had been hastily assembled, including Elidon and a handful of the city's top politicians. "There are many others who will be eager to make your acquaintance, including the other primes, but alas, they were not all available on such short notice."

"No! Because I very rudely arrived without giving you any advance warning at all!"

"I would not call you rude," Darien said.

"You must forgive me my impetuousness," Melissande said. "I had no intention of coming to Welce on this particular trip. I was heading toward Milvendris with a group of trusted advisors when we encountered terrible weather. It is not an exaggeration to say I feared we would founder and sink. We took on water, and the engines needed repairs that took several days, and suddenly we were low on supplies. Welce was the closest nation I could think of where I could be certain of a welcome."

"That's terrifying!" Corene exclaimed. "I don't like being out in the middle of the ocean anyway, but in the middle of a storm—" She shuddered.

"We will be happy to help you restock and send you on your way," Darien said. "But we would be even happier to host you for a nineday or so, if your schedule allows you to linger that long."

"Oh, now that I am here, I would love to stay a nineday at least! I have heard so much about your lovely country, and I have greatly missed Corene since she left us. But I do not want to impose."

"Nonsense. My daughter imposed on Cozique's hospitality for a quintile at least."

Melissande gestured back at the members of her entourage. None of them had stepped forward while introductions were being made, leading Val to suppose that they were high-ranking servants who wouldn't expect to have their names announced to the king. "Yes, but Corene brought only one attendant with her, while I have come with dozens! I cannot expect you to house them all, but perhaps you could direct me to a small inn that I could rent out for the duration of my stay?"

"Give me an hour or two and I will locate someplace suitable. Your soldiers could stay in the city barracks if you like."

"Thank you, but it is best if they are always within call. After the situation in Malinqua—you understand—my mother has insisted that I never travel to any other foreign nation without an entire cadre of guards at my back. It is quite tedious, of course, but I have become accustomed to their attentiveness."

"We can put a few elaymotives at your disposal," Zoe said. "Do you or any of your attendants know how to operate one, or shall we supply drivers as well?"

"Two of the guards are expert drivers. Elaymotives have become quite the symbol of status in Cozique!"

"You mean you haven't learned yet?" Corene scoffed. "I don't believe you."

Melissande conjured a wicked smile. "I have, of course. But my mother does not know it, so I pretend I have not."

"Your mother is like Darien," Corene retorted. "She knows everything."

"In any case, I do not think I would be easy attempting to drive a strange vehicle in an unfamiliar city, so I would leave that chore to my soldiers." She opened her eyes very wide. "Unless there was some terrible and exciting situation! And I had to suddenly escape from determined pursuers!"

Corene grinned. "All right, that's what happened to me in Malinqua, but I promise you, Chialto is much more sedate."

"I try always to be prepared for the most outrageous contingency."

"Usually, the most outrageous contingency is *you*," Corene replied.

Melissande laughed. Zoe stepped forward, laying one hand on Corene's arm, one on Melissande's. "We have no need to continue this discussion standing out here in the courtyard," she said. "Why don't you and all your companions come inside? We will take you upstairs and feed you lunch and find them a comfortable place to wait in one of the public rooms downstairs—if that is close enough to satisfy your mother?"

"Yes, thank you."

"Meanwhile, I will send someone off to find an establishment that can hold all of you for a nineday. I am assuming that you would prefer there be no other guests while you are in residence?"

"Exactly. Thank you again. I am sorry to be so much trouble."

Zoe pulled them both toward the huge open palace doors, and everyone else fell in step behind them. "Nonsense," Zoe said. "I think it will be very entertaining to have you."

The rest of the day was a chaotic montage of meals and conversations and endless interruptions as Zoe and the palace staff worked to get Melissande settled—and everyone in Chialto who had the slightest interest in Cozique found a reason to drop by the palace to get a glimpse of the royal visitor.

Nelson was one of the first to arrive, inviting himself over for lunch and planting himself in the dining hall with the air of someone prepared to stay all day. It turned out that he and Melissande had met before and took great delight in each other's company. They put their heads together and whispered secrets or sat across from each other and told stories that led to raucous bursts of laughter. It was clear they were both hugely enjoying the recognition of a kindred spirit. Corene and Zoe seemed amused at their antics—Darien less so, although he did not appear particularly put out. Elidon, who had a much finer sense of decorum, looked decidedly disapproving.

Naturally, in all the hubbub, there was no chance for Val to slip away and head down to the park on the south side of the city. She told herself it was just as well.

By dinnertime, Val had a headache and even Melissande looked like she was beginning to flag. "If it does not seem unbearably ungrateful, I would like to withdraw to the establishment you have found for me and take a quiet dinner there tonight," she said. "Then I will return in the morning quite refreshed, and we can make plans for the rest of my visit."

"Just let me know how much activity you are willing to endure," Zoe told her. "I myself hate state dinners with all their pomp, but I think you might enjoy them much more than I do! And there are many, many merchants who would love a chance to visit with a princess of Cozique. I could organize a luncheon and a dinner every day for a nineday and find thirty people to attend each one."

"Arrange for me as many activities as you please!" Melissande said. "I am an ambassador for my country, after all, never mind that I am an accidental one. My mother will be delighted if I make friends on her behalf. Now I really must go or I shall fall asleep where I stand."

In another twenty minutes, Melissande and her group had departed. Nelson had finally gone home and Elidon had retired an hour ago, so suddenly the parlor where they had congregated most of the day seemed shockingly quiet. The only ones left were Darien, Zoe, Corene, and Val.

"A nineday!" Zoe said, taking her shoes off and stretching her long legs before her. "I'll barely make it to fourthday before I collapse of exhaustion."

"Nobody expects you to shepherd her around the city," Darien said. "My impression is that Melissande is one woman who is very able to take care of herself."

"She seems so dainty and frivolous," Corene agreed. "But she is more determined than you'd expect. Name any dangerous situation, and I guarantee she'll figure out a way to come out on top."

Darien looked at her a moment. "I did not think her either dainty or frivolous," he said.

The tone caught Zoe's attention. "Something about her you didn't like?"

Darien seemed meditative. "So far, she has not done or said anything I could possibly dislike," he said. "But I wish she would be honest about why she's here."

Corene looked surprised. "You don't believe she was swept off course and running low on supplies?"

"No, do you?"

Corene shrugged. "I haven't really thought about it." She mulled it over, her face gradually pulling into a frown. "What other reason could she have? And why wouldn't she tell us what it was?"

"Two very good questions."

"I can't think she's had a rift with her mother," said Corene. "They argue all the time, but Melissande is completely loyal to the crown."

"Maybe she's run away to be with an unacceptable lover," Zoe suggested.

"Ha. Melissande takes unacceptable lovers all the time. It's part of the agreement she has with Jiramondi."

"Who?" said Val.

"Her husband. He's only interested in men, which she knew when she married him. The arrangement suits them both, and they're very fond of each other."

Darien put up a hand, as if he didn't want to hear any more details. "So if she hasn't come here in defiance of her mother, is she here on her mother's behalf?"

"As an emissary on a delicate mission?" Zoe mused. "Maybe, but then why not say so from the beginning?"

"Because the mission is *too* delicate?" Darien speculated. "And she wants to be sure we can be trusted?"

Corene looked indignant. "Well, of course we can! She knows that!"

"She knows *you*," Darien said gently. "She trusts *you*. It's me she's not sure of."

Zoe grinned and resettled her shoulders against the chair. "Ah, well, if *you* have to set out to charm a skittish young princess, I fear we'll never learn what she really wants."

Darien ignored her. He was still watching Corene. "And the truth is, depending on how desperate her venture is, we might *not* be the safe haven she hopes for," he said. "So tell me honestly. Putting aside the fact that Melissande is your friend. Putting aside the fact that *you* would support her in any reckless personal venture. Can she be trusted? Or does she trail disaster in her wake?"

For a long moment, Corene stared back at him, her forehead furrowed in concentration. "I believe Melissande could have complex motives for doing something," she said at last. "I believe she is capable of deceit on a grand scale. And disaster might result sometimes, I don't know. But I don't believe she would ever *intend* disaster. I truly, honestly believe that she is always working for what she thinks is good and right."

"Good and right for Cozique," Darien replied. "But for Welce?"

Corene lifted her chin. "If you're so suspicious, why don't you just ask her?"

"I do not believe that is a tactic that would work with her until she is ready to share secrets." He paused a moment, his eyes still on his daughter, then spoke again. "While she is in residence in Chialto, I would caution you to remember that you are her friend second—and a princess of Welce first."

Corene's face showed first surprise, then indignation, then thoughtfulness. She returned Darien's steady look with a narrowed gaze of her own. "I hope you didn't really think I might forget that."

"Sometimes we all need reminders," he said.

Zoe smothered a yawn and came to her feet. "I anticipate a very interesting—and exhausting—nineday," she said. "I'm going to get a good night's sleep while I can."

Chapter Thirteen

Rain kept most people confined indoors for the next two days, greatly curtailing any plans for lavish social events to celebrate the princess. Melissande joined them for breakfast both mornings and entertained them all with light and amusing conversation; if she had any darker purpose for coming Welce, she was clearly not in a mood to say so. Corene accompanied her back to her inn both days so they could catch up on their lives. If Melissande shared any secrets on those afternoons, Corene wasn't telling.

The weather had cleared up by the morning of fourthday, and Val wandered out to the courtyard to enjoy the cheerful sunshine and the fresh-washed breeze.

"I'm taking Melissande to tour the Plaza of Women—you should come with us," Corene said, stepping up behind her.

"I don't want to intrude on your time with your friend."

"Don't be silly. We've had two days together. Come with us."

The only other activity Val had considered was heading down to the southern park, and that suddenly seemed both pointless and dreary. "All right," she said. "Let's go."

They ended up being a sizable group by the time they were all assembled. Not only were they accompanied by Foley, but two more of Darien's guards piled into the overlarge elaymotive, and Val was guessing that the driver was also a soldier. When they arrived at Melissande's hotel, the princess emerged with two guards of her own, one of them a Dhonshon man and one a Malinquese woman. All the fighters crammed into the compartment in the back of the vehicle, while the members of the royal families rode in comfort in the capacious main cabin.

"Valentina!" Melissande exclaimed. "How delightful that you have decided to join us! Your king scoffed at the notion of playmates, but that is exactly what we shall all be."

"I'm not very playful," Val felt compelled to say.

"She's more fun than you'd expect for some who's so *very* hunti," Corene said. "And everybody except Darien calls her Val."

Melissande turned her huge blue eyes on Val. "Shall I call you Val, too, or do you prefer formality from a stranger?"

Val liked that Melissande asked the question; it made her warm somewhat to the foreign princess. "Val is fine."

"We could spend all day at the Plaza," Corene said. "What are you looking for? Trinkets to take back to friends at home? Clothes for yourself?"

"I hardly know until I see it."

"And we—but oh!" Corene exclaimed. "We have to go to Leah's first! I can't believe I didn't think of that!"

"Leah is still in Chialto? But yes! Take me to see her immediately."

Corene stretched forward to give directions to the driver. When she leaned back in her seat, Val asked, "Who's Leah?"

"One of Corene's great friends from Malinqua," Melissande said.

"She's one of Darien's spies," Corene explained. "She was living in Malinqua when I ran away there, so Darien had her look out for me."

"And then she bravely helped us arrange for Alette's escape," Melissande supplied.

The name was teasingly familiar. "Alette..."

"A princess from Dhonsho," Corene said. "She was living at the palace with us, but she wanted to get away from her father—"

"The evil king of Dhonsho," Melissande murmured.

"And Leah came up with a very clever plan to get Alette to safety. Now Alette lives in Yorramol with her lover, so there was a happy ending, but the whole adventure was quite scary," Corene said. "And now Leah lives in Chialto, but she's still spying for Darien."

"She is?" Melissande said. "How is she doing that?"

"She runs the cutest little boutique that caters to foreign visitors. And they spend money there, and they tell Leah about their home countries, and Leah reports anything interesting back to Darien. Apparently, she was *quite* helpful last year when the Karkadians were in town."

"Bah," Melissande said in distaste. "The Karkadians."

"Yes, I understand they are quite horrid. Darien says I can never go visit them on any diplomatic mission, but I admit I'm curious."

"You should not be curious enough to visit the Karkades," Melissande said sternly.

It wasn't long before the driver pulled up at an attractive storefront on the boulevard that connected the Plaza of Women with the Plaza of Men. This whole stretch of road, Val knew, was lined with shops carrying every type of high-end merchandise, from shoes to jewelry, all designed to appeal to the wealthiest residents of the city. Many owners lived in small apartments above their businesses and were available night and day to provide anything the rich and capricious might desire to buy.

Their guards, even Foley, remained outside, leaning on the elaymotive while the three women headed inside. They'd only gotten a few steps across the threshold before the woman behind the counter called out a welcome. "Good morning, how may I—oh, Corene, how nice to see you! And *Melissande!* What are you doing in Chialto?"

She hurried around the counter with her hands outstretched, and the three of them exchanged enthusiastic greetings. Within a few moments, they were laughing and trading stories and exclaiming in amazement at details of the others' lives.

Val hovered behind them, a polite smile on her face in case someone tried to draw her into the conversation, but pretty soon it was clear she was on her own. She relaxed and began strolling around the shop, curious to see the wares on display. Fairly quickly she realized that the place was organized by the elemental affiliations, with the items in each grouping reflecting the proper colors and materials.

She had to admit that Leah had accumulated an eclectic and intriguing collection of merchandise. Here in the elay section was a grand headdress of white and yellow feathers that would stand up around the wearer's head like an aureole of light. The coru section included two waist-high sculptures built of seashells and driftwood, each one depicting an alarmingly large but apparently imaginary fish. The sweela corner was set off with a half-unfolded room divider covered with bits of broken mirrors so that it reflected the sun with a blaze almost too bright to endure.

Val wandered through the hunti items, impressed by the minutely detailed carvings contained inside large seed pods and incised into animal bones. But she found herself irresistibly drawn to the torz area of the shop. The foot-high flowering bush made of emeralds, rubies, and gold was striking, though too gaudy for her taste. But she paused for a long time before a simple clay sculpture—a lifesize pair of worn hands, clearly a woman's, held out in a cupped position as if offering a gift. The palms were empty, so obviously the buyer was supposed to fill them with jewelry or blessing coins or some beloved treasure. At the base of the sculpture, a green and brown scarf wound around the place where the forearms rested on the table.

Val couldn't help curling her own hand into a ball and resting it inside the bent fingers. The clay felt warm against her skin. For a moment, she was overwhelmed with a grief so powerful that she found it difficult to draw the next breath. She pressed her free hand against her chest and tried to shove the pain aside.

"Are you torz?" someone behind her asked.

She dropped her arms to her sides and turned around, to find that she had been addressed by a girl who looked like she might be six or seven years old. The child had dark hair, a solemn expression, and a helpful air that made Val think she might consider herself a shop assistant. "No, I'm hunti," she replied. "My mother was torz. The hands—for a minute they reminded me of her."

"I'm torz, too," the girl replied. "So is my mother."

Val smiled. Her chest still hurt. "Torz mothers are the best ones."

"*I* think so." The little girl scanned Val's face. "Is your mother gone?"

Val nodded. She didn't really know how to talk to children, but this girl had an uncommon maturity that made it easier. "Almost two years now."

"Do you have other family?"

"I do. Though I don't live close to them, so I don't see them much."

"Maybe I'm your family," the girl suggested. "If our mothers are both torz."

"Maybe. I don't know how we'd find out."

The girl held out her hands. "I can tell you."

Val glanced over at the others, but Corene, Melissande, and Leah were still talking with great animation. "Really? Why do you think that?"

"Because I'm the heir to the torz prime."

"Ohhhhh!" Now Val was remembering the story about how the girl's identity had been revealed last year. The tale was very dramatic, but she hadn't paid that much attention; the events had seemed so far away from Val's daily life of crops and livestock and property improvements. "You're Leah's daughter, right? Your name is Mally?"

"Yes, and I can tell things about people when I touch them," Mally said. "Just like Taro can."

"All right." Val extended her hands and Mally's fingers closed around them, even warmer than the clay. The grave little face grew more earnest as Mally appeared to sift through whatever information resided in Val's skin before the girl dropped her hands.

"You're not related to *me*," Mally said, "but you're related to Darien. You're his sister."

Val hadn't entirely believed that a small child, even the torz heir, could really decode the mystery of a stranger's heritage, but she was convinced now. "I am."

"I like him."

"I do, too. Usually," Val said.

For the first time, Mally's face lit with a smile. "Darien is *very* hunti," the little girl observed.

Val laughed. "He certainly is. But so am I."

Mally gestured at the sculpture of the cupped hands. "But you can still buy something torz if you want to."

Val realized she had already made the decision. "I do want to. Can you wrap it up for me so I can take it home?"

A middle-aged woman had emerged from some back recess of the shop to take over the responsibilities at the sales counter, and she handled Val's money while Mally covered the sculpture in tissue and settled it in a thick cloth bag. A cheerful group of teen girls and their mothers invaded the shop as Val was concluding her transaction. Leah broke off from her conversation with Corene and Melissande to hurry over and greet the newcomers.

"We'll come back in a couple of days!" Corene called, waving goodbye and drawing Melissande to the door.

"Or you can come to the inn for dinner some night and we can talk till dawn," Melissande suggested.

"I'll do that! It was *so* good to see you!"

The three of them climbed back into the elaymotive for the short ride to the Plaza of Women. This time, when they disembarked, one of Melissande's soldiers and two of Darien's were right behind them. Val supposed an open-air market presented more hazards than a closed shop with guards standing watch outside.

"I don't feel like I'm in any danger," she said. "But if someone wanted to attack us, would three guards be enough to fend them off?"

"It would depend on how many attackers appeared," Melissande said, entering into the debate with some enthusiasm. "And how skilled they were! We could be dead in a very few minutes."

Corene cast them both a look of derision. "You can't actually believe that these three are the only guards watching over us," she said. "There are soldiers all over the Plaza, they're just discreetly placed."

"Yes, my mother does the same sort of thing," Melissande agreed. "I think they would get along quite well, our parents."

"What would you like to do first?" Corene asked. "Eat lunch or start shopping?"

"I would like—oh, I know! I want to visit the famous blind sisters!" Melissande said.

Corene laughed. "You have a question you would ask them?"

"It is said they know everything, and they will tell you if you pay them enough money."

"They know everything about *Welce*," Corene countered. "All the rumors, all the politics, all the history. But what do you think they could tell you about Cozique?"

Melissande was smiling. "Perhaps it is Welce I want to know about," she said. "Secrets neither you nor Darien would tell me, even if I asked."

"How very mysterious!" Corene replied. "All right! We'll go see the blind sisters. And we'll *all* ask them questions."

"I don't have anything I need to know," Val said.

"You'll think of something."

They strolled to the very center of the square, where three women sat on a raised dais for everyone to see. They were all large and soft-bodied, with wide, round faces lifted to the noonday sun. Their eyes were closed and their hands lay relaxed on their knees as they sat in almost identical poses at three perfectly spaced intervals around the circular platform. Val thought they exuded an air of serenity, as if they possessed all the knowledge in the world but did not let it trouble them.

"Good, there are no other customers," Corene said, mounting the steps and motioning the other two forward.

Val followed somewhat helplessly, still having no idea what question she might pose. The blind sisters traded in knowledge. You could ask them anything you wanted to know, and they would tell you how much it would cost you to learn the answer. But you could also buy information with information of your own.

Corene and Melissande had already settled themselves in front of two of the women, so Val dropped down in front of the third. It was hard to guess the woman's age, which could have been anywhere between thirty and sixty. The rumor was that these were not the same three who had originally set up shop here in the Plaza decades ago, but children or grandchildren who had carried on the tradition. Looking at the woman's open, unlined face, Val found it impossible to tell.

"Did you come today to ask me something?" the woman asked in a low, comfortable voice.

"I suppose I did," Val said. The woman waited, showing no sign of impatience. Val pulled out a handful of coins, all silvers and quint-silvers, and the blind sister laid her palm across Val's. Once Val had made her inquiry, the woman would pick out the denominations that covered the cost of her reply. "How long does it take to recover from the loss of someone you love?"

The blind sister withdrew her hand and dropped it back on her knee. "That is a question with no answer," she said. "For some it takes weeks. For others, years. Grief is a spiral path, and we all walk it at our own pace. You think you have moved away from its dense heart, but the next few steps bring you closer to the center again."

"It's just—every time I think I've left it behind, I find it around the corner again."

"It hides behind familiar things," the blind sister agreed. "And it waits."

"Will it ever go away?"

The blind sister reached out again and took Val's hand in her own. "Probably not," she said gently. "But it will grow more manageable. Less like a wild animal and more like the tiny mouse that skitters through your house, startling you, and maybe for a moment stopping your heart. Not perhaps something you welcome, but not something you need to fear."

Val nodded dumbly, knowing the woman couldn't see her. "Thank you," she said. "Most people have told me I'll be fine when enough time has gone by."

"You will be fine. You'll just be different."

The woman had refused Val's coins but now, when the blind sister released her, Val dribbled them all onto the stage between them. "Thank you," she said again, pushing herself to her feet. "I hope the rest of your day is very good."

She was a bit unsteady as she made her way off the dais and waited for the other two to finish their conferences. Corene and her blind sister were both laughing, so Val supposed they were swapping unflattering gossip about some of the highest-placed members of Welchin society. She suspected that this would be an interaction when no money changed hands, though each party gained something of value.

Melissande, by contrast, appeared to be having a very intense conversation with her own counselor. She was leaning forward, speaking quietly; her face was unsmiling. There was a stack of silver coins at the older woman's knee, but Val couldn't tell if they were payments Melissande had already handed over during the session, or tithes left behind by previous visitors.

While Val watched, curious, the blind sister nodded and spoke a few words in a voice so low that Melissande had to lean even closer to hear her. When Melissande responded with a sharp question, the sister held out her hand for another payment. In the drowsy sunlight, Val could see the glint of a gold coin as it passed between the women.

Val couldn't help staring. What could Melissande possibly need to know that would merit such a costly fee? And why would she need to ask about it in secret?

✦

Residual emotion and a nagging sense of distrust kept Val quiet for the rest of the day, but Corene and Melissande were enjoying themselves so much that they didn't seem to notice. Immediately after visiting the blind sisters, Corene announced she could not wait another moment for food, so they found an open-air café with a brightly striped awning and settled in for lunch. Corene also insisted on ordering for Melissande to make sure the foreign visitor had a chance to taste all the most traditional Welchin dishes.

"And we'll each have a glass of sirix, along with a carafe of fruited water," Corene told their server.

Melissande laughed as the girl hurried off. "If I am not mistaken, sirix is a Soechin product, not a Welchin one."

"You're right, of course, but I wanted you to see that even in Welce, we can command all the luxuries on offer in Cozique."

"Do you suppose the sirix they serve here is legitimate or smuggled?" Val asked.

Corene made a face. "Judging by the price, it's legal." She brightened. "So now we'll get a chance to compare the quality."

Melissande looked over with wide eyes. "You have sampled contraband?"

"Only once."

"How did it taste?"

"Like adventure and defiance."

"I imagine your father was not happy to learn of this escapade."

"He didn't know about it."

Melissande shrugged. "You said it before. Like my mother, he knows everything."

"Are you getting smuggled shipments in Cozique?" Val wanted to know.

"Some. My mother has done what she can to discourage the practice, but of course it is impossible to patrol every small dock and port."

"I forget," Corene said innocently. "What are relations like between Cozique and Soeche-Tas?"

Melissande laughed. "You do not forget! They are delicate. Soeche-Tas does not offer us any particular threat, as it is a small country and not close to our borders. Yet it has been making alliances with countries that do not particularly like us, which makes it potentially problematic. So we try to avoid doing anything to anger its top politicians. We would much rather the country view us neutrally than with hostility."

"What nations dislike you?" Val asked.

"Dhonsho and the Karkades in particular," Melissande said.

"And they dislike you *a lot*," Corene observed.

"Yes, if the Karkadians thought they had any chance at harming us, they would mount a full-scale offensive. As it is, they harass us in many small and exhausting ways. Every year there is at least one Karkadian naval captain who is willing to sacrifice himself and his entire crew to engage one of our warships in the hope of causing us a small degree of pain." She shook her head. "Imagine. Sending an entire crew to their deaths merely to prove how much they hate us."

"They are a people of extremes. That's what Darien says," Corene said.

"They are a people without limits," Melissande replied. "Even more dangerous."

"What about Dhonsho?" Val asked. "Have they done you any harm?"

Melissande looked troubled. "Nothing major, but they have more military might than the Karkades. And they have been making alliances with smaller countries to the north and west of Cozique, promising aid to each other if one of them comes under attack."

"Attack from Cozique?" Val asked. "Is that likely?"

"Cozique is never the aggressor. Not in the past fifty years, at any rate. Our tendency toward colonialism is in the past."

"Then you shouldn't have anything to worry about," Val said.

"Exactly. Ah, here is our sirix! Let us toast to old friends and new experiences."

Chapter Fourteen

After the meal and another couple of hours of shopping, Corene and Val dropped Melissande off at her hotel and hurried back to the palace to dress for dinner. This was to be the first formal event of Melissande's visit, though it would be a relatively small one, with only the primes and some of the dowager queens in attendance.

Because this wasn't a full-scale state affair, Val opted for a severely tailored silk jacket in dark blue, heavily embroidered with matching thread, and falling almost to her knees over loose pants in the same shade. To brighten up the dark colors, she added wide bracelets, a heavy necklace, and four hair clips, all made of figured silver. Her face looked even paler than usual, so she brushed a little rouge into her cheeks.

Not that it mattered. Melissande would draw most of the attention of everyone in attendance. But she still felt like she should make an effort.

Before she left the room, she paused in front of her dresser, where she had set her newest acquisition, and traced her fingers over the faint calluses in the cupped palms. Her mother had never done any physical labor while she was married to the hunti prime, but once they'd moved to the smaller house near Aunt Jenty, Merra had taken up gardening. Handling tools and digging in the dirt had roughened her hands to the point that she had to rub cream into them a couple of times a day. But she had enjoyed the work, no question about that. She kept an immense flower garden in the front of the house and tended a vegetable garden in back, and nothing had made her torz soul happier than bringing in armloads of blossoms and produce.

Val gave the hands a final pat and went out.

The royal palace offered dozens of places to sit down to a meal, from the overwhelmingly opulent hall on the ground level to cozy parlors attached to individual suites on the upper floors. Tonight's affair would be laid out in a mid-sized space that could hold up to fifty people and featured decorations that reflected the elements. The cream-colored wallpaper was embossed with a subtle pattern of flowers, birds, and trees in a landscape that included an undulating river and a high sun. The table runner was embroidered with the colors of the five elements—red, black, blue, green, and white—and the same colors appeared on fabric swags over the tall windows. Half of the centerpieces on the table were bouquets of red and orange roses arranged in clear glass vases partly filled with water. The other half were fat pillar candles sitting in wooden holders carved to resemble birds and butterflies.

The hall was big enough to accommodate groupings of furniture set against the wall, a comfortable distance from the main table. When Val entered, the only other people in the room were sitting together in one of these spots. Zoe and Taro. She headed straight toward them.

"There you are," Taro said, making room for her next to him on a dark green sofa. "I was saying that you and I were probably the two people who were most miserable at the thought of attending the dinner tonight, so I hoped Zoe would have the kindness to seat us together."

"I am such a ramshackle hostess that I didn't bother to make table arrangements at all," retorted Zoe. "Sit with your wife if you want to be sure of an agreeable dinner partner! I know you brought her, because I saw her walk in with you." She glanced around. "Though she's not downstairs yet."

"Still primping in honor of the foreign princess," Taro said. "I was surprised she agreed to come with me, since Virrie isn't much of one for pomp and pageantry. But she said she could tolerate it if we only stayed for a day or two. I think the real truth is that she misses Natalie, and she figured Mirti would bring her back to the palace when she came to pay her respects to Melissande."

"She did," Zoe answered. "They arrived a couple of hours ago."

Nelson had strolled up, and now he dropped onto a couch next to Zoe, ruffling her hair with affection. "So what did Mirti tell you?" he asked. "Is Natalie indeed the hunti heir?"

Zoe nodded. "Yes, the whole forest whispered her name, apparently. Mirti said that she herself was thrilled, and she asked Natalie, 'Can you hear that?' And Natalie was completely unimpressed. 'Well, of course I can hear that. That's what all trees sound like.' So apparently trees all over Welce have been calling out to Natalie but she didn't realize it was anything special."

Taro grunted. "Sounds like Natalie. I love her. But that's a child who lives life on her own terms. Says what she thinks. Is unmoved by miracles. Keeps going after things until she gets what she wants. The older she gets, the more she clashes with Romelle."

"Sounds like it might be a good idea for her to start spending more time with the hunti prime," Zoe said. She gestured at someone who had just strolled through the door. "And here she is."

Mirti quickly joined them, choosing a wooden ladderback chair that looked decidedly uncomfortable and sitting there with her back perfectly straight. No slouching for her. All at once, Val was acutely aware of a strange, building buzz of energy, a prickle in her hands and feet. Her skin felt flushed, her head seemed oddly light, and there was a pleasant fizzing in her veins. She hadn't even felt this giddy when she drank her glass of sirix over lunch.

Ah. She was in the close presence of four of the primes, and their powerful auras were blending with and amplifying each other's. She remembered what Darien had said about the primes' healing abilities and she suddenly felt it for herself. They weren't even trying to pour their energy into her, and yet it was pooling around her anyway, practically levitating her from her chair. She concentrated on not floating away.

None of the others seemed to be similarly affected. Val supposed they were so steeped in their own power they were immune to the pull from the others. "We were just talking about you," Zoe said to Mirti. "And how exciting it is that you've found your heir."

Mirti nodded. "Yes, I'm going to ask Romelle if I can keep Natalie with me for the next quintile or so. She knows a great deal already, since she's spent half her life at court and half of it on the estate of a prime, but that was the *torz* prime. Hunti ways are different."

"I feel obscurely insulted," Taro said lazily.

"I find myself wondering what elemental magic lies under the land on Taro's property!" Nelson exclaimed. "First Mally, now Natalie, revealed as primes. Maybe we should foster all of our likely candidates with Taro."

"Not a chance," Taro said promptly. "I'm not having a bunch of Kayle's nieces and nephews wandering around my place, tripping over rabbit holes and falling into streams. They're all absent-minded poets who don't have the sense to come in from the rain, and I'd constantly be having to fetch them from some corner of the property because they got lost and just sat down in the middle of a cornfield." As the others laughed, he smiled at Zoe. "I'd take Celia for a few ninedays, if you wanted. There's a child with potential."

"A potential for mayhem," Zoe said. "I think she'd love to visit, but you'd have to clear it with Virrie first. A person has to be *prepared* before trying to take on Celia for any length of time."

"That's any child," Taro said. "You've only had the one, so you don't know."

"Is this where we're supposed to ask you when you're planning to produce more possible coru primes?" Nelson asked, grinning. "Not to mention, more heirs for the kingdom?"

"No, indeed, that is not a conversation I'm interested in having!" Zoe replied. "In fact, let us talk of other topics entirely! Val—why don't you tell us how you've been spending your time since you've been in Chialto?"

Val felt a moment's resentment at being thrust into the center of attention, something she always hated. She frowned to concentrate her thoughts, which were still drifting. "Well, today I went to the Plaza of Women with

Corene and Princess Melissande," she said.

"What did you think of Melissande after spending a day in her company?" Zoe asked.

"What else could she think, except that the girl is brilliant and charming?" Nelson said.

"We all know *you* like a bright and charismatic woman," Zoe said to him. "But Val generally has a more tempered response."

"It's hard not to like her," Val confessed. "It's not just because she's lively and funny. It's because she will focus on *you* and seem to listen closely to your answers. As if she thinks *you* are as interesting as she is."

Nelson was nodding. "Yes, that's the oldest conversational trick there is. Works every time."

"I hardly think you would know," Mirti said dryly. Zoe and Taro laughed, and even Nelson grinned.

"Well, I always have a great deal to say," he said by way of excuse.

Zoe, like Melissande, was listening intently to Val. "But I sense you were not entirely won over by our foreign visitor."

"I just wondered—after the things Darien said the other night—if she might have some reason to be here that she just hasn't told us yet."

She thought Nelson might leap to Melissande's defense, but he was nodding again. "Yes, that degree of charm is easily deployed to cover a complicated agenda," he said.

"I suppose it's too much to hope that she did something suspicious while you were out with her this afternoon," Zoe said.

Val hesitated. She hadn't had time to mention this to Darien yet. "She wanted to visit the blind sisters. She said she had a question for them. And when I was done asking my own question, she was still talking to one of the other sisters. And I saw her give the woman a gold coin."

That caught everyone's attention. "Difficult to imagine what an overseas visitor might need to know that would cost that kind of money," Mirti said.

"Difficult indeed," Zoe said. "I suppose you didn't ask her."

"It didn't seem likely she would tell me the truth."

"No, although you might have learned something interesting from the lie she elected to tell," Nelson said thoughtfully.

Taro stirred on the sofa. "Well, it's too late now! She already knows whatever it is she wanted to learn, and she'll share that with us or not, as she chooses." He patted Val on the arm in a soothing way, as if he sensed something had distressed her. "So you also had a question for the blind sisters? Is that a secret too, or would you like to share?"

She never would have brought the topic up on her own, but suddenly she felt the same forlorn rush of loss that had overcome her in Leah's boutique. "Nothing grand or important," she said in a low voice. "I asked about—I know it's been a long time since my mother died—but I don't really understand grief. I don't really understand death."

Taro put his arm around her shoulders and pulled her against his comforting bulk. Zoe's eyes filled with compassion. "Grief is different for everyone, I think," Zoe said. "And each loss hits you in a different way. I was young when my mother died, and there were so many other radical changes in my life that it was hard to separate out how much of my despair came from losing her and how much came from general upheaval. My father's death also brought me massive changes, but I was so numb from pain that at first I didn't even notice them. And it seemed like every day I learned about something else that he had concealed from me, so I had to contend with anger right alongside the pain. No death is easy to endure, but both of those tore me apart. Now and then I am still finding a new piece of myself to put back together."

"In its way, death is simpler to understand than grief," Mirti said. "I think of death not so much as a loss, but as a change of form." She extended her arm and turned it this way and that, showing off the shapes of her wrist and elbow. "We are buried, and our bodies return to the earth. Our bones disintegrate to a rich compound that feeds the soil and brings forth new life."

"That's a very torz way to look at it," Taro said. "I completely concur."

"Oh, but there is more to it than that!" Zoe exclaimed. "I look at Celia, and I think, 'The blood in her veins is the same as mine, is the same as my mother's, is the same as my grandmother's—back through generations, connected forever.' Nothing lost. Everything still there."

"But you can have more tangible reminders than that," Nelson said. "Letters and diaries and paintings—everything a man created, every word a woman wrote—all these things remain, living proof of the questing mind. There is no permanent death if this evidence remains."

Taro shifted beside Val as he waved at someone across the room. "Kayle has just arrived," he said. "Surely the elay prime will have the definitive word on what happens to the soul when the body crosses over."

Kayle ambled their way and Val felt a spike in the intensity of the energy field around her. Her lungs felt opalescent; she thought her exhaled breath might hang in the air with a diamond brightness.

"Oh, hello," Kayle said, his voice edged with surprise, as if he hadn't expected to see the primes all assembled in one place, as if he had forgotten the reason they'd been called together. He was a tall man, with the thin awkward body of someone who only rarely remembered to eat and resented the necessity when he did. His white-blonde hair was thin and uncombed, blowing about his head in an invisible breeze, and his blue eyes looked enormous through a pair of thick spectacles. Every time Val had seen him, she had been seized by the thought that he might someday simply turn sideways into a hidden pocket of air and vanish entirely because he had forgotten how to exist on the human plane.

"We're so glad you could join us for dinner tonight with the Coziquela princess," Zoe said, gently reminding him why he was present. "It shows her great honor to have all the primes in attendance."

"Yes," he said. "Well."

He seemed so befuddled that Val couldn't imagine trying to draw him into conversation, but the others seemed less put off by his untethered manner. "We thought you could share your perspective on an important question," Nelson said. "We were discussing what happens when people die—and what the dead leave behind."

Kayle didn't seem to find the topic strange or need a moment to gather his thoughts. He simply replied, "Oh, well, the dead. They are never gone. They are around us everywhere." He made a comprehensive gesture, and Val found herself following the line of his hand, as if she could see spirits drifting through the air. "When one of them comes unexpectedly to mind, you think you are just calling up a memory. But in fact, they are stroking your cheek, whispering in your ear, reminding you how much they love you."

Involuntarily, Val touched her face. She could almost hear her mother's voice, promising her that everything would work out if she would only be patient. She could almost catch her father's laugh, recall the way she felt when he returned home after a long visit to the city. The memories were as sharp as shattered glass, as sweet as a summer garden.

"Ah, that's very nice," Zoe said.

"Maybe so," Nelson said, "but I still want to read the old letters."

There was a commotion at the door, and the entire mood in the hall abruptly shifted. Melissande swept in, Corene at her side, and it was as if a burst of light bounced across the room and rearranged all the seams and angles. Val straightened up and pulled away from Taro, and everyone in her small group seemed galvanized to action. Almost instantly, they were on their feet and headed over toward the new arrivals. The rest of the dinner guests entered behind Melissande—Darien, of course; Taro's wife, Virrie; Nelson's wife, Beccan; Elidon and Seterre; and Josetta and Rafe.

Darien moved to the center of the room to capture the attention of the small crowd. "Welcome, everyone, I'm glad you could join us. You'll see that this is not a formal gathering—just family and the primes—so we all have a chance to get to know our visitor a little better. Never fear, there will be plenty of pomp in the coming days, as I believe Zoe and Elidon have been planning an endless stream of entertainments."

Zoe came to stand beside Darien and gestured at the table. "Sit where you like! It will not be an evening for observing rules."

Elidon sailed past her and took a seat in the very middle of the long side of the table. "The rules of civility will be observed, at least," the elder queen said. "I think we can all agree to that."

Soon enough, they had all found their places. It might have been an informal gathering, but no one had had the nerve to usurp Darien's place at the head of the table. Melissande sat across from Elidon, and Corene and Nelson settled on either side of her. Val found herself felicitously placed between Taro and Virrie. She could bask in torz comfort all evening long and not care what else unfolded around her.

As soon as the staff had finished serving the first course, Darien led them all in a toast to Melissande's health. "So tell us," he said, setting down his glass, "how have you enjoyed your first days in Welce?"

"Very much! Today, your daughter and your sister and I visited the Plaza of Women and spent a great deal of money."

"We visited Leah's," Corene said to Zoe.

"Oh, that's right, you were all friends in Malinqua," Zoe said. "I completely forgot."

"What a very charming place! With goods from all over the world! It makes me think that our Coziquela merchants should bring in more imports."

"I would think Coziquela already trades with every country in the world," Kayle said.

"With many of them, it is true," Melissande said. "But there are some commodities that do not cross all borders, so it is a constant process of figuring out what might be welcome in some market and what might not." She speared a piece of meat with her fork and presented it to the table. "Food, for instance. A delicacy from the Karkades might be repulsive in Malinqua. For cultural reasons. Religious reasons. Or simply due to unfamiliarity."

"Now, culture is something that I would think is not easy to export," Nelson observed.

"The *trappings* of culture are sometimes prized by other countries—the colors, the clothing, the jewelry. But the stories behind the trappings—the religions, the rituals—these do not so easily transfer."

"And yet that does not keep some nations from trying to bring their beliefs to other shores," Darien said.

His voice was mild, but Melissande must have heard a note of censure, because she answered him directly. "Yes, that is Cozique's history," she said. "But our conquering days are over."

"This is heavy talk before we've even gotten through the first course!" Beccan exclaimed. She was a bright, cheerful woman who, as the wife of the sweela prime, had had a great deal of experience guiding philosophical debates among argumentative people. "Can we talk of lighter subjects?"

"But yes! I am perfectly prepared to be shallow!" Melissande answered. "Shall it be fashion? Shall it be gossip? These are the areas in which I excel."

"Ooh, yes, gossip," Corene said. "Are there any scandals brewing in the foreign courts?"

"Indeed, yes, news out of Berringuey! The royal prince and his wife had a son, and now all of his other direct heirs are conveniently dead—his cousin Siacett and her whole family."

A collective shudder went around the table, then several people began talking at once, sharing their impressions of the prince, who had visited Chialto a few years ago. Josetta put her arm around her husband in a comforting way, and Val had to strain to remember. He was related to Berringuey royalty, she thought. Maybe the news made him sad.

"Their customs appall us, yet is it fair to judge their actions by our own standards?" Nelson asked when some of the furor had died down. "Is there such a thing as universal right and wrong?"

"Surely murder is judged a crime in every culture," Darien said.

"Yes, but there is no evidence that the Berringuese heirs were killed," Melissande said. "Generally, they take their own lives as a way to show fealty to the crown—to avoid any chance that their very existence will precipitate civil war."

Darien's expression was sardonic. "That is the official story, certainly."

"I admit I have my doubts as well," Melissande said.

"But the question remains," Nelson insisted. "Just because a nation embraces a practice that *we* find offensive, are we in any position to judge them?"

"We can judge them," Taro said in his rumbling voice. "We can reject their actions. But do we have the right to go in and try to force our own ideals on their citizenry? I say no."

Mirti leaned forward, leaning her elbows inelegantly on the table. "What if they are engaging in wholesale slaughter? What if they are enslaving women? If we merely stand by and let atrocities occur, are we not complicit?"

"But isn't every nation entitled to its own system of beliefs?" Kayle asked. "Its own gods? How can you be certain the rules and precepts you follow are, in fact, correct? The fact that you believe in them with your whole heart proves nothing. Others believe in their own systems with equal fervor."

"I am with Darien," Mirti said flatly. "I believe there are certain things that are simply wrong, and that everyone recognizes as wrong—recognizes as *evil*. The only question then is how far you should go to stamp out that evil."

"That is what Cogli says," Melissande replied, nodding. "He believes there are unquestionable truths but limited responses. He tends to reject the grand solutions like war, and instead favors slower but more comprehensive ways to change cultures. Cogli is passionate about international trade because he says it shows people that different lives are possible, so they clamor to make their own changes."

"That's wise," Nelson said. "I like that."

"Who's Cogli?" Zoe asked.

"An advisor to the queen. And my husband's lover."

There was a moment's studied silence. Melissande raised her eyebrows and looked around in an astonishment that Val guessed was completely feigned. "Oh, what is it? Should I not speak of lovers in public? Or do you disapprove that my husband would choose to consort with a man?"

"Oh, nobody cares about *that*," Corene said.

Nelson and Zoe both looked amused. Val assumed that was because sweela folks were famous for their indiscretions and because Zoe didn't seem to have high standards for behavior. "Many people have lovers, and many people know about them," Zoe said, her voice grave, though her eyes danced. "But yes, generally, such knowledge is spoken of only in private and only in hushed tones."

"But in Cozique, everyone knows about Cogli!" Melissande exclaimed. "He is quite well-respected. Unlike my uncle's most recent mistress, who was beautiful, but stupid and gauche. My aunt had to take her aside and explain how one behaves at state functions, including how to dress. Not in sheer fabrics that showed every detail of her breasts."

This silence was even more uncomfortable. Elidon looked highly disapproving and even the broad-minded Virrie was frowning slightly. Darien put down his fork and regarded his guest steadily.

"You're exhausting," he informed her. "And yet you are neither as stupid nor as gauche as your uncle's young woman. I would wager all the gold in Chialto's coffers that you never make a misstep in conversational gambits, and so you are only trying to shock us. But I wouldn't place a copper on trying to guess why."

Melissande actually laughed. "Merely, I am curious," she said. "How much will your manners cover? How rude must a guest be before you are rude in return?"

"You don't worry," he said, "that I will form an unfavorable opinion of you that will influence the way I deal with you—and, by extension, your country?"

Melissande took a sip of her water. "I do not," she said. "You have treated with the Karkadians and the Soechins, and they must be far more repulsive than I am."

Corene choked down a laugh, and Zoe started grinning. Zoe said, "Well, perhaps you haven't heard all the tales, but I have not always been measured in my response to our foreign visitors. I threatened violence to the Karkadian prince—yes, and I *would* have harmed the Soechin ambassadors the other day if Val hadn't been there to stop me."

Val glanced up in alarm as everyone turned to give her a quick look of appraisal, but the attention quickly returned to Melissande. "See, that interests me," said the Coziquela princess. "I am always curious about what people will do when they are pushed too far."

"That's a dangerous game, though, if you're the one doing the pushing," Nelson observed. "And if the consequences fall on you."

"Yes," said Melissande. "That is certainly a risk."

"I think I have a fairly good idea of what I'm capable of," Zoe said. "Do you have an understanding of your own limits?"

Melissande turned a sunny smile her way. "I think I do, but how can any of us know until we are tested? My reactions might be more violent and ungoverned than I expect. Or I might be frozen in fear, unable to act with the fortitude I believe I have. It is impossible to be sure until the right circumstances arise."

"I would wish for your sake that those circumstances always remain theoretical," Darien said.

Beccan clapped her hands together. "Again! How have we strayed to such sober subjects! You promised us light conversation about fashion and scandal! Tell us quickly, what are the women in Cozique wearing these days? I must replenish my wardrobe and I do not want to be a dowd."

This time, Beccan was successful at turning the conversation to lighter topics, which saw them through the rest of the meal. Afterward, the whole group adjourned to the "lesser ballroom," where screens had been set up to make the space feel even smaller and cozier. Val managed to keep a pleasant smile on her face as she mingled with the others, but she was watching the clock. Surely she could retire by midnight? Maybe she could even leave right now if no one was paying attention.

As she had on the night of the coronation, she slipped out through one of the tall windows and took refuge on the balcony. Just three ninedays later, the air was balmier than it had been that night. Heat was starting to pile up during the days and simmer well into the night. Very soon it would be time to celebrate Quinnatorz changeday, the sign that deep summer had arrived.

Which meant that the last day of Quinnahunti was only five days away.

Val wrapped her hands tightly around the railing of the balcony. She had always been indifferent to the changing of the seasons, except for that one. Her father had died on Quinnatorz changeday, which would have seemed fitting somehow, if it hadn't been so terrible. The hunti prime easing from the world just as Quinnahunti ended. As if all things hunti were to be laid aside, all at once, for what seemed like forever. Knowing that the seasons would turn, and turn again, and that another Quinnahunti would arrive next spring, was no consolation at all. *This* season was over; *this* loss was final.

She had not thought she would be able to bear it, the next year, facing down the anniversary of his death. She had been tense from the moment Quinnahunti changeday dawned, and she had only grown more anxious as the quintile passed. She and her mother were still spending half their time at the estate, where Mirti frequently joined them, but neither of the other women seemed filled with the same level of dread. In case they hadn't remembered the date, Val hadn't mentioned her own unease. She knew how to be stoic. She knew how to be strong. She wouldn't trouble anyone else with her sorrows.

On the last evening of Quinnahunti, as a late sunset spilled gold across the lawn, a courier knocked furiously on their door. Somewhat apprehensive—because such urgency so often portended bad news—Val hurried to answer it. The courier was covered with dust and panting from exertion; his horse stood to one side, drooping, as if it had reached the limits of its strength.

"I was told I had to arrive before nightfall," the courier managed between gasps for breath. "I wasn't sure I would make it. Are you Valentina Serlast?"

Now she was bewildered. "I am."

He handed her a small package wrapped in layers of brown paper and addressed to her in Sebastian's handwriting. "This is for you."

She found herself pressing the package to her heart as if to calm her fevered pulse. "Has something happened to him—to the person who gave you this?"

"No, not at all. He just said you had to have this before changeday."

Val opened the door wider. "You look exhausted. Do you want food and a place to stay? I can send a groom for your horse."

The courier looked grateful. "If it wouldn't be too much trouble."

It was half an hour before she had settled the visitor and given her mother and Mirti a light explanation of the delivery. Half an hour before she could retreat to her room and lock the door and stand for a moment just staring at the unopened package. Sebastian had left Jenty's house a year ago, when he was only fifteen, and taken up what seemed to be a carefree life in Chialto. His letters were short and infrequent, and his visits even more so, but in his random and erratic way, he stayed faithfully in touch.

She knew before she opened the package that he had sent her a gift because he realized this was a day she would be blind with grief. Because he wanted to give her some small measure of joy to set against the bleakness of memory. To remind her that the world was not empty, she was not alone, and someone remembered her.

She sat on the edge of the bed and carefully untied the string, carefully peeled back the paper, carefully unfolded a black velvet cloth to reveal a small rectangular wooden box. It was imperfectly made, as if the craftsman was a mere apprentice, and Val knew at once that Sebastian had been the one to carve the challinbar. The uneven sides had been inexpertly stained with a black glaze but successfully polished to a high shine. A somewhat crooked clasp held the lid in place. She slid the hook free and looked inside. The interior of the box, painted a vivid red, was empty.

Black for hunti. Red for sweela.

Only the underside of the lid was stained a different color, a warm honey tone that was light enough to let the natural grain of the challinbar show through. In the center, a bronze tint overlay the honey in the shape of a single glyph. A flowing V, cut through with a single sweeping line; a nestled S.

Val turned the box to see the lid from an upside-down perspective. A curved S tucked against a confident A.

I am Sebastian Ardelay and I will always remember Valentina Serlast.

She had pressed the box to her lips before she started weeping. It was the first time all day she had felt safe enough to cry.

Since then, Sebastian had sent her a gift every year on the last day of Quinnahunti. Once, two years ago, she thought he had forgotten, or maybe had gotten tired of the ritual. Dark had fallen, and no visitor had arrived, carrying mysterious packages. She had tried not to be hurt. She had told herself that she no longer needed such comforts and remembrances. She had reminded herself that his life was so full, so busy, that he could not possibly be expected to remember the quiet rhythms of her existence.

And she had woken the next morning to find a box outside her front door, delivered sometime in the night. She never knew who had brought it.

But now there was a coolness between them. A gap. A distance. This might be the first year he chose not to honor the tradition. She would not go looking for presents as Quinnahunti wound down. It was time to move beyond such expectations.

She was jerked from her reflections as the door behind her opened and someone stepped through. Val turned, prepared to find that Corene had tracked her down, and was surprised to find Melissande instead.

"Is it permitted that I join you?" the princess asked in her pretty voice. "Or have you crept outside to escape all the people, including me?"

Val managed a smile. "I do feel overwhelmed by too much time spent in crowds," she admitted. "But I would have guessed that you thrive in such settings."

"Yes, the more people who are nearby, the more I feel energized and alive," Melissande replied. "At times I feel quite giddy with sensation. It is marvelous."

"The very thought makes me shudder."

"Then I shall go back inside."

"No—no," Val said awkwardly. "Feel free to stay. It is such a pleasant night."

Melissande glided forward and rested her fingers on the railing. She wore delicate rings on every slim finger. Val tried not to feel overlarge and clumsy in comparison to this exquisite creature. "And such a pretty view. I like the way the moonlight dances on the water."

"I have to think the cities in Cozique are much grander than Chialto."

"Some of them, yes. But every place has its own charms. That is why one travels—to discover how wide the world is, and how full of unfamiliar marvels."

"I've never journeyed outside of Welce."

Melissande turned her head to give Val an open appraisal. "I sense that you are not particularly interested in doing so."

"No. I find it hard to leave behind places and people. Once I arrive somewhere, I put down roots. I settle in place. When I was a girl, I spent one summer with my aunt. Even though I was homesick, even though I missed my mother, I almost couldn't bear to leave when the time came. I cried so hard for so long that I started throwing up. I had to stay an extra day until I recovered enough to travel."

Melissande was smiling. "That is very sweet," she said. "But limiting."

Val shrugged. "It's just the way I am."

"I assume you are—what is it called? The tree element."

"Hunti. Yes."

"Like your brother."

"Yes. I cannot imagine Darien would ever leave Welce either."

Melissande turned her back on the view she had been admiring, rested her spine against the railing, and appeared to think something over. "He is not an easy man to read."

Val was surprised into a laugh. "Darien? No."

"I fear he was not particularly impressed with me tonight."

Val was genuinely curious. "Did you want him to be? It almost seemed like you were trying to offend him."

Melissande laughed. "Did it?" she said lightly, but did not say whether it was true. "People tend to react to me in one of two ways. Either they despise me or they adore me. It is rare they find themselves on some middle ground."

Val hadn't made up her mind about Melissande yet, but she could easily imagine landing at one or the other extreme. "That must make life interesting for you," she said politely. "I don't think I stir such strong reactions in most people."

Melissande turned her head to survey Val again. "Ah, but that just means you are very good at concealing what you are thinking," she said. "You do not want people to know you until you know them."

It was so true that Val felt herself stiffen with surprise that a stranger could see her so clearly. "I think it takes a long time to get to know people."

"Sometimes," Melissande said. "Sometimes they show themselves truly within a day, or an hour."

"You don't," Val said.

Melissande was smiling again. "You think not? I admit there are layers. But—" She pulled away from the railing just enough to make an abbreviated curtsey. "This is my true self."

And why is your true self here in Welce? Val wanted to ask. Instead, she turned to more conventional topics. "I hope you enjoyed the dinner tonight."

"I did! All of your primes have such strong personalities. How much power do they wield at court?"

"Formally, not very much," Val said. "Informally, a great deal. Vernon—the old king—used to rely heavily on the advice of the primes. Darien always consults them, but he makes his own decisions."

"And if I wanted someone to advocate for me? Speak to Darien in my favor? Who would I cultivate? His wife?"

Val could not help an inelegant snort. "Good luck trying to influence Zoe."

"What appeals to him? What interests him? What arguments move him?"

Val stared at her. "You can't expect me to tell you that. He's my brother!" Belatedly she added, "And the *king*."

"I am not asking you to betray him," Melissande said. "Merely to tell me how to approach him."

"Just offer him the truth. That's what he appreciates."

Melissande sighed. "Ah, but the truth is often knife-edged and indiscriminate. It cuts in all directions. It is easier to handle when it is presented in a familiar sheath."

"I don't even know what you're trying to find out."

"Some kings care about enriching their coffers. Some care about securing their borders. Some want their countries to be seen as enlightened, or sophisticated, or filled with opportunity. What does your brother want for his kingdom?"

Val's voice was hard. "I suppose what he wants is to know what kind of bargain you're interested in making."

Melissande sighed a second time and turned around to face the view again. The air seemed cooler, Val thought, the lights of Chialto dimmer. Even the water of the Marisi seemed to have slowed, or stopped, because the lake below them barely shivered in the still air. "I do not even have a bargain to offer," Melissande said. "It is all theoretical, anyway."

The balcony door swung open, sending light and sound spilling out into the night. "Here you are! *Both* of you!" Corene exclaimed. "Everyone has been asking about you for the past ten minutes."

Val grinned. "You're lying. No one even noticed I was gone."

Corene took Val's arm in one hand and Melissande's in the other and pulled them toward the open door. "*I* noticed," she said. "And Taro noticed. And I would bet that Darien did, too. Come on. Zoe's going to serve sirix, and Darien doesn't know it, and I want to see his face."

All three of them laughed, and they quickly stepped back into the warmth and color and motion of the ballroom. But as they joined the others, and sampled the wine, and watched Darien keep an unwaveringly composed expression as he sipped at the most controversial beverage in all of Welce, Val couldn't help wondering. Why was Melissande in Welce if not to strike a bargain—for a trade agreement, a military alliance, an exchange of academic information? By every measure that mattered, Cozique had more to offer than Welce, and yet her words had implied that she saw herself in the role of supplicant. What could Welce have that she needed?

And what would she do to get it?

Chapter Fifteen

Val thought she would probably go mad during those last days of Quinnahunti, counting the hours until changeday. To distract herself, she agreed to every invitation, no matter how unappealing. That meant she spent fifthday having another intimate luncheon with Elidon and a long, exhausting afternoon drinking pretend tea with Celia in her playroom.

That meant she didn't hesitate to accept when, on sixthday, Mirti asked her to accompany her as she took Natalie on a tour of Chialto. "I want to show the girl that the hunti spirit isn't just to be found in the forest," Mirti explained. "It's everywhere."

Even though she was willing to go, Val felt compelled to make a point. "I'm not particularly good with children."

"And you think I am? But she's not a child, she's the heir to the hunti prime."

"You do realize that somebody can be both things at the same time."

Mirti made an indeterminate noise. "Natalie isn't like other children."

Val quickly discovered what that meant. The three of them piled into the back of a midsized elaymotive driven by one of Darien's soldiers, and Natalie instantly turned to Val.

"You're Darien's sister?"

"I am."

"Why have I never met you before?"

"You have, but you were too little to remember me."

"But I come to Chialto all the time and I've never seen you here."

"I've rarely been in the city for the past seven or eight years."

"Why?"

"I prefer living in the country."

"I live with Taro on his estate."

"I know."

"And I like it, but I *miss* the city if I don't come back."

That wasn't a question, so Val didn't respond. But Natalie barely needed time to take another breath.

"Do you hear the trees talking to each other?"

"I don't. Apparently, that's something only hunti primes can do."

"But you *like* trees?"

"I do."

"Which ones are your favorites?"

"The challinbar trees on the hunti estate."

"Oh, yes. They talk *all* the time."

The interrogation went on until they disembarked at a small park in the middle of the city. It was a considerable distance off the Cinque, in a rather unfashionable neighborhood, and Val was pretty sure she'd never been there before. The space featured five trees set around the perimeter at regular intervals, overlooking a scrap of poorly tended lawn. Before each trunk sat a wooden bench painted in one of the elemental colors.

"We should sit in each spot and meditate ourselves into a state of balance," Natalie decreed, dropping immediately onto the red sweela bench.

Mirti and Val chose seats across from her, and they all observed a moment of silence. It was a common practice for anyone who visited a temple, but Val didn't have high hopes that the restless Natalie would be able to remain still for long. Indeed, barely three minutes had passed before Natalie had jumped up and headed to the black hunti bench. Mirti and Val again moved on. In less than ten minutes, Natalie had achieved as much balance as she appeared to be capable of.

"Where are we going next?" she asked.

"Hold on," Mirti said. "I want you listen for a moment."

"But I already know I can hear the trees."

"Just *listen*."

So they all stood as motionless as possible, their heads tilted courteously as they waited for the trees to communicate. Val didn't know what Mirti and Natalie might be overhearing, but nothing came to her ears but the susurration of leaves, the occasional creak of swaying branches, and the distant sound of traffic from the nearest streets.

She watched as Natalie's face drew tight in concentration and loose in surprise. "But—that's so strange."

"What is?"

Natalie brushed her hand down the bark of the nearest trunk. "There are only five trees in the park, but I can hear more."

"How many more?"

"Maybe—ten? A lot of them."

"What are they saying?"

"I can't tell."

Mirti nodded, looking deeply satisfied. Val figured her own expression must be one of complete mystification. "The trees talk to each other," Mirti said.

Natalie's eyes grew big. "All the trees in the city?"

"All the trees across Welce," Mirti corrected. "Across vast distances. Their leaves whisper stories to each other. Their roots travel underground, reaching out to touch the roots of their neighbors, and they pass knowledge back and forth. I can stand in any small grove in Chialto and ask for news of my estate hundreds of miles away."

"I can't do that," Natalie said, disappointed.

"Not yet. But you will."

"Will I have to wait until you're dead?"

Val almost choked, but Mirti seemed unfazed. "Maybe. But my guess is you'll start hearing some of those voices within a year or two. Come on. We have more places to go."

Their next stop was the bustling shop of a woodworker who specialized in large tables and other pieces of furniture. Every item had been so lovingly constructed and polished that it was impossible for Val to refrain from running her hands over the silky finishes. Her favorite items were the heavy tables that were little more than thick slices carved from various trunks, the central rings and ragged perimeters perfectly preserved.

The woodworker's wife brought out a tray of refreshments and they paused to eat chocolates and drink fruited water. "Everything he makes is so beautiful," the woman said with a sigh, "but it bothers me sometimes that these magnificent trees had to *die* just so some rich woman can have a bedframe." Her voice took on a tentative, questioning tone. "I would think the hunti prime might feel the same way."

Mirti raised her eyebrows and glanced at Natalie. Val had to suppose this was a topic the two of them had recently discussed. "All of the elements are celebrated not only for what they *are* but what they can *accomplish*," the girl said in a pedantic tone. "The water in a lake is beautiful, but you also use it to nourish your crops and you drink it to stay alive. The air around you doesn't have much value unless you can breathe it in."

"Yes, but the roots of a tree hold the world together," the woodworker's wife argued. "There's some value in *that*."

"Different trees have different purposes," Natalie said with finality. "As long as we have plenty in the forest and across the land, we can turn some of them to more practical uses." Mirti cleared her throat, and Natalie hastily added, "And as long as we honor and renew them."

"It comforts me to hear you say so," the woman admitted. "I'm elay, and I just can't help but see the holy in everything."

"That's a good attitude," Mirti approved. "You can't ever go wrong if you approach the world that way."

After they left the woodworker's shop, they traveled a few blocks through a district of the city that seemed part industrialized, part professional, dotted with structures of all sizes and materials. Eventually they came to a spot where six buildings of solid white stone were clustered together around an irregular common.

"The university," Val said. "I've only been here a few times."

"Part of the university," Mirti corrected, alighting from the elaymotive. "Where they study the sciences. Kayle practically lives here when he's not at Vernon Harbor."

They made their way to the largest building, passing dozens of students hurrying along the paths, arguing in the courtyard, gathered in the hallways waiting for classes to begin. The light sifting through the big windows bounced off the pale walls, gleamed on the scuffed marble floors, threw shadows behind pillars and shelves. A medley of unfamiliar scents drifted down the corridors, some harsh and bitter, others cloying and heavy.

"The medical building," Mirti explained, leading them toward a broad stairway whose treads were worn smooth by centuries of footsteps.

On the second floor, they turned into a large, high-ceilinged space instantly notable for two main features: the rows of narrow worktables that filled the center of the room, and the ten or twelve skeletons that had been posed around the perimeter.

Val involuntarily started back at the sight, but Natalie crowed with delight and practically danced into the room. "Look at this one!" she cried, and then bounced over to the next specimen. "Oh, and *this* one! It's amazing!"

An older man had been conferring with a group of students when the three of them walked in, but he broke off his conversation and hurried over to greet Val and Mirti. Natalie was already deep in the room, looking at the next set of bones.

"Prime! We're so pleased to see you," the man said, but Val thought he looked harassed instead, maybe slightly anxious. She assumed he was a teacher at the school. "We've all heard the rumors that Princess Natalie is to be your heir."

"Yes, and it turns out she's never seen a complete skeleton before. I know you keep small ones on hand—rats and so forth—and I wondered if I might pick one up for her to take home."

I suppose this is the real reason I could never be hunti prime, Val thought, putting some effort into keeping her expression interested, or at least neutral. *I do not have any interest in filling my pockets with bones.*

"Of course! I have quite a selection in my office, and I'd be happy to let her choose one."

"And didn't you just receive an impressive donation? I heard that a road excavation team came across a gravesite along the western coast. Some of the oldest bones we think we've found."

Now the professor could no longer hide his dismay. "Indeed, the first box arrived this morning! We were all very excited, because we'd been told most of the bones had been perfectly preserved. But whatever fool placed the skeleton in the box didn't know the first thing about packing, because when we pried off the lid—" He gestured, as if words were inadequate to convey his distress. "Just a jumble. Pieces and shards. Not even a fingerbone is intact. It will take us *quintiles* to assemble it."

Mirti nodded once. "Show me."

"It's over here, just heaped on the table."

"Natalie!" Mirti called, and followed the professor to the largest table in the room, set up before one of the generous windows. Val trailed behind her, and soon the students and Natalie had joined them. Val could understand the professor's despair. Spread out on the flat black table was an undifferentiated mess of sharp white fragments, long cylinders of bone snapped in half, round knobs of joints cracked in two, a smooth cup of skull shattered down the middle.

"It's a tragedy," the older man said. "Of course, we've instantly dispatched some of our own faculty to the site to oversee the rest of the excavation, but who knows if they're already too late?"

"Oh, it's never too late," Mirti said in an absent-minded tone of voice. She reached out a finger and traced a loving line down a long thin fragment that looked as if it might once have been part of an arm. "So old," she said, obviously speaking to herself. "I can't even guess—"

One of the students opened her mouth as if to speak, but the professor flung out a hand and shook his head. He was watching Mirti with a sort of hopeful fascination—well, they all were. Her face had taken on a look of intense concentration, and now she was using both hands to stroke the angles and ridges of the crumpled skeleton. The calcified dust that covered the table seemed to swirl and rise, wrapping around her fingers; the pile of bones shifted under her palms with a light and hollow clatter.

Slowly the pieces began to rearrange and reassemble, the splintered shaft of a femur combining with its severed twin, a collapsed assembly of ribs organizing themselves into an arched white canopy. The hands reattached themselves to the wrists and the vertebrae aligned themselves to march down the center of the table. The jaw fitted itself back into its empty hinge, snapping shut to erase an expression of gaping surprise. The great empty eye sockets stared out over the repaired slopes of the cheekbones as if the skeleton was appraising the walls and shadows of its new home.

"There," said Mirti in a tone of satisfaction. "That'll do, I think."

"Prime!" the professor exclaimed over his students' low murmurs of awe. "I have never seen such a demonstration! I would break a thousand bones just to watch you employ elemental magic to weld them back together."

"It's a strange thing," Mirti said, glancing down at the spread fingers of her left hand. Val noticed that Natalie was studying her own hands, back and front, as if gauging how much power she might one day be able to command. "I can break a bone or a slab of wood from a short distance, but to heal either one, I have to be able to touch it. Maybe because destruction requires little more than power and intent, but repair relies on grace and mercy."

One of the students piped up in a hushed, respectful voice. "My father told me that he once saw the old hunti prime stop a rampaging carriage by snapping the wooden axels and sending the wheels flying off. Saved the lives of a woman and three children riding inside."

"That was my brother. He did indeed do that, from halfway across the Plaza of Men. I have never needed to attempt anything so spectacular."

"Based on your exhibition today," said the teacher, "I am certain you could manage it."

"I would rather not find out," said Mirti, "because I would rather see no one's life in danger."

"Of course, prime."

"Maybe I can demolish a building someday," said Natalie hopefully. "Only if it's supposed to be torn down, of course. And nobody is inside. And it's made of wood."

Mirti glanced down at her, faintly amused. "I feel certain," she said, "that you will one day be called on to do spectacular things."

Chapter Sixteen

Seventhday also began in a most agreeable manner, as Melissande and Corene and Val spent most of the morning wandering through the Plaza of Women, followed by guards from two nations. It was clear all the merchants in town were gearing up for changeday, which tended to center around food. Every bakery was busy taking orders for cakes and pies and braided breads; the fish markets and slaughterhouses posted signs listing the special cuts they would have for sale; and bags of caramelized fruit were sold by every vendor in the city, whether they offered shoes or jewelry or housewares.

"I cannot eat any more, not another bite," Melissande proclaimed as the three of them sat in a café and sampled platters of bite-sized pastries. "This is exactly the time I would wish someone in this city sold keerza! I need its dark flavor to temper all the sugar I have consumed."

"What's keerza?" Val asked.

"A bitter drink that everyone in Malinqua consumes as often as possible," Corene answered. "The first five times you try it, you hate it, but then suddenly you find yourself craving it whenever you sit down on a quiet afternoon." She turned to Melissande. "Leah sells it. Want to go ask her for a cup?"

Melissande pushed herself to her feet and fished inside her pocket. "Yes, but first I am supposed to investigate a shop. The clerk at my hotel assured me it was a place I should not miss. I have the address here."

Corene took the paper and frowned over it. "I know the street but not the shop. But it's close enough to walk."

Corene led the way and the rest of them followed. Within two quick turns, they were out of the Plaza proper and on a shadowy back road that had an indefinably disreputable air. Val saw Corene swing her head from side to side, assessing the storefronts with some disapproval. She sensed movement behind her and realized that Foley and the other guards had all stepped closer.

A few blocks later, they arrived at their destination, but the one-story building was shut up tight, its shutters firmly closed and its warped door reinforced with a padlock. The buildings on either side of it appeared to be equally deserted.

"Are you sure this is the right address?" Corene asked.

"Well, I thought so, but now I am not certain."

A voice came out of nowhere, and Val realized that there was a man standing in the shadowed space between the shop and its nearest neighbor.

"Something in particular you're looking for?" he asked. "Maybe I could help you out."

Corene stumbled backward, practically hissing in surprise, but Melissande seemed oddly undisturbed.

"Could you indeed?" said the princess. "I was told that this store sold a certain kind of commodity, but sadly it does not appear to be doing any business today."

"You're in luck," said the stranger. "I deal in all kinds of commodities."

Val frowned. The voice was oddly familiar, but she couldn't place it, and the speaker remained completely out of view between the buildings. Corene had her sharp gaze trained on Melissande, but kept her mouth shut.

"I wonder what the cost might be," the princess said.

Judging by his voice, the man was smiling. "Well, premium goods and services always command high prices."

"No doubt there are others who could provide the service for a more reasonable fee."

"Not as many as you might suppose," the man replied. "Do you think you'll require my assistance?"

"Not today," Melissande said. "But may I return here someday if I do?"

"I'll be expecting you," he said. He inclined his head just enough to expose his face to a sliver of sunlight, then he ducked away and disappeared down the alley. Val stepped back so suddenly that she almost lost her footing. A swift hand under her elbow helped her keep her balance, and she realized that Foley was right at her back, close enough to engage in combat if this stranger offered violence.

"We need to get back to the main road," he said with quiet authority.

Corene nodded dumbly and set a brisk pace as she led the entourage to the sunlight of the Plaza. They traveled mostly in silence. Melissande didn't offer any explanations and Corene didn't make any comments, but anyone who had known Corene longer than a day knew that she would unleash a torrent of questions the minute they were someplace safe.

When they arrived at Leah's, Corene pushed the door open with unnecessary force, almost slamming it against the inner wall. Leah looked up from a table of sweela goods and smiled at them brightly.

"Good afternoon! I didn't know I was expecting you today."

"Do you have a private room somewhere?" Corene demanded. "My friends and I need to talk."

"We do not," Melissande said.

Leah's eyes widened, but she gestured at a discreet door set into the back wall. "Through there. Upstairs. Send Chandran down if you want to be alone."

Five minutes later, the three of them were sitting in the middle of a colorfully chaotic storeroom, sipping hot keerza from small earthenware mugs. Chandran turned out to be a great somber-looking bearded fellow whom Melissande greated with a hug, but he didn't stay long enough to make conversation.

Val found that Corene was right. She didn't like keerza at all. She only took a few more swallows in order to be polite.

"Now," Corene said, as soon as they could no longer hear the echoes of Chandran's feet on the stairs. "*What* was that all about?"

"Nothing to concern yourself with," Melissande said.

"Well, I *am* concerned."

Melissande appeared to be searching for words. "I need something. I have asked who might be able to supply it, and this man was one of the names I was given."

"What do you need? Drugs? I didn't think that was one of your vices."

"As if I have so many vices!"

"Well, is it?"

"Corene, my dearest friend. No. I am much too clever and cool-headed to give myself over to such uncontrolled pursuits."

"Then what is it?"

"It is something—that I wish to give my mother."

Corene stared at her. "You're usually a better liar."

"As it happens, that is the truth."

Val spoke up. "Whatever it is you want, you can't get it from that man."

They both quickly turned their attention to Val. "You know him? How is that possible?" Corene demanded.

"His name is Jodar. I was with a friend the other day, and Jodar approached him and threatened his life."

"You *what?*" Corene said.

"Oh, now, see, this is much more interesting than anything that I have said or done!" Melissande exclaimed. "What friend were you with? Why would someone want to kill him? How astonishing that someone as demure as you should have such extreme acquaintances!"

Corene put her hands to her head. "I think you've both gone mad."

"Well, *you're* the one who dragged me down to the bachelor district to drink illegal sirix," Val argued. "It's not like you're so very proper."

Corene pointed at Val. "We will address your situation later." She pointed at Melissande. "Be honest with me. Or I'll tell Darien you're plotting something dangerous, and you'll never leave the hotel without a phalanx of Welchin guards at your back."

Melissande's smile was strained. "That would not inhibit my actions as much as you might think. Corene! I admit there is some risk to what I am trying to do. But *I* am not in danger. No one is trying to harm me."

Corene watched her steadily. "Is this the real reason you came to Welce?"

"Welce was not, in fact, my intended destination. But yes."

"Whatever it is you're doing, you need to tell Darien."

"This does not concern him."

Val spoke urgently. "Whatever it is you're doing, you need to do it with someone who is *not* Jodar. Believe me, Melissande. He's not someone you can trust."

"How did you find him, anyway?" Corene asked.

"She asked the blind sisters," Val said.

Melissande gave her an admiring look. "Ah. How observant of you."

"I didn't realize they set up questionable assignations in addition to dispensing information," Corene said.

Melissande shrugged slightly. "Knowledge is knowledge."

"So you have to find someone else," Val said doggedly.

"I feel that all choices for this particular enterprise will be equally unsavory," Melissande said. "But I will take care."

Corene shook her head. "I don't think—"

Melissande put her dainty hand on Corene's arm. She was smiling. "This is not your story," she said. "Let it unfold according to my plan."

Corene watched her unhappily a moment. "If something happens to you because I didn't interfere—"

"It will not." Melissande lifted her hand and picked up her cup. "Drink your keerza. And then we shall go home so we can prepare for the night's festivities. Do not trouble yourself, Corene. All will be well."

✤

No sooner had their elaymotive dropped Melissande off at her hotel than Corene turned to Val and said, "Now. You. What friend were you with? Why would anybody threaten him? And why haven't you mentioned anything about this during all the time we've spent together?"

It was ridiculous to want to lie as breezily as Melissande, to refuse to give up even a name, as if Sebastian's mere existence was a secret too precious to display in the ordinary world. She glanced at the front of the elaymotive, where Foley sat beside the driver.

"There's a glass panel between us," Corene said impatiently. "They can't hear us."

It didn't matter who heard. There was nothing to conceal. "I was with Sebastian Ardelay. Someone I've known since we were children. Darien knows him, too—and doesn't like him. I've seen him from time to time since I've been in Chialto." She shook her head. "I'm afraid that he's fallen into some risky habits and made some hazardous friends."

"Ardelay? Is he related to Nelson?"

"In the way that so many rootless young men are," Val said dryly.

Corene's frown dissolved into a grin. "Ah. One of the famous Ardelay indiscretions. But whose?"

"One of Nelson's cousins. Nelson acknowledges him, of course."

"Of course." Corene waited a beat, and when Val didn't offer any more, she said, "So? What's your relationship with him?"

"I told you. We're friends. I've known him since I was eight."

Corene studied her. "You're in love with him."

Val was instantly irritated. "I'm not. Why would you think that?"

"Because you're being so secretive. Nobody ever bothers hiding the fact that they've got a friend. Only an inappropriate lover."

"Well, maybe Sebastian is an inappropriate friend."

"Why? What's he doing that you're so worried about?"

"Smuggling sirix."

Corene's eyes went wide. "No! *Really?* That's very exciting." She frowned. "Also, no wonder Darien doesn't like him."

"Darien didn't like him long before that. He thinks Sebastian is too unsteady."

"Well, is he?"

"In a lot of ways," Val admitted.

Corene tilted her head. "But in some ways he's completely reliable?" When Val didn't answer, Corene prodded. "Like what? What can you rely on him for?"

To remember me when I'm sad. Well, that sounded hopelessly pathetic. *To remember me.* "Just to be a good friend," Val said lamely.

"So he's sweela, I take it? If he's Ardelay."

"Yes."

"And that bothers your hunti soul."

"We're so different. He's so restless and I'm so settled. We don't see each other that often, which is just as well, because we argue all the time."

Corene settled back against the seat, but her eyes were still on Val. The elaymotive was straining up the long hill to the palace, which was already in sight. "Oh, you hunti people," she said with affectionate derision. "You spend so much time trying to determine how things *ought* to be that you don't pay any attention to how you *want* them to be. Whereas sweela people figure out what they want and then they put their energy into getting it."

"Yes, and upend the whole world in the process, not caring who else gets hurt!"

"Sometimes," Corene said, nodding. "Sometimes the world needs to be upended."

Val turned her head and looked out the window. Suddenly she felt tired. It wasn't even sunset yet, but her bones protested that it must be past midnight. Hard to believe there was still a long formal dinner to get through before the day was officially over. Maybe she could tell Zoe that she'd developed a stomachache from the keerza.

The elaymotive pulled up in front of the palace, and they climbed out. "What are you going to tell Darien about Melissande?" Val asked.

Corene pressed her lips together and started toward the open doors. "For now, nothing. Melissande is very clever. She knows how to run her own affairs, and getting Darien involved in a delicate transaction could ruin something I don't even understand. But—I admit I'm worried. I'll be watching."

"She knows you will. That will make her even more careful."

"She could probably stand to be more careful."

Val tried for a smile. "She's not a hunti woman, that's for sure."

"Oh, you'd be surprised. She can be quite steadfast. But right now—" Corene shook her head as they stepped into the great hall. "I'm guessing it's coru all the way. Changing as change is required."

"I hope we find out what's she up to."

"I hope we don't," Corene answered. "Because that will mean everything has gone wrong. And I feel like that could be disastrous."

Eighthday proved to be more fun than Val had anticipated. Zoe had commissioned seamstresses to come to the palace to make new outfits for all the women who would be attending the Quinnatorz changeday ball, and now it was time for the final fittings. Zoe, Corene, Val, Mirti, and Elidon spent the day in one of the private suites in the royal wing, trying on clothes and accessories and experimenting with ways to wear their hair. Even Celia and Natalie joined them for the fun, though they were both too young to attend the ball. Zoe had had special outfits made for them, anyway, and Celia refused to take hers off all afternoon.

Natalie followed Mirti around and asked incessant questions, when she wasn't helpfully pointing out small flaws in someone's hairstyle or hemline. Val thought that even Elidon was starting to get annoyed, but Val had a certain sympathy. Natalie was so very hunti; she had an unshakeable belief that things were either *wrong* or *right*, and she thought that naturally anyone would want to know when something needed to be corrected. It had taken Val a long time to learn that some people preferred their truths with blurred and ragged margins.

Food was brought in every hour or so, and those who weren't in the middle of having something tucked or hemmed lounged around sampling pastries and sipping fruited water. Mirti never cared much about her appearance, but she had gotten into the spirit of the event and commissioned a navy-colored silk tunic embroidered with rays of silver. As she modeled it for the group, she even allowed Corene to fashion her hair with an array of silver clips.

"The look suits you," Elidon pronounced. "Severe but elegant."

At Corene's urging, Val had opted for a fashionable Coziquela sheath dress of shimmering black shot through with vibrant threads of color. When she stood entirely still, the dress appeared to be uniformly dark, but as soon as she moved, the thin vertical lines of crimson, emerald, purple, and gold flashed and disappeared. The high neckline was modest but the sleeveless style was daring. Corene had finally relented and said Val could bring a light wrap with her to the ball in case she got cold.

"But it has to be red," Corene said.

"Black."

"You honestly have no idea how to make an impact when you walk into a room."

"I honestly have no wish to."

Corene sighed, but then she smiled. "Well," she said, "maybe something will happen at the ball to change your mind."

Ninthday dawned overcast and chilly, but that didn't deter Corene. "I hate all my bracelets and necklaces," she said over breakfast. "I have to go to the Plaza of Women and buy something new to wear to the changeday ball tomorrow. Val has to come with me."

"Take Melissande."

"She is spending the day with Kayle Dochenza."

Zoe looked up from helping Celia cut her toast. "Oh, that poor girl," she said, as if she couldn't help herself. "Why?"

"They're making some kind of deal about elaymotives. And I think they're also talking about some kind of—ore? mineral?—*substance* that Kayle wants to import from Cozique. She said that after he leaves she will be so exhausted she will have to rest for the remainder of the day so she will recover in time for the ball tomorrow."

Rest—or leave the hotel on some secret, chancy mission that she didn't want her friends to observe. Val traded a look with Corene, fairly certain they were entertaining the same thought.

"If I had to spend an hour by myself with Kayle, I'd need to rest for a whole nineday," said Elidon.

"Anyway, so Val has to come with me."

Truth be told, a shopping expedition would be a distraction. Val wasn't sure how else she was going to get through the day. The end of Quinnahunti. It was ridiculous to attach so much importance to the date.

"All right," she said. "Let's go."

They wandered through the plaza for hours, grateful that the gathered clouds never made good on their threat to rain. Corene bought half-a-dozen items, but Val couldn't muster any interest in the shoes and tunics and jewelry that every shop owner displayed in honor of the coming holiday. Most of her attention was on the sun as it made an agonizingly slow crawl across the sky.

Was it still morning? How could it barely be noon? Had time actually come a halt shortly after they'd finished lunch? At this rate, they would be traveling the Cinque for a year and eating dinner for centuries. Val wanted to go home and throw herself on her bed and pull the pillows over her ears and sleep until morning.

It wouldn't matter so much if she thought she'd hear from Sebastian. But this year, she couldn't count on him to smooth away the rough edges of the day. She should have stopped relying on him long ago. Grief wore away, that's what everyone said, and no one could ease it out of your heart, no matter what kind gestures they made. You had to heal yourself. You had to lean on your own strength. No other supports could be trusted.

"It's getting late. We have to get back," Corene finally said. "Where do you think the driver is with our elaymotive?"

Corene chattered for the whole drive back and up until the minute they parted at Val's door. Val stepped inside the room, which was dark and cool because she'd left the curtains drawn. She leaned against the door and shut her eyes, mentally planning how to fill the remaining minutes of the day. Maybe she could nap for an hour. Take an hour to bathe and dress for dinner. The meal would be small and quiet, as everyone wanted to be rested for tomorrow's festivities, but that meant Celia was likely to join them. And Zoe and Corene were likely to sit down afterwards to play simple games with Celia, and Val was always welcome to join them, and that would be another hour gone. Maybe two. And eventually she would make her way back to her room, and eventually it would be midnight, and Quinnatorz changeday would officially be upon them, and Val could put aside this unprofitable, pointless malaise. Eight hours, and then another year before she had to face the day again.

She opened her eyes and moved across the room to collect her underclothes from the dresser. She switched on the sconce over the dresser and froze in place, one hand still uplifted. There was a small package in the outstretched hands of the torz sculpture she had bought at Leah's shop. It was slim and flat, a length of black velvet wrapped around what looked like an overlarge coin. There was no note, no card, nothing to indicate who it was from or how it had been delivered to her room.

She barely breathed as she carefully picked it up and slowly pulled back the fabric. Then she sat down right on the floor.

It was a circular pendant made of polished wood so hard and dense she knew it must be from a challinbar tree. The black stain was not quite dark enough to obscure the intricate, complex pattern of the grain. A thin gold loop at the top of the pendant held a serpentine gold chain. Val lifted the charm so it dangled at eye height and she could get a closer look at the swooping V, the cuddled S, picked out in brooding garnets. The initials everyone else would see.

She pinched the loop and turned the disk upside down. An elegant S, a confident A. What she would see any time she lifted the pendant as she wore it around her neck.

He had not forgotten.

She could make it through the day.

Chapter Seventeen

Val is nineteen.

It is three years since her father has died, and she has become more serious than ever. She finds she has little in common with the girls her age, who seem shallow and frivolous, entirely focused on meeting and marrying someone young and attractive. She absolutely hates the quintiles that she and her mother spend in Chialto in a house that Darien has found for them in a fashionable neighborhood. He almost never has any time to spend with them, as he has become Vernon's closest advisor and a fixture at the royal court, and there is no one else in Chialto she can even tolerate.

She spends most of her time in the city pining for a return to the hunti estate, where her mother has spent the past three years acting as Mirti's agent and housekeeper. But now, suddenly, her mother has declared herself done. She has found a small property near her sister's house and made plans to move herself and her daughter a hundred miles away.

Val is both agonized and relieved to leave behind the house where she grew up, the house where she was born. Despite Mirti's generosity, her absolute sincerity when she asked them to stay, Val has begun to feel more and more like a guest in the place that once seemed like home. Part of her believes it will be good for both her mother and herself to make a clean break and start fresh in a new place, but part of her is paralyzed with apprehension at the monumental change this represents. Val hates change, even if it's very small. She can hardly wrap her mind around this comprehensive disruption of her life.

But she dreads the move for another reason. She feels an actual physical pain at the idea of traveling so far from the challinbar grove that she will not be able to wander through its shade any time she chooses. She has the fanciful notion that, the farther she is from the sacred wood, the more soft and formless she will become, her bones turning brittle and dissolving inside the pliant sheath of skin.

The only person she mentions this to is Sebastian. He has most unexpectedly arrived with Aunt Jenty, who has come to help Merra Serlast organize the move. It has been at least six months since Val has seen him, and his presence almost breaks her out of her somber mood.

"I want to go, I do," she tells him. "But I think maybe I'll die if I'm so far from the challinbar grove. If I can't walk out there any time I want and just put my hand against the trunk of the heart tree."

"Take it with you."

"You can't move a *tree*."

"No, but you can take a piece of it. I made you a box out of a stick of challinbar, remember? Find a big fallen branch and hire someone to build you a table or something."

"I suppose I could do that. But it would have to be a pretty big branch."

"And bring a sapling with you to plant at the new house. Challinbar will grow anywhere in Welce, won't it?"

"Yes, but it takes years to reach any size. The heart tree is centuries old."

"So you have a small challinbar tree for the next twenty years. That's better than no challinbar tree."

The very idea is cheering her up immensely. "You're right. Let's go out to the grove."

They pack a lunch, hike through the forest, and picnic in the deep shade under the dense green canopy. It turns out that only two kinds of fallen branches are littering the grove—thin spindly ones not suitable for carving, and massive trunk-sized limbs that are almost too heavy to budge.

"I didn't think to bring a handsaw," Sebastian says as they finish their meal and consider the possibilities. "Or I would just hack off a piece for you to take home with you."

"At least there's plenty of dead fruit on the ground. I'll harvest some of the seeds and take them with me for planting."

Val collects the rotted fruit while Sebastian investigates the fallen limbs. One of the smaller trees looks as if it might have been damaged by lightning sometime in the past quintile; a low branch has snapped off near the trunk and is hanging down at a drunken angle, just barely touching the ground. Sebastian tugs and strains at the outer boughs, trying to break the branch free, but it remains stubbornly attached.

"I don't know what you think you're doing," Val says. "Even if you get it loose, it's too big to carry home."

"It's the smallest branch we've seen," he replies. "I can drag it to the house."

"All that way? I don't think so."

In answer, Sebastian merely grunts. After eyeing the slope of the branch from where it brushes the ground to where it joins the trunk about six feet up, he carefully steps onto the lowest, narrowest part. It trembles and sways under his weight, but he spreads his hands for balance and takes another two steps.

"Sebastian! Get down from there. You'll fall and split your head open."

He takes a few more steps, then a few more, moving with greater confidence as the branch widens under his feet. Val stops gathering challin fruit so she can watch him in silence. As he gets close to the broad trunk, some of the other boughs are within reach, and he grabs one in each hand to hold himself steady. Then he starts jumping up and down on the branch, right where it has sheered away, trying to sever its last jagged bonds with the tree. Val hears the wood shift and groan as Sebastian's boots connect with the uneven surface. Suddenly, with a loud crack, the limb gives way, and the man and the branch crash to the ground in a noisy explosion of leaf and flying bark. Sebastian yells and Val cries out, and for a moment the air is filled with so much debris that she can't tell exactly what has happened.

"*Sebastian!*"

There is a moment of silence except for the sounds of twigs and leaves and shards of wood drifting down and settling into place. Then Sebastian curses. Then he laughs.

"Ow," he says. "Well, that was a little more abrupt than I expected."

Val strides over, pushing aside the thin, flexible outer branches to get to the man on the ground. "Are you all right? Did you break anything?"

He takes her hand and lets her tug him to his feet, though he moves a bit gingerly. "I don't think so. Got the breath knocked out of me."

"That was stupid. You could have killed yourself."

He grins at her. "It was brilliant. It worked."

She surveys the prize. It is maybe ten feet long, possibly a foot in diameter, and she can't even guess how much it weighs. "I don't see how we can possibly get this home."

"I brought a couple of ropes. We'll hook both of us up to it and pull it through the forest. If we don't make it all the way to the house, we'll send some of the footmen back to get it. You'll see. It'll work." He glances at the remains of the picnic. "If you're done picking up fruit, let's get started."

"Give me a couple minutes."

While Val packs up the remains of lunch and carefully wraps the challin fruit in layers of linen napkins, Sebastian knots two long pieces of rope to strategic spots on either side of the downed limb. Hauling hard on a single line, he's able to move the log a good ten feet on his own.

"See?" he says, grinning at her. "We can do it."

She slings the picnic bag over her shoulder and grabs the other rope. "We can do it," she agrees. "Let's go."

※

They make it more than halfway home before Val has to stop. Her hands are so raw that they have started to bleed, and her shoulders and legs are so sore she simply can't exert any more effort. Sebastian drags the log another hundred yards on his own before he, too, finally admits defeat. But they are outside of the forest now, on a wide grassy track that anyone can follow. They can come back tomorrow with horses and better gear.

"That branch is so big you could make a *chair* out of it," Sebastian says. He is enamored of the possibilities. "You could make a dollhouse—a replica of the mansion."

"That might make me sad," she says. "But maybe a picture frame."

"Commission a painting of yourself," Sebastian suggests.

"That's silly. I don't need a painting of my own face. But I could put the frame around the portrait of my father that's in the parlor."

"And then commission a painting of your mother to match."

"That's a good idea."

But when they make it back to the mansion, all such thoughts are driven from Val's head. Her mother has taken ill and collapsed in bed, struggling to breathe. Jenty has sent for the nearest doctor, but he hasn't arrived yet. Val goes straight to the sickroom to do what she can, coaxing her mother to drink water mixed with herbal concoctions, bathing her fevered face and hands with cold water.

Two days later, the danger is past, though her mother remains limp and listless for another nineday, and still hasn't entirely regained her energy by the time they undertake the move. It is the first of the many incidents that will come with increasing frequency over the next six years, as Merra's lungs gradually shut down and her strength gives out. Of course, Val doesn't know that yet. She is too relieved at her mother's recovery to wonder whether trouble might strike again.

Caring for her mother and overseeing their relocation has preoccupied Val so much that she hasn't had time to grieve over leaving behind her childhood home. She's completely forgotten about the fallen challinbar branch, abandoned in a meadow somewhere between the house and the forest.

But Sebastian has gone back sometime during the nineday to rescue that treasure. And since then, every year on the last day of Quinnahunti, he has sent her a gift made from the branch. He is so rootless and unsettled that she doesn't even know where he stores the lumber from year to year. Maybe he has left it with some artisan who consults with him about what wondrous objects to create next. Maybe he's had it carved into chunks and he carries lumpy bags of raw material with him every time he moves to some new questionable set of lodgings. He probably considers the challinbar wood at least as valuable as any of his other possessions.

I am Sebastian Ardelay and I will always remember Valentina Serlast.

Chapter Eighteen

One hundred and fifty people sat down to Changeday dinner at the palace, and all of them seemed focused on Melissande. She was dressed in a brilliant blue sheath dress dotted with random sequins, and every time she moved or even breathed, she shimmered with light. She was seated between Darien and Nelson at the head table, which was on a slight dais, and every other guest in the room watched her as if waiting for her to erupt into flames.

Val had never in her life been so glad to be placed at a side table on the edge of the room, where no one was likely to notice her. She didn't even mind making polite conversation with two Chialto merchants and pretending she knew something about shipping manifests. It was surprisingly easy to smile and nod, to tilt her head as though she was intrigued by the topic. Every dish presented to her smelled wonderful and tasted divine. Her whole body felt light, as if she had shed a shadow soul that weighed almost as much as her own body. It was such a relief to be through the grief of the anniversary.

It was such a comfort to be able to wear Sebastian's latest gift, which perfectly accented her color-streaked gown. Corene had noticed the pendant the minute Val joined her in the dining hall.

"That's so perfect for you! I can't believe you haven't been wearing it every day."

"I was saving it for a special occasion."

"Nonsense. It should be your signature piece. Something people expect to see you wearing."

"Well, maybe." *Well, probably.*

The meal eventually gave way to dancing in what Val's mother had dubbed "the greater ballroom," an enormous space on the ground floor of the palace. The high ceilings had been hung with streamers in all the elemental colors, complemented by banners in a shade of silvery blue that featured heavily in the Coziquela flag. Every man in Chialto seemed determined to partner Melissande at least once, and it was rather entertaining to watch the young ones try to outmaneuver each other for her attention. Val wondered if they didn't realize she had a husband or if, for one dreamy dance with the beautiful visitor, they didn't care.

A significant number of partners solicited Val's hand for the dances, which she assumed was because they thought it politic to make a good impression on the king's unmarried sister. She accepted whenever she was asked, but she much preferred lingering on the sidelines and watching the other guests. Corene appeared to be having a grand time, twirling with great energy and flirting madly. Neither Zoe nor Darien danced while Val watched, but Nelson never missed a number. Val noticed with approval that the only partners he chose were the shy young girls or the formidable dowagers, the women who rarely made it to the dance floor. His warmth and attentiveness put the most awkward girl at ease, made the older women throw back their heads and laugh with delight. He even squired Elidon around for one stately turn, and though the queen did not unbend enough to chuckle, she did smile for the whole dance.

A little before midnight, Val snuck outside for some fresh air, gliding across the great hall and passing a cadre of palace guards as she slipped out the front door. She quickly discovered she was not the only one to seek a change of scenery. A few groups of people had gathered on the broad courtyard to argue or exchange gossip. Couples stood in the shadows that clung to the sides of the building, leaning their heads together so they could whisper or exchange quick kisses.

Braver guests had descended toward the edges of the lake, where rafts had been rowed out to the middle of the water and attached to buoys. Each raft was filled with an assortment of candles and colored lanterns that bobbed and swayed on the rocking waves, creating a scene of festive enchantment. More small boats had been tied up at the dock for the use of visitors who wanted to venture out onto the water to enjoy the lights or the stars or each other's company. Footmen stood on the dock to help guests into the boats and distribute poles and oars.

Finding no allure in the idea of touring the lake by night, Val stayed close to the main entrance, a few paces into the darkness that lay beyond the palace lights. She took just enough time to let the air cool her cheeks before turning back to the big open doorway.

Someone was stepping outside as Val approached. Squinting against the brightness of the interior lights, Val first made out the trim silhouette of a small, muscular woman and then noticed that she wore the uniform of a palace guard.

"Valentina Serlast," the soldier said.

Val came to a halt, trying to make out the woman's features in the uneven lighting. "Yes?"

"We met a few ninedays ago. At the harbor."

"Oh. That's right." Val searched her memory. "Yori?"

Yori smiled. "I'm impressed."

"Most of the details of that day have stuck with me," Val said dryly.

"I'm not surprised." Yori hesitated a moment, then went on. "I can't say much. But you might tell anyone you care about *not* to be at the harbor tomorrow night."

Val felt her body seize with a sudden chill. "What? What's going to happen?"

Yori shook her head. "That's all I can tell you."

"But I—"

Yori sketched a bow and slipped past Val into the shadows that lined the building. Val stared after her and felt her mind churn with feverish speculation, trying to decipher Yori's warning. Her best guess was that Darien was planning a raid on the waterfront, looking for smugglers who trafficked in sirix, and Yori had figured out that Sebastian was part of that network.

She had to alert him. But what could she say? She hadn't even spoken to him in three ninedays. And if she warned him that a raid was planned, he was certain to notify his criminal friends, and they would all disappear like rats from the harbor streets. Darien would be furious and Yori might lose her job.

But if she said nothing—

If he was arrested—

Surely, Darien wouldn't *harm* Sebastian. Val didn't know much about Chialto's judicial system, but she couldn't imagine that Darien allowed prisoners to be mistreated. Even so, he had made it clear that sirix smuggling had steep consequences for international relations, and he might mete out harsh punishments for those who engaged in it. She wasn't certain he would grant clemency just because he was personally acquainted with one of the offenders. In fact, since he actively disliked Sebastian—

Val stood a moment longer just outside the doorway, her body a pillar of ice, her mind a racing chaotic jumble. She could leave right now, hire an elaymotive to take her to the last address she had for Sebastian. But she had a hazy sense that criminals did most of their work by night; there was a good chance he wouldn't be home. Well, she could rise very early and carry out the same plan, being more likely to catch him asleep in his bed. Of course, she would still have to decide what to tell him that would keep him away from the harbor without rousing his suspicions. She could—she could—

She gave one sharp nod and strode into the grand hallway, past the guards, and back into the ballroom. Scarcely fifteen minutes had passed, and yet it seemed like she must have been standing outside agonizing for a quintile at least. The colors in the room looked dull and smeared; the couples whirling across the dance floor seemed graceless and spasmodic. Even Melissande looked washed out and wooden.

It took her a few minutes to spot her target, and then she saw him standing with a cluster of other men, talking with great animation. With no attempt at subtlety, she marched across the room and placed her hand on his arm. Everyone in his small group fell silent to stare at her.

"I need to talk to you," she said. "Privately."

Nelson gazed down at her with an expression that went quickly from surprise to worry. He was the sweela prime; no doubt he could sense the anxiety sparking through her. His eyes narrowed under his red eyebrows, and he laid a warm hand over hers.

"Let's dance," he suggested in a kind voice.

She wanted to scream that she had no time for trivialities, but as he led her out onto the floor, she realized he was right. The music signaled a gentle waltz, not so lively that they would be too breathless to speak, and the sounds of the instruments would cover their conversation. Nelson's hand against her back was unexpectedly comforting, and his steady, concerned regard was reassuring.

"What's put you in such a state?" he asked.

"I need you to do something for me."

"Of course."

"I need you to invite Sebastian Ardelay to your house tomorrow night. It has to be tomorrow. And he can't go home until the next morning."

Now Nelson's expression grew quizzical, although still compassionate and concerned. "I might have imagined dozens of things you could have said to me, but this would never have crossed my mind."

"I can't explain it any better than that."

"And will you be at my house as well?"

She shook her head. "He can't know that this was my idea."

"What exactly would you like me to tell him? How shall I explain my sudden urgent desire to see him?"

"I don't know. Think of something! Family business! How can he decline an invitation from the sweela prime?"

Nelson sighed and swung her in a sedate circle. "So what kind of trouble has the boy gotten himself into now?"

How much was it safe to tell Nelson? She had no idea. "I don't want you to repeat anything to Darien."

He actually laughed. "This gets better every moment. I'm not in the habit of confiding in the king—but you must know, Valentina, that I cannot withhold any information that threatens the safety of the realm."

"No—no—nothing like that," she said hastily. "It's just that—it's possible that Sebastian has gotten involved with sirix smugglers, and it seems that tomorrow night Darien plans to round up as many of them as he can catch."

"Ah." They completed a few more measures in silence. "Yes, I can see such an enterprise appealing to that young man. He is so very bright and so very reckless. If that's all it is—"

"It is, Nelson, I swear it." She opened her eyes to their widest and stared up at him, inviting him to look into her soul. "Read my mind."

He patted her back reassuringly. "Oh, your purity of thought shines through even when you think you are being opaque. I have rarely met anyone less likely to lie."

"So you'll do it? You'll invite him over and keep him safe?"

"If I have to kidnap him and lock him in a room. Yes." He spun her under his arm and brought her back into his light embrace. "But I must ask. What is your interest in my nephew?"

"He's not your nephew."

Nelson waggled his head. "They all are, in their way, those fatherless Ardelay children left to grow up on their own. We make light of it—oh, look, more proof of the wild Ardelay behavior!—but I want all of them to know I see their value. I consider myself uncle to all of them and try to make sure they know it."

"That's kind."

"But you still haven't answered my question. What's your interest in Sebastian?"

"He's my oldest friend. I worry about him."

Nelson lifted his eyebrows but didn't inquire further. "With cause, it seems."

"So you'll keep him safe?" she repeated.

"I will."

The orchestra chose that moment to bring the song to a close. Nelson, with typical extravagance, bowed low to Val and kissed her hand. Then he pressed it briefly to his heart and smiled down at her. "Try not to worry," he said.

She smiled but couldn't answer because *I won't* was a lie and *I can't help it* was rude. Anyway, she didn't have a chance to reply because Corene swept up just then. "Dance with me," she said, tugging on Val's hand.

Nelson bowed again and stepped away. Val tried to put Sebastian out of her mind and focus on Corene, but her mind felt fuzzy. "With you? Is that allowed?"

"Well, it's not common, but nobody cares," Corene said, pulling her out onto the ballroom floor where couples were already forming. "Anyway, look, Mirti and Elidon are dancing. And Melissande has already partnered with three different women. Zoe said she'd dance with Beccan except then everyone in the room would solicit her hand and she can't bear the thought."

The orchestra struck up a lively tune, and Val found it was actually a relief to have something to distract her from thinking about Sebastian. So she accepted Melissande's invitation next, and then offers from a few of the young men she'd met earlier in the evening. And the night wore on, and the hour grew late, and some of the guests began trickling out of the ballroom. Elidon was known for staying at any gathering until every last soul had finally left, but Mirti headed for the exit the minute the clock struck two. Val was right on her heels.

When she made it to her room, she collapsed on her bed and stared up at the ceiling, clasping her pendant in her right hand. She could trust Nelson, of course she could. There was no need to worry. Sebastian would be safe.

✻

Firstday again. Most members of the royal family arrived late to the breakfast table, rumpled, yawning, and casually dressed. Zoe looked exhausted and Corene announced she was going back to bed as soon as she'd eaten. Darien appeared as rested and imperturbable as always, which was annoying. Since everyone was too tired to talk, the meal might have been entirely silent except for Natalie's endless questions about what everyone had worn, eaten, and said. Corene and Zoe took turns answering her when they didn't ignore her altogether.

Val toyed with her food and tried desperately to figure out what to do. Firstday. Would Sebastian be waiting for her at the park? She wanted to see him—so much that the longing was almost a physical sensation, a tightness in her bones—but she didn't trust herself. As Nelson had said, she was not capable of lying, and Sebastian knew her expressions better than anyone. He would instantly sense that she was trying to conceal something, he would badger her until she told him everything—and then? Would he sensibly keep away from the site of the greatest danger or would he run headlong toward trouble in a misguided attempt to warn his friends?

Loyalty, that was the blessing that turned up for him over and over. He would ignore the risk to himself to make sure anyone else in his circle was safe. For his own sake, she had to stay away. She had to trust Nelson.

Firstday would be harder to get through than ninthday had been. She wasn't sure she'd be able to bear it.

✻

An hour in the conservatory, wandering through the plants.

Two hours answering correspondence that she had shamefully neglected, which included writing out a lengthy letter to the property manager to remind him of details he could not possibly have forgotten.

Two hours spent with Mirti and Natalie, telling the next hunti prime details about Damon Serlast's life. She found herself growing unexpectedly animated as she described the experience of walking through the forest on a brisk spring day or sleeping under a challinbar tree in the middle of summer.

An hour with Corene lying back in a small boat as Foley poled it around the lake. Since a dozen small watercraft were still tied up at the dock after last night's party, Corene had declared that it would be a pity not to take advantage of them. The princess trailed her hand in the water and half-heartedly splashed Foley at intermittent intervals, but Val just lounged there, relaxing as much as she could, and tried to gauge the time by the angle of the sun.

Surely Nelson's message had reached Sebastian by now. Surely Sebastian was in the house of the sweela prime. Surely all was well.

She should have accepted Nelson's dinner invitation, so she could be *certain*.

But no. Sebastian would have read the guilt on her face. It was better this way.

She believed that up until the minute Nelson arrived at the palace, looking for her.

Chapter Nineteen

The sweela prime strolled into the dining room as the members of the royal family were halfway through an intimate family meal. He looked relaxed and casual as he leaned over to give Zoe a kiss on the cheek.

"I didn't know we were expecting you for dinner," she said.

"You're not," he replied. "I've come to collect Val."

Val had just spooned some more compote onto her plate, but at that, her head jerked up and her heart started a painful pounding. But Nelson seemed so calm, so unconcerned. Surely nothing had gone wrong? She tried to make her tone match his. "I didn't know I was expecting you, either."

"A young friend of mine has come to call and I thought you would enjoy meeting him," Nelson said. "Are you free or should we arrange another time?"

Val stood a little too quickly. Sebastian must have guessed something was amiss and kept interrogating Nelson until he learned Val's part in tonight's activities. He would be angry with her, but she didn't care. "I'm free. There's nothing special planned tonight."

Zoe waved a lazy hand. "Cold collations left over from yesterday's banquet," she said. "I'm sure Beccan has set a much better table."

Corene looked up. "*I'm* free tonight if anyone's asking."

Val expected Nelson to make some easy refusal, but he tilted his head and considered Corene for a moment. "Why don't you join us, then?"

She was immediately on her feet. "Can Foley come?"

"Of course."

In a matter of minutes, the four of them were stepping out of the great front doors, where a small elaymotive idled in the courtyard. Val was surprised to find no chauffeur in the front seat; she couldn't remember the last time she'd seen any of the primes drive themselves around the city.

"It'll be a tight fit, but you two girls can squeeze in the back," Nelson said. "Foley, would you like to take the wheel?"

That got everyone's attention. "Nelson," Corene exclaimed. "What's this all about?"

Val found that, not intending to, she had gripped Nelson's arm. "What's happened to Sebastian?"

"In the car," Nelson said. His open, relaxed air had entirely disappeared. He looked grim and worried.

Foley was already in the driver's seat as the rest of them clambered in. "Where to?"

"The harbor."

"The harbor!" Corene exclaimed as Foley put the car into motion.

Val hitched herself forward to get as close to Nelson as she could. "What's happened to Sebastian?" she repeated.

Corene divided a look between them. "Wait—this is the friend you were talking about? The sirix smuggler?"

"He accepted my dinner invitation, but a few minutes ago I got a note saying he would have to reschedule. I don't know if he somehow learned about tonight's raids, but—"

"Wait," Corene said again. "Raids? Somebody tell me what's going on!"

"Val has learned that Darien is planning an operation at Vernon Harbor tonight to round up people he suspects of being in the smuggling trade," Nelson said. "She's afraid Sebastian will be one of the people caught in the net."

Corene gazed at Val. "And how did you learn this?"

"Someone warned me." At Corene's expression of disbelief, Val added, "I'm not going to tell you who it was because I'm not getting anyone in trouble."

"Is this person even *reliable*?"

"I verified it," Nelson said. "I have my own sources of information." He blew out a hard breath. "And they tell me that some of these operatives are inclined toward drastic violence. If they're cornered, they'll fight."

Corene glanced around the interior of the elaymotive. They were on the Cinque now, which was fairly heavily trafficked as some people returned from their workdays and others set out for their evening's entertainment. Still, Foley guided the car expertly between the other vehicles and kept up a pretty brisk pace. "And you think the four of us can defend ourselves in the middle of a pitched battle," she said.

"That's why you let Corene come," Val realized. "So Foley could protect us."

"I love him, but Foley can hardly fend off a band of hardened criminals!"

Foley spoke up for the first time. "A smoker car has been following us since we hit the Cinque," he said. "I'm guessing Nelson has a few reinforcements of his own."

Nelson grinned. "House guards," he said. "Very loyal. Very well-informed."

Val felt sick. "You can't bring Corene into this," she said. "Darien will murder you."

"I know," he said. "I *would* like to have Foley with me, but I'm leaving the two of you at one of the inns along the road to the harbor."

"Oh no, you're not," Corene said. "You can't possibly think you can dangle an adventure in front of me and then tell me I can't have it."

"There's no way you're leaving me behind," Val said. "If you force us out of the car, we'll just hire another one and follow you."

"I'll choose a location that doesn't rent elaymotives."

"We'll steal one," Corene said. "Jaker showed me how to start one without a key. Jaker's an old friend of Zoe's," she explained to Val. "He taught me *so* many useful things."

"Fine, I'll leave Foley with you to make sure you don't do anything rash," Nelson said.

Foley just shrugged. "I don't tell Corene what to do."

Nelson spread his hands. "But I can't take Val and Corene into the middle of a military operation!"

"Then you shouldn't have come to get us to begin with," Val said.

They argued about it for the rest of the trip around the Cinque. Traffic eased up once they made the turn onto the southern highway just as the sun was beginning to set. As soon as the road opened up, Foley accelerated to a pace that would have been alarming under any other circumstances. But tonight, all Val could think was *Go faster. Go faster.*

"Fine, you can come to the harbor," Nelson finally said when Val estimated they were about two-thirds of the way to their destination. Foley had turned on the smoker car's external headlamp to illuminate the road in front of them, and all the elaymotives passing them in the other direction half-blinded them with their own bright lights. To either side of them, the landscape alternated between swaths of unrelieved darkness and clusters of brightly lit habitation. "But you'll stay in a safe place far from any action while I go out and reconnoiter."

In the brief flash from a passing car, Corene and Val exchanged glances. They both shook their heads. "All right," Corene said. From the front seat, Nelson sighed.

Sooner than Val would have believed possible, they had arrived at the haphazard neighborhood at the edge of the ocean. By night, it was a patchwork of well-lit blocks and pitch-black alleys, with some streets overrun with a mix of impatient business professionals and cheerful revelers, and others completely deserted. Nelson gave Foley succinct instructions about where to turn on the uneven roads, and it was clear he was making his way toward a specific district very near the water. As they wound through the disorganized streets, they saw fewer and fewer people out and about, and those they passed had a hunched and furtive manner. The air was heavy with the scents of saltwater, fish, and intrigue.

Corene leaned forward. "You seem to have a pretty good idea of where you should be going."

"If a person had an interest in buying, say, illegal goods of any kind, the north edge of the harbor is where he would probably go," Nelson replied.

"And *have* you ever bought illegal goods?"

"Maybe. From time to time. Here, Foley. Pull over. That's the place."

They had stopped in front of a tall, narrow brick building that looked simultaneously impregnable and ramshackle, with thick walls, small windows, and a heavily padlocked door. The four of them disembarked as the second elaymotive pulled up behind them. Nelson produced a key and led the way inside.

It was almost too dark to see. This part of town had very few streetlamps and the lone light from half a block away barely filtered in through the grimy windows and open door. Val cast one quick look around. The place was empty except for a couple of desks and chairs and one large metal box that might be a safe. The floor felt gritty under her shoes, and the smell of dust was almost as strong as the scent of the ocean. In the farthest corner, lost in a pool of shadows, was a column of articulated darkness. A stairwell, most likely. The building could easily be four stories tall.

"What is this place?" Corene asked. "And why do you have a key?"

"It's an office where Kayle and I sometimes meet with buyers and sellers who—might prefer unofficial channels."

"Nelson, are *you* a sirix smuggler?" Corene demanded. "Is Darien going to catch *you* in his net tonight?"

"No, no, we're only interested in minerals that are rare in Welce and that Kayle needs for all his inventions. Nothing illegal. Well, not illegal in Welce, anyway."

Foley had stayed at the threshold and was gazing out. "Seems like there might be something going on close to the water," he said. "I can hear a commotion."

Nelson joined him at the door and cocked his head to listen. "All right. My guards and I will head down that way and see if we can find young Sebastian." He turned back toward Corene and Val. "You two will stay here."

"Of course we will," Corene said in a dulcet voice.

Nelson grunted at Foley. "I'm counting on you. I'm leaving you here with them."

Val waited for Foley to reiterate that he didn't give Corene orders, but the guard just nodded. She wondered how concerned Foley would have to be to disregard Corene's commands in order to keep her safe.

"Here," Nelson said, handing something to Foley. "There's a lantern behind the desk. Light it with this, but keep it shielded. You don't want anyone *outside* realizing there's someone *inside*."

He spoke so soberly that for the first time Val acknowledged the possibility that she and Corene could be in significant danger. She'd been so focused on Sebastian that she had barely considered the fact that foolhardy bystanders could be swept up in random violence just as easily as criminals.

"We'll be careful," Foley said.

Nelson grunted again and was gone. The three of them stood motionless, staring at the closed door, listening as Nelson exchanged a few words with his soldiers. They heard the rhythmic tattoo of heavy feet marching away. Then silence.

"All right, let's go after him," Corene said, heading straight for the exit. The knob rattled under her hand, but the door remained firmly shut. She tugged harder, in mounting frustration. "He locked us in! I can't believe it!"

"The sweela prime is not a stupid man," Foley said. Val couldn't be sure, but she thought he might be smiling.

"What are we going to do? Just stand here in the dark, straining to hear the sounds of fighting five blocks away?"

"At least we don't have to be in the dark," Foley said. He was quickly at the desk, retrieving the lantern and lighting a match. A moment later, a warm circle of amber light threw a welcome illumination across the room.

Corene yanked at the heavy door again, suddenly bad-tempered. "I'll kill him."

"Not if Darien kills him first for bringing us here," Val said. She gestured at the corner. "I wonder if those stairs go all the way up. If there's a window on the top floor, we might be able to see down to the waterfront."

Corene started in that direction. "Yes, but it's just as dark outside as it is inside," she pointed out.

"Let's find out."

The metal stairs were flimsy and filthy, tracing a tight switchback route up three more levels. Foley led the way, holding the lantern high enough to illuminate the path for the other two. Val was quickly out of breath, but Corene didn't seem particularly winded. She even laughed.

"Do you know what this reminds me of?" she asked.

Val had no idea, but Foley answered immediately. "The towers in Malinqua."

"That's right! Although this won't be nearly as high."

"Or as dangerous," he retorted.

Corene glanced down at Val, who was bringing up the rear. "There was this tower in the royal city, and at the very top there was an eternal flame. And I got trapped up there when some people were trying to kill me, but Foley saved me. With Nelson's help."

"You saved yourself first," Foley answered.

"Sounds exciting," Val panted.

"Well, I wouldn't want to do it again."

The uppermost room was a cramped, round space with a conical ceiling that disappeared into shadows. Unexpectedly, the walls were almost entirely constructed of windows, providing a complete view of the city laid out around them. The vistas in most directions were primarily of rooftops, chimneys, and the high walls of nearby buildings. But the scene toward the harbor was open and unobstructed since the land sloped down toward the waterfront and most of the nearby structures were squat offices and impermanent shacks. In the patchy illumination of the occasional streetlamp or window, Val could trace the cluttered web of streets as they wound down toward the harbor. She thought she could make out a few broad docks and piers surrounded by small, bobbing boats—and then, beyond them, the grand vast nothingness of the sea.

Corene pressed up against a window. "I can't see anything," she complained.

Foley carefully set the lantern on the floor so its flickering flame didn't outline their bodies and alert passers-by that three people were inside. Then he went to stand on Corene's right side, while Val took a spot on her left.

"Maybe there's nothing to see yet," he said.

Val cupped her hands around her eyes to block out any reflections in the glass. "I think I can make out shapes moving across the docks," she said. "Maybe they're shadows. Or maybe they're people."

"Carrying cargo from ship to shore," Foley responded. "Maybe."

"I wonder where Darien's soldiers are," Corene said.

"I wonder where Nelson is," Val added. *I wonder where Sebastian is,* she wanted to say. How could Nelson possibly find him? The streets were too dark, too labyrinthine, too full of places to hide. Anyone who wasn't apprehended by guards would simply slip away down some lonely alley.

Suddenly, an arc of flame sizzled across the open space right where the boardwalk of the pier met the cobblestone of the street.

"What was that?" Corene demanded.

On her words, one corner of the wooden dock burst into flame. Even from this distance, they could hear shouts and loud noises, as if heavy objects had been hurled against brick or stone. The indeterminate shadows flitting across the pier became more solid, looked more like men fleeing a scene of disaster, aiming for the safety of shore.

They were met by another line of solid forms charging in from the buildings that ringed the dock. Soldiers, Val guessed, rushing forward to contain the smugglers as they attempted to escape the fire. The sounds of distant shouting intensified, augmented by the clanging of metal as weapons engaged. Another sputtering arc of fire traced a graceful line through the night. A small boat at the very edge of the pier was instantly ablaze.

"They're forcing the men off the boats and into their cordon," Foley said. "They'll catch dozens of them."

Corene smashed her face against the window as if she would push herself all the way through it. "But look—I think some are jumping into the water. I see splashes. They'll be swimming away."

Val's throat felt tight. Was Sebastian in the ocean? Could he swim? Or would he have to fight his way through fire only to find himself in the arms of a royal guard? "What about the people who weren't on the boats?" she asked. "The ones who were in the warehouses picking up cargo. Don't you think some of them will escape?"

Foley glanced at her. "Sure." His voice was kind.

Corene's nose was flattened against the glass and her hands were pressed against the pane. "I can't *see*," she said again. "How can the soldiers see? How can the smugglers? How can they tell who they're fighting or where anybody is?"

Foley pointed. "There's a big mass of bodies right off the pier—can you make it out? Hand-to-hand fighting there, I'm guessing. But you're right. I can glimpse a lot of shadows running away, and the soldiers won't be able to catch all of them in the dark."

Another explosion erupted down below, this one appearing to ignite on land, and the shouting was so loud they could hear the alarm in the raised voices. "What happened?" Corene demanded.

Foley shook his head. "I think that was a mistake. One of the smugglers knocked something out of a soldier's hand and it went up in flames. Look—you can see everyone is scattering."

"People are getting away?" Val asked hopefully.

"Or losing track of who's a guard and who's a felon."

"Look! Another blast!" Val cried.

"I think some of the smugglers got hold of a whole bag of explosives, and they're just throwing them everywhere," Foley said somewhat grimly. "That'll change the outcome for sure. It looks like pure chaos down there."

"If only I could *see*."

Almost on Corene's words, the sky bloomed with eerie incandescence. It was as if every light source in the entire neighborhood was suddenly supercharged with fuel—the streetlamps, the sconces in nearby buildings, even torches that fighters had brought into the fray. The blazes on the pier and the burning boat leapt higher, sending sparks shivering into the water and throwing every combatant into sharp relief. There were renewed shouts of triumph and alarm as the soldiers surged forward, suddenly able to perceive every enemy with unimpeded clarity.

"*Nelson*," Corene breathed. The sweela prime had grasped the need for illumination and he had responded with fire.

Val heard herself whimper as she forced herself even closer to the glass. There—that was a ragged form breaking free of the battling crowd and streaking up the slanted street toward safety. But no—his silhouette was too visible in the mystic light, and two soldiers gave chase and quickly brought him down. A second smuggler tried to flee—a third—but each one was apprehended almost immediately, betrayed by the merciless glare.

More men ran, more followed, and the mass of fighters shifted gradually uphill, closer to where Val and her companions watched in varying degrees of horror. A few of the criminals appeared to have slipped through the royal net and, by twos and threes, were charging up the street as fast as their feet would carry them. They couldn't evade the preternatural light, which seemed to have flared over all of Vernon Harbor, but they were putting some distance between themselves and their pursuers.

Val found herself watching a trio that had outdistanced all the rest. All three were clearly intent on hiding their identities, as they wore dark clothing and hooded cloaks that covered their faces. Two of them were supporting a third man between them, clutching his arms and practically dragging him up the hillside. Val wondered if he had been hurt in the skirmish. He looked thin and frail, and he stumbled along as if he could barely keep to his feet. She supposed it was honorable that his fellows would not leave him behind.

Then the slim man slipped, falling to his knees until his companions jerked him upright. The rough handling caused his hood to slip back from his head, exposing his face in the haunted light.

"Melissande!" Val shrieked. "Corene—that's *Melissande!*"

"What? Where? Oh, I see her, I see her—what's she *doing* here? Why is she with these terrible people?"

Val turned and raced for the stairwell, fumbling for footholds in the dark. The other two were instantly behind her, Foley holding the lantern high enough to show them the steps. "She must have snuck down to the harbor tonight to meet someone," Val said over her shoulder. "Someone dangerous. And then when the raid started—"

Foley finished her sentence. "Her contact decided to keep her as leverage in case he got captured. Or maybe he always intended to keep her."

"We have to get out of here," Corene panted. They were almost at the bottom of the stairwell now, all of them trying to descend even faster as they got closer to the ground. "I think I can crawl out one of those windows if we break the glass and I stand on the desk—"

"Nelson gave me a key when he gave me the matches," Foley said.

"*What?*" Corene demanded. "And you kept us *locked up* in here?"

He didn't answer, but Val figured he had probably just shrugged. *What did you think I would do? I'm here to keep you safe.* But there was no time to argue about anything less dire than Melissande's situation. They were downstairs now and running across the floor, Foley pushing past them to shove the key in the lock and throw the door open.

They dashed outside, then paused uncertainly to get their bearings. The light was so strange, a high white ghostly glow that made all the shadows dance and retreat. Solitary shapes pounded past them right up the middle of the street; other figures sidled between the buildings, so thin and slippery they might not even be real.

Foley pointed. "There!" he shouted, charging forward.

Val and Corene followed on faith, but a second later Val could see the three fugitives struggling up the hill. Melissande was staggering like a drunk, and she cried out in pain as one of her captors yanked her forward. In the ethereal light, Val recognized him as the man who had threatened Sebastian's life. Jodar.

Foley was upon them before Jodar or his companion comprehended that trouble might be coming from the other direction. The two thieves let go of Melissande's arms as they braced to confront their attacker, each of them brandishing knives that glinted wickedly in the light. Val had the sudden awful realization that she did not have the flimsiest weapon she could use to defend herself. Foley could not possibly keep them all safe.

But for the moment, Jodar and his friend ignored the women, dropping into fighting stances as they positioned themselves for a coordinated attack on Foley. Val swallowed a sob and followed Corene as she swerved around the combatants and dropped down next to Melissande, who was on her hands and knees and gasping for air.

"Quick—get up—come with us—"

Melissande didn't waste breath on exclamations of surprise, just nodded and took Val's proffered hand. There was a yell from Jodar as he saw Melissande come to her feet, then a heavy *oof* as Foley must have punched him in the gut. Val didn't have time to look, time to worry. She took half of Melissande's weight while Corene took the other half, and they hobbled toward the building they had just abandoned. Behind them, she could hear horrible sounds of bodies colliding, blades engaging, and fists connecting with bone.

Suddenly, booted footsteps pounded toward them as someone else pelted uphill—Val heard a shout and a jostling sound. A hand grabbed her shoulder, and she cried out and spun around, losing her grip on Melissande. A man had come up behind her, dressed in dark heavy clothing like the other smugglers. His face was scarred and sneering.

"Give me the princess," he snarled, snatching at Melissande's arm.

Corene leapt between them, shoving Melissande at Val so hard both of them nearly tripped. "Get her to Nelson's office!" she ordered. Val was stupefied to see a small silver dagger glinting in her hands.

Melissande and Val were clinging to each other, too stunned to move. "No! Corene! You must not!" Melissande called.

"Get back!" Corene shouted, just as the new combatant lunged forward as if to crush her.

Melissande shrieked. Impossibly, Corene pivoted aside and made a quick slashing motion with her hand. Her attacker howled and whirled around, so angry he was practically hissing. Val looked desperately for Foley, but he had his hands full with Jodar, who was battering him with both fists. Jodar's friend stood nearby, bent over nearly double in pain. But still on his feet. Still a threat.

"Corene!" Melissande wailed.

Val clutched Melissande's arm and dragged her backward. "Quickly— that building belongs to Nelson. We'll run in and find something to use as a weapon—"

"I cannot leave her! Let me go!"

Impossible. Val dropped her hand and sprinted toward the door, but an anguished howl from Melissande jerked her around again. Jodar's friend had recovered his breath and was bashing Foley about the head from behind while Jodar tried to kick Foley's legs out from under him. Corene had been shoved to the ground and her attacker loomed over her, dagger poised to strike home.

As one, Val and Melissande started forward. Before they could take two steps, another figure darted out of the shadows and flung itself at Corene's assailant. The force of the impact carried them both to the cobblestones, and they rolled together, punching and clawing at each other's faces. Corene scrambled to her feet and launched herself at Jodar, waving her blade so wildly that he flung his arm up to shield his face. His other hand snaked out and caught Corene's wrist in a grip so brutal she screamed in pain. Her knife clattered to the street.

Melissande wailed again and rushed forward, just as a wave of bodies crested the hill. Val shouted a warning, but a second later she was almost weeping with relief. These were Welchin soldiers, crisp and efficient, and in moments they had the fighters surrounded. Jodar and his companion struggled and cursed as four guards forced them to their knees and bound their arms. Four more soldiers swiftly separated the two men wrestling on the ground—the one who had attacked Corene, and the one who had rescued her. Both men were hauled upright and secured with more rope.

Melissande ignored all of them and ran to where Corene and Foley sat panting in the street. "Corene! Corene! And Foley! Say you are not harmed! Oh, what a dreadful night!"

Corene reached up a hand to draw her down next to them. "We'll be all right. What are you *doing* here?"

Val didn't get a chance to hear Melissande's answer, because at that moment, two more soldiers strode onto the scene. In the unnatural light, Val could see them clearly. One appeared to be a burly middle-aged man with a stern face and an impatient manner. The way everyone snapped to attention, Val assumed he was the captain in charge of this operation. Beside him marched a small but sturdy figure. A woman. Val couldn't tell if she felt relief or misgiving when she recognized Yori the same minute Yori recognized her.

"Someone tell me what's going on here," the captain barked.

Yori didn't say anything, but she looked at Val with her eyebrows raised. Taking only the briefest moment to think about Darien and the absolute fury he would feel as soon as he heard about the events of this night, Val stepped forward.

"I'm Valentina Serlast," she said as coolly as she could. That got the officer's attention; his hawk eyes instantly focused on her face. "And that's Princess Corene."

The captain broke his stare long enough to glance at Corene, then he returned his gaze to Val. "And why are you here, if I may ask?"

Really, lying was so easy when the stakes were so high. "Corene and I learned that a friend of ours was meeting a man down at the harbor tonight and we were afraid she might have made a mistake in judgment. So we followed her, but before we could find her—" She made a shaky gesture and allowed a tremulous note to creep into her voice. "Suddenly there were explosions and fighting. We didn't know what was going on. It was terrifying."

The captain narrowed his eyes. It was clear he didn't believe her, but equally clear he wasn't certain how to proceed when confronted with someone of such high status. *Just wait*, Val thought. "And your friend? Did you find her?"

Val pointed. "As you see. Princess Melissande of Cozique."

At that, both the captain and Yori spun around, gaping. Corene and Melissande had helped Foley up, and the two women were fussing over him enough that Val guessed he had been badly hurt. He was swaying on his feet, and his face was a mass of bruises, but he didn't look like to be in danger of passing out. Melissande appeared to be favoring one arm, but otherwise seemed unharmed. If Corene had taken any injury tonight, she showed no sign.

"The foreign princess," the captain breathed.

"So you see we had no choice."

They both turned to face her again. It seemed incredible, but Val thought Yori might be wearing the slightest smile. "And how did you get to Vernon Harbor?" the captain wanted to know.

Well, everyone in the palace had seen them walking out together, so there was no way to shield Nelson now. She shaded the truth just a little. "In an elaymotive driven by the sweela prime."

The captain couldn't stifle a groan as he briefly lifted a hand to his forehead. No doubt about it now, Yori was grinning.

"Nelson is the one who told us about Melissande," Val added, since that particular falsehood might keep Darien from murdering him.

"Do you know *why* the princess was meeting some questionable contact down at the harbor on the most dangerous night of the quintile?"

"I don't." Time to play the highest trump card she had. "I imagine my brother the king will ask her that very question."

"I imagine he will," the captain said.

Yori jerked her thumb toward the four captives. Three were still arguing and struggling with the guards; the fourth stood quietly, head bowed, weary, a dark hood still over his face. "What do you want to do with this lot? Put them with all the rest, or—"

The captain grunted. "If they were threatening the foreign princess, we'll need to set them aside for extra attention," he said. "Do you recognize any of them?"

"I didn't get a good look yet," Yori said. She turned on one heel to survey the first two. "Oh yeah. Jodar and Korbic. We've seen a lot of them."

"Jodar," the captain muttered. He sounded tired.

Yori made a quarter turn. "And that one—don't know his name, but we've arrested him before. Hey, Serl!" she called to one of the soldiers. "Pull back the cloak on that man's face so I can see it. No, the other one. Yes, that's right—*oh*."

The captain glanced at her in surprise. "Someone else you know?"

"He's one of my informants. I asked him to come down here tonight and mingle with the smugglers to see if he could provide me with any useful information." She raised her voice again. "Serl! Untie him! He's not one of the criminals!"

"So we've got these three to take back with us for a special interrogation," the captain said. He gave Val a long, comprehensive look. "And we need to make sure Valentina Serlast and her companions are also safely returned to the city."

More bodies were moving along the street, and someone clattering up the hill shouted out a question. The ghostlight overhead briefly brightened to a hard glare, then began fading. "I'm guessing that's Nelson," Val said. "We'll go back with him."

Just then, Nelson charged into view, his guards in formation around him. "What's this? What's this? I thought you were safely locked inside!"

"We had to rescue Melissande," Corene answered.

"*Melissande!* Are you—and Foley! My good man, are you hurt? What's been going on here?"

Yori and the captain paid him no attention. "What about your informant?" the captain asked. "Do you want him to ride with us or come in and make a report in the morning?"

Yori said, "We've got enough to handle tonight. I'll let him make his report tomorrow."

"He looks as disreputable as the rest," the captain commented.

Yori grinned again. "That's what makes him a useful spy."

Curious now, Val turned her head to get a good look at Yori's agent. He was rubbing his wrists where the rope had been cut away, and he was beginning to edge back into the shadows as if hoping he could simply disappear before anyone realized he was gone. The eerie light summoned by the sweela prime had dimmed considerably by now, but there was just enough illumination to paint a glow across his slanted cheekbones, coax a note of red from his tousled hair.

He seemed to feel her gaze on him and he turned to meet her eyes for one long, unsmiling moment.

Sebastian.

Val felt her whole body ossify; her lungs became granite in her chest. If someone had knocked her over, she would have crashed to the ground like a marble statue and shattered into a thousand pieces.

Her brain tried frantically to process too many thoughts at once. He was alive; he had survived this wretched night. He had—oh, but he had been the one to save Corene! He had leapt into the fight to save her life, when he could have escaped into the darkness before the soldiers arrived. And now he was caught in Darien's net—except, no, he had been playing a deep, dangerous game, working for Darien all this time—

Sebastian looked away, glanced around, realized none of the guards was paying any attention to him. He inched backward, never looking in Val's direction again. No one stopped him. He took a few more steps, a few more—and then suddenly, with a flare of his cloak, he ducked behind a building and was gone.

Val stared at the spot where he had been and felt her body prickle with heat as her flesh resumed its customary texture. Yori had lied to the captain just as coolly as Val had. Sebastian had not been playing any double role; such a game was completely alien to his nature. Loyalty and authenticity were his watchwords—even if he was loyal to disaster and authentically stupid.

But he had saved Corene.

And Yori had recognized him.

And he was still alive.

Not until she started breathing again did Val realize that she had stopped. Not until her heart began pounding did she realize it had abandoned its work. She folded her knees and simply dropped to the cobblestones and now, when it hardly mattered, she started sobbing.

Chapter Twenty

The return trip seemed endless. It turned out they could not all fit in Nelson's elaymotive, which Foley was too injured to drive anyway. Yori commandeered a troop transport, a utilitarian vehicle without much cushioning, but it was large enough to allow Foley to lie on the floor while Corene knelt solicitously beside him. Melissande and Val sat in cramped, uncomfortable seats that were bolted onto one side of the vehicle and seemed to slam into their spines with every bump in the road. Yori took her place in front with the driver, glancing back now and then to make sure none of them needed anything, but otherwise offering no conversation.

Corene was too focused on Foley, and Val was too weary, to demand explanations of Melissande. The princess didn't appear to be inclined to talk anyway, as she rested her head against the wall and closed her eyes. Her lovely face was pinched with pain or worry, though she had assured Corene she had no need of medical attention. Val supposed that, whatever had brought her to the harbor this evening, her mission remained unfulfilled. It was possible that her night had been even more catastrophic than theirs.

Or maybe, looked at another way, Val's night had not been so terrible after all. Sebastian was alive. He was free. He hadn't had his throat cut by Jodar, and he hadn't been scooped up in Darien's raid. Val could let herself drift down from her state of agonized terror.

So why did she still feel this restless worry along her bones? Why did she have the sense of spiders on her skin? If she could just see him. If she could just talk to him. If she could just explain why she had been avoiding him—but why had she been avoiding him? Why had she been so angry? What would she have done with all that anger if this night had gone another way, if she had found his broken body lying in a gutter behind a harbor alley? The very thought made her blood heat and curdle in her veins, made her want to throw her head back and start screaming.

Instead, she clutched the edge of her uncomfortable seat and only moved when the motion of the transport once more sent her bumping into the walls.

After what seemed like hours, Val saw the lights of Chialto start to form on the horizon. It was so late that most of the buildings were dark, but streetlamps and a few bright windows sketched out the shapes of the boulevards and neighborhoods. Almost home.

Once they crossed the canal and turned onto the Cinque, Corene pulled herself from Foley's side and seated herself across from the other two. "We have to decide what story we're going to tell Darien." She gazed steadily at Melissande. "I mean, Val and I have to decide how we're going to explain ourselves. *You* have to tell him the truth."

Melissande did not bother to open her eyes. "Yes, I have realized that. I will be most explicit with him in the morning."

"He'll want to see you tonight," Corene said.

"He may want to, but he will not." She lifted her eyelids and gave Corene a most somber look. "I must return to my hotel tonight. It is imperative. But I swear to you I will come to the palace tomorrow and explain everything."

Corene looked unconvinced. "I think Darien would say that, even if you keep your secrets until the morning, you would be safer at the palace tonight. I think he would want me to insist."

Yori had half-turned in her seat as soon as they started talking. "Don't worry about it," the guard said. "We'll leave a full detail at her hotel tonight. No harm will come to her."

Melissande turned a reproachful glance in Yori's direction. "You want to make certain that I do not disappear into the night."

Yori grinned. "That too."

"All right," Corene said. "You come to the palace in the morning. *Don't* tell Darien anything until we're in the room! You owe us that much."

"I do indeed."

Corene looked at Val. "Now. How do we explain how *we* ended up at the harbor?"

Val liked the lie she had already come up with. "Nelson told us Melissande was in danger. We had to go look for her."

"How did *he* know?"

"He's the sweela prime. When he danced with her at the changeday ball, he sensed that she was preoccupied and afraid. He had some of his men follow her and learn what they could."

"Yes, but why did he tell us and not Darien?" Corene objected.

"He thought we might be able to persuade her not to go. But once we got to the hotel, she had already left."

"That works," Corene decided.

Yori spoke up again. She sounded amused. "You realize I'm going to tell the king the truth."

Corene faced her. "Really? And why do *you* think we went to the harbor tonight?"

Yori's eyes were on Val's face. "I don't know, but I'm guessing it had something to do with that young man."

"What young man? Sebastian? We didn't even find him."

"He found us," Val said in a constricted voice. "He's the one who came to your aid when that man was about to stab you."

"That was *Sebastian*? You never said!" Corene looked around. "So where is he?"

"Yori told the captain he'd been working as her informant, and they just let him leave."

"He's been spying for Darien all along? Every time I think I know what's going on, something else happens!"

Now Val was watching Yori. The guard glanced at her driver and glanced away, but Val was able to interpret the swift action. Yori had lied to her captain, but she would just as soon not have someone else report that fact to her superior officer. Well, Val owed her an immense debt. Another fib was a very small downpayment. "I was surprised, too," she said.

Yori grinned and turned her face forward again.

Fifteen minutes later, they were dropping Melissande off at her hotel, where Val could spot a swarm of Welchin soldiers awaiting her. In another fifteen minutes, the transport was straining up the hill toward the palace. Its solid bulk loomed out of the shadows, discernable only because of a few strategically placed lights along the entrance and the roofline. The vehicle hadn't even come to a halt before half a dozen figures hurried out of the front door—staff or soldiers, Val couldn't be certain in the dark.

"I suppose you sent someone ahead of us to alert Darien," she said to Yori.

"I suppose I did."

On the words, the back doors of the transport were drawn open and two men stuck their heads in. "Is the wounded guard back here? Yes? All right, someone bring a litter."

Corene and Val climbed out first, but Corene instantly turned around to supervise Foley's extraction. Yori stood back and watched. Val approached her and spoke in a low voice.

"It's not true, is it? About Sebastian."

"No."

"Then why did you say it?"

Yori considered. "Sometimes the truth does more harm than a lie. And we'd already rounded up the major players. We could let the small ones go."

"He's not a bad person. He's *not*."

"That's what I'm hoping. If he is—" Yori shrugged. "Sooner or later, it will catch up with him. I know what it means to teeter on the edge. Sometimes it doesn't take much to push you to one side or the other."

"Thank you."

Yori smiled, but in the dim light her face looked serious. "Maybe you have to be the one to give him that push."

"I've—never tried to do that with anyone."

"Maybe it's time to figure out how."

Val nodded dumbly and turned to find Corene. She must have already followed the phalanx of soldiers into the great hall, because none of them were anywhere in sight. Instead, a still and solitary figure stood in the doorway, a backlit silhouette of a patient, inexorable presence. Val couldn't see his face, but she didn't have to. Darien.

He was not the kind of man to rant and rave, to yell, to wave his arms. He simply said, "Come up to my office and explain everything."

※

Corene was waiting for them in his office. So was Zoe, who looked rumpled and tired, but not particularly upset. She was also arranging cups and plates on a small side table, and Val suddenly realized she was famished. She'd eaten only half her dinner, and the night's exertions had drained her body of all its reserves.

Corene was already at the table, taking a huge bite of bread and jam. Val had swallowed a slice of fruit before she even sat down. Zoe and Darien seated themselves, and the room seemed, for a moment, ominously quiet.

"So," Darien said in an even voice. "Tell me what you did. And why."

Corene talked around a mouthful of food. "We knew something was wrong with Melissande. She'd been evasive about how she planned to spend some of her time. But I thought she was just—" Corene shrugged. "Carrying out diplomatic duties that had nothing to do with us."

"Then Nelson danced with her at the ball and said he could sense something was wrong," Val took up the tale. "He had some of his house guards follow her. When she left for the harbor, he came to get us."

Darien rested his gaze first on his sister, then on his daughter. "Why the two of you? Why not me?"

"Because you lack subtlety," Corene said with great zest. "He thought she might talk to us when she wouldn't talk to you."

Darien's face was impassive. "Whose idea was it to follow her all the way to the harbor?"

"Mine," Corene said. "Nelson didn't want to take us, because he suspected that Melissande might be in some kind of trouble. But Val and I said we'd go without him if he tried to leave us behind. And we would have."

"That's the first thing you've said that I believe."

"Oh, really?" Corene demanded, instantly on the offensive. "Then why do *you* think we were down at the harbor tonight?"

"That's what concerns me. I have no idea."

"Well, we *did* go to the harbor and we *did* find Melissande," Val said.

"And we saw her being *kidnapped*," Corene added. "So we rescued her."

Darien nodded politely, making no attempt to hide his incredulity. "And did she explain to you what reason had taken her to the waterfront tonight?"

"Well, you have to understand, things were very jumbled just then," Corene said. "Foley had practically been killed! So we were trying to save him, too, and then your guards arrived, and then Nelson came back—"

"Came back?" Darien interjected. "He had left you alone somewhere in the harbor streets?"

Corene eyed him, silently mulling over her response. Val had a sudden vivid memory of the tumultuous times that had gripped Chialto when she lived in the city eight years ago. When Zoe had been revealed as the coru prime. When one of her first actions from her new position of power had been to rescue the sweela prime—her uncle Nelson—from a disgrace that had kept him estranged from the king for nearly a decade. Surely Darien would not—could not—banish Nelson again for his role in tonight's disaster.

"He locked us in some squalid office that he and Kayle have down near the docks," Val said, hoping her voice sounded indignant. "He said we would be safe."

"We didn't want to be *safe*," Corene added, picking up the cue. "We wanted to find Melissande. It took us forever to break the lock."

Val thought Darien infinitesimally relaxed. Zoe glanced at him, but didn't offer a comment. "So you rescued the princess," he said, returning to the main story. "What explanation did she give for her presence there?"

Corene shook her head. "She wouldn't say. But she agreed to come here in the morning and tell you everything."

"You don't have a clue?"

Corene looked troubled. "We found her with some men that your soldiers arrested for being sirix smugglers. But I can't imagine—" She shrugged. "Why would a Coziquela emissary need to obtain sirix illegally? It makes no sense."

"Nothing about this evening makes any sense," Darien said. "Beginning with Melissande's actions and continuing with your own."

Val let a little raw emotion seep into her voice. The distress was genuine, even if the words weren't. "We didn't have any reason to think we'd be in danger. We didn't realize there would be some kind of *war* down on the waterfront where we could have been *killed*."

"My dears, we have been so worried," Zoe said gently. "Tonight of all nights—!"

"Well, maybe if Darien would ever tell people what he had planned, people wouldn't accidentally stumble into his disasters," Corene said with supreme unfairness.

Darien's mouth tightened. "I cannot promise to be more forthcoming in the future, but perhaps I can ensure your safety by taking steps to keep you contained whenever I have organized anything of a hazardous nature—that will be carried out *miles* from you in a location you could never be expected to visit for any reason whatsoever at that particular hour."

Corene was completely unimpressed. "Of course, you've never successfully locked me up before, and you have *no idea* how much danger I've been in when I've been visiting half the countries in the southern seas, but certainly, go ahead and try to *contain* me."

Zoe reached over and placed a hand on Corene's arm. "Just because he knows you are an independent adult, just because he knows you have led an adventurous life in the past two years, doesn't mean that he can't be worried about you every single minute. The two things are not incompatible."

"In fact, I should have expected Corene to be squarely in the middle of trouble," Darien said. "It's Valentina who surprises me. She usually behaves so sensibly."

She came to her feet, suddenly filled with a boiling rage. "What do you know about me and who I am and how I behave?" she demanded. "Have you even spent a whole nineday in my company over the past eight years? How could I expect you to worry about my safety when you've barely seemed to remember that I'm alive? I'm fine, Darien—I can take care of myself. I've been doing it for years. I certainly wouldn't rely on *you* if I was looking for someone to watch over me."

She swept from the room, not quite so blinded by tears that she couldn't see the shock on all three of their faces. Even Darien, who never let his composure slip, looked both astonished and stricken. She didn't care. She didn't turn back. She didn't apologize. She just ran out the door and down the hall and into her room, where she threw herself on her bed and sobbed until she thought her body would crack from the pressure of the pain.

But Sebastian was alive. It was the only thing that allowed her to finally uncurl and calm down and close her eyes and sleep. At least she wouldn't have to spend the rest of her life without Sebastian in it.

Chapter Twenty-One

V AL IS TWENTY-ONE.
She and her mother have been living near Aunt Jenty for almost two years, and the lives of the households are inextricably intertwined. Jenty and her husband are the foremost landowners in the area, so Jenty is the most prominent hostess, a responsibility she takes seriously. She holds formal entertainments two or three times per quintile and casual lunches and dinners almost every nineday. Val and her mother are part of every event and have become fixtures on the social scene themselves. Merra relishes the role with her entire torz being, but Val only tolerates it. She knows how to be polite and she has learned how to pretend she is interested in someone else's conversation, but she still finds the necessity for subterfuge abhorrent.

"Don't think of it as *lying*," Saska tells her one evening as they help each other dress for a summer dinner. "Think of it as being kind. Maybe the young man you're talking to is feeling uncertain and insecure, and he's just hoping he's not going to make a fool of himself. And if you smile and nod, he will start to feel more confident. You are supporting him. A hunti person lives to provide support, right? The great challinbar tree that holds together the world."

Saska is eighteen and a lack of confidence is not her issue. She is a quicksilver well of radiance, interested in everyone and everything, but not for long—charming, delightful, and easily bored. She has taken up and discarded passions for horses, dogs, roses, literature, music, and too many other subjects for Val to keep track of. An incorrigible flirt, she has broken more than a few hearts in their neighborhood, though no one seems to bear her any ill will.

Val finds Saska's coru ways utterly mystifying, but her cousin remains one of her favorite people. And, indeed, Saska's advice has always helped Val manage better in the world, so she takes this instruction to heart. "All right. That's how I'll try to think of it when I'm talking to some dull man over dinner."

"Maybe you'll be partnered with someone who isn't dull," Saska teases. "I know who's on the guest list. There's someone you'll like."

Val sighs. For the last year, Jenty has been inviting eligible young men to all her parties and making sure Val has a chance to meet them. Like Merra, Jenty believes that the best spouse is a torz spouse, so most of these eligible bachelors have been sons of local landowners or young farmers running their own properties. To a man, they have all been earnest and solid and prosperous, and Val is certain they would make ideal husbands. But so far, she has found herself unmoved in their presence. She has never expected to make a marriage of great passion, but she has always assumed she will feel an easy affection for her spouse. If she can't generate such a response, she is beginning to think, she might be better off not marrying at all.

"I do appreciate Aunt Jenty's efforts," she said. "But her matchmaking doesn't seem to be doing me much good."

Saska sets a final clip in Val's dark hair. "Oh, this isn't someone you'll want to *marry*," she says. "Just someone you will enjoy."

Val doesn't believe it until they head to the parlor where the guests will gather, and she sees who is chatting with her mother. "Sebastian!" she exclaims, running over to fling her arms around him. "You didn't tell me you would be visiting Jenty!"

He returns the hug with enthusiasm. "How very fashionable you look! Your hair is particularly nice."

"Saska did it for me. What are you doing here? How long are you staying?"

"I'm making business inquiries for my father."

She draws him to one side of the room so they can talk privately. "Your father? I thought you weren't speaking to him."

He makes an uncertain motion with his hand. "We got back in touch, talked a few things out. He's running a new enterprise and asked if I would join him."

She remembers that she is supposed to be supportive, but this is not something she can endorse with a nod and a smile. "Don't you remember how his last business venture turned out? He went bankrupt and all his creditors lost money."

"I know, but this one is different. He's running a transport service between one of the northern mines and the harbor outside of Chialto. Supplying ore that Kayle Dochenza needs for his elaymotives. When sales take off, my father says we'll be rich."

"Where did he get the money to start the business?"

"He has investors."

"You're not one of them, I hope." When he doesn't answer, she frowns. "Sebastian! You didn't give him any money, did you?"

"I don't *have* any money."

"Did you take out a loan?"

He laughs and grabs her hands to give them a reassuring squeeze. "You worry too much! Everything is fine. Tell me about you! Saska says Aunt Jenty is introducing you to all the most promising young men of the northern provinces. That sounds exciting."

"It isn't, though," she says gloomily. "I thought torz men would be more interesting than they actually are."

"Oh, now. I always thought you wanted some respectable, settled man with a large property and sizable income. And it turns out that's not the case?"

She is instantly antagonized. "I wanted to marry a torz man because I thought he would be steady and reliable and *kind*. I didn't care about money."

"It's hard to be steady and reliable without money."

"Maybe. But you can be kind if you're poor."

"Not in my experience," he says cynically. "If you're poor, you're always scheming to find the next meal or the next bed. You don't care who else gets hurt as long as *you're* well-fed and off the streets."

That catches her attention. "Are you in trouble?" she asks directly. "Are you hungry?"

He squeezes her hands again, and then drops them. He is smiling, but she recognizes the expression as a mask. "Tina, Tina, don't worry about me! I have never been starving in the streets! I am too creative for that."

"You know Aunt Jenty would let you stay here. And my mother and I would always take you in."

"I don't want anyone to *take me in*. My life is an adventure and I am enjoying it very much."

She wants to press the issue, but she knows better. Too much questioning makes Sebastian edgy, too much concern makes him irritable. She hunts for a way to change the subject. "So what kinds of adventures are you having that are so enjoyable?"

His eyes glint as he considers her. "We-ellll...I suppose Saska has told you about some of my romantic entanglements."

Val endures a spike of jealousy so strong it feels like physical pain. That Sebastian would confide in *Saska* instead of her! The two have always been close, growing up almost like brother and sister, but Val has always believed she is the only one Sebastian truly trusts. It feels like the worst kind of betrayal to discover someone else knows some of his secrets. She hopes her voice sounds light and playful. "Romantic entanglements! More than one? No, Saska has kept those details to herself."

He laughs. "It turns out city girls are much freer with their affections than girls in the country," he says. "Show a woman some attention, buy her a trinket or two in the Plaza, and a man can have a pretty good time."

She can't let a comment like that pass unquestioned. "But Sebastian—you're not raising false hopes with these women, are you? You're not making them think you are falling in love? That would be so unfair. So unkind."

"No, no, trust me, Tina. Everyone is playing, and everyone knows it.

These are girls who want to have a good time but are far from ready to settle down." A note of mockery creeps into his voice. "And if they *were* thinking of marrying and starting a family, they wouldn't pick *me*. A penniless bastard who lives on his wit and charm? Hardly a good catch."

"It still seems like a dangerous game," she says. "*You* might fall in love, while *she* is still playing, and then where would you be?"

"I would be exactly where I am now, which is heart-whole and fancy-free," he says firmly.

"I still think you should be careful."

He makes a scoffing sound. "*You* will be married before *I* am."

She sighs. "Lately I am not so sure of that."

"You simply have to overcome all your ridiculous hunti rules."

"I don't have rules!"

"Requirements, then."

"And anyway, they're not ridiculous."

He counts off on his fingertips. "He has to be torz. He has to be older than you. He has to be a respectable member of the community. He has to have a good heart. Does he need to have a certain height and hair color, too? I'm not sure I ever asked."

She is so annoyed that she finds it hard to believe she'd been so excited to see him when she first walked in. "Of course not! I am open to meeting anyone. But I do think our chances of happiness would be better if he met certain standards. I would think any thoughtful man would also have standards for the woman he wants to marry."

"That just proves I'm not a thoughtful man," Sebastian answers. "I think any woman has the potential to be delightful. And I hope to have the chance to prove it dozens of times over the course of my life."

She isn't sure how to reply to that, but fortunately Saska descends on them just then. "Val! You're supposed to be mingling with the guests. Sebastian, come with me. One of our old neighbors was asking about you and he wants to know how you're doing."

The two of them move off, already laughing and talking together. Val allows herself a moment to calm her irritation before she summons a smile and steps up to greet one of the guests, an older women who owns a shop in the nearest town. She has rarely felt less sociable, and she's sure the visitor will sense her coldness, but in fact the other woman doesn't seem to realize that anything is amiss. Val isn't sure if she is a better actress than she had always believed, or if most people are simply too self-involved to notice when someone else is distant or struggling. The thought turns her even cooler.

Therefore, she is quite surprised when, twenty minutes through the meal, her dinner companion asks her if something is wrong. He is a man in his early thirties, not particularly tall, a little stocky, with dark hair already beginning to thin in the back. She has met him once or twice when he has been in the area visiting his parents, but he lives fifty-some miles away on his own property. She can't remember all the details, but she does recall that he owns a small business and his mother is proud of him.

"I don't mean to be rude," he says in an apologetic voice. "But you seem so quiet. I wondered if you had a headache."

"No—I'm the one who's being rude," she says. "Someone made me angry earlier, and it's made me disagreeable! I apologize."

His smile is tentative but sweet. "Well, if this is you being angry and disagreeable, I have to say I'm not very impressed. You should be throwing objects around the room! Yelling at the servants!"

She thinks he is joking but she's not sure. "Is that how you behave when you're in a temper?"

"Oh, no. I tend to find displays of rage a waste of time and energy. I'm more likely to utter a few curt words and then walk away so I can consider my next course of action."

"Which would be what?"

"Deciding how important the quarrel is. Can I shrug it off as something trivial? Do I need to request a longer discussion when we're both calmer so we can figure out how to fix whatever went wrong? Might I need to end the relationship altogether? Sometimes the answer is obvious. Sometimes it takes a little time."

She toys with her glass of fruited water. She likes his answer. "I usually mull it over to decide what I think went wrong. And if it doesn't seem important, I forget about it. And if it does, I do what I can to avoid that person in the future." She takes a sip. "People say I can be inflexible, but I *try* to see all sides before I make a decision."

He smiles. "Sounds like you might be a hunti woman."

"I am. You?"

"Torz."

Six months later, they are engaged.

Chapter Twenty-two

Despite the fact that she had gone to bed so late, Val woke up while dawn was still balancing indecisively on the horizon, trying to decide whether or not it would actually tip over into morning. *Sebastian,* she thought, and climbed out of bed.

In terms of dressing for the day, she didn't do much more than brush her hair and make sure the tunic she pulled from the armoire was clean. She was already wearing her new pendant, of course; she hadn't taken it off since she put it on. A pair of shoes and she was ready to go.

She was hungry enough to consider swinging by the breakfast room to see if food was already laid out, but since the only person who was likely to be up at this hour was Darien, she decided it wasn't worth the risk. Therefore, she had to listen to her stomach grumble as she took her seat on the big public transport that had conveniently pulled up in the courtyard to drop off the morning workers. She thought she could ignore it for an hour or two, and she stared determinedly out the window as the elaymotive lurched into gear and began its descent. Twenty minutes later, as the ungainly vehicle lumbered through the Plaza of Women on its circuit of the Cinque, she changed her mind. She hopped off at the first stop and visited the closest food stalls she could find.

Well, who knew how long it would be before she found Sebastian? She better buy enough to get her through the day. She purchased two loaves of bread, some fruit, a wrapper of nuts, and a canvas bag to carry them all. Ten minutes later she paid way too much for a decorative container of fancy fruited water, because what if she got thirsty and couldn't find another vendor? She had no idea what the day would hold.

Once she'd gathered all her supplies, she didn't have to wait long until the next omnibus wheezed into view. It was older, creakier, dingier, and much more crowded than the first one. No seats were available, so she stood in the aisle, the canvas bag over her shoulder, her hand wrapped around a greasy railing. She didn't feel particularly impatient as the vehicle traveled and paused, traveled and paused, as it made its laborious way around the city, and she wondered why that was. As if checking her body for wounds, she investigated her mind for turmoil.

Nothing there but hard, implacable determination. She had to see Sebastian. Until she laid eyes on his face, she wouldn't worry, wouldn't scheme, wouldn't analyze, wouldn't debate her best course of action. There was nothing in her head at all except the desire to find him.

Only then would she start thinking.

The transport made its cautious turn around the bottom loop of the Cinque and began its journey east. Two more stops, and it was time for Val to disembark. She hefted the bag over her shoulder and hiked toward the park.

She had no idea how likely it was that Sebastian would meet her there. By this point, he had probably given up expecting her to make their regular rendezvous—which would have been yesterday, in any case. But she decided she would wait here a couple of hours before she went looking elsewhere. She had an address for him, but Sebastian changed locations as often as an alley cat, so he might easily have moved during the time she'd been in Chialto. But if he didn't come to the park, she'd try the apartment next. Then she'd go to the restaurant where she and Corene had sipped their illegal sirix and see if the proprietor would divulge his supplier's whereabouts. After that—well, after that, she didn't know. She'd figure something out.

The walk wasn't long, but the bag was unexpectedly heavy, and the crisp morning air was already showing signs of a sullen heat. Val switched the strap to her other shoulder as she arrived at the tree-lined perimeter of the park. Ducking her head to clear the lowest branches, she stepped into the cool green circle.

Sebastian was sleeping on the sweela bench, wrapped in a tattered black cloak, his red head pillowed on a lumpy pack. His right hand rested on his chest, loosely grasping the hilt of a dagger so he would be ready to fight if danger woke him abruptly. His face showed an assortment of cuts and bruises, and one of his eyes was puffy. But his breathing was steady and untroubled. None of his arms and legs appeared to be broken. He was alive.

She stood there a long time just looking at him. The strangest little prickling bubbles started collecting under her skin, at the bends of her elbows, at the backs of her knees, and then spread through her veins like a hiss of heat. She felt her cheeks flush and her fingers tingle; she almost thought her hair was standing on end. It was the oddest feeling. She didn't understand it.

She was caught wholly by surprise when she dropped her bag to the ground and began weeping into her hands.

Through the clamor of her own sobbing, she heard a smaller commotion—a body turning, boots hitting the ground, an exclamation and an oath.

Then a swirl of motion and suddenly she was enveloped in warmth and cloth and darkness. Sebastian had taken her into his arms, under the shelter of his black cloak.

"Tina, Tina, Tina!" he chanted, his voice hoarse. "Oh, my love, I'm so sorry! Don't cry, don't cry—we'll sort it all out—"

She was sobbing so hard she could hardly force the words out. "I thought you might—you might *die* and you—I hadn't even talked to you for so long—and I—and then you—and I don't *know!* I don't know what to do about anything—"

For a moment, she felt his arms tighten around her, then he scooped her off her feet and carried her back to the red bench, cradling her against his body. She had thrown her arms around his neck, and now she buried her face in his shirt and wept into the soft cotton. She could feel small metal buttons dig into her cheek, feel the fabric grow damp against her skin. Could hear Sebastian repeating her name over and over, with infinite patience, infinite tenderness.

Oh, my love, I'm so sorry.

Had he really said that?

Finally, her tears slowed, her ragged breaths became more even. She still had her eyes pressed against his shirt, but she could feel him bending his head over hers, feel his hand smoothing down her hair, stroking her cheek, tucking itself under her chin.

"Better now?" he said, lifting her head. "Ready to talk?"

She stared into his eyes and felt some of her flat determination return to stiffen her spine. "Why did you go down to the harbor last night?"

He dropped his hand and stared back at her. "Why did *you?*"

"Because you were not safely at Nelson's house."

He shook his head. "I don't understand. What was your part in this whole misadventure?"

"Someone told me there was going to be a raid at the harbor on firstday night. I didn't want—"

"Wait, who told you that?"

"I don't think I'm supposed to tell anyone." He looked like he might make a stormy rejoinder, so she hurried on. "I didn't want you to get caught, so I asked Nelson to invite you over—"

"Why didn't you come to *me?*"

"Because I thought you would go to the harbor anyway and warn your friends. Which you obviously did."

"I couldn't let them walk into a *trap!*"

"How did you find out about it?"

He looked affronted. "I'm not telling you if you're not telling me."

She assumed some other royal guard had friends among the smugglers and had dropped a timely word. Not that it mattered. "So when Nelson told me you weren't with him last night, I insisted on coming to look for you."

"He had no right to bring you someplace that he knew would be so dangerous."

She just looked at him. "I would have gone by myself if he hadn't taken me, and he eventually figured that out."

"Well, then, you would have been stupid," he said roughly. "A woman like you running around in the middle of street fights and fire bombs—"

She pulled back just a little. "Then you were equally stupid, because it was just as risky for you," she said.

"Maybe, but at least this is the life I have chosen. You were just—"

"And *why* is this the life you have chosen?" she interrupted, suddenly and completely furious. "Living in the shadows, living outside the law, making deals with *criminals*, risking your life every day, and *why*? For *what*?"

"Because it's fun," he shot back. "It's exciting. I like to see how much smarter I am than the people who try to stop me."

"Well, you're not, are you? You could have been arrested last night—"

He leaned forward till their faces were inches apart. "Oh, no, I had already escaped the net," he said. "I was safely on my way out of the battle zone, when I saw *you* and your frirends wrestling with killers in the street. You think you came down to the harbor to save me? I had to save *you!* If I'd been snared in the raid, it would have been your fault."

"I guess you should think about that the next time you try to throw your life away," she flashed back. "Ask yourself, 'Do I want Val unexpectedly showing up in the middle of this nonsense?' And if you don't, maybe you shouldn't do it. Because if you keep doing stupid things, I'm going to keep trying to stop you."

He made a sound of frustration. "It's not your job to watch out for me."

She lifted her hands and slammed them against his shoulders. "I was *terrified* for you!" she cried. "I thought you would *die!* Do you even understand what that *means*? Do you know what it's like to be so afraid for someone else that you can't even *think* about yourself?"

"What do you think I was feeling last night?" he demanded. "When I saw you and your friends in a knife fight with *Jodar* and his men? I know my heart stopped beating! Tina, why did you—"

She hit him a second time, harder, feeling the tears unexpectedly rise again. "I can't *live* in a world that you're not in, Sebastian!" she wailed. "How can you not understand that?"

A moment longer he stared at her, his eyes so close to hers there was nothing else to see. Then he crushed her against him and brought his mouth down hard on hers.

It was the first time he had ever kissed her, and yet it seemed like the thousandth time. It felt so familiar, so essential, so much a part of her day-to-day existence that she could not survive without it any more than she could survive without air. She could not remember a time in her life that did not include Sebastian kissing her. She could not imagine a future without such a thing. The world reordered itself, or maybe it finally revealed the patterns it had held all along. The kiss lasted nearly forever.

Finally, slowly, Sebastian pulled away, then leaned in again to rest his forehead against hers. "Well," he said, "this complicates things."

She found herself surprised. "Do you think so? It seems to make everything simpler. Or at least clearer."

He strangled a laugh. One of his hands stayed wrapped around her waist, the other came up to toy with her hair. Their foreheads were still touching. His eyes looked huge. "Oh, Tina, I do love you. But I've never known what to do about that."

She was surprised again. "You mean, you've known before today? Before right now?"

He laughed again. "Yes. I've always known."

"But you never said!"

"It seemed to be a pointless confession. You had made it clear I was not a candidate."

She pulled back enough to be able to see his whole face. "I never said that!"

His soft laugh was rueful. "Well, you were very specific about your determination to marry some settled, sober, mature torz landowner. What part of that description suggests Sebastian Ardelay?"

"Yes, but I didn't think I would *love* him."

He traced his thumb along her cheekbone. "And you think you love me?"

"Of course I do. Apparently, I always have. Or I would feel different."

She wasn't sure why that was amusing, but he seemed to be struggling to contain mirth. "And you don't feel any different since I kissed you?"

"No! Except that now I understand things. It's like—" She wasn't sure how to put it into words. "It's like when I was a little girl, and I was looking around the room and I could see these halos around the windows and the furniture and even my hands when I held them up. And everything just felt strange and when I walked across the room I was dizzy enough to fall down. And my mother found me and said I had a fever. And I thought, 'Oh! I'm sick! *Now* it makes sense!'"

He dropped his face into his hand and started laughing uncontrollably. Val tugged at his shoulder. "Why? Why is that funny?"

Sebastian lifted his head, but he couldn't stop laughing. "You're comparing me to a *disease!*"

"No, I'm just trying to explain."

"And you're doing a most excellent job of it."

"But I don't think you're telling the truth when you say you've always known you loved me."

"Oh, you have to tell me why."

"Because you said so! Well, you said you were never going to marry anyone. Don't you remember? We were sitting in the challinbar tree, and you said you never wanted to marry anyone because you didn't want to be tied down to one place."

"I was *thirteen*."

"You said you would never change your mind."

"I didn't say I wouldn't fall in love. I just said I didn't want to be married."

Val leaned back even more, suddenly troubled. "And have you changed your mind about that?"

Sebastian's laughter had faded, to be replaced by a rueful smile. He stroked her cheek again, as if something about the texture of the skin or the shape of the bone beneath it was mysteriously delightful. "And that's why this is so complicated."

"So you *don't* want to marry me."

He gestured at his body. "Tina, I'm a thief, a smuggler, a small-time criminal, a landless *bastard* with no prospects! You're the daughter of a prime and the sister of the king! No one in the entire country of Welce would consider that a good match."

She nodded slightly, then shrugged. "All right."

"All right what?"

"All right, it doesn't matter. I don't care about getting married."

Another one of those sounds that was half-laugh, half-groan. "So—what? How do you envision moving on from this moment? You return to your farm, I return to my illicit ways, and we meet for the occasional assignation?"

"Well, I haven't thought that far ahead—because I hadn't thought of this *at all*," she said. "So I don't know! Our lives are very different, but they've *always* been different." She put her hands around the back of his head and pulled him close enough to give him a quick kiss. It had been too long since that other one, that first one, that millionth one. "And we've always managed. We've always stayed connected. It will be different now, but we'll figure it out."

He rested his head against hers again. His expression was somewhere between unconvinced and admiring. "How are you so calm?" he said. "How is this not the cataclysm for you that it is for me? I look ahead and all I see are obstacles and impossibilities, but you—the world is remade but you're walking around in it like this is the way you always remembered it."

"Not the way I remembered it," she said. "The way it was always supposed to be."

"That's my hunti girl," he said. "Once you've discovered a truth, it's an absolute."

"Of course. And the truth is I love you."

He kissed her again, bending her slightly backward with his urgency. His mouth left hers, began traveling along her cheekbone, down her jaw, up to her ear. His hands began roving, caressing first the undulating topography of her spine, then the curved keyboard of her ribs. Everywhere his body touched hers, she felt again that spike of heat, that intoxicating rush of bubbles just beneath the skin.

His mouth returned to hers. "I feel," he whispered against her lips, "I believe we should go someplace more private than a park in the middle of the city."

"Yes," she murmured back. "How close is your apartment?"

He made a despairing sound. "Ugh. It's a disaster. I wouldn't even bring a smuggler back there if I was trying to swindle him."

"Well, we can hardly go to the palace."

He choked on another laugh. "No."

"There must be a hotel nearby."

"That's so tawdry."

"Not if we pick a *nice* one."

"Even so. Tina—"

She kissed him. "Nothing matters except a chance to be with you," she said. "Everything else just—falls away."

He seemed to be thinking rapidly. "All right. There's a place—back up toward the Plaza of Women. It's respectable but caters to a lot of foreign guests, so the management isn't too picky. Let's go there." He inspected her for a moment. "Although—will someone recognize you? I would think enterprising business proprietors would know what the king's sister looks like."

She stood up, tugging at his hand. "Sebastian. I'm not some frail teenage girl who has to be protected from scoundrels. I'm a grown woman who has been managing her own life for *years*. I can sleep with any man I choose."

He allowed her to pull him to his feet. "Yes, but—the last thing I want to do is damage you, even if I'm just harming your reputation."

She drew him toward the exit, pausing to pick up her fallen bag of eclectic food. At the moment, she was too full of elation to feel hunger, but who knew how long they would be at the hotel? Best to bring supplies. "I hope you're not under the impression I'm a virgin," she said as they ducked under the canopy of branches and headed toward the Cinque. They were still holding hands.

"No, of course not!" he said. "But I'm glad to hear it. I wouldn't want to add that sin to all the others the king will lay at my door."

"My brother has absolutely nothing to say about my life," she replied. She remembered the last words she had flung at Darien when she stormed out of his office last night. *I certainly wouldn't rely on you if I was looking for someone to watch over me.* "Just like I have nothing to say about his."

"He might see it differently."

"Let's just leave Darien out of our conversation for the rest of the day," she suggested. "Let's only talk about us."

He laughed. "I can agree to that. But speaking of virgins—I hope you don't have any illusions about *me* when it comes to that condition."

"Sebastian," she said calmly, "I have never had any illusions about you at all."

The hotel was solidly built, only mildly fashionable, with a small kierten, an efficient middle-aged woman running the front desk, and plenty of vacancies. Their room was on the second floor, with a view of a narrow alley and the brickwork of the professional building next door. It contained a bed, a dresser, two chairs, and bathing facilities.

It held the whole world.

"I didn't think your body would look like this."

"Like what?"

"So lean. Like you've never eaten enough. But also—all these muscles. They're very nice."

Muffled laughter. "What did you think I'd look like?"

"I never thought about it."

"Not once?"

"No. Why? Did you think about my body?"

"Often and often."

"What did you expect?"

"This beautiful breast and *this* beautiful breast, only they're so much more beautiful than I imagined. And this—the curve, right here. Between your rib and your hip. Perfection."

"Well, I'm surprised at how perfect a man's body can be."

"What else surprises you?"

"This necklace you're wearing. It's so heavy, and there's so many charms attached to the chain."

"They're all the blessings you've given me over the years."

"All of them? Wait—you *kept* them?"

"Yes. Unless they were ones you'd already given me."

"You must have a complete set here."

"Except for one."

"Which one is missing?"

"I'll tell you when you draw it for me."

"I'm wearing my necklace, too. The one you gave me."

"I saw that. It makes me happy that you have it on."
"I'm never going to take it off."
"Your initials."
"*Your* initials."
"Love letters. All these gifts. All these years."
"I've kept every one of them. But this is the best."

※

"You're very good at this, you know. It's delightful."
"I *have* had three lovers."
Teasing. "So many? I'm impressed."
"Why is that amusing?"
"You're so *particular*. I wouldn't have thought even three men would have met your standards."
"Well, how many women have you been with?"
"Seven."
"Now *I'm* surprised. I thought it would be more."
"I like the game. The flirting. But any time it turned serious—" A shrug. "It didn't feel right."
"I was always serious."
"Yes, I imagine you were. There was that one fellow. The torz man. You thought you would marry him, didn't you? I must say, he sounded ideal for you."
"I thought he was."
"So what happened?"
"It's hard to explain. I liked his house and I could imagine myself running it. I could picture our children racing across the lawn. It all seemed right. But I looked at him and it seemed wrong. I couldn't fit both of us in the picture at the same time."
"So you broke it off with him. That must have been hard to do."
"It would have been, except I knew there was no other choice. I don't know how to live a lie."
"You don't. Do you think you broke his heart?"
"I think he was sad. I don't think he was surprised. I think he knew me better then I knew him. Anyway, he married a nice torz girl the following spring and they seem to be happy."
"I can't imagine that."
"Marrying a nice torz girl? Or being happy?"
"Loving you. And then managing to fall in love with someone else. Six months later. Six years later. Ever."
"Well. You won't have to."
"Hunti means forever."

"And sweela?"

"Sweela means the fire that never goes out."

※

"I don't want to leave."

"Then don't."

"No one knows where I am. After last night, everyone will be worried if they can't find me."

"Just a little longer. Just another kiss."

"Yes."

A long silence.

"And another kiss."

"My aunt Jenty used to say, in the most dire voice, *'Kisses lead to other things.'* I had no idea what she was talking about."

"Let's prove her wrong. Many kisses. Just kisses. No other things."

Many kisses. More than kisses. Laughter. The sounds of desire.

Whispered. "I guess Jenty was right after all."

※

"I *have* to go."

"When can I see you again?"

"I don't know. Tomorrow, maybe? There's so much—oh! I forgot! Melissande was supposed to come to the palace today and explain why she was down at the harbor last night."

"Melissande? The princess from Cozique? *She* was there in the middle of that mess?"

"Yes—in fact, that's one of the people you rescued last night! Maybe that's why Yori let you go."

"Who's Yori?"

"The guard who said you were her informant."

"Is she the same one who interfered when Jodar was going to try to murder me a few ninedays ago?"

"She is."

"Then I'm grateful to her."

"Let me up. I have to get dressed."

"But I don't want you to go."

"I have to go anyway."

"So. Tomorrow?"

"Maybe. It depends on what happens this afternoon. If I can get away, where shall I meet you?"

"The park."

"There's no privacy in the park."

"We can go somewhere else once we've met up. Find another hotel. By the end of Quinnatorz, maybe we'll have taken a tour of all the hotels in southern Chialto."

"You could clean your apartment. We could go there."

"A year of cleaning would not make it an inviting place to bring a woman."

"What time?"

"Early afternoon. I have business to attend to, so I'll have to leave before nightfall."

"What kind of business?"

A long sigh. "Ah, Tina. That's a conversation for another day."

"I think it's an important conversation."

"This is one of the reasons I said everything was complicated."

"Complicated doesn't mean impossible."

Laughter. "I don't suppose it does."

"So tomorrow afternoon at the park if I can."

"I'm counting on it."

Another kiss. "So am I."

Chapter Twenty-three

Corene pounced on Val the minute she stepped into the great kierten of the palace. It was clear she had been loitering there, waiting for Val to arrive.

"Where have you *been* all day?"

"I had some things I needed to do. What's going on? What did Melissande say?"

"She hasn't been here yet. She sent a note saying she would come for dinner and explain everything. But that is not a good enough answer! *What things were you doing?*"

Val intended to make a cool, evasive reply, since there was no reason she needed to share the very personal events of this day with the inquisitive princess. But though she tried to keep her expression impassive, she felt a smile lift the corners of her mouth. "Just. Things."

Corene squealed and grabbed her arm. "You went off to find him, didn't you? What's his name—Sebastian? And? *And?*"

"Hush. I have to go change clothes and get ready for dinner."

"Darien's been looking for you. He's been worried."

"I can take care of myself."

Corene's smile was a little lopsided. "Well, that's the thing. Darien never thinks *anyone* can take care of themselves."

Val turned and headed for the stairs, ready for this conversation to be over. Naturally, Corene followed. "Really? Because he let me do it for years."

"You mean, at the house you shared with your mother? I have to think there were guards nearby, maybe ones you didn't notice. Stationed there to watch over you just in case there was trouble."

Val thought about that as she climbed the steps. Maybe. There had always been a couple of workers on the estate who were a little bigger and more powerful than the average groom or gardener—workers her mother had hired with vague comments about needing a strong pair of hands for some project or another. And Val had noticed more than once that the posting house a couple of miles down the road frequently had royal soldiers staying overnight, though she had always assumed they were on their way to some assignment for the crown. But maybe *she* had been the assignment. Maybe she had been more closely guarded than she knew.

"That was never the kind of care I needed," she said. "Or the kind of attention I wanted."

"Maybe not," Corene said. "But everybody shows love in their own way."

They arrived at Val's door. "Go away. I need to clean up and get dressed."

"But then you're coming downstairs? I think Melissande will be here in an hour. And Nelson and Mirti are joining us for the meal."

"Yes. I'll be right there."

Once she was in her room, Val quickly stripped and stepped into the bathing room. As she soaped up and rinsed off, her hands paused now and then, hovering over her body. Sebastian had touched her *here*. Left a small mark *there*. Kissed this spot over and over. She could hardly wait until nighttime, so she could lie in her soft bed and deliberately recall everything they had said, everything they had done. She could hardly wait until tomorrow afternoon when they could do it all again.

After she'd dried herself off, she dressed in a simple black tunic and leggings. There would be a foreign princess and three primes at the dinner table, so perhaps she ought to wear something more formal, but she had a feeling formality was about to go out the window. She was glad she hadn't missed Melissande's explanation. She wondered how much of it would be true.

When she stepped out of the bathing cubicle, she found Darien waiting for her in the main room. He was standing at her dresser, absently looking through the items on display. At her small sound of surprise, he turned in her direction. Despite his slight smile, his face was somber.

"I like this sculpture," he said, briefly touching the upraised fingertips of the cupped hands.

"I bought it at Leah's shop. It reminded me of our mother."

"That was exactly what I was thinking."

She came close enough to pick up a comb so she could attempt to detangle her damp hair. "I suppose you've come to interrogate me about where I've been."

"Not at all," he said. To her astonishment, he looked uncertain. She had never seen him wear such an expression. "I thought we should talk."

The combination of too much tousling and too much humidity had left her thick hair an impossible mess. She coiled it up into a knot and found a few clips to pin it in place. There wasn't much else she could do. "About what?"

"About my failings as a brother."

She couldn't help an incredulous laugh. "I didn't think you realized you had any imperfections."

"Nonsense. My wife and my primes and my oldest daughter point them out on a regular basis. Even my youngest daughter has started to articulate them."

She studied him a moment. "I don't think Zoe or Celia—or even Corene—would ever accuse you of abandoning them."

"No. And I did not realize you thought I had abandoned *you*."

"I told you. When I first arrived here. I told you how much help I needed with our mother, and you weren't there to give it."

He shook his head. "No. You think I left *you* behind. You think I didn't care enough about *you*."

She felt suddenly awkward, almost shy. "It's just. You were gone so much when I was growing up. I was a little girl, and I thought you were so glamorous. I could hardly wait until the next time you came home and told me all the stories about the palace. But you never wanted to stay. There was always so much waiting for you in Chialto. I kept thinking that once Vernon died, you would come back home, but you were gone even more. Sometimes I felt like I'd lost you, but other times I felt like I'd never had you at all."

"I'm sorry," he said. "It's not like I ever *forgot* about you or our mother. You were always there, at the back of my mind, a place of—solidity. Familiarity, maybe. The two of you were always what I pictured when I pictured *home*. But I didn't think you *needed* me. I never met anyone who seemed as self-complete as you. I never knew anyone I worried about less. Not because I didn't care, but because I trusted you. It never occurred to me that you might need someone to lean on sometimes, but it should have. Everybody does."

She tilted her head. "You don't."

"Not often. But sometimes."

"But *everybody* leans on you," she said. "You're like the challinbar tree that holds the world together. *I* shouldn't need you, too."

He held his hand out, a simple gesture, and she laid her palm hesitantly in his. "Maybe we need each other," he said. "I will be more generous if you will."

Now she closed her fingers around his, but she was laughing. "Wait, I have a feeling that's a sneaky way for you to try to get something you want," she said. "What am I bargaining for?"

He laughed back. "Well, even you must acknowledge that it is not easy for me to escape Chialto often, so if you expect me to be more present in your life, you will have to spend some portion of your days here."

She dropped his hand, but only so she could shake a finger in his face. "See? I knew it! You seem to be hunti through and through, but you are as devious as a sweela man."

"Now that is truly an insult. But you have to admit my argument is sound."

She had no idea how her life with Sebastian might go forward, but it seemed safe to assume that he, too, would be largely based in Chialto. One way or the other, Val was probably going to be back in the royal city more often in the future.

"Maybe," she said. "I'll think about it."

"We can discuss everything at length in the coming days," he said. "But for now, I believe we have a mysterious princess to contend with. Let's go down to dinner and see what she has to tell us."

※

Kayle had been summoned from the harbor, so four primes were actually present at dinner, and Elidon joined them as well. Darien, Corene, Val, and Melissande rounded out the numbers. The nine of them had managed to squeeze around the table in the breakfast room, preferring the intimate feel of the small space where it seemed like important conversations could be had in confidence.

Melissande's face had a pale, bruised look, which she had tried to counteract by dressing in a brightly patterned dress of teal and sapphire. She maintained an easy flow of conversation with Corene on her right and Nelson on her left, but it was clear she couldn't summon her usual vivaciousness. The footmen served everyone, then set all the dishes on the table and left the room, closing the door firmly behind them.

"Shall we eat first or attempt to talk through our meal?" Darien asked.

"I am still hoping to return to the harbor tonight so that *some* part of this day might be salvaged," Kayle said. "I don't mind listening to the sound of everyone chewing if it means this conference is quickly finished."

"As usual, Kayle demonstrates social grace for all of us," Nelson murmured, toasting him with his glass of fruited water.

Kayle instantly fired up. "Oh, and I suppose *you* were down at the waterfront all day helping clean up the mess left behind by the king's military operation."

"I did send some of my house guards to assist with the work."

"Repairing trust with business owners is not work that soldiers can be expected to perform."

"I suppose not. Well, then, as always, I rely on your skill and delicacy. We shall proceed with all haste." Nelson glanced at Melissande. "Princess?"

Melissande pushed the food around on her plate. "I am not very hungry, anyway. I would prefer to talk."

"Then please begin," Darien said. They sat across from each other, he at the head of the table and she at the foot, and he watched her steadily. "What is the real reason you came to Welce?"

Melissande laid down her fork. "I had no intention of coming here. My original destination was Haskonia."

Everyone was surprised at that. It was a small island nation distinguished for very little except its location near the middle of the shipping routes to the far southern continents. It boasted little agriculture and few natural resources worth trading for, but it was convenient, and it had developed a reputation as a reasonable stopover for ships that needed to restock or refuel.

"Is your mother seeking to lay claim to the island?" Darien inquired.

"An interesting strategy," said Elidon, always the tactician. "Potentially quite lucrative. Cozique could offer to provide military protection to the citizens, and in exchange it would have the right to charge fees to ships from every nation that wanted to dock there."

Melissande's smile was rote. "I told you, our imperialist days are over. It is true we have had some discussions with Haskonia, but they were instigated by the governor. We no longer go where we are not wanted."

"So why Haskonia?" Darien asked.

"Because I hoped to deliver a package there and have it sent on its way to Yorramol."

The name was taken up and repeated by half the people sitting at the table. Val knew almost nothing about the country, the only inhabitable stretch of land on the southernmost continent in the world. It was so far away that for years she had thought it was an imaginary place.

Corene was staring fixedly at Melissande. "Were you sending a package to Alette?"

"Who's Alette?" Kayle demanded.

Zoe answered him in a low voice. "One of the daughters of the king of Dhonsho. A year or so ago, Corene and Melissande helped her escape her father's vengeance, and she found haven in Yorramol."

"Is she looking for trading partners?" Kayle asked. "I don't have any contacts in Yorramol, but I'd like to."

"You might discuss that at some other time," Zoe said gravely, though she appeared to be trying not to laugh. She returned her attention to Melissande. "Forgive the interruption. But I think we'd all like to hear the answer to Corene's question."

"Yes, I'm trying to deliver something to Alette," the princess replied. "Her brother Kendol."

Darien's voice cut through the resulting exclamations of astonishment. "My understanding is that the king of Dhonsho has more than a dozen children. Why is this one so special?"

"He is the king's third oldest son, the only one by his favorite wife—who is dead now, because he had her killed when she bore him too many daughters." Melissande paused long enough to let their horror and disgust subside. "While his oldest son is the crown prince, he is greatly disliked, and a faction of Dhonshon society would like to see Kendol on the throne instead."

"I assume that is what Kendol would like as well," Darien said.

"Indeed, he is ambitious. But he is also an intelligent, educated man with a strong moral sense. He studied international law for a time in Cozique, and he has traveled widely among the northwestern nations, and so he does not have the insular views of many of his countrymen. If he were on the throne, my mother believes that Dhonsho might become a more civilized place."

Darien leaned back in his chair. "So Cozique is fomenting revolution in Dhonsho."

"No," Melissande said forcefully. "Kendol approached us—very carefully, through intermediaries—more than a year ago. We have carried out the most tortuously intricate dance you can imagine as we tried to determine if his overtures were genuine and if we could in fact provide him any kind of reasonable assistance. We considered extending him an offer of sanctuary—"

"Which Dhonsho would have seen as an act of war," Darien interjected.

"Exactly. And while we would love to see the current king replaced by Kendol, there is every possibility that Kendol will end up dead instead, murdered by an enraged father. We would just as soon not have his blood spilled on Coziquela soil."

"So is Prince Kendol with you now?" Mirti asked. "If you never allowed him to visit Cozique, how did he fall into your hands?"

"He was smuggled out of his country last quintile. One of my mother's ships met him in the middle of the ocean some three hundred miles from Dhonsho. I set sail on a different ship and met him at another rendezvous point far out to sea. We wanted to make sure there was no one in any harbor who might get a glimpse of the rebel son of Dhonsho climbing aboard a Coziquela vessel." Melissande took a sip of water and followed it with a swallow of wine. "And then I set my course for Haskonia, where I planned to turn him over to a merchant captain who has deep ties to Cozique."

"But the merchant betrayed you," Nelson guessed.

"Possibly. Or possibly I am nervous and overcautious and all would have been well had we continued on toward Haskonia as planned. But as we docked in Botchka for a day to take on supplies, I noticed two Dhonshon ships in the harbor. They didn't hail us or ask to come aboard. I stayed another day—and another—deciding I wouldn't leave until they did. But they remained tied up at in port. I wasn't sure what to do."

Val tried to envision how nerve-wracking that must have been. Not knowing whether everything was perfectly fine or whether disaster was about to strike. But knowing with absolute certainty that a mistake not only could cost one man his life, but also launch a war.

"Finally, I decided to set sail again, but not toward Haskonia. I headed east instead. I reasoned that I could change my course once I was far enough out to sea that no one could observe me." She took another drink of wine.

"But we had not been on the move more than a day before my captain told me it appeared we were being followed. He could not be certain they were tracking us, but there were certainly two ships in our wake."

"I suppose they weren't helpfully flying the Dhonshon flag," Zoe remarked.

Melissande managed a small smile. "No. In fact, my captain's opinion was that they might be mercenaries looking for an easy target. Which could have been just as bad as being boarded by Dhonshon soldiers. Well—it would have better in that our deaths probably would not have sparked a war if we were killed by raiders. But still not a very good outcome for me *or* the prince."

"So you decided to head to Welce," Darien said in a neutral voice.

"No, in fact, I seized on an opportunity to head toward Soeche-Tas. On our second day out to sea, we encountered Soechin vessels that appeared to be heading home, so I turned to follow them. I reasoned that neither a mercenary nor a Dhonshon soldier was likely to board my ship if there were witnesses. Besides, my mother keeps an embassy in Soeche-Tas, so it seemed like the perfect destination." She took a deep breath. "Unfortunately, as we sailed, the Dhonshon ships stayed always to the north of us, always between us and Soeche-Tas. I saw no clear path to the Soechin harbors. So I turned south to dock at Chialto instead."

"With Prince Kendol on board," said Darien.

"Yes."

"Which means that instead of seeking sanctuary in Cozique, which has the greatest naval fleet in the southern seas, the prince is seeking sanctuary in Welce. A small country with a small military force and a bent toward peace."

"We have not been able to leave," Melissande said. "The Dhonshon ships that followed us are still patrolling the waters some distance out from your harbor."

"Indeed, I had received reports of their presence, but I had not been able to determine why they were in this vicinity." Darien studied Melissande for a moment. "You potentially have brought a war to my borders."

"I have tried not to," Melissande replied. For the first time since Val had met her, the princess seemed to be speaking with utter openness and honesty. "It is why I did not tell you the real reason I arrived in Chialto. It is why Kendol has not thrown himself on your mercy. You did not ask for this entanglement, and I have tried to undo it on my own. Up to this point, my schemes have failed. That does not mean my next one will be unsuccessful."

"What have you tried so far?" Nelson asked. "I presume you were meeting someone at the harbor last night."

Melissande grimaced. "That was my third attempt to find a boat that could smuggle Kendol out of Welce. My mother maintains a small network in Welce, but none of her agents could supply me with names of captains who might be reliable. I began to make discreet inquiries—"

"That's what you asked the blind sisters," Val said, surprising everyone by speaking up.

Melissande nodded. "And they gave me some names. But I found myself wary of trusting the first man I was directed to."

"Jodar," Val said. "No, he's a *terrible* man."

Darien briefly transferred his attention to Val. "I think at some point I will ask you how you are acquainted with such an individual."

Val ignored him. "Then why were you with Jodar last night at the harbor?"

Melissande sighed. "I thought I was meeting someone else. It was a shock to find him waiting for me. At first I was angry, but quite soon I became afraid, since it appeared that he had shifted his plans from betraying the prince to betraying *me* and holding me for ransom. I was actually relieved when the first explosion went off, because I thought I would be able to get away from him in the chaos. Unfortunately, I would not have been successful if Corene and Val had not come to my rescue."

"Yes, we shall forever be grateful that they were so fortuitously on hand," Darien said dryly.

"But I don't see that anything has been solved," Kayle said with his usual complete lack of subtlety. "I mean, the prince is still in your company, isn't he? What are we going to do about him?"

"That is exactly the question," Darien replied.

"He would not ask you to give him sanctuary," Melissande said. "He knows that would be tantamount to setting you at war with his father."

"Giving him aid might result in the same outcome," Mirti said.

"It might," Zoe said. "But we can't possibly return him to his countrymen to be slaughtered."

Nelson appeared to be momentarily distracted by the opportunity to debate. "It's an interesting ethical dilemma," he said. "The life of one man set against the lives of what could be thousands."

Zoe just looked at him. "This is not theoretical," she said.

"It's not," he said. "But it's not simple or clear-cut, either."

"Well, I don't see that we have a lot of choices," Mirti said. "We give him sanctuary. We help him escape. Or we turn him over to the waiting ships. If we're not going to turn him over, that leaves two options."

"We could destroy the Dhonshon ships," Kayle said. Everyone turned to stare at him. "What? We *could*. Just because you don't like the idea doesn't mean it's not possible."

"If our goal is to prove ourselves righteous and humane, killing an uncounted number of foreign nationals does not seem like the way to accomplish it," said Darien.

"No, but we might simply take them into custody," Nelson said thoughtfully. "Find some trumped-up charge—accuse them of spying! Hold them for a few ninedays until the prince has had an opportunity to sail away."

Darien glanced at Melissande. "Would that answer? Or would they respond with violence if we tried to board?"

"I cannot imagine they would tamely submit."

"And we do not want to trade a life for a life," Zoe said. "Who's to say that a prince is worth more than a soldier? If even one man died in such a maneuver, we would have failed."

"A prince *is* worth more than a soldier," Elidon said firmly. "Otherwise, why have a monarchy at all?"

"Maybe if you judge by the potential contributions each one could make to society at large," Nelson said. "But a prince could be villainous, in which case his contributions are negative, while a soldier might—who knows? Carry out some daring maneuver that saves dozens of people. Giving his life a more positive weight."

"Again, this is not a theoretical discussion," Darien said, his voice edged. Val saw Zoe look away to hide a smile. "If our goal is to avoid bloodshed, we do not want to engage the Dhonshon soldiers."

"But would you have to engage them?" asked Mirti, always the most practical of the primes. "Could you not simply surround them? Bring a dozen Welchin warships to encircle them but don't exchange cannon fire?"

Darien looked intrigued. "It's an idea," he said. "Though they might attempt to fire on us anyway, out of frustration."

Now Zoe was grinning openly. "I might be able to keep them off-balance," she said. "Roil up the ocean under their hulls. They'll be so busy bailing water and trying to lash everything down that they won't have time to load their guns."

Mirta gestured at the elay prime. "And Kayle could make himself useful by whipping up some heavy wind."

"I am always useful," Kayle said. "It is just that sometimes I don't see the value in your schemes."

"I like it," Darien decided. "We neutralize the Dhonshon contingent while we try to figure out how to move Prince Kendol to someplace safer. That is not Welce."

"It is a good plan," Melissande said apologetically. "But it might not be good enough."

"It seems like you have nothing but obstacles," Kayle complained.

Darien quieted him with a glance. "What have we overlooked?"

"I feel certain that some Dhonshon operatives are already on Welchin soil looking for an opportunity to assassinate the prince. Like you, they are reluctant to initiate a war, so they would prefer not to kill Welchin soldiers. But if they think the prince might possibly escape, they will take ruthless action."

Darien nodded. "That's a good point. Then we must simultaneously monitor the activities of anyone in Welce who appears to be of Dhonshon descent. They do not make up a large portion of our population and should be tracked easily enough."

Melissande leaned toward him across the table. "I would urge you not to be naïve, King Darien," she said. "There are plenty of fair-skinned men who can be hired to carry out a task for a Dhonshon king. The man who does not look like you is not the only one who can be your enemy."

Darien bent forward as well, his expression as intense as hers. "I have never been so foolish as to think someone is my ally merely because he resembles me," he said. "Just as I have never believed people can be trusted simply because they are charming and beautiful."

Val almost gasped at the implied insult, and even Zoe's eyes grew wide. Nelson snorted. "No, in fact, it's the charming ones who are often the most deceitful," he observed.

"Well, you would know," Kayle said.

"Come now, it's pointless to bandy words," Mirti said. "If the prince is in danger no matter what we do, what is our next step?"

"That *is* the logical question," Zoe said. "How do we get him to safety? Princess, what were your plans before they went awry?"

"At the moment, I believe my best course of action is to get him to the Coziquela embassy in Soeche-Tas, where my mother's youngest brother is installed. If I can deliver Kendol to the embassy, my uncle can secure him passage on an outbound ship. And from there he can sail to Haskonia and on to Yorramol."

Darien tilted his head. "Still hazardous for him."

Melissande nodded. "But the risk for Welce is greatly reduced."

"So you have just been trying to book passage for Kendol from Chialto to Soeche-Tas?" Zoe asked. "I wouldn't have thought it would be so difficult."

"Neither would I. But it turns out your ordinary Welchin mercenaries are reluctant to ferry a Dhonshon passenger to Soeche-Tas, and Soechins flatly refuse."

"Yes, Soeche-Tas has a hatred for Dhonsho," Darien said. "Even if a Soechin accepted the commission, he would probably throw the prince overboard—not knowing who he was, and not caring."

"Once I could not find a way to send him by water, I looked into the overland route," Melissande said. "But, as far as I can tell, there *is* no overland route between Welce and Soeche-Tas."

"No, the mountain range that divides us is impassable except by small groups moving slowly and on foot," Darien said. "From time to time, our governments have debated the merits of working together to blast through the stone and create an open trading road. But then we remember how different our customs are and how much we distrust each other, and we decide we already are as close as we need to be. That mountain range has ensured us relative peace for generations."

"I am certain it has. But it has complicated my own task."

"Water is probably the way to go," Darien said. "Let me look into what kind of craft my own navy can supply and get back to you quickly with a set of options."

"I would be more grateful than I can say."

"I still think there is a question that hasn't been answered," Mirti said. "Where *is* the prince? Have you left him on your ship this whole time? Is he safe there?"

"Ah. No."

They all just looked at her. After a long moment, Darien said, "You brought him ashore."

"My vessel was too easily identified. I thought it possible the Dhonshon soldiers might simply sail into harbor and set it on fire."

"But instead they've stayed out to sea."

"The ships have, certainly. But at least a dozen Dhonshon soldiers have landed. And twice they have raided my ship."

Corene straightened up in her chair. "You never told us that!"

"There was no bloodshed. My captain knew he should bluster and complain, but offer no resistance. The Dhonshons searched every hold and locked cabinet, looking for evidence of the prince. I do not believe he is safe on board."

"So instead he is walking around on Welchin soil, appearing to be a guest of the Welchin crown."

"They cannot prove he is here. They cannot prove he was ever on my ship. If they never find him, they can never have a grievance against you."

"Darien," Elidon said urgently. "We must get him out of our country. If he dies in Welce—"

Darien nodded. His face was as cold and closed as Val had ever seen it. "I hope Cozique is prepared to be our allies in the war that will inevitably follow."

"Tell me, then," Melissande said, as passionate as he was calm, "what would *you* have done in my place? Ignored his initial requests for help? And then, once having offered him assistance, would you have turned him over to his enemies the minute they posed a threat? Or would you have tried to find safe haven for him while you desperately looked for an alternative plan?"

"I would not have sought shelter on the shores of a friendly nation without informing my hosts just what kind of disaster I had brought to their doors."

"Yes, you would have," Corene objected. "You never tell anyone *anything*. You keep every secret until someone forces it from you, and even then you don't tell everything."

The interruption lightened the mood, as everyone around the table tried to muffle a laugh or hide a grin. Even Darien looked slightly less furious. "In this case," he said, "I believe I would have been at least somewhat more open."

"My apologies," said Melissande. "I was trying to reduce the chances you would be drawn into the conflict. Perhaps it was the wrong decision, I do not know."

"Again," Mirti said. "Where *exactly* is the prince of Dhonsho?"

Val knew. "He's at the hotel with her," she said. "Acting as one of her guards."

Several people exclaimed *"What?"* but Melissande nodded at her approvingly. "Very observant," she said. "Dhonshons are integrated fairly evenly into Coziquela society. Their numbers are not large, but they hold jobs in all sectors from commerce to science to the military. I reasoned that no one would expect me to parade the Dhonshon prince around so publicly."

"Your audacity leaves me breathless," Darien said.

Melissande smiled at him. "I admit I was counting on your officiousness," she said. "I knew you would station Welchin soldiers around my hotel even if I explicitly asked you not to. Your motive would have been to keep *me* safe, but the end result would have been adequate protection for Kendol."

Zoe appealed to Darien. "Should we bring him here? I would not call the palace impregnable, but it is the most well-defended spot in the city."

"No. I don't want to meet him. I don't want to be in the same building with him. I don't want there to be a chance that any spy from any country in the southern seas might see me conversing with him. I want there always to be at least a shred of doubt about whether or not Welce provided him aid."

"Very wise," Melissande said. "So then what is our next step?"

"I will see what kind of transport I can arrange. You will ensure that the prince is ready to leave at a moment's notice."

"And perhaps increase your guard around the hotel?" Elidon suggested.

Darien's smile was sardonic. "Oh, trust me, ensuring the princess's safety already necessitated the presence of a considerable force. Much as I would hate to have the Dhonshon prince perish in Chialto, I have even less interest in seeing an heir to Cozique die while under my protection. Cozique would absolutely destroy Welce in retaliation."

Melissande laughed. "No, indeed, my mother would send you a letter of commiseration, expressing her belief that I came to a sad end due to my own carelessness. I am the only one she would blame."

"Darien feels exactly the same way about me," Corene assured her.

"At any rate, you can do nothing until I lay my plans," Darien said. "I would suggest you return to your room and recuperate from your recent exertions."

"You will have to continue to entertain," Elidon said. "Invitations have been issued, and people are expecting to meet Melissande. Indeed, we will need to continue feting the princess until a few days after Kendol is safety away, just to allay the suspicions of the Dhonshons who might believe he is still with her."

Zoe groaned. "Much as I hate to admit it, Elidon is right. But at least we have a couple of days before the next party is planned."

Melissande came to her feet, and everyone else did the same. "Then I shall take Darien's excellent advice and rest while I can." She nodded at him, her expression suddenly grave. "I thank you. You have been more gracious than perhaps I deserve. I am sure I have made mistakes, but please believe me when I say my every action and my entire intent was for good."

Nelson took her hand and bowed over it. "*I* believe you," he said. "And you know the sweela prime can read the truth of a person's heart."

"I believe you, too," Darien said. "But it does not make my situation any easier."

Her smile had a tinge of its usual mischievousness. "But then, you are a king. By definition, your life will never be easy."

Corene grabbed her other arm. "Come on. I'll go back with you, and you can tell me everything you didn't tell Darien."

Corene glanced at Val, but Val shook her head. The tumultuous night and the momentous day were beginning to catch up with her. She needed to return to her room, lie down, sleep. Dream. Entertain disbelief and wonder. She needed to marvel at how her life had contorted and leveled out to deliver her to the astonishing place she was now.

Chapter Twenty-Four

On thirdday, everyone at the palace was so preoccupied with discussing the events of the last two days that no one paid much attention to Val. She spent the morning with Elidon and Mirti and Natalie, answering a barrage of questions from the hunti heir, before slipping out right after lunch. It was a simple thing to board a public transport and ride it halfway around the Cinque before exiting at her usual stop.

Sebastian was in the park before her, pacing. As soon as he saw her, he spread his arms wide and she flung herself into his embrace.

"It hasn't even been a day and I've missed you unbearably," he murmured into her hair. "I kept thinking you wouldn't be able to get away today and I didn't know when I could see you again, and that made me miss you so much it *hurt* me. I mean, I felt actual pain in my gut."

She lifted one hand from his back to gently pat his stomach. "Maybe you're sick. Maybe what you think is love is really some dreadful illness."

He laughed and kissed her. "No, I feel utterly fine now that you're here."

"Well, good. Have you cleaned your apartment? Or picked out the next stop on our hotel tour of Chialto?"

"Neither. But come on. I have a place for us to go."

They caught the next transport headed back to the more respectable neighborhoods near the Plaza of Women. Here, there were rows of well-kept buildings where working professionals and ambitious merchants had their lodgings. The district wasn't fancy, but it was decent, and every few blocks the streets were brightened by small parks and gardens.

Sebastian guided them to a long three-story building of rough beige stone, where all the doors and shutters were painted a dusky blue. They went through one of ten identical exterior doors, climbed to the second floor, and entered a small apartment. From the kierten, Val could see the main room, a large square shape lit by a generous panel of windows, and a side door that might lead to a bedroom. The place felt serene and spacious, but perhaps because it was entirely empty.

"What is this?" Val asked.

"My new apartment. I rented it this morning."

"*What?*"

"I wanted to be able to bring you somewhere nice."

"You know I don't care about things like that."

He shrugged. "I was tired of the old place. It was dingy and dark. I'd been thinking about moving anyway." He swept a hand out as if presenting it to her. "Do you like it?"

"It might need furniture."

"I did manage to get a mattress. But I didn't have time for chairs or tables or dishes. Anyway, I wanted to make sure it was all right with you before I actually tried to furnish it."

Val wandered away from him, exploring. A set of shelves had been built into one wall and painted the same off-white color. Hooks were set above the wide windows, apparently to hold curtain panels. The floor was scuffed and scarred in places, but looked as if it had been recently waxed and polished. She glanced into the second, smaller room, where there was indeed a mattress on the floor, covered with a red blanket and a couple of blue pillows. Next to it was a small table, holding a jug of water and a basket of food. If anything, the sun in this room seemed even brighter, cheerier, almost delighted.

"I do like it," she said. "I think it will be one of the happiest places I've ever been."

※

They spent the next three hours at the apartment, making love, talking, napping, making love again. By late afternoon, they were both starving, but Sebastian had brought enough provisions to blunt the edge of their hunger.

"You can stay as long as you like," he said once evening began to creep over the horizon line. "But I need to leave."

Val was sitting on the edge of the mattress, putting on her shoes and watching Sebastian stuff the remains of their meal into a bag. "I don't particularly want to be here without you. Where are you going?" When he hesitated, she continued in a calm voice, "Don't lie to me. Even if you're going to tell me something you know I won't like."

"The firstday raid removed a lot of enterprising fellows from the streets of Chialto," he said. "That means there are additional opportunities for someone like me. Cargos to pick up and deliver. I need to make a few inquiries."

She considered him a moment. "Maybe it's time for you to think about some other means of making money."

He sat down next her and took her hands. "I love you, Tina. Having you in my life like that is making me insanely happy. But you can't expect me to suddenly change who I am, who I have been all my life."

"I don't. But you could change what you *do* with your life. Take up a new career that's full of excitement and danger but doesn't come with the risk of you ending up in a royal jail cell."

"I don't know what that life would look like."

"I don't either, but you might think about it."

He clasped her hands even more tightly. "Would you leave me if I was a smuggler forever?"

"Sebastian. No one knows better than I do that it's impossible to remake another person. I'm hunti—I *never* change. But I can grow, I think. I can find new ways to be the same person in the same place. I can branch in another direction, seek a different source of sunlight."

"And will you do that for me?"

"I think I'll have no *choice* but to do it for you. If I want to be with you, I can't spend all my time on my property hundreds of miles from Chialto. But I'm not sure I can leave it entirely behind, either. I will have to find a way to bring together all the things I care about. I don't know how I'll do that. I think we'll both have to come up with ideas."

He took a deep breath. "Maybe. I mean—yes. Of course. I just don't—you can't expect me to stand in the middle of a bean field and talk about crop rotation with the neighbors."

"Surely there is some middle ground between being a farmer and being a felon."

"Yes. We'll find it. We *will*."

She leaned in and kissed him. "We will. Until then—be careful as you engage in your illegal pursuits. I have just discovered I love you. You wouldn't be so cruel as to disappear from my life two days later, would you?"

He brought her hands to his mouth and kissed her knuckles. "I will never be cruel to you," he whispered.

"Then whatever you're doing tonight," she whispered in reply, "come back to me tomorrow."

Back at the palace, Val found everyone walking around with a suppressed air of excitement, although no one actually seemed to know what was going *on*. Well, Corene didn't know, and if Zoe and Mirti knew, they weren't telling.

"How can we find out?" Corene speculated as the two of them sat in the conservatory, eating sweets purloined from the kitchen. "I know! Let's pull blessings and see if they tell us anything."

Val didn't move. "I'm too tired to go traipsing out to a temple."

"I have a set in my room. Josetta sent them to me when I was in Malinqua, and it was very comforting to have them. Come on."

A few minutes later, they were in Corene's quarters, an untidy suite decorated in warm ochre tones and filled with overstuffed pillows and vases of riotously colored flowers. It couldn't have said *sweela* any louder if all of the furnishings had actually been shouting.

Corene pawed through the items in a dresser drawer—Val noted with disapproval that the contents were a complete jumble—until she found a red velvet sack tied shut with a golden cord. "They're so cute and little, I just love them," she said. She made a few token efforts at straightening the unmade bed, then climbed onto the coverlet. "Come on, sit up here with me."

Val complied, but she was frowning. "Why is it so messy in here?"

Corene waved a hand. "I wouldn't let the maids in because I was trying to catch up on my sleep. I suppose you always make your own bed and line up your shoes just so."

"Well, it's just more *comfortable* when everything is in its place."

Corene rolled her eyes but gave it up. She poured the coins out onto the bed, where they made a musical sound and a glittering pile. Unlike a temple barrel, which might hold several hundred coins, this set appeared to have only one coin for each blessing. No duplicates, then. Probably no ghost coins, either, unless Josetta had specifically commissioned one.

"What exactly are we trying to find out?" Val asked.

"The fate of tonight's enterprise, whatever it is. Let's each draw one blessing and show them at the same time."

Val waited while Corene closed her eyes, picked up a coin, dropped it, picked up another one, dropped it, and finally kept the third one she drew. Val just sifted once through the pile before she made her selection.

"Now show them," Corene commanded, and they extended their palms. The princess frowned when her own blessing was resilience and Val's was flexibility. "Hmm. I was hoping for something more emphatic. Like triumph or luck. Something that would indicate the Dhonshon prince was safely on his way."

"You think they're trying to get him out of the city tonight?"

"I think Darien doesn't want him here a day longer than necessary."

"Maybe they've had to adapt their plans because of a change in circumstances," Val said. "That's not *bad*, precisely."

"Maybe. Let's draw blessings for Kendol and see what we get."

This time they pulled courage and patience. "Again, not entirely reassuring," Corene remarked, "and I say this as someone who very much likes her own blessing of courage."

"It does sound like his road out of Chialto will not be an easy one," Val said.

"Maybe the coins are just in a cautious mood tonight," Corene answered. "Let's pick blessings for ourselves and see if they're just as grim."

"You first."

Corene repeated her ritual of choosing, discarding, and choosing again. "Travel," she said. "Happy to get it for myself but a little anxious that it didn't show up for Kendol."

"Maybe the coins just can't read him because he's not Welchin."

"Maybe. But his sister Alette never seemed to have any trouble pulling blessings, and she did it more than once."

"Well—then—I don't know."

Corene nodded, then sighed. "All right. Pick one for yourself."

Val dipped her hand into the cool metallic pile and pulled the first coin she touched. Heat rose to her cheeks when she saw the design etched into the smooth surface. Love.

"Now, that's a *very* interesting blessing," Corene exclaimed. "I think it's time that you tell me just what you've been doing the past few days."

Val was still blushing. "I shouldn't." She dropped the coin. "But I want to."

Corene wriggled back until she was leaning against the rumpled pillows. "Well, now you have to. Tell me everything."

※

They talked until dinnertime. Val was surprised to find Corene an excellent listener who followed up with searching questions that showed she had paid attention both to what was said and what was left in silence.

"I'm not a particularly good authority on love, but I do know it's never as easy as you think it's going to be," she said when Val had talked herself out. "Even though you've known him most of your life. Even though you think there won't be surprises. Even if you're committed to him body and soul, and he feels the same way about you. There will be times he makes you angry and times he disappoints you—"

"Trust me, there have already been plenty of those times," Val interjected.

"Right, but you think things will be *different* once you know he loves you. And some things will be, but at the core, he'll still be the same person he always was. And so will you. And you can't expect that to change."

Val hugged a frilly red pillow to her chest and rested her chin on the flounced border. "I think I've always seen Sebastian pretty clearly," she said slowly. "And I don't want him to be different. If he changed, he wouldn't be the person I love. But I *do* want him to think about his life. Where it's headed. What he wants from it if he wants me in it. Maybe that's asking too much, I don't know. We haven't even begun figuring this out yet."

Corene grinned. "Seems like the figuring-out part could be fun, though."

Val laughed out loud. "It has been so far."

※

Darien was absent from dinner, but enough other family members were present to make it a lively affair—Celia, Natalie, Josetta, and Rafe all bringing their very different energy to the table. They stayed up late playing games that would appeal to the children, but Darien never made an appearance.

Val was still on edge by the time she retired about an hour before midnight. She should have been exhausted, but she was too restless to sleep. She paced the room, rearranged objects on the spotless dresser, sorted the clothes in her closet by color, and then re-sorted them by season. She tried lying down but couldn't keep her eyes closed, so she got up and paced some more.

A clatter of wheels and a hum of voices drew her attention to the world outside, and she crossed the room to gaze out the window. The courtyard was faintly illuminated by gas lamps that were never extinguished, and in their light Val could see three troop transports pulled up in front of the palace door. From her high vantage point, all the cars appeared empty, so she assumed the occupants had already gone inside. Guards completing a routine patrol of the city and returning at the end of their shift? Or hand-picked soldiers reporting back to Darien after a surreptitious assignment?

Val watched for another half hour, but no one emerged and the elaymotives stayed parked in the courtyard. No other living creature seemed alive at this hour. Even the lake appeared completely still, not a single wrinkled wave winking with reflected light under an overcast sky. It was as if the whole world waited.

※

Fourthday. Not much different than thirdday, though Corene and Val did spend the morning with Melissande, carefully not talking about political topics in case anyone might overhear. Then there was another astonishing, gratifying, satisfying, luxurious afternoon tryst with Sebastian, who had survived unscathed his mysterious activities of the night before. Another evening meal that Darien did not attend. Another midnight vigil at the window, another late-night arrival of a group of royal soldiers. This time Val was watching when they pulled up. Was that Yori hurrying from the car, not bothering to wait for the others to climb out before she slipped through the palace doors? Val pushed the casement open and leaned out as far as she dared, but by then, the guard was already out of sight.

※

Fifthday. The daylight hours were a repeat of the previous days, but the evening was devoted to a formal dinner designed to allow a small group of Chialto merchants to meet with Melissande. Val watched covertly all evening and marveled at Melissande's ability to appear engaged in every conversation, genuinely delighted at each new introduction. Every Welchin who bowed and stepped away from the princess looked dizzy with bedazzlement, unsteady with enchantment. Val wondered how Melissande could manage such magic on little sleep and an unalloyed diet of anxiety. It was a masterful performance.

Darien was present at the meal, but both he and Zoe disappeared as soon as the guests departed, much to his daughter's annoyance. "He's been avoiding me the last three days," Corene fumed. "I swear I'm going to track him down tomorrow and make him tell me what's going on."

Val laughed. "You'll have to let me know how well that works."

Corene laughed back. "I can tell you already. I won't discover a thing."

But it was Val, unexpectedly, who learned what enterprise had kept Darien so preoccupied over the past few days, and she learned it that very night.

Chapter Twenty-five

As it had the past three days, sleep eluded Val, and this time she was too restless to stay cooped up in her room. She threw on a light robe and wandered down the hallways of the residential wing, but there was no light on under Corene's door. Maybe Mirti was still awake in the opposite wing of the palace. Val made the trek down the grand marble stairwell, soon wishing she'd put on slippers. The smooth stone of the stairwell was icy beneath her feet, even this deep in summer. Maybe Mirti would lend her a pair of socks.

She stepped into the grand hallway, marveling at how different it seemed at this hour. The high ceiling was a flicker of shadows from wall sconces turned low for the night. The tiniest sounds echoed from the sleek walls—the light patter of her footsteps, the musical tinkle of the decorative fountain, a low murmur drifting in from servants still at work in the kitchens.

Abruptly, these minor noises were swallowed by a larger commotion outside. Cars rumbling, doors slamming, voices calling, and then a sudden eruption of people through the front doors. Soldiers. Val lost count at fifteen. Most of them poured into the great empty bowl of the hall and swirled to a halt, but one of them headed directly toward the stairwell that led to the royal quarters.

Yori.

Almost without thinking, Val followed.

Yori headed straight to Darien's study on the second floor, the place he conducted most of his business. She paused at the open door and announced herself with a simple, "Majesty."

Val couldn't see Darien, but she heard him say, "Come in." His invitation was quickly followed by Zoe asking, "Should I send for refreshments?"

Still in the doorway, Yori replied, "If you've got water, that's all I need."

"Yes. Please join us."

Yori looked over her shoulder, a slight smile on her face. Val shrank into the shadows, but she knew it was too late. "Do you mind if your sister hears our conversation, or shall I shut the door?"

Val stepped forward so she was close enough to see into the room. Darien sat on a navy blue sofa, where he appeared to have spent the evening leafing through a stack of official-looking documents. Zoe was curled up next to him, a book open on her lap. The light was adequate but low, giving the room a welcoming ambiance. Val said defiantly, "I *would* like to know what's going on. Everyone would."

Darien sighed but motioned her forward. "Fine. You know enough about what's happening that you may as well hear the rest."

In a few moments, she and Yori were seated across from Darien and Zoe, and the guard began her report. "I'm not sure we're going to be able to transport him by water. So far every route out of the harbor has failed."

Val was sure silence was the only thing buying her presence in the room, but she couldn't help asking a question. "You're trying to get Kendol out of Chialto?"

Yori glanced at her. "We've made few dry runs to see what might work before we risk the prince himself." She counted on her fingers. "Last night and the night before, we set out in small fishing boats, the kind that a smuggler might use to slip along the coastline. Three men in one, four in another. All soldiers, but dressed like ordinary fishermen. We weren't a quarter mile from land when we were hailed by slightly larger boats. We were running without lights, but so were they—until they shined some kind of powerful torch into our boat, bright enough to show every occupant. They didn't try to board us, but only because we'd made no attempt to hide a cargo under tarps. They could see everything and everyone in the boat, and they could tell none of us were Dhonshon."

"I wonder if they're accosting every illegal craft that's trying to sail out under cover of darkness," Darien said.

"That's my guess," Yori said. "There might be a few they've missed—but it would be sheer luck if so."

Zoe was grinning. "I'm sure it's been a great inconvenience to our ordinary everyday smugglers. But it's not like they can complain to the crown."

"So I would assess the risk as high if we attempted to remove the prince from our shores in small vessel," Yori finished up.

"And tonight you made a different experiment," Darien said.

Yori nodded. "We took out a merchant-class ship. Two decks, plenty of room to hide a man or two. Crewed by eight soldiers with some experience as sailors. About half a mile out of the harbor, we were hailed by a Dhonshon ship. Again, no lights. This time, it was a distress call, asking for assistance. When we stopped, they asked for permission to send someone across to pick up supplies—and when the men boarded, they asked for a tour of the ship. Very polite, very restrained, and of course we complied. I had the definite sense that if we had failed to answer the hail, or refused permission to board, or denied the tour, we would have quickly been in a battle. The Dhonshons are looking for any crew that looks like it has something to hide."

"But they can hardly stop and search every Welchin ship that leaves the harbor," Darien said.

Yori blew out her breath. "They can stop enough of them," she said ruefully. "The two that we knew about have been joined by four others that are staying farther out to sea. And there might be some even farther out."

"Perhaps the answer is to avoid the appearance of stealth," Darien said. "Boldly send out a ship by daylight with the prince on board."

"We haven't tried that yet," Yori said. "But I wouldn't be surprised if they are using similar tactics even by day."

"None of our legal merchants have reported unwelcome searches."

"I'm guessing because they have only made the outbound trip, and they were not inconvenienced enough to send a message back to the palace. Maybe when they return to the harbor in a nineday or so, and spy the Dhonshon ships still patrolling the waters, they might alert you."

"Perhaps you're right." Darien tapped his fingers against his thigh. "So you think a daylight exit would be just as risky."

"Potentially. And that's not all. I'm fairly certain the harbor is closely watched—that Dhonshon operatives are paying attention to who is boarding every ship. And some of these operatives are not Dhonshon, so we can't easily identify them."

Val found herself unable to resist asking a second question. "Are the Dhonshons only boarding Welchin ships?"

"I don't know for sure," Yori said, "but I'm guessing they're approaching Coziquela vessels as well."

"Maybe they're not watching ships from Malinqua or Berringuey. Book him a passage on one of those."

Darien shook his head. "Too risky. If the Dhonshons discovered their runaway prince on board the ship of another country, we could drag a third nation into war. Bad as our current situation is, that would only make it worse."

"There is always the chance," Yori said, "that a ship could make it through unmolested. A little luck, a little maneuvering. It could be done. But the odds are so poor that I would say you need to abandon hope of helping the prince escape by sea. I think you'd have a better shot at getting him to safety by land."

Darien nodded, but he was frowning. "Send him with a small group of guards north toward the mountains—but then the problem is the crossing into Soeche-Tas. My naval captains know the Soechin ports, but I don't have many soldiers who have experience navigating the overland routes. And certainly not the back ways in and out of the country."

"Your spies have failed you," Zoe said. "It must be for the first time."

"What you need," said Yori, "is someone who's crossed Soeche-Tas in stealth with an illegal cargo."

Darien snorted. "You mean, a sirix smuggler? Unfortunately, I don't happen to have one of those in my back pocket."

Yori very deliberately turned to gaze at Val. "You don't?" she asked.

Darien glanced at Val, looked back at Yori, then more slowly turned to focus on Val. His frown had returned. "You mean, you believe my sister has managed to scrape an acquaintance with one of these fellows? It seems impossible."

Val was staring open-mouthed at Yori. "I thought you were my friend," she said, then immediately wished she hadn't. Not only did it sound childish, it essentially was a confession.

Yori smiled. "I'm an agent of the crown."

"I need details," Darien said. "Who is this person? Why would you think I could trust him? Or her?"

Val crossed her arms and refused to answer. She was still glaring at Yori. Who was still smiling. "I don't know if *you* can trust him, but your sister does. And I'm guessing he would do almost anything to please her."

"A romantic entanglement? In just the few ninedays that Val has been in the city? Unless—" Darien's face loosened to pure incredulity. "You don't mean *Sebastian?*"

"I believe that's his name, yes."

"Is this the boy you've been friends with your whole life?" Zoe asked. When both Darien and Val turned startled looks in her direction, she added, "Corene told me."

"He's not a boy," Darien said, reverting to his usual steely calm. "He's a wild and dangerous young man. Of course I can believe he's turned smuggler. It's exactly what I should have expected of him."

"Well, as Yori says, that might prove to be a handy thing right about now," Zoe pointed out.

"I'm disappointed, though. Val told me she wasn't involved with him. I hadn't expected her to lie."

She couldn't let that pass. "I didn't lie. I wasn't then, but I am now."

"Maybe you could bring him over for dinner some night," Zoe suggested. Darien turned a quelling look on her, and she shrugged. "Well, if your sister's in *love* with him."

"More to the point," said Yori, who appeared to be enjoying this whole nightmare conversation to a ridiculous degree, "he might be able to help you spirit Prince Kendol out of Welce."

"I wouldn't trust Sebastian Ardelay to help an old man up out of a ditch."

"That's not fair!" Val exclaimed. "You don't even *know* him. It's true he's wild, and he's done some things that I don't approve of, but he's—there's so many good things about him. And he's never failed me. Never." She closed her mouth over the next words, but she was pretty sure Darien could hear them unsaid. *Which is more than I can say about you.*

"Wait, did you say Ardelay?" Zoe demanded. "Is he related to Nelson? Wait, wait. Did this young man have something to do with you and Nelson rushing off to the harbor on firstday?"

Again Val refused to answer, and again Yori filled in the void. "I have to take some of the blame for that," she said. "I let Valentina know that the raid was planned. I believe she enlisted the help of the sweela prime to try to keep Sebastian Ardelay away from the waterfront that night, but the plan didn't work. So she and Princess Corene headed down there to try to save him."

Darien rested his gaze briefly on the guard's face. "I suppose you had your reasons for sharing that information with my sister."

"At the time, merely trying to save her some heartache," Yori said. "But I think the decision may repay us tenfold."

"Or cost us a hundredfold."

"Well," said Yori, "he *did* save your daughter's life. That was certainly a fair tradeoff for whispering a warning in your sister's ear."

"*Sebastian* is the one who chased off Corene's attackers? No one thought to mention that fact a couple of days ago."

Zoe went off into a peal of laughter that even Darien's irate glare could not dampen. "No, this is all straight out of a melodrama!" she exclaimed. "Val, I don't care what Darien says. I *have* to meet this young man. If he's an Ardelay, I'm related to him in some fashion, so that's just one more incentive."

Val had no idea how to answer this. She found herself unaccountably nervous. "I don't think he would be interested in making a visit to the palace."

"Then take me to him." Zoe waved a hand. "It can be anywhere. I'm not fancy folk."

"You're no better than a street urchin, but this is not about you making overtures of friendship to Valentina's unfortunate suitor," Darien said. "This is about trying to solve the desperate challenge of moving Prince Kendol out of Welce."

"Perhaps Sebastian would be more likely to help us if he thought we didn't despise him," Zoe said cheerfully.

"I am not certain I trust Sebastian Ardelay enough to even ask him the question," Darien said. "It seems very dangerous to share such an incendiary secret with such a rash young man. Who knows where he might sell the information?"

"He wouldn't!" Val said hotly. "Do you know why he was down at the harbor on firstday? Because someone—not me!—told him about the raid, and he wanted to save his friends."

"Protect his lucrative business contacts, you mean."

Val shook her head. "He doesn't—you don't—he would *never* betray anyone he was committed to. One of his blessings is loyalty."

"A man can be loyal to many things and still not be trusted with a mission of this urgency."

"It seems worth asking him, though," Yori said diplomatically. "Bring him in, tell him some of the story, and see what he says. He might not even know of a way to smuggle a man across the mountains. But he might."

Darien was frowning again, and Val had a fair idea of what he was thinking. He hated being in a situation with such impossible choices, forced to override his own convictions for the sake of a higher imperative.

"I suppose," he said, "it is worth it to ask him what he knows. And what he might be willing to do for the crown." He looked at Val. "Would you invite him to come to the palace at his earliest convenience?"

She lifted her chin. "I'll ask him. But I won't beg him to come."

"*I* could ask him, if you think my invitation would carry more weight," Yori offered. She was grinning again.

Val scowled at her. "If you could find him."

"I thought I might show up at the door of his new apartment?"

Val stared at her, knocked sideways by surprise and a rising fury. "You've been spying on—" But she quickly realized the truth and turned her blazing eyes on her brother. "You've had me followed! For how long? Since I've been in the city? I *hate* you!"

"No, unfortunately, it didn't occur to me at first that you, of all people, would take leave of your senses and start flinging yourself into mad adventures. Corene, yes—Zoe, unquestionably—but previously I'd thought you were completely rational."

"The added attention is a mark of affection," Zoe assured her. "I always have guards trailing behind me, even when I don't want them."

Val was on her feet, so angry, so tired, and so confused that she could practically feel the room spinning around her. "You're a cold, controlling, calculating *bastard*," she spit at Darien. "And I wouldn't help you right now if it meant saving Chialto itself. *No*, I won't talk to Sebastian for you. And if you send Yori to ask him to do you favors, I hope he laughs in her face. And I hope the stupid prince dies and we end up in a war and the whole palace burns down. And I never want to speak to you again."

And she turned on her heel and fled back to her room, sobbing the whole way.

Chapter Twenty-six

When Val woke up, the sun was shining so feverishly through her window that she crimped her eyes shut against the glare. Her room had never been this bright in previous mornings; it had to be well past noon. Or the curtains were open. Or both. But she always slept with the curtains closed because she hated being pushed from dreaming by an insistent, invasive dawn—

Someone had come to her room while she lay sleeping—

She snapped her eyes wide and found Corene perched on a chair just inches from the bed. "Good, you're awake," the princess said. "I was just about to start poking you."

Val put a forearm over her eyes. "Go away."

"Oh, I am not leaving your side until I hear every word of your conversation with Darien last night."

Val groaned and turned over on her side, pulling a pillow over her head. "Obviously, you've already heard it from Darien."

Corene hooted. "From Zoe. Darien hasn't said a word to me."

"Well, I'm not saying anything either."

She heard Corene jump up from the chair, and seconds later, the pillow was yanked from her hands and the covers were pulled down past her ankles. "Come on. Get up. You get dressed and I'll send someone for breakfast. Or, well, lunch."

Val turned facedown into the mattress. "I don't deserve food. After what I said."

"Probably not," Corene said. "But I can't judge that until *after* you've told me what it was, can I? Now get up."

"Has he already sent someone to fetch Sebastian?" Val asked, her voice muffled against the sheets.

"I can't even hear you."

Val sat up, sighing and pushing back the tangles of her hair. "I *said*, has he already sent someone for Sebastian?"

"That's the best part. He won't. Not until you tell him he can."

Val felt herself gaping in astonishment. "I don't believe you."

"Well, *I'm* not the one going around telling lies and keeping secrets."

"No, but—Darien never cares what anyone else says. Or thinks. Or does."

Corene grabbed her by the wrist and pulled her out of bed. "Come *on*. Get *up*. I want to hear everything. But you have to get dressed first, because I think this is going to end up being a very busy day, and you have to be prepared."

Val was ravenous and Corene was an admirably responsive listener, so the hour spent recounting the evening's revelations would have been enjoyable if Val wasn't squirming with such discomfort.

"I never should have said those things. I didn't mean them. I *never* say things I don't mean."

"Darien's smug righteousness can turn the kindest and most serene person utterly hostile. Darien can even put Josetta in a temper, and she's the steadiest person I know."

Val finished off her meal, wiped her hands on her napkin, and realized she had no more excuse to delay an appearance in Darien's office. "Does Zoe ever get mad at him?"

"If she does, she doesn't show it. I think Darien knows he can't control Zoe, so he doesn't try. She chooses—most of the time—to follow his lead, because she trusts his judgment. But sometimes she just calmly does or says something that is exactly the opposite of what he wants, and he just has to accept it. Meanwhile, *she* doesn't try to change *him*. But he will make adjustments to please her when he knows it's important. They're very different in almost every way. But they've figured out how to accommodate each other."

"Hunti and coru. You wouldn't think they could make it work."

"Sweela and hunti. You can make anything work if you try hard enough," Corene said, jumping to her feet. "Come on. Let's go find him."

Darien was, as expected, in his office. When Val entered—followed by Corene, who obviously was determined not to miss any more excitement—he was having a low-voiced conversation with a single visitor. It was the tall, thin, bald man she had seen once before in Darien's presence. When he turned to give Val one quick appraisal, she felt a chill brush over her skin. She was more certain than ever that this was one of Darien's spies, perhaps his most senior and ruthless one, here to deliver reports of deeds done in darkness.

"Thank you," Darien said and the man departed, shutting the study door behind him.

There was a short silence while Val stood in front of Darien's desk, lacing and unlacing her fingers while she tried to decide what to say. She was relieved when he spoke first.

"I believe we each owe the other an apology," he said. "I am willing to start. I cannot in honesty say I am sorry for placing a guard on you—particularly as Yori apprised me of some of your other escapades about which I had heretofore been unaware."

"What escapades?" Corene demanded, giving Val a slight shove in the arm. "Why don't you ever tell me anything?"

"Hush," Darien said to her, before continuing to address Val. "But I probably—I certainly—should have let you know I was doing it." He paused, clearly reluctant to speak the next part, and then continued. "And I am sorry for—for not being more open to the possibility that someone you care about has virtues, even if those qualities are invisible to me."

"If that's your idea of an apology—!" Corene exclaimed.

This time he didn't even look at his daughter. "I have never known you to judge anyone too leniently, so if you believe Sebastian can be trusted, then I believe it as well. And if you are willing to approach him on my behalf, I would be grateful."

"That's better," Corene said.

Val took a deep breath. "And I apologize for saying I hope the prince would die and there would be a war and the palace would burn down because I didn't mean any of those things and I am mortified that I even said them. I am horrified that they even crossed my mind."

There was the slightest hint of amusement on Darien's face. "But you don't regret calling me a cold and calculating bastard?"

"Well," said Val, with the glimmer of an answering smile, "we know you're not illegitimate."

"No need to apologize for telling the truth," Corene said.

"So do you think Sebastian would be willing to meet with me?"

"I don't know. I think he'd come and hear what you have to say, but I don't know if he'd be interested in helping you."

"What would win him to my cause?"

She tilted her head to consider that. Was that one of the reasons Darien was so successful at getting what he wanted—because he also tried to figure out what other people wanted, too? "Don't try to convince him to do it on my account," she advised him. "Don't say that if he helps you, you won't try to prevent me from seeing him. That will just make him angry."

"And you're not a bargaining chip in someone else's game," Corene said in a scolding voice.

"I like to believe I would not have taken that tack anyway, but it's good to know it wouldn't work," Darien said. "But what will?"

"I think just be honest with him," Val said. "Tell him the life of a man is at stake. He won't care so much about politics, about the risk of war. But he cares passionately about justice. He knows life generally isn't fair, and that makes him furious, and he does whatever he can to right that balance."

"That's admirable," Darien said. "That's not even an argument it would pain me to make."

"But he still might not want to help you. Or might not think he *can* help you."

"Well," said Darien. "I suppose there is only one way to find out."

※

Sebastian was about as dumbstruck as Val had ever seen him. Seen anybody.

"The king. Has a favor. To ask of *me*."

"Will you come see him? Today, if possible."

Sebastian's gaze went from Val to Yori, who stood in the kierten trying to look like she wasn't eavesdropping. "How can I be sure this isn't just some elaborate scheme to get me to the palace so he can arrest me?"

Yori did look up at that. "If he'd wanted to arrest you, he could have done it any time these past five days. We knew exactly where you were."

"How long have you been having me watched?" he asked in a hard voice.

Yori waggled her head back and forth. "We try to maintain a general awareness of all the unlawful players in the city, so you'd come to our attention a couple of times. But not until the king's sister enlisted our help down at the harbor did you become—interesting."

Sebastian gave Val a reproachful look. "Sorry," she said.

As usual, Yori seemed to be enjoying herself. "And once you rescued Princess Corene, you became valuable."

"I didn't rescue her. I didn't even know who she was," Sebastian said in irritation. "I was trying to protect Tina."

Val saw Yori lift her eyebrows at his use of the pet name, though she wasn't quite sure what the guard's reaction meant. Satisfaction, maybe? Confirmation? *Yes, this is a man who cares about something other than himself. We can work with him.* Or maybe her expression revealed nothing at all.

"So will you come with us to confer with the king?" Yori asked.

Sebastian was still irritable. "I suppose you'll drag me up to the palace if I refuse."

"I have been specifically instructed not to coerce you."

Sebastian inclined his head. Val could tell he was trying to gather the shreds of his usual insouciant confidence. "Then, yes, I shall come."

※

Val had expected Darien's study to be full of gawkers—Corene and Zoe at a minimum, maybe another prime or two, even a dowager queen. But

Darien was sitting alone at his desk, impassively reading some report, when Val and Sebastian entered. He instantly stood up and circled around the desk to greet them.

"Thank you for coming," he said.

Sebastian's voice was almost breezy. "Of course." His bow wasn't quite deep enough to be suitable for a king, but at least he made the attempt.

Darien surveyed Sebastian for a moment, his expression unreadable. Easy to read Sebastian's face, though—bravado and defiance masking a core of uncertainty. Val thought it had probably been ten years since the two had seen each other face-to-face. Perhaps they had last met even longer ago than that, when Sebastian was still a scruffy child, largely abandoned by his father, scrambling to figure out who he might be in a world that was mostly indifferent to his existence. And Darien was the burningly earnest politician's son determined to make his mark on the world. Smuggler and king . . . were they really so different now?

Darien's mind had apparently been following a similar line of thought. "You know, Sebastian," he said, "I'm not sure I've seen you since you were thirteen, and yet you look exactly the same."

"Less gangly and awkward, I hope," Sebastian said with a laugh. "You look the same, too, but more so."

Darien's face relaxed into the slightest of smiles. "More dull and frowny, I suppose."

"What? No, of course not!"

"Those were your exact words to me when you were—oh, eight or nine, I believe."

Val said, "Well, you *are* very frowny, but I wouldn't call you dull."

"I can't express how much I appreciate that," Darien said, and they all laughed. Darien gestured at a grouping of comfortable seats placed before the window. "Let's sit a moment and talk."

They settled into the chairs, though none of them truly relaxed. Darien folded his hands together before him. "I'm not sure how much Valentina or Yori told you about the situation in which I currently find myself."

Sebastian shook his head. "Almost nothing. Just that you thought I could—possibly, in some fashion—aid you." He made no attempt to hide his disbelief.

Darien nodded. "I have a package that needs to be delivered in stealth to a contact in Soeche-Tas," he said. "For various reasons, it has become clear we cannot get the package out of Welce through the harbor. So we want to explore the overland option. Unfortunately, as you are no doubt aware, there are few easy routes across the mountains because we so deeply distrust our Soechin neighbors. It was suggested that someone who routinely moves illegal goods across the border might have some success getting our package safely to its destination."

For a moment, Sebastian just stared at Darien. "You'll have to forgive me," he finally said, "if I say this seems too preposterous to be true. The king is asking a smuggler to exploit his knowledge and his contacts on behalf of the crown?"

"I know," Darien said. "I would find it ridiculous as well if the situation weren't so dire."

Sebastian leaned forward. "It's a mortifying position for you to find yourself in, to be sure. But look at it from my perspective, and it's even worse. It takes *years* to set up a reliable network, you know. This is not a group of people who give their trust easily! You cannot expect me to lead a brigade of the king's men straight to their doorsteps."

Darien nodded. "I wouldn't ask you to. I would ask you—if you are willing—to take this package by the safest route all the way to the main harbor in Soeche-Tas. Not telling me, or anyone, how you get there or who helps you. I will not have you followed. I will not send soldiers behind you to harass your contacts or even note them for future surveillance. I would hand you my bundle and let you go." He glanced at Val and back at Sebastian, adding softly, "My sister tells me in absolute terms that I can trust you, and I believe her."

It took Sebastian a moment to recover from this. "Your package must be of incalculable worth."

"Yes. It is the key to preventing a war."

"That's not what it is," Val objected. "I mean, it is, but it's more."

Sebastian glanced between the two of them. "My only guess," he said, "is that we're talking about a person."

"We are," Darien said. "I'm curious how you came to that conclusion."

"A document you can copy—or destroy. A cargo you can dump. Gold you can spend and scatter. And any of those goods can be thrown in a trunk and hauled across the country. But people are inconvenient. And they're frail. And they can set the world on fire."

"All of those things," Darien murmured.

"I told Darien you would only help him if you knew that a man's life was at stake," Val said.

"I would like to know who the man is."

Darien studied Sebastian for a moment. "Information about his whereabouts must not be disclosed to anyone. I meant it when I said his existence could start a war."

Sebastian's teeth briefly showed in a smile. "I'd wager I've kept more secrets than even you have, Darien."

"I doubt it," was Darien's dry reply, "but I'll believe you've kept a great many."

"So who is it?"

"One of the younger princes of Dhonsho. Who has abandoned his country in hopes of returning to lead a rebellion later. His father has reason to believe he is in Welce. If he is actually found here, seeking sanctuary—I have the darkest fears about what might happen next."

"Not Prince Kendol?" Sebastian asked.

Darien and Val both stared at him. "How could you possibly know his name?" Darien demanded.

"One of my contacts down at the harbor is a refugee from Dhonsho. His main topic of conversation is how brutal the king is and how Kendol is the only hope the country has."

"I am not entirely certain that a civil war in Dhonsho will have the results even the most fervent rebels desire," Darien said. "But that is not my concern. My concern is to make sure the prince does not die on Welchin soil before he can even make the attempt to overturn his father."

"Where is he now?"

"In the train of Princess Melissande, pretending to be one of her guards."

"What's your plan for getting him out of the city?"

For a moment, Darien's face showed weariness. "The hotel he is staying at is closely watched. We would have to get him through a ring of Dhonshon soldiers to set him on the road to Soeche-Tas. We could station you at some point along the northwest route out of the city and hand him over once we had gotten him that far." He hesitated. "If you wish, I am willing to send a handful of trusted soldiers with you to provide protection—"

"No," said Sebastian. "I wouldn't be able to get close to any of my own safe houses if I had additional men in tow."

Darien nodded. "As I anticipated. It seems wildly hazardous to send the prince of Dhonsho across Welce without a single guard, and deeply unfair to make you solely responsible for him, but there might be no other options."

"It is the *only* option. Or I cannot make the trip."

"Do you generally travel all the way across Soeche-Tas by yourself, or do you meet a confederate at the mountains?"

Sebastian smiled. "Sirix is a heavy cargo, my friend. I travel alone to the Soechin harbor and personally oversee the selection of barrels. But I have trusted friends who help me carry the goods back to Welce. I do not inquire if they pick up other items while they are on our side of the mountain and before they return to their own."

"Undoubtedly a wise precaution," Darien said.

"Is there a safe place to go once we reach the harbor in Soeche-Tas?"

"Yes, Princess Melissande has a reliable contact there."

"If he can, in fact, be trusted. If he is still alive." Sebastian shrugged. "When your work is underground, you learn to plan for sudden unforeseen adjustments. What if this contact is not available? What would I do with the prince then?"

"I admit I have not thought that far."

"My Dhonshon friends have taught me that there is no love lost between the Soechins and the Dhonshons. I could not leave him alone to wander the streets."

Darien briefly touched his fingertips to his eyelids. "This is impossible."

"I think you have some details to work out before you send me off into the night with the prince," Sebastian said.

Darien dropped his hand and looked up. "But you will accept the commission?"

Sebastian steadily returned his gaze. "If I like the payment you offer."

Val made a small infuriated noise. They were discussing a man's life; it did not seem to be the time to think about money. But Darien merely nodded. "It must be obvious that you could, within reason, name your price."

"A friend of mine is sitting in one of your jail cells even now. Release him."

Val thought that her own face must show as much surprise as her brother's, though Darien recovered more quickly. "What is his crime?"

"He killed a man."

Val gasped and Darien's frown returned. "I can't put murderers back out on the street."

"The dead man killed my friend's daughter. In a way so brutal I don't want to describe it in front of Tina. I think even you, Darien, understand the urge for vengeance. He never hurt anyone before that day. Never."

Darien nodded. "Let me investigate. I can't promise. I can't fix one monstrous wrong by perpetrating another one."

Sebastian's smile was crooked. "And yet, people try to do it all the time."

"But if I agree? You will agree?"

Sebastian hesitated a moment, but it was clear to everyone in the room that he had already made up his mind. Val wasn't sure what had appealed to him more—the moral obligation to save another man's life, the chance to prove himself worthy to Val's brother, or the opportunity to take on a dangerous and potentially deadly assignment. Or all of those things in combination. "I will agree."

Darien's face stayed impassive, but Val thought she saw him relax a little. "Then I am in your debt."

Sebastian flashed another smile. "Not if you pay me what I ask. Then we are even. That is the point of payments."

Darien came to his feet, so the other two quickly rose as well. "How very pure of heart you must be to actually believe that."

Sebastian was still laughing when there was a knock on the door, and Zoe stuck her head in. "I don't want to disturb you, but I thought perhaps I could interest you in some refreshments?"

"We've just finished up," Darien said. "Sebastian, this is Zoe Ardelay, the coru prime and my wife."

Sebastian offered a much more flourishing bow to Zoe than he had to Darien. "It is an honor to meet you."

She came deeper into the room. "And you have no idea how much I have longed to meet you! Val has been very mysterious about you, so all of us have just been guessing."

Sebastian looked bemused. "All of who?"

Corene pushed in behind Zoe. "Zoe and *me*," she said. "I'm Corene. *Thank* you so much for saving us the other night down at the harbor!"

"Princess," Sebastian said, bowing again.

"Sebastian was just leaving," Darien said.

"But surely he'll stay and have an early dinner with us?" Zoe asked.

"It's a kind offer," Sebastian said, "but I have many plans to make."

"You will be much better equipped to make them once you have a full stomach," Zoe said.

"That's quite thoughtful, but I—"

Corene waltzed up to him, took his arm, and pulled him to the door. He was so stunned he didn't even resist, though he did send Val one quick, panicked look. She was biting her lip to keep from laughing out loud.

"Nonsense," Corene said. "You're not running away this time. Come on. The table is already set."

※

Although Val was too on edge to enjoy the conversation, and Darien appeared to be too deep in thought to expend much effort in being sociable, the meal proceeded at a rather rollicking pace. Corene and Sebastian lived up to their sweela affiliation and were quickly making each other laugh and exclaim in delight. It seemed possible they might declare themselves best friends before the meal was over. Zoe seemed to thoroughly enjoy their antics, added a few cheerful comments of her own, and presided over the meal with her usual haphazard grace.

"Tell me again how the two of you know each other," she said.

"You've met my Aunt Jenty," Val said. "Sebastian's mother was the sister of Jenty's husband. Jenty raised Sebastian from the time he was about seven."

"My mother died. And my father was unreliable," Sebastian explained.

"If he was an Ardelay, as it seems he was, that almost goes without saying," Zoe answered.

"Nelson's reliable," Corene objected.

"Nelson always comes through," Zoe said. "But he will follow his own agenda if it suits him. You have to pay attention when you're making deals with the sweela prime."

"He's been very good to me," Sebastian said.

"And I adore him with all my heart. But he's still—Nelson." She surveyed Sebastian a moment. "If you're related to Nelson, you're related to me, since my father was Nelson's brother."

"I am, but the connection is distant."

She held out her hand. "I could trace the story in your blood, if you would trust me to learn it."

He glanced uncertainly at Val, and she nodded, so he laid his palm in Zoe's. Her fingers closed gently around his, and she seemed to lose herself in thought for a moment. Counting his heartbeats, maybe. Matching them to her own.

She was smiling as she released him. "Indeed. It appears we are some type of cousins through a patriarchal line. So you share a heritage with *two* primes. Of course, any of Nelson's relatives also can claim that distinction, but it still makes you a little special."

"Indeed, I feel quite extraordinary."

"You must consider yourself free to come and go at the palace as often as you like," she said.

At this, Sebastian looked at Darien and Darien looked at Zoe and Corene looked at Val and Val looked at the table. "Yes," Darien said in an expressionless tone, "we will always be glad to see you here."

"Well," Sebastian said. "First I have to figure out how I might carry out the commission you have for me. And then we'll think about what happens next."

The door opened, but it wasn't a servant who stepped through, it was the elay prime. "Oh, good, you're eating," said Kayle, picking up a clean plate from the sideboard and pulling another chair up to the table. "I've been traveling all day and I'm starving."

"Please feel free to join us," Darien said in an edged voice. Zoe and Corene could hardly contain their mirth. Sebastian's face showed awe, as if he had not imagined such rudeness existed in the world.

"You asked me to let you know if there was more Dhonshon activity in the harbor," Kayle said, around a mouthful of meat.

Darien frowned. "There hasn't been. At least, I haven't gotten a report to that effect from my guards stationed on the waterfront."

Kayle shook his head and gulped down half a glass of water. "No, they haven't come in through the docks. One of my aeromotive pilots was flying over the coastline this morning and he saw a handful of small boats tied up at a small cove. A very inhospitable spot, rocky and subject to strong waves. But these boats were small enough to navigate to shore. And large enough to carry maybe five men each."

"How many boats?"

"Three."

"So potentially another fifteen Dhonshon men prowling the city," Zoe said.

"I wonder if they're tired of waiting," Darien said. "Ready to take action."

"Or perhaps the first warships have had time to send word back to Dhonsho and get a directive from their king," Kayle said.

"We must act quickly," Darien said. He turned to Sebastian. "If you would. Make arrangements as swiftly as you can. I will take care of matters on my end."

Sebastian pushed his chair back. "I will. When can I expect to hear from you next?"

"No later than tomorrow evening."

Kayle, who had not seemed to notice that anyone except Darien was present, suddenly fixed his gaze on Sebastian. "Oh, hello there," he said. "It is good to see you again."

"Again?" Corene repeated.

Sebastian inclined his head respectfully. "Prime. I did not expect you to recognize me."

"Nonsense. I never forget anybody."

"That's a complete lie!" Zoe said. "You never *remember* anybody."

"I do if they're important to me," Kayle defended himself. "I remember you. And Darien. And Corene. And—" He paused, eying Val doubtfully.

"My sister Valentina," Darien said dryly.

"Well, she's not important to me," Kayle said. Before Val could reply in kind, he added, "Although I could see where she *might* be someday. So I will make a special effort to recall her."

Zoe and Corene were almost in convulsions as they tried to hold back their laughter. Darien said merely, "I'm sure Valentina will appreciate that."

Zoe recovered enough to ask somewhat breathlessly, "So how do you know our guest?"

Kayle was wiping his plate with a thick slice of bread. "Oh, I did business with him and his father some years ago." He shook his head. "The products were desirable, but the finances proved to be untenable." He studied Sebastian as he chewed his bread. "It was admirable of you to make good on all your father's debts. Many men would not have."

Now Val looked over at Sebastian, her eyebrows knitted in worry. She had known that the business had ultimately folded, but she hadn't heard about the debts. And the repayment. Sebastian never had any extra cash. How had he managed to scrape up the funds?

"It seemed like the least I could do for people who had trusted us," Sebastian said.

"Well, I like an honorable man," said Kayle.

Darien was also appraising Sebastian. "As do we all," he said.

"I suppose some people might prefer villains or fools," Kayle argued. "Then there's no guilt when you do them wrong."

Darien opened his mouth as if to challenge this, and then almost visibly gave himself a mental shake. "Just so."

Even Sebastian was smiling as he stood up. "I've greatly enjoyed our conversation, but if you'll forgive me, I have much to do." He nodded at the various occupants of the table. "Majesty. Prime. Prime. Princess."

Val was on her feet before his gaze came to rest on her. "I'll walk you out."

She waited until they were downstairs, through the busy great hall, and outside in the courtyard before she turned into his arms and kissed him. He returned the kiss with commendable ardor but broke away almost at once, though he kept his hands wrapped around her elbows.

"That wasn't so *entirely* terrible, was it?" she asked.

"Well, becoming king certainly hasn't made Darien any warmer or less opaque," Sebastian said. "But he's—broader in his thinking, maybe. He was such a self-righteous and unyielding *prig* when he was younger. Absolutely convinced no one else could have an opinion that mattered. And that seems to have changed a little."

She couldn't help giggling, because it seemed so true. "I think he's the same at heart. He still thinks he knows what the best *outcome* should be. But he's willing to try unconventional solutions if they get him what he wants."

"Partnering with me is certainly unconventional."

"Will you do it, though?"

"I said I would. Don't you want me to?"

"I don't like the idea that you'll be in danger," she said honestly. "But I would feel awful if you were able to save a man's life and you didn't do it."

He grinned and dropped a quick kiss on her mouth. "And I'd feel awful if I passed up a chance to make your brother like me."

She looked up at him somberly. "I told him that he shouldn't appeal to you on those grounds. I told him it wouldn't work."

He shook his head. "Oh no. If he'd said, 'Save the prince, and I'll let you marry my sister,' I would have refused the job. And then eloped with you the next day, just to spite him."

"I thought you didn't want to get married."

"Well, maybe just to annoy Darien."

"You've been thinking about it," she speculated. "Ever since we talked about it. And you're thinking maybe you want to get married after all."

He laughed, sighed, and hugged her tightly. "I'm thinking I don't know anything anymore," he said. "Except that I love you. And I have a chance to do something spectacular. And I have to go and make plans."

"I love you, too," she said. "It makes me happy to say it."

He kissed her again and stepped away. "It makes me happy to hear it. We'll talk tomorrow when I come back to tell Darien anything I've learned."

"I'll be here."

Chapter Twenty-seven

Val waited with Sebastian on the edge of Chialto. The sun was a bright coin that had rolled halfway down the slope of afternoon as it headed toward the precipice of twilight. They had been in the same spot since mid-morning and were prepared to linger past nightfall, if necessary.

The plan that had eventually been worked out was relatively simple and involved several different parties leaving Melissande's hotel over the space of a couple of hours. The largest group would include Melissande and one of the other Dhonshons in her entourage, and the assumption was that most of the watching foreigners would follow her. A second group would depart from the rear of the hotel in feigned stealth, clustered protectively around a man dressed in traditional Dhonshon clothing. Yori expected that a few of the king's men would have stayed behind, anticipating this kind of trick, and they would trail behind the second decoy. Finally, Kendol would exit the hotel accompanied by a few Welchin soldiers, all of them dressed like wealthy merchants and stepping boldly out into the open. The hope was that only one or two Dhonshon guards would be left behind to see him emerge, and they might not realize who he was.

Yori hadn't been sure when, exactly, each of these groups would set out, so she had wanted Sebastian in place well before noon. Val had offered to help him while away the tedium. He had originally made a half-hearted refusal, but he had given in without much persuading.

So now they were perched on top of the back storage compartment of a royal elaymotive, an act that required them to constantly rebalance on the slick metal of the frame. They were parked on a side street about half a mile out from the Cinque, within sight of the northernmost bridge that crossed the canal that encircled the entire city. It wasn't a particularly well-traveled route, since the narrow bridge led to a back road that took a somewhat meandering route to the northern border of Welce before it intersected with the wider and more well-maintained highways. But the fact that it was half-deserted was the reason that Sebastian preferred it. Fewer people to see them leave, fewer to notice them in transit. Now all they had to do was await the prince.

"I'll have to duck away the minute we see the guards arriving with Kendol," Val said. "Darien wants to be able to deny that anyone in the royal family has had any conversation with the prince."

"Not that the Dhonshons will believe him."

"Darien sets great store by the truth, even when everyone else assumes it's a lie."

Despite the fact that they were, simultaneously, tremendously bored and constantly on high alert, they had had a delightful day. The weather was perfect, a refreshing mix of lavish sunshine and playful breezes, and they had been required to do nothing except delight in each other's company. It had not been difficult.

Darien had supplied the sleek, stylish elaymotive that looked like it had come straight from one of Kayle's factories. At the moment, it was open to the elements, but Val saw a retractable leather canopy folded and lashed behind the passenger compartment, and she assumed this could be pulled up to form a reasonable roof. The car sat low to the ground and featured a design that was almost triangular, with a pointed nose, long body, and slightly wider back end. Val supposed three people could fit inside—one in the narrow front seat and two crammed into the rear—but it wouldn't be comfortable for long. But it was fast, Darien had assured Sebastian, the fastest model Kayle had yet produced, and outfitted with powerful headlamps that would enable a driver to take it out by night, even over uncertain roads.

Sebastian was the one who'd stocked it with provisions, and he proudly showed them off to Val as they waited. There were multiple cannisters of the compressed gas that powered the vehicle, so they wouldn't have to worry about running out of fuel. There were a few nondescript tunics and leggings, as well as some heavier jackets, in case anyone needed a change of clothes. Two blankets. An assortment of knives.

The most important items were the many gallons of water, bags of dried fruit, packets of nuts, and strips of cured meat. All the foodstuffs were neatly packed into canvas carriers that could be strapped over someone's back or slung over a shoulder. "Keep your hands free for climbing. Or fighting," Sebastian explained.

"It seems like a lot of food for two people," she said. "How long do you think you'll be on the road?"

"Depends on what we encounter. Bad weather. Enemy soldiers across the border. Old friends who no longer want the risk of housing a smuggler for the night. We might have to take a longer route than I anticipate. One of us might even get wounded."

Not for the first time, Val felt a clutch of worry in her chest. Well, honestly, she'd noticed a tense compression around her heart ever since this plan had been proposed. "And *then* what? It's not like you'll be anywhere you can seek help."

He pointed to a small metal box under the front seat. "Bandages and salve," he said a bit smugly. "I try to think of everything."

She was sure that plenty of potential misfortunes hadn't occurred to him, but all she said was, "I hope you're careful. I hope you stay safe."

He put a finger to her lips. He was smiling. "Everything will be fine. I've made this trip a hundred times."

"With much less dangerous cargo in hand."

"Eh, maybe not. Any Soechin soldier I might encounter on the road would instantly be able to identify a load of contraband sirix. But who will recognize the Dhonshon prince?"

"Aren't you even a little afraid?"

He considered. "I feel a great need to be circumspect, certainly. I am acutely aware of the hazards—and I understand how disastrous the consequences will be if I fail. But I'm not afraid."

"You're looking forward to it."

He laughed. "It will certainly be an adventure."

"And what happens after you return?"

"That," he admitted, "is an interesting question."

"Do you think that Darien—"

He flung up a hand, turning his head sharply. The pinched nose of the car was pointed directly at the bridge, but Val and Sebastian had spent most of the day looking the other way, toward the noise and bustle and color of Chialto. Watching and waiting for their precious and problematic passenger to arrive.

Sebastian was squinting down the road that, for most of the day, had only accommodated a handful of elaymotives and one or two horse-drawn carts. "I think I see a vehicle coming our way. Moving fast," he said.

They both slid to their feet, poised to act quickly. Val felt an unaccountable sense of uneasiness. "I thought the plan was to travel at an ordinary pace so they wouldn't draw attention," she said.

"Well," he answered, "plans change."

Even as he spoke, she could make out the car he had spotted. It was a small elaymotive, designed for one or two riders, and it was careering down the road at a breakneck speed. The vehicles in its path swerved out of its way, one of them dropping off into a shallow ditch. The car sped even closer, bouncing so violently over the road that the wheels occasionally left the pavement. It didn't slow down as it barreled in their direction, and Val uttered a faint cry and scrambled out of the way.

With a screech of brakes and a spray of gravel, the car wrenched to a halt a few yards past their own elaymotive, and the occupants clambered out. Val did little more than register that one was a fair-skinned Welchin and one was a dark-complected Dhonshon before she realized that both of them were bleeding.

They staggered toward the waiting elaymotive. Sebastian raced over to support the Welchin guard, but she motioned him to the prince's side. "Ambushed a mile from the hotel," she panted. "We fought them off and left them behind, but I'm guessing their friends will follow in our tracks quickly enough. Go *now*. As fast as you can."

"You're hurt," Sebastian exclaimed. "We can't leave you—"

"I'll be fine," she said. "But the prince needs tending to or I'm afraid he'll bleed out. Bandage him up before you go."

Val's attention had been caught by motion down the road. A mid-sized elaymotive weaving through the light traffic at a fast and deadly pace. "No time," she said. "They're almost here."

"Go!" the guard shouted. "Now! *Go!*"

"But the prince—"

Val grabbed Kendol's arm, feeling blood smear slickly along her palm, and urged him toward the elaymotive. "I'll treat him while you drive!" she cried. "We have to go!"

Sebastian had grabbed the prince's other arm and was helping him into the back of the car. "Tina, you can't come with us—"

"Hush," she said, climbing in next to the prince. He sank almost bonelessly to the seat, his head thrown back, his eyes closed, his left hand clutching his right arm. Blood oozed between his fingers. "Just get in and *drive*."

A moment only Sebastian hesitated, then he vaulted into the front seat and slammed the car into motion. Val saw the Welchin guard yelp and jump back. Within seconds, the elaymotive was thundering across the bridge and accelerating as the tires hit the rutted pavement of the northern passage. Two cars traveling in the other direction veered abruptly to get out of their way. Val thought she heard the drivers shouting invective as Sebastian raced past.

She tried to ignore the swaying and jouncing so she could concentrate on her patient. She bent down to retrieve the box of medical supplies, then cradled it against her body as she opened it, so nothing would fall out. As Sebastian had promised, it contained gauze, medicated creams, a bottle of antiseptic, and not much else. That might be a packet of needle and thread for sewing up bigger wounds, but as she couldn't possibly perform such a delicate operation while the elaymotive was rattling down the uneven road, she didn't bother looking more closely.

Holding the essential supplies in her lap, she turned as best as she could to examine the prince. He was on her left, which made it easy for her to pull his injured right arm into her lap. The purple sleeve of his embroidered silk jacket was sliced to tatters, so she just ripped it in half from the shoulder to the wrist.

Five wounds made raw red gaping marks along the rich brown of his skin. Three of the cuts were superficial, already beginning to clot, but the other two were deep and worrisome, still pumping out blood. Val hesitated, unsure which required the most immediate attention, terrified of guessing wrong. Then she simply closed her mind to panic. Choose; act; move on.

Unspooling a length of gauze, she folded it over and over to make a thick pad, then tore off another measure of cloth. She bound the pad tightly over the gouge that was high on the prince's arm, trying to create enough pressure to staunch the bleeding. Repeated the process with the other cut, which was closer to the wrist but running horizontally across the vein. Maybe not bleeding quite so much. The actions were simple: Make a pad, apply pressure, bind.

Not knowing if it would help or not, she spent the next ten minutes with her fingers wrapped around the prince's arm in both spots, adding the strength of her hands to the pressure of the bandages. She felt the cloth grow damp under each palm, saw the seeping scarlet stain the woven white, but neither pad grew saturated enough to start dripping. She thought the dressings were holding.

Carefully, she lifted her hands, and anxiously, she watched. Maybe the upper dressing grew a little redder; maybe a droplet trickled down Kendol's wrist. But there were no gouts of blood. The white cloth turned pink but not crimson.

She tore off another strip of cloth, wet it with alcohol, and cleaned her hands. Another length of gauze, more alcohol, so she could wipe Kendol's lesser wounds. As soon as she touched the moistened fabric to one of the half-closed welts, the prince jerked reflexively at the pain. Val barely caught the bottle before it tipped over. Her gaze flew to his face.

He still sat with his head thrown back against the cushions, his shoulders slumped down, seeming unable even to muster the strength to brace himself against the elaymotive's rough passage. Val thought that, if it weren't for the fact that his body was crammed awkwardly into the inadequate space, he would have rolled and flopped at every lurch and bounce.

"I'm sorry," she whispered in Coziquela. "I didn't mean to hurt you."

His eyelids lifted, revealing eyes of a startling amber color. Against the darkness of his skin, they were vivid as firelight in a night vista. "You did not," he murmured in response. "I thank you for your attentions."

She was not supposed to be talking to him—she was not even supposed to *be* here, in this car, on this journey, part of this desperate adventure—but now she could not glance away. She thought his face was a study in pain, but it was more than the physical wounds that harmed him. He appeared to be a man who had been molded by suffering, scraped by it, reshaped by it, bone-weary but unbroken. The bright eyes held an expression that was infinitely sad and infinitely enduring. The round face looked as if it had been elongated somehow by unrewarded patience; the full lips seemed compressed by sorrow. He watched her.

"I'm Valentina," she offered, since she couldn't think of anything else to say.

"I am Kendol," he replied. "Do you think I will live?"

"I've done my best."

"It is all I can expect." He closed his eyes again.

Sebastian seemed to have caught the sound of their voices over the noise of wheels and wind. "How is he?" he called from the front seat.

"I think I've stopped the bleeding. Other than that, I don't know."

"Darien will kill me. You shouldn't be here. I don't even know where I can leave you that will be safe—"

She leaned forward so her mouth was closer to his ear. "We can't worry about that now," she said impatiently. "We just have to go as far and as fast as we can."

"Can you look behind us and see if anyone is following us?"

She craned her neck so she could peer over shoulder. Most of the cars on the road behind them were vehicles that Sebastian had passed in their intemperate flight. But she didn't have to look too far back to see a cloud of dust raised by another traveler moving almost as fast as they were.

"Yes. But we seem to be outrunning them."

Sebastian almost laughed. "I've never been in an elaymotive this fast. In five hours, I bet we could put ten miles between us."

"That's good, isn't it?"

"It would be good if we only had to go fifty miles. But we have to cover around three hundred. We'll have to stop and eat. Change the fuel tanks." He shook his head, never lifting his gaze from the road ahead. "And once it's dark, we'll have to slow down significantly. Headlamps won't help us much. I like the back roads, but they're full of unexpected breaks and hazards. Can't risk going at this pace, but we'll lose a lot of time. And if I pull over to sleep a few hours—"

"I'll spell you."

Now he risked one brief glance at her. "You can drive an elaymotive?"

"Why would you think I couldn't?"

"I just—it didn't occur to me—"

"I got one of the big old clunky ones to take all over the property. I didn't think I'd like it, but I love it. It's so practical."

"All right then. I'll go for a couple more hours. We'll stop to eat, we'll switch places. I'll try to sleep so that I'm alert enough to drive at night."

"Maybe the Dhonshons won't be able to drive in the dark. Maybe they don't have headlamps."

"Maybe, but I don't want to count on that. And if there are a lot of them, they'll be able to change drivers a lot more often than we will."

"We're faster. We know the terrain. We have a plan."

She was close enough to his profile that she could see his grimace. "It's not much of a plan. Get to the border and run. And what I'm going to do about you—"

She reached out to stroke his red curls, wild and tangled from the wind of passage. She could tell that her own hair was already a disaster. "You don't have to do anything about me. We'll figure it out together."

"Right," he said. He accelerated to weave around a horse-drawn cart before an oncoming elaymotive could block his path. The horse shied and almost dragged the wagon off the road, and the other elaymotive braked dramatically to allow them room. Both drivers were yelling. Sebastian simply wrenched the car back into their own lane and kept going. "For now, just drive."

※

Val had been jittery with adrenaline when they first jumped into the car and took off; she had been stressed and frantic as she tended to Kendol's wounds. But it was hard to stay at a fever pitch of terror when there was nothing to do except hope that Sebastian's wild maneuvering didn't land them in a gutter. Kendol had closed his eyes again and hadn't bothered to reopen them. Val could tell, because she kept checking, that he was still breathing and his wounds had stopped bleeding. There didn't seem to be any other way she could help him.

And the only way she could help Sebastian was to occasionally check the road behind for any sign of their pursuers. But by now they seemed to have outdistanced the Dhonshons by so much that she couldn't even pick out shapes and shadows that might be their enemies. Was Sebastian right? Would they really be able to gain ten miles before the afternoon was over? What did that translate to in terms of time? How much time was a safe margin between them and the prince's would-be assassins?

At what point would they be out of danger?

She didn't know the answers, and there was nothing she could do. Trying to avoid crowding the prince, Val scrunched down in the seat until she could rest her head against the back cushion, and she closed her eyes. She wasn't surprised that she couldn't really sleep, but she was able to stop the ceaseless circling of her thoughts long enough to drowse.

They had been traveling at that bone-jarring clip for about three hours when Val felt the elaymotive begin to shudder and slow. She stirred and lifted her head, feeling her muscles spark with protest. Beside her, Kendol opened his tawny eyes and looked at her, though he didn't speak.

"I think we're stopping," she said.

Five minutes later, Sebastian had pulled off the road into a circle of patchy shade. They had traveled far enough from the city that they were in an altogether different landscape—not quite barren, not quite fertile, a tired mix of low, rocky hills, sparse grass, struggling underbrush, and the occasional defiant stand of trees too thin and too stubborn to be defeated by this unwelcoming terrain. Val was sure they must have passed any number of small towns and farmsteads while she was dozing, but at the moment they appeared to be in a wholly uninhabited stretch of land that felt like it could be a hundred miles from civilization. She had a hazy idea that, to the north, the landscape grew rockier, unfriendlier, and even less populated, but she wasn't sure she'd ever spent much time traveling down the northern road that ambled alongside the mountain border.

"Are we taking a break?" she asked. Her voice sounded as fuzzy as her mouth felt. She realized she was parched with thirst.

"For fifteen minutes. Then you can drive for a while."

Sebastian parked in the wispy shade and swung himself over the side of the car. Val climbed out more gingerly. Kendol opened his eyes and straightened in his seat.

"I am afraid I might need assistance to disembark," he said.

Sebastian helped him from the vehicle while Val opened the back compartment and pulled out supplies. In a few minutes, she had spread a blanket on the uneven ground and laid out a selection of food. Sebastian and Kendol had disappeared behind the trees to relieve themselves, and she kept her back decorously turned until they reappeared.

"Everyone should eat something. Drink something," Sebastian ordered. "But hurry." Val had never heard him speak Coziquela before and thought it sounded funny on his lips. Or maybe it was that his accent was unfamiliar to her. She supposed he'd learned a street dialect from various dubious colleagues, while she'd been trained in the version used in the queen's court.

They didn't have dishes or utensils, so they ate with their fingers and drank directly from a communal jug. No one felt like sitting on the blanket—in fact, Sebastian and Val paced to limber up their joints. Kendol shifted his weight from foot to foot but didn't look like he had the energy to try anything more taxing.

"How are you feeling?" Val asked him in Coziquela.

"I am in some pain, but it is not excessive," he said.

"Would you like to change out of your bloody clothes? There are some things in the car that you could wear."

"That would be pleasant, thank you."

Val gave him a soft gray tunic from the storage compartment and accepted his soiled purple shirt in return. The royal silk was luxuriously smooth against her fingertips; the bright embroidery looked to be actual gold. "It's too beautiful to throw away," she said.

"You can't drop it here, anyway," Sebastian said. "We don't want to leave any traces of the prince behind. And that is very much a Dhonshon item."

Val sighed, wadded it up, and stuffed it under the car seat. Before Kendol had buttoned the tunic over his bare chest, she motioned for him to pause so she could do a cursory check of his wounds. Nothing seemed to have started bleeding again, which she took as a good sign.

"I don't think I should change your bandages yet," she told him. "I'm sorry, I don't know much about nursing."

"We'll take the first aid kit with us when we leave the car behind," Sebastian said.

Val frowned. "You're abandoning the elaymotive?"

"Have to. Have to cross the mountain pass on foot."

"But—" She could think of so many objections. "But it's Darien's car."

He smiled briefly. "I was very clear about what would happen to it."

"And—I'm not sure Kendol will be in good enough shape to walk very far."

Sebastian shrugged. "He'll have to. There's no other choice."

"But—"

"I will manage," said the prince with his precise diction.

She blew out her breath. "All right. I'll manage, too. I don't have the right shoes for a trek across the mountains—"

"You're not coming with us," Sebastian interrupted.

"Where do you think I'm going?"

"You're going to drop us off and then drive as fast as you can somewhere else. Where the Dhonshons won't find you."

"But I—"

"Eat something," Sebastian said. "We need to leave here as soon as we can."

She scowled but stopped arguing. Of course it made sense that she wouldn't accompany Sebastian and Kendol into Soeche-Tas, but once she had jumped into the elaymotive, she had considered herself locked into this adventure. It seemed anticlimactic to be left behind at some lonely crossroads, but Sebastian had already made it clear that his Soechin contacts were wary of strangers. They might not even be willing to tolerate Kendol—particularly given the mutual distrust between Dhonsho and Soeche-Tas.

She hastily consumed some meat and a piece of fruit, stepped behind the trees for a moment of privacy, and then spent five minutes freshening up. A handful of water splashed across her face and hands, a comb dragged painfully through her knotted hair, a scrap of leftover gauze commandeered to hold a tight braid in place. Sebastian had returned to the car and was fussing with the fuel cannisters, swapping out an empty one for a full one, and placing the used one in the rear compartment so he would leave no clues behind for their pursuers.

Kendol was chewing with dogged intensity, as if he wasn't hungry but knew it was his responsibility as a dispossessed prince to maintain his strength. She tried to imagine what he was thinking. Surely he was wondering if he could trust the two of them—foreigners, people he had never seen before this day, who had no particular reason to risk their lives to keep him safe. Ever since he had been picked up by the first Coziquela ship, he had been completely at the mercy of strangers, helpless to change or even influence his fate. He couldn't even have been entirely certain that Melissande would not betray him, and yet he had put himself unreservedly in her hands. And now she had handed him off to people she herself barely knew and he had been wounded in his desperate attempt to escape.

What kept him going? What made him submit to their directives, acquiesce to every instruction? Was it simply that he had no choice except to hope that they were honorable? Or did he have faith that a higher power was watching over him, protecting him—not just as he endured this leg of his tortuous journey, but as he pursued his grander scheme of challenging his father for the crown? Was he a fatalist or a righteous believer? Or too numb and exhausted and buffeted by events to be either?

She didn't know how she could reassure him, didn't know if anything approaching reassurance could be offered in a situation like this. But she searched her memory to come up with a word that Saska had taught her just a few ninedays ago when she was sighing over the memory of her Dhonshon lover. "Friend," she said to Kendol in his own language, pointing first at herself and then at Sebastian, using the word reserved for the most heartfelt of relationships. "Friend."

The change in the prince was remarkable. His face loosened into an awestruck smile, his amber eyes lit with gratitude. Setting down the last of his food, he pressed his palms together, touched them to his forehead, and then bowed from the waist. "Friend," he repeated.

"I'm afraid I don't know many other words in your language," she said in Coziquela.

He straightened, still smiling. "The one word is enough."

"Is everybody ready? Let's go," Sebastian said, offering his arm to the prince.

Val slid into the driver's seat, quickly checking that she understood the levers and dials of this fancy new model. Everything seemed familiar enough, though shinier and handsomer than the battered old smoker she drove at home. She glanced at the horizon line. Probably three hours till sundown.

"Do I just keep driving on this road forever?" she asked Sebastian as he settled Kendol into the back.

He climbed in next to prince, folding his legs in a position that looked distinctly uncomfortable. "In about two hours, we should intersect with the Great Central Highway. Do you think you'll recognize it?"

She nodded. "If you take it south, it goes straight to the hunti estate. Mirti's place."

"Exactly. You want to go north. Toward the mountains. Pull over once you get tired—or once it gets dark—and wake me up."

She turned the car on and steered it back onto the pavement. Despite the need for haste, she kept the elaymotive at a sedate pace until she got a better feel for the responsiveness of the controls. But this new model handled as smoothly as she would have expected; on a better track, she thought, it would have proceeded with an almost imperceptible glide. She increased her speed as her confidence grew, and within twenty minutes she was passing every other vehicle in her path. Her face, now completely exposed to the elements, was soon both chilled and numb. If she hadn't braided her hair, she might never have been able to untangle it.

Well, no need to worry about that. No need to think about anything except distance. She stared straight at the horizon line and sped toward it as fast as she could.

Chapter Twenty-eight

Val had been traveling along the Great Central Highway for about an hour when she started thinking about stopping. Sunset had begun loitering over the landscape to her left, shaking out its flame-dyed hair to catch the attention of the brooding night. The car might be equipped with headlamps, but she didn't know where they were or how well they would illuminate the path ahead. Not only that, her eyes had begun to burn with strain and every muscle in her body ached from the combined hours of sitting in the car. It had been ten minutes since she'd passed a cluster of buildings where other people might be expected to gather, where someone might notice if an elaymotive rolled up with a Dhonshon in the back. Surely it would be safe to pull over to the side of the road again. Even if someone noticed them, soon it would be too dark for anyone to get a good look at the passengers in their car.

She slackened her pace and began searching for a likely spot. Trees were hard to come by in this part of the country, but all she really needed was a flat stretch of land that wasn't separated from the road by an insurmountable ditch. After a few more minutes, as the sky got progressively darker and her shoulders grew increasingly tense, she found an acceptable site on the opposite side of the road. She crossed the empty lane and eased the wheels over the edge of the pavement to the sandy ground below.

Careful as she was, the transition was bumpy enough to wake her passengers. She heard the two men stirring in the back seat, muttering a quick question and answer, then she felt Sebastian lean forward over the back of her seat.

"Where are we?" he asked.

"Maybe fifty miles down the Central Highway. I'm sorry, I had to stop."

"No, this is good. I've slept for three hours, and I feel pretty alert."

"I can't believe you could actually sleep under these conditions."

"I can sleep anywhere."

"For the first time in my life, I'm jealous of you."

He laughed. "All my dreams accomplished."

They pulled themselves cautiously from the car, moving slowly as if making sure their bodies actually still worked before they tried anything too strenuous. Kendol had shoved himself into a half-standing position, but he didn't try to disembark until Sebastian lent him a hand.

"Let's have dinner and switch drivers again," he said.

This time all three of them sank gratefully to the blanket that Val laid out over the rocky ground. The elaymotive was between them and the road, so Sebastian was willing to light a candle so they could see what they were eating. Val stretched out on her stomach and propped herself up on her elbows just to feel a different stretch in her back. She thought she was finally starting to get some feeling back in her face.

Kendol asked something in Dhonshon, shook his head as if to clear it, and repeated the question in Coziquela. "How much farther?"

"This road goes all the way north until it hits the main east-west highway along the border. If we turned west on that and followed it to the coast, we'd end up at the northwest harbor. That's the second-biggest port in Welce," he explained.

"Is that where you're going?" Val asked.

He shook his head. "No, but I hope it's where our pursuers *think* we're going. Just past the east-west road there's a small track that goes straight to the northern border. You can take a cart over it, or a single horse, but not an elaymotive. We'll go on foot from there. It's about twenty-five miles from there to the mountains."

Val raised her eyebrows. "That's a long way to travel under your own power."

Sebastian made an indeterminate gesture. "There are—people—who roam that area. Stake out a few campsites. Rent out a few horses. They're not always there. They won't always take a paying customer. But I think they'll help us."

"And once you cross the mountains?"

She could barely make out his face by the light of the single candle, but the smile in his voice was unmistakable. "There are a lot of variables. People who might help. Who might not. We could get to the coast in five days, or it might take a nineday and a half. Have to travel the route to see."

She wanted to protest. She wanted to beg him to be careful. Wanted to demand he turn back, insist they could find another way, say she didn't care if the prince made it to safety after all. But that would be pointless, she knew. They were committed to this venture, not just for the sake of Welce, but for the sake of this man who had no other hope in the world but them. If Sebastian had abandoned them here on this stretch of land in the middle of a lightless highway, Val still would have considered herself honor-bound to get the prince to freedom. It was one of the rules of the world. You did what you promised. No matter what it cost.

Sebastian reached over to pat her cheek. "I've done this a hundred times," he said softly, switching to Welchin. "If I didn't have Kendol with me, I'd be here just the same. Carrying a different cargo. But on the identical path."

"I'm not sure that reassures me as much as you think it should."

"I can't help it if you're the kind of person who senselessly frets herself to death." She gave him an indignant look and he laughed. "We'll be fine. I know what I'm doing."

"I don't have a choice but to hope you do."

His smile faded. "I'm more worried about you, frankly. I've been trying to figure out what you should do once you've dropped us off."

She was surprised. "Can't I just go back the way I came? I don't think I'll get lost. And if I do, I'll just stop at one of the places we passed on the way."

He looked troubled. "But if you retrace our route, you're bound to pass our pursuers as they come after us. I'm thinking it might be better for you to turn west on the highway once we intersect it. There's a small military outpost nearby—maybe fifty soldiers. They're stationed there to patrol the border, but any captain on assignment would be happy to spare a few guards to escort you back to Chialto."

"It seems like a lot of bother," Val said. "I don't see why it would matter if I pass the Dhonshons as I head back to the city. I mean, they won't have any idea who I am, will they? I could be anyone."

He gestured at the elaymotive, a looming bulk of shadows in the dark. "I would agree, except you'll be driving this car, and it's pretty distinctive. I've never seen one shaped like it, have you?"

"No, but they were pretty far behind us as we drove out of the city. They could hardly have seen enough to take in details."

"Unless they had field glasses. Which seems possible, even likely." He made a low sound of frustration. "*We* had some, tucked right under the front seat, but I completely forgot about them when we were racing away from the city. It would have been useful to get a good look at our pursuers."

She was skeptical. "How far can you really see with them? How clearly?"

His voice sounded grim. "They were close enough to us in the city that they probably would have been able to make out your face."

Val frowned and pulled herself into a seated position. All her bones protested. "Very well. So what if they did? It will be obvious you're no longer with me, so they'll just keep driving. They'll know they're on the right track, once they see me. That will put *you* in more danger, not me."

He shook his head. "I don't think so. I think they'll see you, and intercept you, and drag you from the car. And I think they'll—interrogate you. And it will be more dreadful than you can imagine."

She leaned forward to place a comforting hand on his leg. "I won't say anything. I'd never tell them where you are."

"That's what I'm afraid of!" he burst out. "You and you stubborn hunti heart! You'd let them beat you and torture you, and you'd never say a word! It stops my blood in my veins just to think about it, it really does. I'd rather think that you'd betray me at the first sign of violence."

She couldn't help a slight laugh. "You wouldn't betray me either, even if you were being threatened with your life."

"I would. I'm a feckless sweela man, I only care about my own skin. I'd tell them anything they wanted to know."

"No, you wouldn't. Oh, you'd answer them right away, but you'd make up some story so complex and detailed that they'd think it had to be true. *That's* the sweela way."

"Well, it's not me they're likely to find, so I'm still concerned about you."

She rose to her knees and kissed him, then settled back down in a cross-legged pose. Kendol watched this byplay with a close attention, but she couldn't tell if his expression was shocked, approving, or speculative. Would he think he was safer or more at risk if his two companions appeared to be in love? Did he even know what they were arguing about? She didn't think he understood Welchin, but he could probably guess that they were debating plans that involved him. Everything involved him right now.

She didn't know how to reassure him, so she answered Sebastian instead, her voice affectionately mocking. "Now who's fretting senselessly?"

"I have to say, between this trip and the misadventures down at Vernon Harbor, you have caused me no end of grief lately. I am not used to *worrying* about you."

"Well, I am very accustomed to worrying about *you,* so I'm pleased to think you finally know what it feels like."

He groaned. "Life was so much easier when you were safe on your country estate. Too far away from me, of course, but living your placid life, surrounded by your unalarming friends. I knew right where you were, and it was like a beacon in my mind. A small, welcome clearing in a great dark wood. Just knowing you existed in the world was a refuge for my heart. And now—" He swept a hand out to indicate the swooping darkness that unrolled around them in every direction from the central point of their single tiny flame. "You're on a perilous jaunt across the country and I can't even stay with you to protect you and it will be *days* before I even know if you're all right and the fear will eat at me every single minute until I see your face again. I'd almost rather go back to how we were before I knew you loved me, because at least then you weren't in danger."

She kissed him again. "You don't mean that."

He sighed, kissed her back, and came to his feet, drawing her up beside him. "I don't," he agreed. "But it's a very near-run thing."

Kendol managed to stand under his own power, but he looked a little shaky. "It is time to go now?" he asked in Coziquela.

"It is," Sebastian said, answering in kind. "Is there anything you need before we get back in the elaymotive? Do you want us to look at your wounds again?"

"I think it is best that they remain untouched. I am ready to go on."

They climbed into the smoker car, which felt just as small and cramped as before. "Try to sleep," Sebastian told them both. "We've got another couple hours before the turnoff. Rest while you can."

Despite this admonition, Val spent the first fifteen minutes of the drive sitting stiffly upright in the back seat, watching the road ahead. Brief though their stop had been, night had completely overtaken them. A faint line of exhausted gray still lingered low on the western horizon, but darkness had dropped over them like a cage of velvet. Val couldn't spot the moon, so either it hadn't risen yet or it was unhelpfully hiding its lustrous face. The starlight, while impressive, did nothing to illuminate their route.

But Sebastian had switched on the headlamp affixed to the front of the elaymotive, and the single beam cast a cone of eerie light ahead of them. It was more like a lambent mist than a useful torch, Val thought, creating a dreamy chiaroscuro landscape of featureless shapes against flat, pale surfaces. Nothing had any sense of depth or texture; the whole scene looked like a pencil sketch surrounded by an ink-black border.

Hazards were hard to see and, not surprisingly, Sebastian had dramatically slowed his speed. Even so, they frequently hit rough patches in the road with a little too much force, or banked unnervingly around a curve that had been invisible until the last moment. Three times, Sebastian slammed on the brakes when small creatures darted into his path. Val had to assume that any humans who were fools enough to be walking this road at night would be smart enough to leap out of the way when they heard or saw the elaymotive bearing down on them. And she had to hope that any drivers coming in the other direction would be outfitted with their own headlamps that would warn of their imminent approach. But it was all too easy to imagine collisions and catastrophes.

Once Sebastian had reached his turnoff point, Val would be continuing on alone. She wanted to study the manner of driving by night, watched only by the constellations. She observed for another mile, another five, as the road unfolded before them, a few hundred feet at a time. So the trick was to feel her way forward and not be spooked by shadows. She could do that, she thought. She was used to setting a course and sticking to it. She knew how to ignore distractions.

"Better get some sleep," Sebastian said from the front seat.

She leaned forward to kiss the back of his head. "All right. Be careful."

There was a laugh in his voice. "Always."

She settled in next to Kendol, whose deep breathing indicated he was already dreaming. Closing her eyes, she gave herself over to the uneven rhythm of motion and was quickly lulled to sleep.

※

The abrupt cessation of motion jerked Val awake. She sat up, fighting a sense of disorientation, struggling to open her eyes only to realize they were already open. The world was completely dark; that was why she couldn't see anything. Sebastian had turned off the elaymotive's front light, and night had crowded in from all directions.

"Val. Prince Kendol. It's time."

Val felt Kendol start and sit up. "This is where we leave the elaymotive and continue to travel on foot?"

"Yes."

"Then I am ready."

They all climbed out, stiffly and with infinite care. The warm air of summer had cooled considerably, making the night seem even unfriendlier. In the dark, even the slightest sound seemed magnified, freighted with significance. Their footsteps crunched on the road with all the noise of boulders falling.

Suddenly, a beam of light cut a swath through the suffocating darkness, and Val saw that Sebastian had turned on some kind of flameless lantern. She almost sighed with relief at being able to see something, anything, within the limitless sea of black.

"That looks like the headlamp on the car," she said. "I don't think I've ever come across one before."

"Similar principle, but the power source only lasts a few hours," he said as he opened the back compartment of the car. "I've got three with me, but I try to use them sparingly."

He had her hold the torch for him as he switched out the empty fuel tank for a full one, then he began lifting out bags of supplies and setting them on the ground at his feet. "I'm leaving one pack of food and a couple cannisters of water for you," he told her. "I've turned the car so it's facing west. It's just fifteen or twenty miles to the army outpost, and you should make that tonight, but I want you to have provisions in case something goes wrong. If you have to pull over to sleep, don't linger too long. We don't want our friends to catch up with you."

"Maybe they've given up by now. How far ahead of them do you think we are?"

"Two hours? Certainly no more than three. Plenty of time for you to get to the base, even if you travel slowly."

"All right."

"Did you see me turn on the headlamp? Do you need me to show you how it works?"

"Yes, please. I watched you but—"

After giving her a quick demonstration, Sebastian repeated the directions to the army outpost, then began slinging the supply bags over his shoulders. Kendol stepped forward. "I can handle some of our provisions," he said.

"I'd rather not risk having you open a wound or two," Sebastian said, a smile in his voice. "I'd rather carry the food than carry you."

"It does not seem fair."

"You can take charge of the first-aid kit if Val will get it for us."

Val quickly retrieved the satchel from under the seat and handed it to Kendol. "It's not very heavy."

"Thank you."

"Let's get going," Sebastian said.

He turned toward Val. She had already stepped so close to him that they were instantly face to face, chest to chest. The lumpy bags hanging around his body made it too hard to hug him, but she rested her palms on his chest and stretched her face up to his. It was so dark that the first kiss missed, and she felt the rough brush of his whiskers along the corner of her lips. But the second kiss was perfectly placed, mouth against mouth, tasting of unspoken words, banked desire, and reckless promises.

Sebastian lifted his head. "Be careful."

"*You* be careful."

"I'll see you again as soon as I possibly can."

Sebastian switched on his handheld torch, and by its light Val saw him trace a faint path that led from the road through a border of low bushes. She thought she could make out a hulking shape a few yards down this track—a hillside, maybe, some kind of geographical feature that would hide fugitives within a few swift paces. She waited until the tiny light was swallowed by the countryside, until she couldn't even imagine she could still follow its fey impossible sparkle.

At last, she climbed back into the elaymotive, which was parked at the T-shaped intersection of the two main roads, its pointed nose aiming toward the western border. She started the motor, turned on the headlamp, and edged onto the road.

Surely the Dhonshons would come to this intersection, assume the prince had fled west toward the coast, and follow as fast as they could. Surely the Dhonshons would miss that little footpath winding toward the northern border.

But what if they didn't?

What if some scuff in the dirt, an overturned rock, a broken branch, made them suspect that Kendol had headed for Soeche-Tas instead of the sea? What if they abandoned their own elaymotive to continue the pursuit on foot? What if Kendol's injuries had weakened him so much that he had collapsed on the trail?

What if the Dhonshons found him—and Sebastian?

Val couldn't allow that to happen.

She pulled the car in a quarter-circle, turned onto the Central Highway, and headed directly south. She knew exactly what she had to do.

※

Driving by the dim light of the single headlamp was even more disorienting than observing as someone else did it. Val proceeded at such a slow pace that she thought it might have been quicker to walk. She sat with her hands clenched on the controls, her body hunched forward so she could peer out into the dimness, senses alert for anything that might indicate danger. A sound. A flash of movement. An unexpected dip in the road. Trouble could come from anywhere.

She thought it was most likely to come roaring straight at her from the very direction she was headed.

She wondered if the Dhonshons would actually travel at night, if they were really only a few hours behind, if they had managed to follow Prince Kendol's trail this far, or if they had given up hours ago. If she *did* encounter them on the road, would they recognize her car, as Sebastian suspected? Or would they race toward her, see a solitary woman on a lonely journey, and speed right by?

She didn't want them to speed right by.

After she had been traveling for about an hour, she pulled off the road for a short break. It took a monumental act of courage to turn off the headlamp and let the darkness swallow her whole. The moon had risen when she hadn't been paying attention, though it was only half full and clearly not interested in making her life any easier. Still, it provided a wisp of illumination, an exhalation of foggy light. After she stood still for a few minutes, her eyes adjusted enough to let her step away from the car and be fairly certain she could find her way back.

Though she only stepped a few feet away and very quickly returned.

She freshened up, checked her supplies by feel, took a few sips of water and ate a piece of fruit. It took some digging around under the front seat to find the wadded up ball of fabric that was Kendol's shirt, and for a moment she was afraid it had fallen out of the car on one of their infrequent stops. But no, there it was. Wrinkled and stiff with metal thread and dried blood. She smoothed it out on the front seat. Then she felt around some more until she discovered the field glasses that Sebastian had so inconveniently forgotten.

She dropped these on top of the shirt to keep it from flying out of the car once she started moving again.

Back on the road. The headlamp's thin, brave wedge of light was the most welcome sight she had ever seen. She was starting to get the trick of night driving by now, so she increased her speed slightly, though she was nowhere near the pace Sebastian had set. But she had time, she thought. She just had to get to the main intersection before the Dhonshons did. Surely she had time.

Although time was a concept with almost no meaning at this point. She had no idea if it was midnight, if it was almost dawn; she couldn't gauge when a minute had passed, or an hour. Similarly, she had no way to measure distance. Had she traveled five miles, or a hundred? There was nothing in the world but this mysterious, shadowed road—this slow, ponderous vehicle—moonlight and starlight above her, dancing mistlight just ahead of her, always just ahead. Nothing else moved, beckoned, or even existed.

She could not remember a time in her life she had ever been this alone. She drove on.

Chapter Twenty-Nine

It was still full dark when Val arrived at the junction of the Great Central Highway and the road they had taken northwest out of Chialto. Still, she didn't think dawn was too far off. The moon had drifted toward the horizon and the eastern sky had lightened from onyx to shale. Surely any travelers who had stopped for the night would soon be on the move again.

She turned onto the intersecting road and traveled about a mile in the direction of Chialto. She slowed enough to sweep the car in a grand semi-circle so that she was once again facing away from the city, then she pulled off onto the side of the road.

This would be the tricky part.

Well, in truth, it had all been a little dicey.

She got out of the car and paced slowly beside it, back and forth, running her finger along the sleek metal to help her keep her balance and make sure she didn't accidentally step too far away. She was so tired by now that she couldn't stay seated, because she was too likely to fall asleep. She was so tired that she knew she might start making stupid mistakes.

But the eastern sky was definitely showing signs of lightening; now it was a transparent silver. She could almost make out shapes along the side of the road, trees and boulders and undulations of land. She could almost see to help herself to a tasty breakfast of dried meat, stale bread, and tin-flavored water.

Just so it was handy, she picked up Kendol's embroidered shirt and settled it over her head like the hood of a cloak. It was as long as a tunic and flowed down her back, covering her hair and shoulders. To hold it in place, she fastened a few buttons around her throat and led the hood fall back. She tried not to think too much about the blood decorating the fabric almost as much as the gold embroidery.

There. The sky was even lighter now. Was that motion on the road behind her? Had the day's traffic already started to run?

Val picked up the field glasses and peered through them, fiddling with the knobs until her view abruptly came into perfect focus. Yes, there was one large vehicle lumbering in her direction—it looked like it might be a public transport, or maybe even a commercial hauler ferrying goods from one end of the kingdom to the other. It was hard to tell if any other cars were behind it on the road. Were those dancing black spots faraway elaymotives or were they simply hallucinations conjured by her bleary vision?

Val dropped the glasses and rubbed her eyes. She tried not to think about how long she had been awake, but she assured herself that it hadn't been that long. Certainly there had been other times in her life when day blended into night into day, and she had suffered no ill effects. When the creek on her property flooded, threatening the lower fields, and she and her staff had worked through the night to move grain and equipment from various sheds and outbuildings. When one of the horses had had a difficult birth and the groom was inconveniently gone for the nineday.

When her mother lay dying, moaning from pain, and only Val's hands could soothe her.

She closed her eyes against memory and weariness. The sound of a motor rumbling by jerked her awake, and she felt her heart pound with apprehension. Had she slept? For how long? A moment—an hour? Had the Dhonshons slipped by her? No—no. The sky was barely two shades lighter, and the road in both directions was still largely empty. Everything was fine. But she couldn't fall asleep again. Couldn't close her eyes.

She bent over and pawed through the dirt until she found a small, spiky rock. She debated putting it in her shoe, but what if she unexpectedly had to run? So instead she clutched it in her hand, tight enough to feel its points practically pierce her skin. She had learned long ago that pain was the antidote to slumber. She just hoped this pain was powerful enough to overcome the overwhelming urge to sleep.

She squinted toward Chialto again. The road was starting to come alive now; the movement of traffic made it appear as if the pavement itself was rippling. She lifted the field glasses to her eyes again to study the oncoming vehicles. Another transport, which looked as if it might be carrying farm animals. A wagon behind a pair of horses and a carriage behind a team, traveling at two very different rates. Smoker cars weaving around the slower-moving vehicles. The one in the lead was low and sporty and—if her burning eyes could be believed—held only a driver.

But the one behind it . . .

She rubbed her eyes again and then stared grimly through the lenses, willing her vision to sharpen. The second elaymotive wasn't moving as fast, but it was covering ground at a brisk and steady pace. It was larger than her own car, but smaller than a transport—big enough to hold maybe six people, she thought. The closer it came, the more convinced she was that at least some of the passengers had the dark skin and bright wardrobe of the typical Dhonshon man.

She was so engrossed in the scene behind her that she had been paying no attention to traffic coming from the other direction. When an elaymotive whipped by her from the north, she was so startled she exclaimed out loud.

Steady, she admonished herself, catching her breath. *Focus. Almost there.*

But the spike of adrenaline chased some of her exhaustion away. She tossed aside her spiny little rock and climbed back into the front seat, pulling the purple shirt over her head as both a beacon and a disguise. She waited until the transport lumbered by, followed seconds later by the speeding driver in the sporty smoker car. Now the road behind her was empty except for the vehicle carrying the Dhonshons and, far behind it, the two horsedrawn conveyances.

She took a deep breath, then started the car and edged it onto the road, choosing a speed that would allow the Dhonshons to catch up to her within a few minutes. Her eyes felt like hot embers embedded in her face. Her fingers were clenched around the controls so tightly her bones ached. Her whole body was tense with trying to listen over the sound of her own motor to gauge the distance between her and the following car.

And then she heard it. A shout of interrogation, a yelp of triumph, and a growl of power as the pursuing vehicle leapt into a higher gear.

Val slammed open the fuel throttles and tore down the road as fast as she could go.

The flare of adrenaline had burst into a wave of fire that flushed her whole body with excitement and fear. Had she waited too long? Were they too close? Could she outdistance them over a short track, or would they catch up to her before she was able to hit her top speed? She felt the purple fabric billowing behind her as she raced away, heard another shout behind her, sounding slightly fainter.

The farm transport was just ahead of her and she veered into the other lane to pass it, then swerved back to her own side of the road just in time to avoid being hit by an oncoming smoker car. Once it passed her, she darted back into the other lane and this time made it safely around the slower vehicle. The sporty little car was nowhere in sight. Nothing but open road ahead of her for the next half mile...the next quarter mile...

Just as she spotted the Great Central Highway cutting across the route directly ahead of her, she heard the pursuing car squeal around the big transport, throwing debris up as it skidded back to its lane. Another whoop of elation from the Dhonshons.

Closer than she'd thought. She had to slow to make the turn, but she couldn't afford to lose too much time. She eased up on the controls just enough so she thought she could handle the curve without tipping over.

There was another shout behind her.

At the juncture, she wrenched the car hard to the left, hearing the wheels whine in protest. For a moment she thought she'd misjudged and would be thrown over the side onto the pavement, but the car righted and steadied. Instantly, she slammed in more fuel and felt the car leap forward in response.

The road before her stretched out level and empty for as far as she could see, but she knew that wouldn't last for long. Within a few miles, the land would start bulking up into gentle hills and dipping down into narrow valleys. The scrubby shrubbery that unrolled on either side of the road would give way to a few stands of short, hardy trees, which would soon be intermixed with taller specimens in thicker groves. And it wouldn't be long before the whole western margin of the road would be defined and bordered by the forest.

The forest.

She kept the car running at the fastest pace she could manage without careering into a ditch. She didn't think she was attaining the speeds Sebastian had managed, but she thought she was slowly drawing away from her pursuers. Not too far away, of course. The whole point of this exercise was to have them follow her.

She couldn't look behind her to check. She had to concentrate on the vista ahead of her. Road. Sky. Bushes and trees. The occasional lonely cluster of buildings that represented a small community or a sprawling homestead. More trees, taller and more looming with every mile.

With increasing frequency, she encountered other vehicles, either coming toward her in the opposite lane or clogging the route ahead of her. While the Great Central Highway was a major artery for the entire country, it was also heavily used as a local road, so she most often came upon horse-drawn carriages or early-model elaymotives that rumbled along at a sedate pace. She passed everything in her way as soon as she had an opening. More than once, she heard startled drivers berate her with indignant curses. She never bothered to even look their way.

She began to get nervous as she was stuck behind a farm cart pulled by a single horse that dawdled its way up a steep incline. She was afraid to try to pass it when she had no idea what might come flying over the hill, but her shoulders itched with the conviction that Dhonshons were staring and gesturing at her in mounting glee. How close were they now? How slim was her margin of safety?

The pointed front of her elaymotive was crowding the back boards of the wagon when they crested the hill. Ready to open the controls to full throttle, Val was forced to crawl along behind the wagon when she saw a convoy of three transports laboring up the grade. She wanted to scream from impatience and a growing sense of fear. Was it her imagination, or could she hear cheers of excitement from the Dhonshons closing in?

The second the last transport wheezed past, she wrenched her elaymotive around the wagon and urged it to its highest level of speed. She couldn't tell if the furious shouts from behind her came from the irate drivers or the thwarted pursuers. But wait—that was a word Saska had taught her. A Dhonshon oath. They were close, too close, she could almost feel their breath upon her skin, their hands upon her body—

But then she skidded violently around a curve, and none of it mattered.

There it was. The hunti estate. The land she knew as well as she knew her father's voice, her mother's scent. The one place she could lose herself and never be found.

The formal entrance to the property was another half-mile down the road, but Val wasn't aiming for the house. She had no desire to bring murderous foreigners into the living quarters of the property to menace the servants and staff. All she needed was to set a foot inside the forest.

And it was right there. The ancient wood. Crowding up against the edge of the road as if curious to see who might go flashing by. Extending west for acres and acres, filled with every variety of tree native to Welce. Hardwoods and softwoods, fruit trees and flowering trees, short ones that huddled together so thickly hikers could hardly push through them, tall ones whose long bare trunks suddenly exploded into greenery high overhead. Trees that collected rainwater, sheltered wild creatures, fed the earth, caressed the sky, held the whole world together.

Trees that had protected Valentina Serlast her entire life.

She simply steered the elaymotive off the road, into a narrow lane between two smooth slim trunks, and slammed to a halt so hard all her bones reverberated. Snatching up the folded blanket, two water cannisters, and the one remaining pack of supplies, she vaulted over the side of the car and sprinted forward.

Into the forest. Into her place of safety.

The moment the canopy of leaves blocked the sunlight from her face, she felt better. It hadn't occurred to her that she wasn't breathing, but suddenly she was sucking in great gusts of air, flavored with cedar and pine and wet leaves and damp soil and a spice she simply thought of as *green*. Her feet had no trouble navigating the hazardous, uneven ground. She did not trip over the protruding roots, slip on the slick half-decomposed needles. Sunlight was sparse, but she found it easy to see.

She ran.

Behind her she heard ominous noises—another elaymotive crunching off the road and up to the edge of the forest. Car doors slamming. Voices raised in sharp cries and swift responses. Heavy feet crashing through the undergrowth, impatient hands shoving aside low-hanging limbs until they snapped. One man yelled something in an eager tone, and she was sure he had just exclaimed *I see her!* although she didn't understand his words. The footsteps behind her grew louder, more urgent. The shouts grew delirious with excitement. *We have her!*

She kept running.

There was no path through this part of the forest, not even one of the faint trails that could be found closer to the main house. But she knew exactly where she was going and exactly how to get there.

And no one would be able to keep up with her.

She detoured around clustered trees that intertwined their limbs so tightly even she could not slip between them. She skimmed over fallen trunks that were so new they still sported freshly unfurled leaves and so old they were slick with moss. She ducked under heavy branches and clambered over masses of thick and tangled roots. All the while she breathed that rich, fragrant air, felt it fill her body with strength and her mind with light. Felt it nourish her soul.

The voices behind her grew fainter but no less urgent. Now it seemed likely the Dhonshons were shouting out a different set of questions. *Where is she? Can you see her? Have we lost her?*

Deeper in the forest now, so deep that in some spots the sunlight couldn't penetrate at all. Even on this warm day, a chill clung to these cluttered caverns; whatever grew in those shadows thrived in the dark. All around her she could hear the chatter and scatter of birds and insects and small forest creatures; now and then, she saw eyes peering out from under a braid of branches. She knew there were dozens more, hundreds more, of forest denizens, silent and invisible, who watched her pass.

She kept running.

Now the only human sounds she heard were her own—her shoes snapping dry twigs underfoot, her breath beginning to labor. She slowed a little, just enough to recover her strength, and strained to catch any noises from behind her. That might have been a man yelling in frustration, but it might have been a forest bird cawing in alarm. She slowed even more, adopting a steady but reasonable pace. Not much farther now—not much farther—

She pushed through a screen of shrubbery and there she was. In the stand of challinbar trees. She stood motionless for a moment, panting, feeling the last of her fear drain away.

She was sure she didn't imagine the sudden soughing of the upper boughs, as if the trees were conferring, waking each other from a pleasant drowsing to make sure they didn't miss this momentous event. *Look who's here! See who's come to visit! Valentina Serlast! Back again after so long away.*

She dropped her bundles in the middle of the clearing and made a quick circuit of the grove, laying a hand first on one rough trunk and then the next.

I've missed you, she thought each time she moved on. *I remember you.*

Each time, the echo came back. *We missed you. We remember you.*

She stopped last at the heartwood tree, the massive sentinel that watched over this forest, this estate, this nation—the great indestructible guardian whose roots encircled the world. *I need you,* she thought. *Take care of me.*

She would have sworn she heard the words spoken out loud. *Step into my arms.*

Pausing only to stuff the blanket into the back of the pack and sling the various straps over her shoulders, Val began scaling the tree. As always, the hardest part of the climb was on the lowest section of the trunk, when she had to search for knots and gnarls to serve as handholds. But she had done this a hundred times, a thousand. Her foot might slip and scrabble against the deep ridges of the bark, her hand might search fruitlessly for a purchase, but then suddenly there it would be—a burl, a bump, a cranny. A place to fit her fingers, tuck her toes. And she pushed herself up another inch, another yard.

Finally she reached the lowest branches and hauled herself up. She gained her footing and rested a moment, gazing at the green weave above her. How high did she need to go? What were the chances the Dhonshons could make their way to this holy spot in the center of the forest? Even Sebastian couldn't find this place if he wasn't with Val. She wasn't sure anyone could these days, except Mirti. And now maybe Natalie.

But sometimes people got lucky, stumbling across a treasure when they weren't even looking. Val resettled the bundles over her back and resumed climbing. Another five feet up. Another ten. She wasn't dizzy when she looked down, but the ground seemed very far away.

She decided this spot would do.

The massive trunk was narrower here, although still too thick for her to encircle it with her arms. The branches were thinner, springier, than those that spread out directly above the ground; they curved upward at the ends as if seeking the kiss of sunlight. But they were still solid enough to bear her weight, especially if she didn't edge out too far. Even better, there was a spot where two limbs met and interlaced, forming a natural shelf. A place where a woman could come to rest and lay her burdens down.

For a long moment, Val simply sat there, her back against the tree, her legs drawn up tightly to her body, her forehead on her knees. All the exhaustion that she had banished during her mad escape came crashing back in one devastating wave; she was suddenly shaking with fatigue. Her eyes, still burning from strain, now blurred with weariness. Her body ached from exertion, and her skin smarted with stings and scratches. She wanted nothing so much as sleep.

She forced her eyes open. She must take a few precautions first. She unfastened the strap of her pack, looped it over a branch, and fastened it again so it wouldn't fall, then she secured the two small water cannisters. She took a few sips of water, a few bites of food. She shook out the blanket and wrapped it around her shoulders, knotting it around her throat.

Nothing else was likely to drop to the ground below and betray her location. Well, *she* might unwarily shift position, jerk abruptly awake, lose her sense of balance and go crashing down through the plait of branches to her probable death below. It was doubtful; she had never tumbled out of any tree at any point in her life, even when she was a small girl just learning to climb. Still, she was so tired she didn't trust her usual senses. She pressed herself as deeply as she could into the join of trunk and branches, tried to anchor herself securely in place.

She thought she heard the murmuring of the challinbar tree, a voice as sibilant and soothing as the rustle of leaves. *I have you, hunti girl*, the voice whispered. *I will not let you fall.*

Comforted, cradled, secure, Val closed her eyes and slept.

Something woke her. A sound, too close. The cry of a hunting bird or a wild cat? The crack of an old tree limb coming down?

The footsteps of a man, stalking through the forest?

Stiff and sore and drugged with dreaming, Val struggled to come fully awake. It was hard to tell in the forest's perpetual gloom, but she thought it might be late afternoon. Not sure where danger lay, she kept her body entirely still and strained to listen. Were those voices, distant but urgent? Or simply the cries of small creatures announcing their presence in the woods?

The sounds came closer, grew more distinct. Those were definitely men calling out to each other, asking questions, trading information. She desperately wished Saska was here to interpret what they were saying. Had they somehow tracked her progress through the woods, following broken branches and footsteps in the moss? Were they simply making a methodical survey of the forest, combing through it acre by acre? How close would they come? Would they find her?

Even though they weren't near enough to hear, she held her breath. She stayed so motionless on her perch that no branch creaked, no leaf quivered. She waited.

The voices grew closer, changed in tone, as if the pursuers were asking more questions, displaying more confusion. Then one man spoke in a louder, peremptory tone. *Look over there!* he might have been saying. Val felt her whole body tighten with alarm, but whatever he had spotted, it wasn't her shape coiled high in the tree. She caught the distant sounds of people moving through undergrowth, and then the noise faded. The next time a Dhonshon voice came floating her way, it was fainter, farther away.

They hadn't found her hiding place within the challinbar grove. Whether the pursuers had been lured away by some false trail or whether the trees themselves had closed ranks and erased all sign of her passage, she didn't know. She just knew that for the moment, she was safe.

She was sure the Dhonshons would keep looking.

Night fell, and the Dhonshons didn't return. Feeling somewhat braver in the dark, Val made one cautious trip to the ground to relieve herself, then scrambled back up the tree. Despite her earlier nap, she still felt light-headed from lack of sleep and accumulated tension. She ate sparingly, supplementing her meal with a few ripe challin fruits. They tasted like summer and memory.

There was nothing else to do but try to survive the night. Val wrapped herself in the blanket, snuggled back into the niche of branches, and slept as well as she could. She kept jerking awake, uncomfortable, chilled, troubled by dreaming, needing a moment to remember where she was and why the night felt so ominous. Each time, she held her breath and listened, but the only sounds that came her way were the hoots and rustles of forest creatures who belonged here more than she did.

You belong, she thought the heart tree responded.

Each time, she was able to shift to a new position and fall into another uneasy slumber. Only to wake again, wonder again, wait again for any signal of danger.

Morning found her shivering and aching, not even certain if that *was* sunlight filtering so flimsily through the leaves. Clinging to one of the overhead branches, she came awkwardly to her feet to stretch her cramped muscles. Her grip shook loose a light spray of condensation. *Water,* she thought. *I'm going to run out of water soon.* Better make good use of whatever extra moisture had been sent her way. She carefully bent the upper limbs down and licked the dew off the smooth leaves. Inched out a couple of feet and reached for the next branch. Not enough, obviously not enough, but she still felt comforted by making the effort.

For the first time it occurred to her to wonder what would happen if the Dhonshons didn't stop looking for her. Her plan had always been drastically simple. She would lure them away from Sebastian and lead them to the forest, where no one would be able to find her. But she couldn't live in the challinbar grove forever. She could eat fruit from this tree, and others; she knew the locations of hidden springs where she could replenish her water. But she had no hunting skills and no cooking supplies, and she would soon use up all her food. And any time she climbed down from her hiding place, she ran the risk of discovery.

How long before they gave up? How long before she did?

Longer than a day, she thought.

She tugged down another branch, to find the leaves already dry. But three ripe red challin fruits dangled from their stems, a hedge against both thirst and hunger. She picked all three, pocketed two, and ate the third one.

She was hunti. Whatever the storm, she would not bend and she would not break.

※

Late in the day, the voices were back, but coming from a different part of the forest, as if the Dhonshons had made a great circle around the challinbar grove, a tightening spiral of exploration. Val had descended to the forest floor again for a short break, but at the sound, she shinnied back up and took up her post on the high branch.

As before, the voices drifted away before they got too close. As before, Val wondered what had thrown them off her scent.

As before, she sat there for long hours, strung with anxiety, tense with the strain of listening. The air around her grew chillier, denser, filled with the sounds of nocturnal animals. By that she knew that night had fallen, and she could relax, even sleep, till dawn.

The challinbar grove had kept her secret.

Chapter Thirty

V AL IS TWENTY-FIVE AND HER MOTHER HAS JUST DIED.
The event is both long expected and absolutely catastrophic. Val had thought she was prepared for grief, but she finds that the expectation of loss and the reality of loss are such totally different experiences that they bear absolutely no resemblance to one another. She had been sad before, prone to cry over small things, stupid things—a wounded bird, a shattered vase, a sweet and random memory. But now she is broken.

She expected grief to be an emotional reaction, but instead it is almost physical. She feels as though her body has been hollowed out, her insides scraped clean. Her stomach and her lungs and her heart are no longer functioning; her feet trip constantly, her hands are clumsy, she does not seem to be able to judge speed or distance.

Her head, by contrast, is hot and dense and packed with a tangled swirl of words and images and thoughts she cannot pin down. Her nose and cheeks are as flushed as if she has been sobbing incessantly, but she hasn't cried since the hour of her mother's death. Her gaze cannot settle, so she can only take in the world around her in small, sidelong glances. This makes it hard to converse with people, difficult to navigate the house without walking into walls.

Many of the funeral arrangements have already been made, since it has been obvious over the past quintile that her mother did not have much time remaining. There is much left to do, including greeting the many visitors who drop by and planning the ceremony itself, but Val cannot bring herself to do any of it. She can't think clearly enough. She doesn't have the energy or the will. Aunt Jenty, who has stayed at the house for the past nineday, handles everything with her usual compassionate competence.

Saska arrives two days before the funeral and promptly takes Val in hand, arranging for her to get a haircut, finding the appropriate clothes from Val's wardrobe, and insisting that Val eat.

"I'm not hungry."

"I don't care. If you don't eat everything on your plate, I'll call the footmen and have them hold you still so I can force it down your throat."

This is so extreme that it catches Val's wandering attention. "They wouldn't do that."

"Yes they would. They're as worried about you as I am."

"I'd bite your fingers."

Saska actually laughs. "Thanks for the warning! I'll use a spoon."

Val picks up her fork and attempts a bite of fruit compote. She's so surprised at the taste that she swallows it quickly so she can exclaim out loud. "That's challin fruit! Where did that come from?"

"Mirti brought some."

"I didn't even know she was here."

"I told her you didn't feel like dealing with company right now."

Val takes another mouthful. *"You're* company."

"No, I'm not. I'm Saska."

That is so indisputable it almost makes Val smile.

※

Darien and Zoe arrive the day before the funeral. Val allows both of them to hug her, but the embraces mean nothing to her. She's too angry at Darien for *not being here* to allow him to comfort her now, but she's too exhausted to fight with him. Zoe is still practically a stranger, so her expressions of sympathy come across as mere politeness. The coru prime seems intuitive enough to realize that her presence is not particularly welcome, so she makes no effort to draw Val into conversation. She sticks close to Darien for the whole visit, and constantly touches his wrist or his cheek or his chest, as if checking to make sure his heart is still beating, he has no fever, he is remembering to breathe.

"I love how much Zoe loves Darien," Saska murmurs that afternoon, but Val doesn't care. She wouldn't have cared if her brother and his wife hadn't bothered to come at all.

She is so numb by this point that she expects to get through tomorrow's ceremony dry-eyed and stony-faced—and in fact, she hopes she does. A hunti woman doesn't break, even in the face of grief. She doesn't bow under the weight of it. She is as solid as the heartwood tree in the challinbar grove, and just as impervious to cataclysms.

But Val has forgotten there are other primes in Welce, and some of them love her.

When Taro walks in the front door, Virrie at his side, Val feels something inside of her crumble. Her intransigent bones turn brittle, they betray her, she is weak, she is falling. Virrie cries out and Taro heaves his big body across the kierten so fast he catches Val before she has done more than sway on her feet. As soon as his arms go around her, she is sobbing; her chest seems to be cracking open with the force of her cries. No one could absorb that much pain from another person's heart, but Taro can. His arms tighten around her waist, his voice murmurs in her ear. *My darling girl,* he says, *lean on me.*

When he finally lets her go, she is alive again, but she almost wishes she wasn't. "It hurts so much," she whimpers.

"It does," he says. "It always does."

"I don't think I'm strong enough to do this."

He puts his arm around her shoulders and says it again. "Val. Lean on me."

�

For the next two days, when Val isn't with Saska, she's with Taro, and that's how she survives the ceremony, the visitation afterward, the conversations about what her mother would want done with her effects. Darien is already gone before most of these conversations conclude, but before he leaves, he does take the time to sit down with Val and the property manager to discuss the estate.

"It's in good shape financially if Valentina wants to stay here, but it would fetch a high price if she wanted to sell."

She is surprised. "Why would I want to sell?"

Darien seems equally surprised. "Do you want to stay here all by yourself?"

This seems like a stupid thing to say. "I'm hardly by myself with so many staff members on the property."

"Yes, but—"

"Anyway, this is my *home*. Where else would I go?"

"You could come to Chialto and live with me. I always thought you would."

The possibility has never occurred to her. She knows her expression must be one of blank shock, because after a moment, he sighs. "Well, any time you change your mind, just let me know."

She just stops herself from asking, *Why would I change my mind?* She turns to the estate manager and says, "What else do I need to know?"

✦

It is a relief when Darien and Zoe take off the next day. Val is sad to see Taro and Virrie depart, but they have lingered almost a nineday, and she is feeling steadier by the time they call for their carriage and hug her fiercely goodbye. Saska has announced that she has nowhere to be and she will stay as long as Val needs her, but Val can tell her coru soul is restless. At the end of the second nineday, she practically pushes Saska out of the house.

"Promise you'll let me know if you need me," Saska demands, and Val agrees. "And you never lie," Saska adds, "so I know you'll keep your word."

The house feels so empty once all the company is gone. Val has recovered some of her energy, so she is able to start chipping away at the many tasks that await her. Overseeing the cleaning that is always necessitated by any large house party. Answering the hundreds of condolence letters. Taking care of estate business that she has partially neglected over the past half a quintile and wholly abandoned for the past three ninedays. Speaking with the neighbors who continue to drop by to check on her, to invite her over for afternoon teas and family dinners.

She needs to go through her mother's personal items—clothes, jewelry, papers—but the task is too monumental to even contemplate right now. Jenty had said, "Don't even attempt it on your own. Let's take some time to catch our breath, and then we can work on it together. We'll bring Lissa, too." Val feels like she should be strong enough to handle this task by herself, that it is cowardly to wait for her aunts to help. But she simply cannot manage it on her own.

A nineday after everyone has left, she spends the whole day walking the boundaries of the property, noting where fences need to be repaired or trees have come down and need to be carted away. The estate manager has suggested turning a level stretch of ground into an extensive vegetable garden. Obviously, it would yield more produce than the estate can use, but his daughter has started to run a small business in cooking and canning, and she would happily oversee the cultivation if she could enjoy the results. Val spends a few minutes surveying the field in question, but she has already decided to agree to the proposal. Why not? Why shouldn't someone bring more living things into the world to replace all the ones that die?

She walks back toward the house with the slow, tentative gait she has adopted since the funeral. She moves as awkwardly as a woman on stilts, trying to keep her balance on legs that are not her own. That hollowed-out feeling has returned; she feels like her whole body is constructed of empty tubes that have been stuck together and bent at the joints. It is hard to predict how these semblances of limbs will coordinate with each other, and sometimes they don't. She has fallen more than once simply because her legs couldn't keep to a course and her flailing arms couldn't provide the proper ballast. Sometimes, when her foot strikes a hard flagstone on the garden path or her heel hits the smooth marble of the kierten, she feels an echo reverberate throughout her cavernous bones. The sound even rings through the vacant bowl of her skull. She has learned to set her feet with care.

By the time she makes it back to the house, she is dusty and cranky and overwhelmingly weary. She welcomes the exhaustion, because she thinks it might help her fall asleep and stay asleep. Then again, almost nothing does.

"There's company in the front parlor," the cook tells her as Val comes in through the kitchen door.

Val glances doubtfully at her wrinkled trousers and muddy boots and then decides she doesn't have the energy to change into something more acceptable. "All right," she says. "When do you think dinner will be ready? I might go to bed early."

"Half an hour is all I need."

"Thank you."

Val heads to the parlor, trying to summon the courteous smile that her caller deserves simply for the kindness of dropping by. But that expression turns to stunned surprise when she steps into the room and finds Sebastian waiting for her.

She had wondered if he'd heard her news, but she can tell by his expression that he has. Saska must have written him, or maybe Jenty. Val herself has had no time to communicate with anyone, and anyway, he has been on the move so much lately that she isn't even sure she has a good address for him.

"Sebastian," she says, because that is all she can think of.

He is moving toward her across the room, but cautiously, the way he might approach a wild animal, wounded and unpredictable. "I understand your mother died," he says. "I'll hug you if you want."

The sound in her throat is a choked cry. She flings herself across the room and lands in his arms, and he gathers her closer in a tight embrace. She feels the empty spaces in her body begin to fill; her hollow bones grow solid again. It is almost as if his touch is healing her. She scrubs her face against his jacket and can't stop crying.

Chapter Thirty-one

Val's second full day in the forest passed much like the first one. She huddled anxiously in her high nest, straining to catch any intimations of danger and making periodic forays onto the ground below. She was so low on water that she risked creeping through the forest to a nearby dell where an underground spring broke through layers of rock and soil to form a small, gently rippling pond in an almost lightless clearing. The place was a draw for creatures from throughout the forest, and her arrival startled away so many of them that the rustle of wings and hoots of alarm sounded like a cacophony. How close were the Dhonshons? Would they come to investigate the disturbance? She hurriedly refilled her containers and threaded her way down the unmarked paths to her own place of refuge.

A few hours later, she heard men's voices again, but she couldn't tell where they were coming from. The tension and the restricted rations and the lack of sleep were beginning to tell on her. She was thinking too dully, reacting too slowly. How would she ever be able to judge when it was safe to try to make her way out of the forest? She couldn't even assess if a sound was coming from her left or her right.

She was hungry, but despite her careful rationing, there was little left in her bag of supplies. All the boughs within reach of her hand had been picked clean of challin fruit; she would need to climb higher to find more. What if she was here another day? Another five? She simply hadn't thought that far ahead.

I will feed you, she thought she heard a voice say. She had started to distrust her senses, but maybe the heartwood tree had been speaking to her all along, just as she had imagined. She remembered a story her father had told her when she was so young she would have believed anything, about how he had spent a summer in the woods. He had brought no food with him, no water, just lived off the bounty of the forest. Not only had he gathered fruits and nuts and berries, he had partaken of a more elemental sustenance, or so he claimed, sucking the sap straight from the trunks of the challinbar trees.

Could he have been telling the truth?

I will feed you, the voice repeated.

Val came to her knees and crept as close as she could to the central trunk and began running her hands along the rough bark. Here—right at the height of her head—there was a smooth patch where the bark had worn away. In the center of that patch was a cylindrical hole, where a bird had pecked at the wood or an insect had bored its way in. Val cautiously poked a finger inside, but no ants or bees came bustling out, angry at her intrusion.

She hesitated, not certain she was thinking clearly, then she shrugged. Bending closer, she put her mouth to the small opening and dreamed of the sap rising through the wood, the heart blood of the heart tree, flowing to every heavy branch, every springy limb, every thin twig, every curled leaf. She thought of the alchemy of sun and soil, of rain and timber, blending and churning and flowering forth in small blossoms and tart fruits. *I will feed you,* the tree whispered. *I will feed the world.*

Her mouth was filled with a sweet syrup, thicker than honey and spiked with a rich patchouli flavor. She gulped it down and her mouth was filled again. She pulled her head back and saw beads of sap gather and spill down onto the bark. She grabbed one of her empty water cannisters and positioned it under the fissure, and watched as the sap continued to puddle and fall, slowly, steadily, drop by amber drop.

Not enough to live on, not for a whole summer, not as her father had claimed. But enough for a day. Enough to get her through till morning.

The night was long and chilly. Val felt like she barely slept, but when she startled awake, she knew that she had been anxiously dreaming. Even so, she didn't feel at all rested. Her eyes burned with weariness and her whole body ached, even her stomach, which clenched with hunger. She leaned her heavy head against the trunk and tried to catch her wandering thoughts. What day was it? How long had she been here? Was there something else she should be doing?

It is time for you to go, said the voice of the forest.

She sat up and shook her head, trying to clear her mind. *It's not safe,* she thought.

The voice came again, more insistent. *It is time for you to go.*

But where would she go? Back to the elaymotive? Was it still parked on the side of the road where she had left it, or had some enterprising passer-by seen an opportunity to acquire a fine new vehicle? Was she even alert enough to drive it down the road? Should she head for the main house? Could she make it there without being observed by the Dhonshons? Were they even still in the forest looking for her? When was the last time she had heard their voices? Maybe they had given up. Maybe she was all alone in the forest.

She was afraid to risk it. She didn't trust her own judgment. *I'll just stay another day,* she thought.

The next moment she cried out in alarm as the branches beneath her bent and shuddered in a nonexistent wind. Half-ripe challin fruits dropped noisily to the ground; a couple of dead limbs cracked and tumbled down. She felt the whole tree shivering, shaking itself off, as if trying to rid itself of unnecessary burdens. She clung to the nearest branch only so she didn't fall, but the message was clear.

It was time for her to go.

Once the tree seemed to sigh and settle into its usual placid state, Val gathered her survival gear and her shredded courage. She ate the last stale heel of bread, took two sips of water, and carefully descended to the forest floor. It was a moment before she could bring herself to step away from the challinbar tree—she stood there with her hand pressed against the bark, flooded with feelings of gratitude and unease, hoping the voice would speak again and whisper, *Stay.* But the tree remained silent.

Stifling a sigh, Val settled the pack more securely over her shoulder and began hiking out of the forest. Back to her car, if it was still there; back to the road. She would only head to the manor house if it seemed safe or if she had no other options. The last thing she wanted was to endanger everyone else living on the property.

She'd been threading her way through the forest for about half an hour when she came to another one of those small hidden ponds, this one ringed by supple grasswood trees that swayed in the faintest breeze. She sank gratefully to her knees, cupping her hands to swallow mouthfuls of water. Then she splashed her face and neck and forearms, trying to wash off some of the accumulated grime. She couldn't remember a time in her life she'd felt so wretched and dirty. It might almost be worth it to strip naked and try to get her whole body clean.

A sound behind her made her lift her head and turn around. She found herself face-to-face with a Dhonshon soldier.

He seemed as surprised as she was; for a split second they just stared at each other through the undergrowth. Then he let out a victorious yell and dove through the greenery toward her. She leapt to her feet and tried to scrabble away, but he caught her in a few quick steps with a grip that nearly crushed her arm. She cried out and struggled against his hold, but she was weak with sleeplessness and hunger. He yanked her against him and began dragging her forward, causing her to stumble over deadfalls and gnarled roots. All around her, the grasswood trees reached down their lowest branches and brushed their spindly fingers across her cheeks. None of them could save her.

Her captor kept calling out his news, and in a few minutes, more figures broke through the trees as fast as they could run. Soon six Dhonshons had gathered around her, arguing in a language she didn't understand. Were they trying to decide whether to kill her or take her back to Chialto as an item to barter? Or were they just trying to figure out how to get out of the maze of the forest? Except for the one with the painful grip on her arm, they all ignored her. But when she tried to yank loose and lunge for freedom, her captor backhanded her across her face so hard she felt her cheek bruise. Shoving his face into hers, he shook her forcefully and yelled a threat that she didn't have to translate to understand. She tried not to whimper, but she wanted to drop to her knees and weep.

One of the Dhonshons made a decisive gesture, pointed to his right, and began forcing his way through the cluttered woods. Val didn't know if she should be relieved or terrified that he had guessed correctly and was leading the other men directly back to the road. She tripped along behind them, her arm still caught in that viselike grip, as they broke through tangle after tangle of underbrush. How could he be so certain of his route? How could he not lose his way, double back on his path, get turned around, head off in the opposite direction? But he kept striding forward with perfect confidence, breaking through a screen of vines and branches, and the rest of them straggled along behind him.

Val was parched and scratched up and exhausted when, after more than an hour, the Dhonshon in the lead almost laughed in satisfaction. He pointed again, and they all peered around him to see a brightness ahead of them, an end to the emerald darkness that had enveloped them for three days. They started moving faster, weaving through the thinning forest, feeling the sunshine stroke their lips and cheeks. Val could hardly keep up as the soldier hauled her along at a quickening pace. She squinted against the brilliance, feeling her eyes fill with tears. She was so utterly wretched and she had failed so miserably. She could not even stretch her tired mind enough to guess what might come next.

The two lead Dhonshons were the first to break through the treeline into the sunlight, and then they shouted and recoiled. Instantly there was more shouting, a great chaos and clamor, and a second Dhonshon rushed back to grab Val's other arm. Before she could try to wrench away from him, she felt a sudden bite of metal against her side.

Her original captor leaned closer and whispered in Coziquela, "Be very careful, or you will die." That was when she realized he had a knife aimed at her ribs. The second Dhonshon was using one hand to grip her arm and the other to brandish a second blade right below her chin.

Now she tried to plant her feet; now she tried to take root right there in the forest. But with a slow, awkward, intertwined gait, the two men dragged her inexorably forward, past the last tree, into the blinding sunshine.

Val blinked and tried desperately to make out what she was seeing. Instead of an empty road, there was a crowded vista, dozens of looming figures appearing as nothing more than tall shadows in the blistering sun. She blinked again and narrowed her eyes, trying to clear her vision. Those were soldiers—twenty, maybe thirty—dressed in the dark blue of the Welchin livery, weapons at the ready, completely focused on the foreigners emerging from the woods. Incongruously, pulled up on the side of road was an open elaymotive with an old woman and a young girl cowering inside. Val could only guess they'd been meandering down the road on a gentle drive when they were suddenly swept up in a convoy of troop transports.

She had no time for them. One of the Welchin soldiers stepped forward and demanded in Coziquela, "Release your prisoner. We do not want to harm you, but we will." Val couldn't see clearly enough to make out the speaker's face, but she thought she recognized Yori's voice. How had Yori found her? And how could it possibly matter?

The men holding Val dragged her forward a few more paces so it was very, very clear that they had knives positioned at her throat and her heart. "Give us safe passage!" the Dhonshon leader bellowed. "Or we will kill her before your eyes!"

"Then you will all die," Yori said calmly. "You're not leaving here with this woman in your possession."

Don't let them murder me! Val wanted to cry. But her throat was too dry, her body too weak, for her to produce a single word. She was only standing because her enemies were holding her up. There was no way the Welchin soldiers could save her before one or both of the knife points went home. She had reached the end of her life here in the shadow of the place she loved best.

"Then we will all die, and she will be the first," the leader called, and he turned to gesture at Val's captors.

Who both screamed in pain and dropped to the ground as if their legs had suddenly snapped in two. Val almost pitched over beside them. She was still gaping at them in astonishment when—*one, two, three, four*—the other Dhonshons all cried out and crumpled to the dirt, writhing and moaning.

Dumbfounded, Val lifted her eyes just in time to see three Welchin soldiers racing to her side. One caught her before she could collapse; the other two knelt beside the fallen Dhonshons, grabbing their weapons and rolling their bodies out of Val's way.

"What—I don't—how—" she stammered.

No one answered her directly, but she heard another voice speaking out clearly over the groans of the Dhonshons and the urgent questioning of the Welchin soldier asking if Val was all right.

"You see, Natalie?" said the woman in the elaymotive. "I shattered all their bones right where they stood. *That* is why you don't want to cross the hunti prime."

Chapter Thirty-two

They headed to the estate to give Val a place to recover. Well, half the soldiers and all the Dhonshons departed immediately to return to Chialto, pausing only long enough for Mirti to repair the bodies she had broken. The others accompanied Val and her rescuers to the manor house because, as Mirti said, "I don't think Darien would like it if we dismissed *all* of his guards before we got you safely home."

Val was still a bit dizzy and disoriented as they arrived at the great house, though euphoria was making her almost as giddy as sleeplessness and hunger. She hardly knew what she wanted to do first—eat, bathe, or sleep—but she quickly decided to restore herself in that exact order.

"But how did you *find* me?" she demanded through a mouthful of food as she and Mirti and Natalie shared a meal in the cozy breakfast room.

Mirti glanced at her heir. "Would you care to explain?"

Natalie straightened self-importantly in her chair. "The *trees* told us, of course," she said. "You had been gone for two days, and Darien was very worried, and he sent soldiers after you but no one *really* knew where you had gone. And then Mirti and I were doing our lessons in the park and all of the trees started rustling and swaying, even though there wasn't any wind."

"Letting me know they had something to communicate," Mirti explained.

"So we put our hands on the trunks and listened," Natalie continued. She frowned. "I couldn't understand precisely what they were saying, but I could hear—it wasn't words exactly, but it was something. Like when you're supposed to be asleep but Virrie and Taro are in the other room talking and you can almost tell what they're saying. Like that."

"I knew right away, of course," Mirti said. "We set out that very afternoon, but I at least was reassured. I knew you were still alive, and safe in the arms of the heart tree."

Val had stuffed an entire piece of bread in her mouth, so she had to quickly chew and swallow before she asked the next question. "And then—once you got to the forest—did *you* speak to the trees?" It sounded ridiculous, said out loud, and yet she was sure that was what had happened. "Because it was as if they suddenly pushed me out of the grove. Insisted I leave. And I'd hardly traveled any distance at all before the Dhonshons found me."

Mirti nodded. "It was time for all of you to come out. I simply made that clear."

"I couldn't understand how the Dhonshons could find their way out of the forest so easily. *Everyone* gets lost there except me."

"*I* don't get lost," Natalie said.

"Indeed, I asked for their way to be made plain and smooth. And apparently it was."

"I was so afraid. I didn't even recognize you when we stepped out of the woods. And then when they just—fell to the ground like that—"

"I'm going to do that when I'm hunti prime," Natalie said eagerly. "Break all the bones of my enemies."

Mirti frowned at her. "It is not a thing to be done lightly. Or in the heat of anger. It is a radical act for a desperate time." She sipped at her water. "But sometimes it is a useful ability."

Val was still hungry, but she was yawning so much she barely had time to take another bite. "I think I need to sleep," she said. "We'll talk about this more in the morning."

But her fastidious soul could not bear to slide between cool, fresh sheets until she had cleaned herself from head to toe. Her hair was so matted she couldn't even comb it out, so she just soaped and rinsed the tangles, promising herself she would figure it out later. Her hair and skin were both damp as she climbed into the high, soft bed that had been hers as a child, in the room that still held her old furniture. She wanted to spend a moment sorting out her emotions, acknowledging memory and loss, but she absolutely could not keep her eyes open. She was asleep within a minute.

When she opened her eyes, it was nearly dark, though a rime of sunset outlined the window frames with fire. She remembered instantly where she was and what had brought her here, but sleep seemed to have infused her with a delicious nonchalance. Or maybe it was rescue and safety. At any rate, she lay there a few moments, luxuriating in a sense of well-being.

She was so relaxed that she barely reacted when she turned over and suddenly realized someone was standing beside her bed. It was only a second or two before she recognized the small shape as Natalie. She couldn't even summon outrage, though she tried for a scolding tone when she said, "You shouldn't sneak into people's rooms when they're sleeping."

"I thought you would be awake."

Val shoved herself to a sitting position. "I am now."

"Can I turn on the light?"

"Yes."

The gaslight from the sconce over the bedside table gave the room a soft, almost romantic glow. Natalie surveyed her with some displeasure. "You look terrible."

"I'm not surprised."

"And your hair is the worst."

"I'm not sure I'll be able to get a comb through it," Val admitted.

"Maybe you should just cut it all off."

"Maybe I should."

"I could do it for you."

"Are you any good at cutting hair?"

"I do it for my mother all the time."

Val couldn't remember the last time she'd seen Romelle, so she couldn't judge if this was a solid recommendation. Her hair had always been one of Val's few points of vanity and it was hard to imagine what her face would look like if it wasn't framed by those thick, dark curls. Then again, so many things about her life were unfamiliar to her now. Why not change her appearance as well?

"There used to be a pair of scissors in the top drawer of the dresser."

Natalie glanced over her shoulder but didn't move. "How do you know that?"

"This was my room when I was your age."

"I like this house."

"So do I."

"Mirti says it will be mine one day." She reconsidered and corrected herself. "No, she says that when I am the hunti prime, it will be mine to hold in trust for the *next* prime. That I must be a good steward of the land and the forest."

Val swung her legs over the side of the bed. "And I have no doubt that you will be excellent at the job. Now give me a couple of moments to freshen up, and then you can cut my hair."

※

Val sat with her back to the mirror while Natalie gravely undertook her task. She felt a sharp qualm the first time the scissors snicked shut, but after that she was fine. It was actually almost soothing to feel the matted locks fall away and watch them accumulate on the floor, symbols of a self she felt she had left behind. Ridiculous as it seemed, her head felt noticeably lighter with each snap of the scissors.

"I'm done now," Natalie announced.

Val ran a hand through what was left, feeling the freshly cut curls twine around her fingers. "How does it look?"

"Well, *I* like it. Turn around and see."

Val swiveled on her stool and spent a moment staring at herself in the mirror. The woman who stared back was not exactly a stranger, but not exactly familiar, either. The short style put all the focus on her face, making her eyes look huge, her cheekbones more prominent, her mouth full and determined. She touched her hair again and her reflection did the same. This was a woman who was less certain of the world than she used to be, but more sure about her place in it. This was a woman who had figured out what she wanted, and was surprised by it, but was still resolved to get it.

"You did a very good job," she told Natalie. "I like it."

"I made a mess," Natalie said. "We'll have to clean that up. But then let's go show Mirti."

※

Mirti approved of the new haircut, but then she was a woman who wore a short style herself because she simply couldn't be bothered to fuss over her appearance. She also was not inclined to spend much time discussing other people's fashion choices, so she quickly turned the subject.

"Will you be ready to leave in the morning, or do you need another day to recover?"

"I'd like to spend a little time showing Natalie around, if I can," Val said. "There are all sorts of special places in the house and on the estate that I think only children know about. She shouldn't miss out."

Natalie's eyes grew big. "Are there secret passageways?"

Val smiled at her. "Maybe."

"And hidden rooms?"

"Not exactly. But I'll show you tomorrow."

They spent the entire next day exploring the grounds and the manor. Val would have thought it would be sad and painful to escort someone else around her old house, revealing her favorite spots—the nook in the library, the cubbyhole behind the dresser in Darien's old room, the concealed door on the second landing of the servants' stairwell, which led to a tiny room barely big enough for two people to stand in. There were still two ancient velvet cushions on the floor, which appeared to have become nests for mice, and the small square window still opened, though it required a lot of force.

"I *love* this!" Natalie exclaimed. "This is where I'll bring my sister Odelia whenever she comes to visit. She'll never want to leave!"

"This is where my mother would always look for me when she couldn't find me anywhere else."

But Val wasn't sad, not at all. Natalie could be an exhausting companion, full of endless questions and uncompromising opinions, but her curiosity about the house and her appreciation of its quirks gave Val a sense of deep happiness. Another person would love this place as much as Val had, and so, with a light heart, Val could move somewhere else.

She still wasn't sure where that *somewhere else* might be.

※

They set off early in the morning, a cavalcade of vehicles. Mirti took the controls of the elaymotive she had driven all the way from Chialto, and Val and Natalie settled in behind her. Two troop transports followed. Not entirely to Val's surprise, the sleek expensive smoker car she had abandoned on the side of the road had disappeared before rescue arrived, but she figured even Darien would consider that a good trade for the safety of his sister.

But had her action ensured the safety of the prince? And Sebastian?

"Is there any word?" Val asked as they set out. It was a question she'd tried not to ask more than once an hour since she'd emerged from her bedroom with her new haircut.

Mirti just shook her head. Either Sebastian and Kendol had not spent any time camping near the woods, or the trees in Soeche-Tas didn't bother to communicate with their colleagues across the mountains. Mirti wasn't sure. It hardly mattered, since the end result was the same—she knew nothing about Kendol's perilous passage. She had no idea if the prince and his escort were even still alive.

But of course they were. Sebastian had made this trip dozens of times and always emerged unscathed. He was clever, he was resourceful, and he had an uncanny ability to make friends in the unlikeliest of circumstances. He would be fine. Of course he would be fine.

But anything could have happened. They could have gotten caught in a rockslide on the northern slope of the mountains and cartwheeled to their deaths. They could have fallen into a river and drowned. They could have been attacked by wild animals that surely must be roving the unfriendly countryside of Soeche-Tas. They could have been betrayed by the contacts Sebastian had always trusted in the past or encountered random strangers who had a passionate, unreasoning hatred for Dhonshons. There were so many ways to be unlucky.

One of Sebastian's blessings is luck, Val reminded herself. It had always buoyed him through a life of chaos and danger. Surely this was not the time the blessing would fail him.

Natalie was too restless to sit still for long and Mirti was not in any particular hurry, so they stopped frequently on the journey. When they were near any small town or settlement, Mirti hunted up an establishment that served food, but twice they pulled over on the side of the road just to stretch their legs. Each time, Mirti chose a spot graced by at least a single tree and made a point of striding over so she could rest her hand against the trunk.

Each time, she looked back at Val and shook her head.

No news.

Maybe there was nothing to know.

Val would not let herself dissolve into worry. She was hunti; her spirit was even more unbreakable than her bones. She stiffened her spine and climbed back into the elaymotive and kept her face turned toward Chialto.

※

They spent two nights on the road at small but comfortable inns where the proprietors were delighted to welcome the hunti prime. Finally, around noon on the third day, they made it to Chialto. The soldiers took the first opportunity to turn off toward the guardhouse, while Mirti drove straight to the palace. Val was surprised at the jolt of warmth she felt when its white walls and gracious lines first moved into view. When had this place come to feel like home?

She had to suppose that fleet-footed sentries had been posted somewhere along their route and raced back to the palace to alert Darien, because he was standing out in the courtyard when Mirti pulled up. His arms were crossed over his chest and his face was unsmiling, but Val was convinced he was happy to see her.

The three of them climbed out of the elaymotive, taking a moment to stretch their cramped limbs, then strolled over to greet him.

"I suppose Yori gave you a report when she arrived with the prisoners?" Mirti asked.

"She did. Although I would like to hear your version of events, too."

"We broke all the bones of the Dhonshon soldiers," Natalie boasted. Mirti frowned at her, and the girl lowered her gaze, abashed. "*Mirti* broke all their bones," she amended. "But that's not something the hunti prime should do unless the situation is dire."

"An excellent philosophy," Darien approved.

"Is there any news from Sebastian and the prince?" Mirti asked a second before Val could voice the question.

Darien shook his head. "We are all impatient, but even once they make it to the embassy, Sebastian will need to find his way back. That will take some time."

"Not too much time, I hope," Mirti said, nudging Val with her elbow. "Or this one will expire with worry."

Darien nodded and changed the subject. "Why don't you give yourselves an hour to unpack and recover, then meet me in my study?"

He waited until Mirti and Natalie had stepped through the door before uncrossing his arms and resting his hands on Val's shoulders. His face was still its usual grave mask. "I was more worried about you than I have ever been at any point in my life," he said. "You were not supposed to be on this journey at all."

"I didn't plan to be. But the Dhonshons were racing toward us and the prince was bleeding and I couldn't let him *die*."

"The sister I remember would not have been on *any* of the adventures you have embarked on since you have come to Chialto. Have you changed, or have I been wrong about you all along?"

She considered that. "Both, I think," she said at last.

"Change is difficult for a Serlast."

"*You've* changed."

His smile was fleeting. "In what ways am I different?"

"For one thing, you fell in love with a coru woman."

The smile lingered longer this time. "That indeed saw me completely remade. And yet at the same time it made me more sure of who I am. It is as if I saw myself in contrast to Zoe and so it made all my own traits clearer and more certain."

"And you've become *king*."

"I was always interested in power."

"Yes, but you liked to work in secret. Moving pieces around. Not putting yourself forward. Now everyone is watching you and your life is very public."

"I still have secrets."

Val snorted. "*That* is not a surprise at all."

"But we are not talking about me," he said. "You are the one who has suddenly become someone I do not entirely recognize."

"I'm not sure I recognize myself either," Val confessed. "And yet, I feel such a certainty about everything I've done. Everything I want to do. Sometimes I don't think I have changed so much as become more of who I am."

"An interesting thought."

"Elidon said something the other day. One tree might live in the forest and stay there forever, holding onto the soil, drinking in the light. Another tree might grow until it achieves full height, and then it's harvested and turned into an object of beauty and value. I always thought I would stay rooted in the forest. But now I think I'm meant to go out into the world. Same person. Different purpose."

"And what exactly will this purpose be?"

"I don't know," she admitted.

"I would tell you to be careful not to let Sebastian make your choices for you," Darien said. "But I cannot imagine anyone who is less in need of that advice."

She laughed. "No. But he will be the reason for some of my choices."

"Then I hope he realizes just how beautiful and valuable this particular harvest is."

"I think he always did."

"Well, I am glad you are home safely," he said, drawing her into one of his rare embraces. It was almost like hugging the challinbar tree. He was that solid, that elemental, that necessary for binding the world together. Val rested her head against his chest and felt for a moment like a lost child who had stumbled into safety.

She stepped away and lifted her head, but before she could speak, she heard running footsteps. They both turned to find Corene bounding out of the door and heading straight in their direction.

"You're back, you're safe!" Corene exclaimed, almost knocking Val over with the force of her greeting. Then she pulled back to get a better look and had to muffle a scream. "Valentina! What have you done to your *hair?*"

Chapter Thirty-three

The next five days were a glacial form of agony.

No word from Sebastian. No word from any of Darien's spies. Mirti made regular forays into the various city parks to make her own unconventional inquiries, but returned unsmiling and uninformed.

Val could barely stand it.

She distracted herself with more activities than she could generally tolerate in a quintile. There were lunches with Melissande, who strove for her usual bright vivacity, though her smile was strained and her laugh was often missing. There were two large dinners with local business owners, and two smaller ones with family and close friends. Nelson draped his arm around Val's shoulders and whispered, "He's a sly and wily sweela man. Too smart to be caught in any trap. He'll be fine, just you wait and see."

There was a visit from Saska, who dragged her to an evening performance at a theater just barely on the respectable side of the southern loop of the Cinque. The play was ambitious and confusing, punctuated by a great deal of shouting and loud, random noises from offstage. Saska loved it, but Val got a headache.

They paused for a drink on the way back to the palace. Val amused herself by trying to guess which of the patrons in the bar might be one of Darien's soldiers, sent to discreetly guard her. "Why weren't you *in* the play instead of watching it?" she asked.

"Oh, I've given up the theater."

"You have? How have you been spending your time, then?"

Saska grew even more animated than she usually was. "I've been volunteering at the shelters run by Princess Josetta. She's just amazing. She seems like this soft and kind-souled elay dreamer, but she has such strength of will. She can do anything."

"I don't know her very well, but she seems like one of those people everybody likes."

"Yes, and people trust her. There's this new project—maybe you know about it?—the Soechins are recruiting impoverished girls who might want to move to Soeche-Tas and marry rich old men. Well, it's more complicated than that—"

"I do know about it," Val said, amused.

"And Josetta helps the girls understand exactly what the life would be like and helps them decide if it would be good for them, and people just put their faith in her. It's so inspiring to watch."

They talked a while longer about the elay princess and her charitable work, but Val couldn't keep her mind entirely on the conversation. What if she was sitting here, laughing and at ease, while Sebastian was lying in a ditch somewhere, painfully dying?

Saska obviously noticed. "Stop worrying," she said. "Everything will be all right."

Val spread her hands helplessly. "I don't care about *everything*. I care about Sebastian."

"That's what I meant. Nothing has happened to him."

"You have no way of knowing that."

"No, but you do. If he was hurt, you would sense it. You would *feel* it, all the way in the core of your body."

"That's a fanciful and ridiculous notion."

Saska grinned. "Well, I *am* fanciful and ridiculous."

Val shook her head. "I don't believe it. I need proof. I need to see his face."

Saska reached across the table and squeezed Val's hand. "You will. Any day now. I know it."

Val didn't believe her. But the fifth day of waiting was almost over, so now all she had to do was get through the next one. And the next. And maybe the next.

A hunti woman could endure anything.

※

The question on Val's mind was: Where would Sebastian go first?

When he made it back to Chialto, he would come looking for her, of that she had no doubt. It made sense that he would come straight to the palace, where he knew she was living, and where he knew the king would be impatiently awaiting his report.

But she was fairly certain he would prefer his first reunion with Val to be away from Darien's cool regard. She would prefer it, too. But where would he look for her? The park on the southern edge of the city? His new apartment? Maybe her better strategy would be to await him at the canal bridge on the northwestern corner of the city, where they had been parked before speeding off on the first round of the adventure. It made sense that he would return by the same path he had taken on the outbound trip—or did it? He must know every route into and out of Chialto. If he had somehow been discovered by Dhonshons, if Soechins had caught him in the company of fellow smugglers, he might be fleeing angry pursuers. No telling what bridge he might take into the city. He might even travel by sea. She had no way of knowing.

"Don't you realize that Darien has guards stationed at every possible entrance?" Corene demanded the morning of the sixth day. "It doesn't matter where you go. One of Darien's people will find him before you do."

"I can't sit here another minute. If he gets here and I'm gone—tell him I'll be back before nightfall."

"I'll come with you."

Val stopped her with a look. "I don't want *you* with me any more than I want my *brother*."

Corene was grinning. "How rude. And if you don't think there will be guards following *you*—"

Val put her hands up to stop her. "I'm leaving now. I'll be back later."

"If he arrives," Corene said innocently, "where should I tell him you've gone?"

Val just shook her head and walked away.

In the end, the park seemed like the most logical choice. As before, she took several transports to her destination, changing vehicles three times in the hopes of throwing off any unwanted escort. She'd been so eager to get away from the palace that she left without bringing any supplies, so she stopped at a small corner market for food and water. But the weather was mild enough to make it a pleasant prospect to sit outdoors all day, dreaming of the return of an absent beloved.

The park was empty when she arrived. She dropped her bundles on the sweela bench, then paced around idly, wondering if she should have brought a book to help her pass the time. Her attention kept being pulled to the metal cauldron in the very center of the space. She was so worried about Sebastian that she was almost afraid to pull blessings for him. What if she pulled three ghost coins, or three that exhorted her to have courage? They would provide no reassurance at all.

But she had to try. She had to know.

She knelt beside the kettle and plunged her hand into the cool pile of metal disks, stirring them around with her fingers and trying to convince herself to choose one. They were blessings, after all. Surely any guidance they offered would be a comfort. She closed her eyes, took a deep breath, and drew three very quickly, one right after the other, placing them facedown on the ground.

Taking another long breath, she opened her eyes and turned over the first coin. Intelligence. That was good, that meant Sebastian would use his quick wit to outsmart his enemies and travel safely back to Welce.

She picked up the second coin. Luck. One of Sebastian's own blessings, and possibly his favorite. A propitious sign for a man on a dangerous mission.

She spun the third coin between her fingers for a few moments before finally flipping it face-up to read the glyph. Love. The last time she had pulled this blessing, she had been with Corene, and she had been coaxed into telling the truth about Sebastian. For the first time.

But she didn't remember ever pulling this coin for him before, not in all the time they'd known each other. She remembered what he'd said the first time they made love, when she had discovered that he wore a necklace hung with all the blessings she'd given him over the years. He'd told her only one was missing, but he hadn't told her which one, and she hadn't had time to sort through the charms on the chain to figure it out.

But she was pretty sure she had pulled it now.

She clutched the three coins in her hand, made a fist, and pressed it against her forehead. *I love this intelligent and lucky man*, she thought. *May he come back to me very soon.*

※

In the next five hours, three sets of people strolled through the park. Two were families, one was a pair of lovers. The two women headed straight for the barrel under its slanted roof, and then glanced around to see if anyone was nearby. The shorter one, a small-boned and fair-haired woman, motioned Val over.

"We've come for blessings," she said. "We're getting married tomorrow. If we each pull one, would you choose the third?"

"I'd be happy to," said Val. No one ever turned down the opportunity to pull blessings for someone else. Besides, she was desperate for a distraction.

Her taller companion had a somber expression that lightened beautifully when she smiled, which she did when she drew the first coin. "Time," she said. "A lifetime together."

"Oh, I hope so," the smaller one replied. Her face looked tense as she mixed the coins, but it relaxed when she glanced at the one she pulled. "Love," she announced. "Not that we need a blessing to tell us what we already have, but I'm so happy to see it."

Val bent over and stirred the kettle, almost as anxious as she'd been when she was choosing coins for Sebastian. The last thing she wanted to do was provide an awkward blessing for a couple just starting out together. So she felt profound relief when she read the glyph in her hand. "Kindness," she said.

The blonde impetuously threw her arms around Val. "Oh, thank you so much! It could not be better!"

"Her last lover was anything but kind," the other woman explained.

The small woman stepped back, smiling up at Val. "Can we pull coins for *you*?"

Val hesitated, but a stranger's blessing always carried a greater power. "I would appreciate it," she said.

This time, the blonde picked first. "Change," she said uncertainly. "Is that good or bad?"

Val smiled. "I used to hate it," she admitted. "But right now I'm in the middle of it and I think—I hope—it's a good thing."

The tall woman wasted no time plucking a disk from the cauldron. "Loyalty," she said.

Val's smiled widened. "One of my own blessings. My favorite, in fact."

They waited, so she was obliged to step forward and pull the third coin herself. "Travel," she said, and she actually laughed.

"You don't seem unhappy," the smaller one said cautiously. "I'm a homebody myself, so it's not a blessing I like to see."

Val nodded. "Like change, it used to be something I hated," she said. "But now I might be looking forward to it. Thank you."

"Thank *you*," the tall woman said. "We have to go, but we're glad we met you here today. We'll remember you at our wedding."

"I hope your marriage is attended by all the blessings," Val replied. "Every single one."

The incident left Val feeling suffused with warmth and too restless to settle back on her bench. Maybe she should hike back toward the Cinque, see if she could find shops nearby where she could browse for a while just to kill the time. Maybe buy more food. Or a book. Paper and ink, so she could write to her long-neglected estate agent—

But those were footsteps hurrying down the street. One set of footsteps. Running. She felt her breath tangle in her throat, and she clasped her hands against her heart as she turned toward the break in the trees and simply waited. She found she could not take a single step.

The branches parted and Sebastian stepped through.

They both cried out wordless exclamations of joy and relief and flung themselves into each other's arms. The next few minutes were nothing but disjointed explanations and protestations. *So worried! . . . But there was no way to hear from you . . . And you're safe? You're all right? . . . Did the Dhonshons find you? . . . Did the Soechins let you pass? . . . I took refuge in the forest . . . I was never in any danger . . . I can't believe you're all right . . . I love you . . . I love you . . .*

At last, Sebastian groaned and drew Val against his chest in a crushing hold. "I cannot believe I am saying this, but we have to go talk to Darien. I am obliged to report to him as soon as I can."

Val lifted her head, beset by a new concern. "Did anything happen to Kendol?"

"No, I delivered him as planned. If the Coziquela ambassador can't get him to safety, well, I've done my part."

"Did any of his wounds get infected?"

"His injuries slowed him down and we had to rest more often than I would have liked, but I didn't see any sign of fever. He never complained. I don't know that I would have had that much fortitude."

"I wonder if we'll ever learn about the end of this adventure. Will he make it safely to Yorramol? Will he challenge his father?"

"I imagine if he overthrows the Dhonshon king, the news will spread throughout the southern seas," Sebastian said. "So we'll know *then*."

"It seems like a long time to wait."

"Some stories take years to unfold."

"Like ours."

He dropped a kiss on her mouth. "Like ours, indeed."

"I chose blessings for you while I waited."

"Did you? What did you pick?"

"Intelligence and luck. I threw them back."

"And the third one?"

She pulled the coin from her pocket and showed it to him. "Am I right? Is this the only one you're missing?"

He took it from her, cradling it in both hands and smiling in delight. "It is! The last one. The best one." He kissed her again. Then, slipping the disk in his own pocket, he wrapped his arms around her and drew her closer. "I've changed my mind," he whispered against her mouth. "I think we should stop at my apartment before we head on to the palace. Darien can wait another hour or two."

"I was thinking the same thing," she whispered back.

They were holding hands and not quite running as they pushed through the leafy overhang on the path out of the park. They had only gone three steps when Yori stepped forward from a spot where she had clearly been loitering.

"All done talking?" she asked, grinning at their expressions of surprise and dismay. "Let's go to the palace. I've got an elaymotive waiting just up the street."

Chapter Thirty-Four

Darien listened intently to Sebastian's narration of his passage across the mountains and through Soeche-Tas. It did not escape Val's attention, so she was sure it hadn't escaped Darien's, that Sebastian was never specific about exactly where he and Kendol had stopped for the night or who they had sheltered with. It would have been hard to reconstruct his path.

"I have to assume there were costs involved in some of these arrangements," Darien said when Sebastian described hiding overnight in a secret room beneath a tavern when Soechin soldiers stopped for a meal. "Obviously, I will bear those expenses."

Sebastian grinned. "I'll happily take any reimbursement you care to hand over," he said, "but I was making a few transactions of my own. I had plenty to trade for a bed here and there."

Darien's eyes sharpened. "You were carrying contraband in addition to the prince?"

"I had to make a profit somehow. I always carry cargo both into and out of Welce."

"What was the product?"

Val was wondering the same thing. Sebastian had been too loaded down with survival essentials to be carrying anything larger than a bag of jewels. Maybe he was lying.

"I think that's why it's considered contraband," Sebastian drawled. "Because it isn't sanctioned by the king."

Darien sat back in his chair and eyed Sebastian for a long moment. Val felt her chest tighten up with worry in a way it hadn't while Sebastian was recounting his sometimes terrifying tale. It was always unnerving when Darien started to think things over.

"I have to assume," Darien said at last, "that you realize you don't have much to gain by antagonizing me right now. When you've just done me a signal favor. When you've announced you're in love with my sister. When every reasonable man would consider this an auspicious time to stay in my good graces. So you're only doing it to prove that no change of circumstances will ever truly tame you."

Sebastian laughed out loud. "Well, I'm not sure I can count on remaining in your good graces," he explained. "So I can't afford to lose my best sources of income."

"I'm rather hoping you'll accept a job offer from me."

Sebastian stopped laughing. "What?"

"Surely you know I maintain spies all over the southern seas. I thought I might convince you to gather information for the crown."

Now Sebastian was pale with anger. "I would never turn over evidence on my friends. If you think that, you know *nothing* about me."

Darien shook his head. "Oh, I know what I need to know about the thieves and smugglers of Welce. It's Soeche-Tas where I've never been able to get a foothold. I wouldn't ask you to betray the members of your trusted network. But you could certainly share news that I might not be able to acquire in any other fashion. Carry messages I have found it difficult to deliver. Listen for and repeat to me the rumors you hear in taverns and brothels." He glanced at Val. "Perhaps not brothels."

"You're serious."

"I am not generally considered a prankster."

"No, but—you're *serious*. You're asking me to work for you."

"You would not be the first man whose dubious morals I was willing to overlook in the interests of achieving an important goal."

"What would I have to give up? Obviously, you wouldn't want me to keep smuggling sirix, but I—"

"You'd have to keep smuggling," Darien interrupted. "Or your friends would become suspicious."

Sebastian stared at him.

"Smuggling in both directions," Darien added. "Though I'd feel more comfortable if I knew what you were spiriting *out* of the country."

"Information, mostly," Sebastian said in a subdued voice.

"Not about national security, I hope."

Sebastian shook his head. "Names of merchants who will take unauthorized products. Harbormasters who will look the other way. That sort of thing."

"I can live with that," Darien said.

"But I—but you—" Sebastian rubbed a hand across his eyes, as if the world had suddenly become blurry and he was trying to bring it back in focus. "I need some time to absorb what this might mean. If I even want to do it."

"Certainly. I imagine it must be a momentous decision for a man like you to consider turning respectable."

Sebastian glared at him. "There are all kinds of insults in that sentence."

Darien was smiling faintly. "My apologies. I'll pretend we like each other if you will."

Now Sebastian laughed. "You're a cool bastard."

"I am. And you're a hotheaded rogue. But we can be valuable to each other, I think, if you're willing."

Val couldn't contain herself any longer. "How do I fit into this new role you have planned for Sebastian?"

Darien rested his opaque gray gaze on her. "Any way you like, I imagine."

She appealed to Sebastian. "Will your disreputable friends trust you less if they think you're involved with me?"

He gave a crack of laughter. "On the contrary. They'll trust me even more. They'll think you're learning things from your brother and passing them on to me." He glared at Darien again. "Of course, that only works as long as he doesn't lie to me."

Darien lifted both hands in a gesture of innocence. "I can envision times I might want you to share misinformation. But I'll let you know when I'm asking you to spread lies. Is that fair enough?"

"I'll think about it," Sebastian said.

"You didn't answer the question," Val insisted. "Where do I fit in?"

"You could come with me on smuggling runs," Sebastian said with a grin. "You were pretty handy when Kendol needed help."

"I have been thinking," Darien said. "Soeche-Tas has always been almost impervious to my attempts to gather knowledge. I've never successfully established a network of spies, and my straightforward diplomatic efforts have netted me little gain. But we are about to set up an office there to help patriate the Welchin girls who are recruited as Soechin brides. It will function somewhat as a dormitory and place of refuge for the Welchin girls whose marriages don't work out—but it can certainly double as an information-gathering outpost. I'll need someone to run it. I was wondering if it would be a job you might enjoy."

Val felt her mouth drop open.

"You aren't particularly fond of Chialto, so you have no incentive to stay in the city," he continued. "You dealt well with the Soechins when they bargained with Zoe last quintile. I think it is because you have such a strong set of rules for yourself that once you understand the rules other people have for themselves, you can communicate with them. I have been limited in my own interactions with the Soechins, because they have many personal traits I consider—unpleasant. I think you would do better than I."

Now she was almost as speechless as Sebastian. "But I—how long would I—I mean, do you think I'd live there *forever*? And handle the place by *myself*?"

"Not forever. Perhaps a year, while I find others to run the operation on a more permanent basis. And of course you wouldn't be alone. I would expect Sebastian to spend a good deal of his time in the country. And there would be maybe a dozen other Welchins there to staff the place." He tapped a finger on his knee. "One might be Corene. In the past year, she has been remarkably effective as an ambassador for Welce, and I can tell she's getting restless. She'll want to move on, and Soeche-Tas is a possible destination. I haven't asked her yet, however, and she hates the Soechins. So she might say no."

"I might say no, too," Val said. She felt dizzy enough to be clutching the arms of her chair, just on the off chance that she might fall over.

"Indeed, you might. It would be quite an enormous change and responsibility. I wouldn't want anyone to make such a decision lightly."

Sebastian grinned, grabbed Val's hand, and brought it to his lips. "I will if you will," he teased.

"I'm not sure I would want the participation of anyone who accepted a job on a dare," Darien said.

Val ignored him. It was getting easier all the time to ignore Darien. "I'll think about it," she said. "But we have a lot to discuss."

Darien came to his feet. "I'm sure we will have many, many conversations before all the details are settled," he said. "But for now, would you like to join me for an early dinner? I believe a small group has already gathered. Mostly family."

Sebastian stood up, pulling Val along with him, as he still had not released her hand. "I'm trying to remember the last time I ate anything," he said. "So, yes. Let's go to dinner."

The "small group" consisted of seven people in addition to Val and Sebastian—Darien and Zoe, Corene and Melissande, Mirti and Elidon and Nelson. The sweela prime slapped Sebastian heartily on the back and said he'd never doubted that the rescue would be successful. Corene and Melissande demanded to know every detail of Sebastian's trip through Soeche-Tas, so Val got to hear the stories for the third time in the space of a few hours. Melissande questioned him closely about Kendol's welfare and asked for any messages from her uncle.

"I assume it was a code," Sebastian answered, "but he said to let you know the lassenberry harvest is spectacular this year."

"Well, *I* could have come up with that," Corene said, disappointed. "I've had lassenberries and they're divine."

"Ah, that is a most excellent message," Melissande replied, smiling. "My mother will be glad to hear it."

"Don't tell us you're planning to leave Welce and return to Cozique," Zoe said.

"I must. I have been gone so very long, and so very much has happened. But I do not believe I can express the depths of my gratitude for your hospitality and your aid in a desperate time." Her expression was unwontedly serious as she looked at Darien. "I hope this will only strengthen the bonds of friendship between our countries."

"That is my hope as well," he replied.

Corene passed a plate of fruit to Zoe. "Well, life will seem very boring when Melissande leaves and Val stops pretending Sebastian doesn't exist and Sebastian starts living an honest life." A thought occurred to her, and she gave Val an accusing stare. "You're not planning to go back to your estate, are you? You and Sebastian, to be farmers? That would be *terrible*."

"I think I'd make an excellent farmer," Sebastian said. "I'd tramp around the property in muddy boots and make plans to breed all the best pigs."

"You'd be setting up gambling dens for all the wild young men of the neighborhood," Nelson said. "The ones whose mothers won't let them come to Chialto because they're afraid their sons will get in trouble."

"You're right, that's more likely," Sebastian said with a grin.

Darien broke a piece of bread in half. "As it happens, I've asked both Sebastian and Val to come work for me."

Clearly this came as news to everyone except Zoe, who demanded, "And what did they say?"

"They're not sure yet. But I think I can convince them. I am very persuasive."

"I'd be interested in knowing what jobs you might offer them," Elidon said.

"Overseeing the arrival and installation of the Welchin women who are recruited to Soeche-Tas to marry men who are looking for brides."

Corene grimaced. "Ugh. Since I think any woman would be a fool to make such a bargain, I think it sounds like an awful job. But Josetta is very excited about the possibilities."

Val turned to her. "Darien said you might come with us and help set up the operation."

"*Me?*" Corene exclaimed. "Go to *Soeche-Tas*? Are you mad?"

Zoe was trying not to laugh. "You could look up the old viceroy. See if he still wants to marry you." She surveyed Corene for a moment. "Of course, you're much too old for him now."

"They really do have some of the most repulsive habits," Melissande observed. "Though I have found some of the more ordinary people can be quite likable. But those who are powerful and wealthy—" She shuddered elaborately. "They sometimes leave me with an actual chill."

"I'm very familiar with that chill," Corene said. "I'm not going."

"I've been thinking," Val said to Darien. "Saska might be willing to come with me. She's been volunteering at some of Josetta's charities and this is the kind of adventure that might appeal to her."

Darien looked intrigued. "That hadn't occurred to me. But that's an excellent suggestion. Can you invite her to the palace so we can talk things over?"

Nelson toasted him with a glass of wine. "That's our enterprising king," he said. "Always trying to put everyone to good use in some fashion."

Darien smiled slightly and signaled to the footmen to bring in dessert. "I do find it useful to always consider how to best deploy the talents of everyone in the most advantageous way."

Corene glanced at Melissande. "Just wait. Before you leave, he'll probably recruit you, too."

Melissande opened her blue eyes very wide. "But Corene! He told me no one would know!"

Everyone laughed, even Darien, but Val had to wonder if Darien and Melissande had already had a very intense, very private conversation on exactly this topic. It was one of the things that was most impressive—and most exhausting—about Darien. He was always thinking ahead. Always considering how any person, any situation, could be turned into an advantage for Welce. Melissande could be a powerful asset, strengthening Welce's ties to Cozique even more.

A footman entered, carrying an assortment of pastries to the sideboard. A second followed right behind him but came directly to Darien's side to hand him a hinged wooden box. It was about the size of Darien's two fists put together and was held closed with an ornate metal clasp.

"Even if Sebastian does not take me up on my proposal, I wanted to express to him my deep appreciation for the splendid work he did on the rescue of Prince Kendol," said Darien. "And I wanted to do so in front of all of you."

He turned to face Sebastian, who looked both slightly uncomfortable and deeply pleased. "You were generous with your aid, decisive in your actions, bold, intelligent, and brave. I have not always had the highest opinion of you in the past, but you have proved me wrong. I am grateful for your efforts and hope we have a long history of working together in the years to come." He handed the box to Sebastian, who sat on his right. "I hope this shows you how much I value you."

Flushing a little, Sebastian accepted the gift and gave a brief nod. "I was glad I was in a position to do some good."

"Please," said Darien. "Open it."

Sebastian glanced at Val, gave her a private smile, and swung back the lid of the box. Then he yelped in alarm as a small black frog jumped out, bounced off his chest, landed on the table, knocked over a water glass, sent two forks flying, and hopped to the floor and out the door.

Zoe, Melissande, and Corene had scrambled to their feet and were screaming with panic and merriment. Nelson was convulsed with laughter, bent so low to the table that his face was practically on his plate. Mirti looked amused, though Elidon's face showed a frown of disapproval. Val could do nothing but gape.

Sebastian turned to stare at Darien as if he had never seen the king before. He seemed incapable of speech.

Darien wore his usual faint, cool smile. He said, "Welcome to royal service."

Chapter Thirty-Five

Val is twenty-seven.

She's aboard a small but luxurious cruiser heading out of the Chialto harbor and turning north toward Soeche-Tas. She's accompanied by her cousin, a few redoubtable women hand-picked by Princess Josetta, a young man who has been designated her secretary, and ten royal soldiers. Her lover is bound for the same destination by a completely different route, but she expects to be reunited with him in a couple of ninedays.

Nothing about her life is familiar. She has left behind everything that, a quintile ago, she believed she wanted. Having uprooted herself, she is no longer sure exactly where she belongs. She is unaccustomed to uncertainty, and she has never much cared for the headlong sensation of excitement.

But she's not afraid. Standing at the prow of the ship as it plows through the dancing waters, she finds herself feeling confident, ready, assured. Keeping her left hand wrapped around the railing, she lifts her right hand and examines it. Her bones bear the same shape they always have; she is different, but she still recognizes herself. She has been bent to a new purpose, but at her core she is unchanged.

She leans out over the railing to better feel the brisk air of the salt wind against her cheek, and she smiles.

ABOUT THE AUTHOR

Sharon Shinn has published 31 novels, three short fiction collections, and one graphic novel since she joined the science fiction and fantasy world in 1995. She has written about angels, shape-shifters, elemental powers, magical portals, and echoes. She has won the William C. Crawford Award for Outstanding New Fantasy Writer, a Reviewer's Choice Award from the *Romantic Times*, and the 2010 RT Book Reviews Career Achievement Award in the Science Fiction/Fantasy category. Follow her at SharonShinnBooks on Facebook or visit her website at sharonshinn.net.

OTHER TITLES FROM FAIRWOOD PRESS

Hellhounds
by David Sandner & Jacob Weisman
small paperback $9.00
ISBN: 978-1-933846-19-4

Embrace of the Wolf
by Jack Cady & Carol Orlock
trade paper $18.99
ISBN: 978-1-958880-06-7

The Whole Mess
by Jack Skillingstead
trade paper $20.95
ISBN: 978-1-958880-12-8

Geometries of Belonging
by R.B. Lemberg
trade paper $18.99
ISBN: 978-1-958880-01-2

After the Tide
by Jessie Kwak
small paperback $9.00
ISBN: 978-1-958880-11-1

Liberty's Daughter
by Naomi Kritzer
trade paper $18.99
ISBN: 978-1-958880-16-6

The Ultra Long Goodbye
by Patrick Swenson
HC & trade paper reprint
$19.99 / $31
ISBNs: 978-1-958880-15-9
978-1-958880-10-4

Being Michael Swanwick
by Alvaro Zinos-Amaro
trade paper $19.99
ISBN: 978-1-958880-14-2

Find us at:
www.fairwoodpress.com
Bonney Lake, Washington